THE HAWLEY BOOK OF THE DEAD

THE HAWLEY BOOK OF THE DEAD

CHRYSLER SZARLAN

arrow books

Published by Arrow 2015

1 3 5 7 9 10 8 6 4 2

This is a work of fiction. Names and characters are the product of the author's imagination and any resemblance to actual persons, living or dead, is entirely coincidental

Grateful acknowledgement is made to Henry Holt and Company, LLC, for permission to reprint an excerpt from 'Stopping by Woods on a Snowy Evening' from *The Poetry of Robert Frost*, edited by Edward Connery Lathem, copyright © 1923, 1969 by Henry Holt and Company, copyright © 1951 by Robert Frost. Reprinted by arrangement with Henry Holt and Company, LLC

First published in Great Britain in 2014 by Century

Arrow Books
Random House, 20 Vauxhall Bridge Road,
London SW1V 2SA

www.randomhouse.co.uk

Addresses for companies within The Random House Group Limited can be found at: www.randomhouse.co.uk/offices.htm

The Random House Group Limited Reg. No. 954009

A CIP catalogue record for this book is available from the British Library

ISBN 9780099584780

Typeset in Fournier by SX Composing DTP, Rayleigh, Essex
Printed and bound by CPI Group (UK) Ltd, Croydon, CR0 4YY

FSC www.fsc.org MIX Paper from responsible sources FSC® C016897

Penguin Random House is committed to a sustainable future for our business, our readers and our planet. This book is made from Forest Stewardship Council® certified paper.

To the memory of my father, Frank Karpinski, who taught me the first lesson a writer must learn: how to love the world.

Magic is a form of storytelling, with each trick a small, self-contained drama. The stories it tells are closely akin to dreams and fairy tales.

—Harry Blackstone, Sr.

Hawley Five Corners, Massachusetts, November 2, 2013

I hold in my hands *The Hawley Book of the Dead*. The ink freshly drying, the pages spiced with the scent of meadows, or the smell of blood. Book from the past, book of magic, book of life and death. Even if I weren't the Keeper of this Book, I would have written on napkins tonight, in the margins of my daughters' schoolbooks, on the walls themselves. Just to be able to tell and keep on telling, to make sense of the world I find myself in. I wait in the darkness, writing by candlelight, a storm raging, two dead men outside. My daughters still gone from me.

Misdirection

Las Vegas, Nevada—August 2013

1

On the day I killed my husband, the scent of lilacs startled me awake. We lived in the desert south of Las Vegas, where no lilacs bloomed for a hundred miles. I might expect to smell bee brush or desert lavender in the fragrant air, but never lilacs.

I pulled a strand of coppery hair across my face. The tang of magic lingered on me from our show the night before: the sweet of stage makeup, the bitter of smoke powder.

Jeremy was fast asleep, one arm flung out, reaching for something invisible, which he often did in his waking, working life. Never a white rabbit, a paper bouquet. Sometimes he'd conjure a peacock when a dove would suffice for other magicians, a javelin instead of a knife. I nuzzled his golden head. My lovely husband smelled the same as I did, of the theater, of magic.

He reached for me with his long hands, pulled me close. "Good morning, love," he murmured, his voice thick with sleep. "Sniffing for contraband?"

My sense of smell has always been keen. I use it to discover the secrets our daughters carry. Years ago, our twins Grace and Fai stuffed their backpacks full of Halloween candy, meaning to eat up every last scrap on the playground at school. I caught the scent of Snickers on them, nixed that plan. On their first day of seventh grade I began snuffling for cigarettes or pot on their clothes like a German Shepherd. They had just marked their fifteenth smoke-free birthday. Ten-year-old Caleigh only needed to be given the once-over for stray bits of cheese, her strange craving. She'd fill her pockets with cheese at school, come home reeking like a wheel of cheddar. At the theater, and at the barn where we kept our horses, I was always on the alert for any hint of smoke, of fire.

I curled my body into Jeremy's while he smoothed my tangled hair, his eyes still closed. He wasn't ready to leave his dreams yet.

"No, not contraband," I told him. "Lilacs. I woke up smelling lilacs."

His blue eyes sprang open. "I was dreaming of lilacs," he said. "Masses of them, growing by a white house. But no matter how many I cut, they always disappeared from my hands."

"Like magic," I said lightly, trying to shake the feeling of something impending, a shadow passing over us. The image made me shiver, and not with cold. "Imagine that."

He pulled me closer. "In the dream, I was trying to bring them back for you, Reve."

I searched his eyes for trouble, found none. I kissed his cheek, rubbed his face with mine, an old trick, older than our act together, older than our marriage. My way of claiming him.

By nighttime, he was dead. I had shot him, while the odor of lilacs still clung to us. Stronger than ever.

It haunted me all day, that purple, heady scent.

Jeremy rose first. He showered, then made us breakfast. Black coffee, fresh eggs scrambled with our housekeeper Marisol's green salsa, prosciutto pink as the Nevada dawn outside the window. Caleigh's version of green eggs and ham. It was a Saturday. The twins slept in, but Caleigh waited at the table for her food, weaving the supple white string she favored for her games. Caleigh, the prodigy of string. She fashioned intricate webs that seemed to foretell our future—patterns she named "Chuck E. Cheese Sunday," or "Listen to the Rain" when Marisol complained her plants needed a real soaking. Somehow we would end up at Chuck E. Cheese's most Sundays, which we all despised except Caleigh, and it always did rain after she'd been weaving her rainy string pattern.

She plied the string that morning. She didn't look up when she asked if we were going to the barn.

"I don't think so. Grace and Fai need new sneakers."

"We get to go to the mall!" Up she jumped, did a little dance in her penguin pajamas, and showed us the pattern I recognized as "The Mall," an escalator she kept in motion with her busy hands. I poured coffee for myself, then grabbed a mug for Jeremy, the one that told him he was the World's Best Dad. The lilac smell was beginning to annoy me. I checked the collar of my robe. Not there.

Jeremy leaned into me, reaching for his coffee, a casual hand on my waist. "If you think of it, stop at Madame Lee's. We need more glow sticks for the fireworks illusion."

"I thought we got three cases last time."

"Went through them. Dan ordered more, but we need them tonight."

With a cast of nearly a hundred, performing illusions and tricks six nights a week, we were always running out of something, something was forever breaking. Jeremy was resigned. I was impatient.

"What do those girls do with them all?"

"I'll leave it to you to ask them, Revelation." He used my full name only when I became stern, when it suited me better than my dreamy nickname.

"You're afraid of them."

"Big strapping American showgirls? I should think so. Any of them could land me in the hospital with one swift chorus-girl kick to the bu . . . behind."

Caleigh twirled up to Jeremy. "Bum, bum, bum, you were going to say *bum*!" she sang. He swooped her up, smacked her cheek with a kiss.

"I can't get away with anything in this house, can I? So I'm off to the theater, where I might get some respect." He set Caleigh down, gave me a quick kiss, and there it was again. Lilacs. I pulled him to me, stuck my nose in his shirt collar. No. Only the scent of him. A nutmeg smell, and something indefinable, clean like freshly cut hay. I held him tighter, felt him breathe into me. He took my face in his hands and kissed me again, a deep kiss. Then he walked out into the Nevada sun, which was sharp as a knife that morning, the heat already settled into every crevice of the day.

Beyond that moment I'd never know what he thought, what he felt. He'd never tell me, after we'd gotten home and the girls were in bed. Not that night or any night after. Instead, what happened at the theater haunts me, in the dark and in the daylight. Whenever I close my eyes, the images come rushing at me, as crystalline and sharply focused as a movie in 3-D.

This is the way Defying the Bullets works: The magician appears to prepare the gun before volunteer audience members who examine the bullets, testify that they are real. It appears that the magician loads the gun, but he or she palms the bullets, the gun having been previously loaded with blanks. No real shot is ever fired. Unless someone switches the blanks for bullets. That had happened to magicians before. It happened to Chung Ling Soo in 1918. Whether it was an accident or not was never discovered. But Chung Ling Soo was no less dead.

2

I arrived at the theater early, just after four. I walked under the ladder of a man updating the marquee. The Bijoux was an old theater, and we liked to keep some things a little old-fashioned to match its age. We hadn't yet gone completely digital, like most of the Strip. The marquee proclaimed THE GREAT REVELATION AND THE MASKELYNE MIND—THE AMAZING MASKELYNES' VENETIAN CARNEVALE—MASCHERARI.

When Jeremy and I began our act together, we played small houses, just the two of us, sometimes even bars and the occasional wedding. The basis of magic is a good story, and the stories we told at first were simple, like the Something Out of Nothing story, turning thin air into doves or ravens, always adding something a little disruptive, lovely, or large. We worked our way up, and in time the illusions got bigger and more splendid. We built enough of a reputation and audience to justify leasing our own theater. We discovered the Bijoux then, the magical elements still in place after all its incarnations.

The Bijoux's history mirrored the unsettled nature of our ever-changing city in the desert. Originally a vaudeville house built in 1913 on Fremont Street, it was revamped for magic when Harry Houdini came through, and trapdoors for every possible purpose were installed. In a fit of nostalgia, its owner moved it to the Strip in the 1960s, when Fremont Street was dying, and the Bijoux was repurposed as a supper club. Then the New York–New York Casino was built around it, and it became a movie palace under the Statue of Liberty. When we leased it for our shows, we added lighting and fly elements. We built a turntable to revolve sets, and a huge lift. But much of the theater remained the way we'd found it, mysterious. The feeling prevailed that at any moment the ghost of Houdini or Al Jolson or Judy Garland might wander by.

An ancient man let us in through the stage door the day we first viewed it. He wore a stained red cardigan, faded overalls, and bedroom slippers. His hair was cropped short, his pink scalp showing through the white stubble. His eyes shone silver, clouded with cataracts. He locked the door behind us and shuffled down the hall without a word. He motioned to us to follow.

He led us backstage, through a maze of fraying curtains. Racks of sequined costumes bloomed with dust, last worn by chorus girls who were now grandmothers. Steamer trunks were stacked or spilled open, revealing the stage props of another age: top hats and bouquets of disintegrating paper flowers. A ventriloquist's dummy stared at us with his shrewd doll's eyes. The old man stopped at the edge of the stage but signaled us to walk onto it. Then he threw a switch and we stood blinking out at the candy box house, row upon row of velvet seats, gold balconies.

I jumped when he spoke. "You're standing on a trapdoor built for Harry Houdini. 1921. Of course, Houdini wasn't a true magician. Really only an escape artist." He said it dismissively.

"I saw Devant's 'Asrah' here. Now *that* was magic. The lady I fell in love with was his assistant. 1919. And Chung Ling Soo was here, when I was a boy. 1914. Performed one of the greatest illusions I've ever seen. The one that finally killed him."

Jeremy and I glanced at each other, and I knew with the sure knowledge of the married that he was thinking the same thing I was. If this man was telling the truth, he'd have been over a hundred years old.

"Born with the century. December thirty-first, 1899." Maybe the old guy had a career as a psychic. "Never did see your great-great-grandfather, John Nevil," he said to Jeremy. "But your great-uncle played this theater. 1923."

Jeremy was descended from a magical family. Jeremy's great-great-grandfather, John Nevil Maskelyne, had been one of the few innovators in the long history of magic. He invented magical levitation, and when he retired, he sold that trick and others for an obscene amount of money. Some descendants of John Nevil struggled to make magic pay, squandering their inheritance from the Original Levitating Girl on magic ephemera, on water torture boxes and fancy dress for the stage and hiring the prettiest assistants. But Jeremy's grandfather and father coddled their share of John Nevil's profit. They shunned the stage, were bankers both, performed another kind of magic by making money appear. Jeremy didn't grow up with the magical arts as a kind of second language, touring England and the Continent with magician parents as some of his cousins had. But when he was a boy, in the attic of the family home in Devonshire, he came across an old leather-bound book, scratched and shredding, full of odd symbols and drawings of elaborate machinery, written in code it would take him months to decipher. One of John Nevil's magic notebooks. It was

Jeremy's start in stage magic, the start of his journey to Las Vegas, to me, and then the Bijoux. John Nevil Maskelyne's history was the spark to our success as magicians, in the tiny minority who actually made a living from magic. The old man seemed to know all about it.

On that first day in what would become our theater, Jeremy told him, "You have the advantage of us, I'm afraid."

He extended a gnarled hand for Jeremy to shake. "Pleased to meet you. Wesley Knowles. Otherwise known as one of the Five Chinese Brothers. Not Chinese, not even Asian. Not brothers. Don't expect you ever heard of us. We were tumblers and jugglers. Minor act. Stopped performing after the Oriental craze went bust with the country. 1929. I stayed on here. Marooned. Before Vegas was even Vegas, only a railroad town. I'm the sole survivor. Now the oldest living authority on theatrical magic of the twentieth century. Last magic act to play this house was Blackstone. The father, not the son. 1957. Until you, that is. If you stay. Hope you do. Bring the magic back."

Wesley had a keen knowledge of every trick or illusion ever performed, and often gave us ideas, solving problems we came up against with simple and elegant machinations. For he stayed with us or, rather, with the theater. He had rooms above the stage. As far as we could tell, he never left the building. Wesley was frail but not decrepit, whatever his age. If he was 103 when we met him, he would have been 113 on the day Jeremy died. He was there on that day of the lilacs. He always was.

Dan Liston, the prop master and general technician, worked with Jeremy on a new and improved water escape on the floor below the stage. Dan maintained every prop, from fly mechanisms we relied on to hoist us forty feet in the air, to every coin Jeremy palmed. He was a perfectionist, but I made it a point to go over the props before every performance. It was my old habit to check, clipboard in hand. Before each show I literally checked off every prop used by even the lowliest cast member.

That day, the prop tables were the same as they ever were. The guns we used for Defying the Bullets lay shining in their case when I opened the box.

Dan had outlined and numbered every item so we all knew which prop we needed to pick up for each trick. Wesley shuffled by, saluting me, as if I were a general and he a foot soldier in an army of magicians. Were his eyes bluer than usual, less watery? Did he seem taller? The silvery wisps of his hair combed over his pink scalp darker than usual? Not that I noticed. He seemed the same.

When I examined my conscience later, I could never say for sure. What I did remember was the scent of lilacs perfuming the air near the prop table.

Wesley called ten minutes, then five. I could hear the dancers getting ready in the big green room, the currents of gossip and laughter drifting through my dressing room as they changed into their Carnevale costumes for the second scene. The opening scene, though, was just the two of us, Jeremy and I in a kind of silent passion play that ended in a magician's duel, our version of Defying the Bullets.

Jeremy played the brilliant Faustian magician, the rival of my dark Mephistopheles. The interplay of darkness and light, God and the devil, was an iconic component of our magic. For Defying the Bullets, we didn't speak at all. Later in the show, there was plenty of music and banter to set up the tricks, but for that first scene, we'd found that silence was more powerful than speech. We vied for the audience's applause and love, until I challenged Jeremy to a duel. Two audience members were selected to act as seconds, to examine the guns that were "loaded" before their eyes. Then we would pace off, turn, and fire. I always aimed true, to complete the illusion. Anyone watching from the front row could see the angle of my aim, and its verity. Jeremy would stagger, then fall to his knees pretending to be mortally wounded while I feigned triumph. Then he'd pluck a gleaming bullet from his mouth, hold it up for the audience and the "seconds" to see, and rise to great applause. That was how it was supposed to be.

That night, we played against each other as usual, producing all kinds of unlikely things from the air, mailboxes and tea sets, fireballs and cascades of water to quench them, until I threw down the gauntlet. We chose our seconds, took up weapons, paced, turned, and fired.

But when I pulled the trigger, a red mist exploded behind Jeremy, spattering the gold curtain. Instead of taking a bullet from between his teeth, after he fell to his knees he kept falling, a look of surprise on his face. A woman screamed. I ran to him, caught him before he dropped to the stage. He fell into my arms, his weight already dead weight. I cradled his head, tried to hold in all the blood and bone and everything that made him my Maskelyne, my love. We were only mortal, after all.

After all the shrieking and running for exits was over, after the EMTs had tried and failed to work their magic, Jeremy's body was taken away. In the quiet of the nearly empty theater two police officers handcuffed me, led me out.

There was chaos outside the theater. Detectives questioned members of the audience, and our performers in their Carnevale costumes. They all looked wilted by the heat, still fierce in the August night. Even faces I recognized looked unreal to me, lit by the twirling, flashing firework lights of the Vegas Strip, like mannequins I'd once seen come to life in a *Twilight Zone* episode. At the top of the theater steps I stumbled, my knees buckling. The dark velvet cloak I was wearing was heavy with its own weight and Jeremy's blood. My body and mind throbbed dully. Nothing was familiar, or whole, or right. When the policemen pulled me to my feet again, my head jerked up, and I thought I saw Wesley Knowles walking away, his blood-red cardigan flapping, his silver hair lit by neon. Leaving the theater, which I'd never known him to do, and walking faster than I'd ever seen him walk. He glanced back once, glanced back and smiled.

Nico, our lawyer, found me in a holding cell that stank of urine and vomit with overtones of Lysol. I was pacing, the same three steps over and over across that cell. I hadn't spoken. I hadn't cried, either. The closest I'd come was when one of the woman guards had told another, "Yeah, I'd kill my old man, too, if I had the guts. I wouldn't do it onstage, though."

I grabbed at the sleeve of Nico's pinstriped suit, still perfectly pressed at midnight. "The girls?"

"Marisol is with them."

"Do they know?"

"Marisol just told them you'd be late at the theater, made them go to bed." That happened often enough. My girls would have at least one more untroubled night. But the next day I would have to tell them of Jeremy's death. It would be the worst thing that they'd faced in their young lives. I had shot their father. And now they would be alone, without father or mother. I'd spend their childhoods in jail. With these thoughts running through my head, the next thing Nico said made no sense.

"They're going to release you. You want to change, Dan packed your clothes."

I only pulled the cloak more tightly around me. Jeremy's blood had soaked through, and I could feel it drying on my skin. It seemed like the last thing I had of him.

"It doesn't matter, Nico," I told him. I started shaking. I thought I'd never be warm again. "I killed him. I belong here. I *shot* him."

"Shit, Reve, you're in shock. Listen to me. They're going to release you because *you* didn't kill him. You didn't have the intent, even if you did pull the trigger. You pulled it every night. It was a trick, an illusion, just part of the show. But it gave somebody an opportunity to switch your gun. Somebody who knew you always used the same one. Jeremy was *his* target, not yours."

I did always use the same gun. Mine was on the left of the case, Jeremy's on the right. Nico told me that a different pistol had been exchanged for mine, identical to it but for a hidden chamber that housed one bullet. I hadn't noticed the difference, it was done so cleverly. I hadn't noticed it was any heavier or changed at all. If I had, everything would have been different. Jeremy would be alive.

"But why? Why would anyone want to kill Jeremy?"

Nico shook his head. "That's anybody's guess right now. But that isn't all. The old guy who lives in the theater?"

"You mean Wesley?"

"Yeah. Wesley Knowles."

"What about him?" I couldn't believe that Wesley had any part in this, but then I remembered the old man's taunting smile.

"The cops found him tucked in a bathtub at an abandoned motel out on Sahara. They got an anonymous call from a phone booth at the airport. The last thing he remembers was heading to the theater bathroom sometime last night. He woke up duct taped and gagged, no idea who'd taken him there, or how. But from then on, some guy was impersonating him."

So the Wesley I'd glimpsed that day hadn't been Wesley at all. "*That* guy is Jeremy's killer," Nico told me. "Got to be."

3

That first morning of our bereavement I woke the girls and gathered them all in Fai's room. I tried not to cry, but my voice shook as I told them the bare facts: that someone had switched the gun I used in Defying the Bullets, that their father was dead. Grace threw herself down on the bed and howled. Caleigh latched on to me, buried her face in my hair. Fai collapsed to the floor, hugged my knees, whispered, "Please no, please no." After that first surge of anguish, we lay curled together on the bed, suspended in grief like bees in amber.

I had to make arrangements for the funeral, or I wouldn't have left the house. I couldn't bear for anyone else, no matter how close, to do those needful things. Choose a venue for the private funeral, plan for the service. Choose the coffin. Buy funeral clothes for myself, our daughters. These were the very last things I could do for my husband. My parents couldn't get a flight until the evening, so the next day Jeremy's cousin Nathan stayed with the girls while I discharged my terrible errands.

Nathan Landry had come to us when he was sixteen. He was

the son of Jeremy's only American cousin. Nathan grew up in New Orleans. He also grew up gay in a family of Catholic Republicans. When he came out they disowned him, and he fled west on a Greyhound, to Las Vegas, to us. We were glad to have him. We were building our act and our career, and the twins were three-year-old terrors who needed constant supervision. Nathan finished high school while learning the family trade and helping with the girls. He'd always been interested in fencing and swordsmanship, and that became his domain. After graduating with a first in Renaissance studies from Oxford, he returned to us, almost unrecognizable from the shy boy he'd been. He'd transformed into a remarkable man: a swashbuckling blond Errol Flynn crossed with an easygoing, bookish southern gentleman. Nathan could wield a broadsword or the poetry of William Blake with equal aplomb. He choreographed all the staged sword fights and dances in our shows, and tutored the girls when we went on the road. He was like a son to us. He steeped the girls in Shakespeare, and they called him "coz."

He hadn't been in the theater that night, but when he heard what had happened, Nathan left his apartment in town to stay with us. "You're the only family I have left," he told me. "At least the only family who ever stuck by me. Let me return the favor, Reve." I let him. I needed to surround myself and the girls with people I could trust. However final it seemed, Jeremy's death wasn't an end. It was the beginning of a kind of hell I was not prepared for, beyond the usual grief and shock when one loses a spouse too young.

I was still a suspect in his murder. Nico told me the police would have me followed, hoping I'd lead them to Jeremy's killer. Maybe they were thinking they'd catch me in a tryst, or a business arrangement that would explain my husband's death.

They still believed I was involved, especially since I'd inherited money, as well as our Henderson, Nevada, home, Jeremy's family home in England, and the cottage in Ireland where we sometimes spent summers. I was hardly on the *Forbes* 400 list, but it was a tidy sum, one that a woman less completely in love with her husband, less destroyed by losing the father of her children, might have thought worth killing for.

Nico was right. I spotted the unmarked car as soon as I pulled out of our driveway. It was parked in a less prominent place than the *Las Vegas Star News* van that had been there since the previous day. They both followed as I made my way from the Desert Palms Funeral Home to the District to pick up the girls' funeral dresses. A caravan for God's sake. But I didn't really care. I didn't feel much, couldn't feel much. I moved from choosing the coffin to choosing the service to choosing dresses for the girls mechanically. There was a veil of grief and shock between me and the rest of the world.

What I remember about that day, besides the despair that clutched me, was being *cold*. The District in Henderson is an open-air shopping mall, pretty enough on a fine day, but that day was not fine. It was too chill for the desert in summer, too wintry for Henderson. Rain threatened; the sky was gray as ashes. I'd thrown on clothes without thinking, had no coat, only a thin sweater. After I was done buying the girls' clothes, I had a long walk to the end of the shops for my widow's weeds. I was frozen at the core by the time I'd got to the café in the complex. I ducked in for something warm. I just wanted to hold a hot cup. The plainclothes policewoman followed me in at a discreet distance. I'd been pretending not to notice her as she'd pretended to shop for children's clothes. Maybe she'd pretend to get a coffee now. The boys in the news van had more respect. They just snapped pictures of me with their long lenses from inside the van.

I went up to the counter, ordered a large tea. A duck-tailed barista was moving in slow motion, listening to Elvis on his iPod. A wisp of "Love Me Tender" escaped his earbuds. The barista mouthed the words. A Young Elvis impersonator. I looked around. A man sat near the gas fire, in one of the leather chairs. His face was turned from me, toward the flames. He was dressed in a dark suit, reading a newspaper. Dark hair, I thought, but it was hard to tell in the shifting firelight. It was eleven in the morning, a strange time of day for an office worker to be lolling in a café, so the suit was probably the woman detective's partner.

When my tea arrived, I held it with both hands, made my way to the hearth, sat in the other leather chair. The woman detective fluttered near us, pretending to linger over her choice of milk or cream, raw or fake sugar. Still the man by the fire did not turn to look at me; he kept his eyes focused on his paper. I wondered how he could see to read. There were no windows in that corner of the shop; the fire was the only source of light.

"Not a very nice day," the man said.

I looked away, looked out the glass doors at the flat gray sky. I had no intention of engaging in conversation. I wanted only the warmth of the fire, and no detective could keep me from it.

"The weather's changed since last week," he persisted, his gaze fixed on his paper. I didn't see a headset for a cell phone, though, so he had to be talking to me.

"Now, last week," he continued, "it was sunny. Sunny altogether. Not too hot, either, for once. Last week you could think you were living in a kind of paradise."

I flinched. It was strange that a detective would bother to give me a weather report, but the man was right. It *had* been warm. It *had* been paradise. I'd been in the District, too, the week before, looking for a new bathrobe for Jeremy, and was informed at the menswear store that bathrobes were seasonal items. Not for summer. That night, when I told Jeremy bathrobes were seasonal, we'd laughed at the silliness of it. He flung his old terry cloth one off with a grand gesture. "A pox upon the man who wears bathrobes out of season. I will not be that man!"

My Jeremy. My Maskelyne. He'd be in the ground soon, where it was always cold. I rose, grasping my cup, the only heat I had. My hands were not steady, and it almost slid through my fingers.

"You'd better hang on to that," the man warned. "It's going to be colder soon, I'd say." His face remained in the shadows, his eyes now riveted on the fire, watching the lick of flames. I turned and rushed out the door.

When I was finished with my last grim chore, I jogged to the car. The woman detective followed at a distance. I threw my bags in the backseat, started the engine, turned the heat all the way up. Then I saw the piece of paper fluttering under the wiper blade. I thought of turning on the wipers, letting it fly away altogether. But I leapt out again and grabbed it. A copy of an old handbill for a magic show. CHUNG LING SOO, DEFYING THE BULLETS. A scream rose nearly to my lips before I bit it back. I ran to the car my detective friend had just stepped into. She and her male partner looked at each other in confusion when I signaled to them. The man rolled down the window. He was dressed in gray sweats, had a shaved head, might have been trying out for a remake of *Kojak*. Definitely not the stranger by the fire.

"It was him," I said, and held out the flyer. "It was the guy sitting by the fire in the café. He killed my husband." I don't know how I knew. I just did. But the man was gone. Young Elvis hadn't noticed him leave. He wasn't a regular, either. I found out later that when my new detective friends had analyzed the flyer and the cup that remained on the table by the fire, neither held fingerprints, DNA from saliva—anything at all that might identify him. The man in the dark suit had vanished.

4

The funeral was a blur. My parents had come from Massachusetts. My aunts, Viv and Gwen, flew in from California. Jeremy's parents had both died when the twins were small: his mother from cancer, his father from grief-fueled alcoholism a few years later. Only one Maskelyne relative came over from England, Jeremy's cousin Bertie, who had to fly back immediately for his own wedding. We left Hope in the Desert Church after the brief service. It was finally raining, a rare desert rain that splattered up mud from the dry ground. The smell of the air was electric.

I knew I'd need a few minutes alone before I could gather my strength again. The girls were with my parents and aunts, talking to the pastor under the church portico. I slipped away, walked through the rain toward the car. I tried to ignore the photographers and news vans clustered outside the church gates, the police detail assigned to keep them out.

Before I could reach the car, a man appeared from the labyrinth walk beside the church. He was big-boned and tall, and so dirty he might have come through the desert on foot. Or perhaps was homeless. One of the funeral directors stepped between us, but I asked him to move aside. I had recognized the breeks the dirty man wore, the long wool socks, the pocketed waistcoat. Homeless or not, this man was dressed as a falconer. The only thing he was lacking was a bird on his leather glove. He held a small blue envelope instead of a hawk, and I reached for it, recognizing Nan's handwriting. My Nan, my mother's mother, at ninety-seven years old did not travel, although she was a master falconer and still held falconry clinics. Since Jeremy's murder I had been hoping for some word from her. I'd grown up in Nan's imposing presence. But as close as she and my mother had been when I was a child, a breach between them opened after I was grown and gone away from home. A breach I couldn't fathom, although I tried for years to understand it. They held an uneasy truce at holidays, but I'd hardly seen or heard from Nan other than at Thanksgiving, Christmas, birthdays. Now here was a letter from her, brought to me in this strange way.

"You're to open that before no one," the falconer told me. I looked down at the turquoise envelope, the letters running in the rain, and when I looked up, the man was gone, had melted back into the desert. I tucked the letter into my bag.

I meant to read it when I was finally alone in the funeral limo, but I broke down instead. The leather upholstery smelled of other people's grief, and I added mine to it. My sobs were drowned out by the howl of the wind, and I let myself keen along with it. Just for a moment. Just as a rest from the stunned shock that had gripped me since the night of Jeremy's death.

When I looked up, I saw Grace stumbling toward the car. She was crying, too. Her flaming hair was wild, and the white dress she'd wanted for her father's funeral clung to her long, stockinged legs. Our beautiful girl, undone by her grief. She seemed impossibly fragile. Of our girls, Grace was closest to Jeremy, but most resembled me. Grace had my temper. Only Jeremy could stanch our sudden flares of anger, soothe us, turn us to our best selves. What could I do for her? We were too much alike.

She flung her dripping body into the car, slammed the door. I braced myself for the storm I could see coming in her face. She turned to me, wet with tears and rain, her breathing hard and shallow, like water tumbling over rocks.

"I have to know. You have to tell me." Her voice was rough and hopeless. "Did you mean to kill Dad?" Her blue eyes pierced me, held me as if I were a butterfly pinned in a specimen case.

"Oh, Gracie, no. Oh, honey . . . of course I didn't mean to kill your father!" The simple words couldn't exonerate me in my own mind, but when I reached for her, she collapsed against me, spent. Sobs racked her thin body, and I held her close until they stopped.

I'd forgotten about the letter, until after the grave site, after all the tears and hugs and Marisol's feast at the house that we scarcely touched. Until everyone else was in bed, the girls with my mom in the guest bedroom, Nathan in his room, my dad snoring finally on the couch after keeping vigil with me. I didn't think I'd ever sleep again. I shook the letter out of its rain-pocked envelope and read the spidery handwriting of an old and frail woman.

My Dearest Reve,

I trust Falcon Eddy will bear this message to you. You need to come home. Hawley Five Corners is waiting for you. You'll be safe there. Don't be your stubborn self. Find a way. Remember the story of the Fetch. And remember, history often repeats itself.

Yours in Haste,
Nan

My heart slammed in my chest when I read the word *Fetch*. Of course I remembered that story. I closed my eyes and tried to breathe, calm and steady. Crushed the letter in my hand.

But our home was here. I would stay, and damn Nan's tangle of stories. This was the real world, with a real killer who would be found. When that happened I would cobble our lives together again. What happens in Vegas stays in Vegas.

Yet I thought, too, every day from then on, of Nan's letter, of what she had written. For of all her many stories, it had been the story of the Fetch that sparked nightmares when I was a child. I could still hear her voice beating inside my head, telling it.

"It was the winter of 1832," Nan would begin in the dusky light of my nighttime bedroom. She held my hand, and hers was warm and supple, not like a witch's claw at all. She dressed in practical clothes, jeans and flannel shirts, things her hawks couldn't ruin. But her thin face was steeped in shadow, her voice pitched to the timeless resonance of fairy tale, so she seemed otherworldly. She told a story better than anyone, and I always thrilled to hear her tell even this story, the one that terrified me so.

"The snow was deep. Lucius Gowdy could hear the wolves howl just past his fence line. But his family was safe now, he thought. He had cut enough wood to supply the five fireplaces in the house through the harshest winter. They had food stored in the cellar, venison dried to jerky, the good big pig killed in the fall smoked and hanging from a rafter. His wife had canned and pickled and preserved; row upon row of jeweled colors in glass bottles glowed in the shadows. He had moved his family more times than he could count, and he was determined to stay in the big house on the Plainfield flats that seemed to suit them so well. But it was a wraith that forced these frequent moves on him. A wraith that looked exactly like him. Often and often, when he was out mending fences, it would come in and sit down at the table in their other homes, and his wife would set a plate down before it, thinking it was her Lucius.

"The spirit began to follow him everywhere. When he plowed the fields, it would follow. When he went to hunt, it would appear clambering over rock walls and downed trees to get to him.

"His wife told him, 'It's surely a Fetch, come to take you. We must move, we must confound it.' For a Fetch was a shadowy figure, a creature made from earth by a wizard, meant to 'fetch' a living person to the fairy world. Lucius did not want to go to his grave, or to any fairy world. So they moved and moved. Each time his wife began packing their belongings, the Fetch would appear and cry out, 'No matter where you go, I'll find you! For I shall take you to my master after all! He'll have you yet.' And it was true: The Fetch always found the Gowdys, until they moved to the Plainfield house. There Lucius had gone through the summer and fall, and now in the midst of the harsh winter, neither he nor his wife or children had seen the dreaded thing.

"Then one day, the wind howled and the storm raged around them, more fierce than ever. Lucius had banked the fires well that morning, but by midday, the flames were nearly out. It wasn't like him at all to let the fires die on such a day, so his wife sought him from the top of the house to the bottom. In the cold cellar, she found the Fetch curled on the dirt floor. The thing was shivering, sick and pale, its skin nearly transparent. It scarcely resembled her husband anymore, and it seemed to be fading. Even so, it was full of venom. 'You'll not see your husband more in this life,' it hissed at her. 'I knew I should have him, and now I've taken him away.'

" 'Where have you taken him?'

" 'He is with my master, where no mortal can follow.'

"But the wife was stubborn, and not exactly mortal. She took a warm cloak and went out into the snow and wind. She saw her husband's tracks and followed them to where their field met the edge of the wood. There his tracks ended, and the tracks of wolves circled. One drop of bright red besmirched the blinding white of the snow. She thought of her husband, then of her children. She'd left them alone with the Fetch! The thing was weakened from its soul stealing, but might it recover, take another form, seek another soul? One of her children's, while she had left them unprotected?

"Her tears froze on her cheeks as she turned and ran through the heavy drifts back to the house, where she found her children safe and warm, the Fetch nowhere to be seen. Lucius Gowdy's wife hugged their children to her, and cried some, and sat with them around the leaping fire that seemed to be laughing and winking at her. For the fires in every hearth mysteriously blazed hot once more. And the fires burned merrily in every hearth all winter, without even the need for her to add a log. Sometimes, in the dead of night, the woman thought she saw eyes in the flames, watching her, watching her children, watching as she wrote in a book of her own keeping.

"The woman never saw her husband again. The next spring, they moved from that place, and kept on moving. The one thing she was certain of was that they'd never be entirely safe from the Fetch. For who knew what would satisfy his master?"

I tried mightily to put Nan's story of Lucius Gowdy from me. Yet it haunted me, the tale of the Fetch, the stealer of souls. I tried to act like myself in the strange weeks that followed, made the girls go through the motions of regular meals and bedtimes, never let them see me when I wept. But every night I would go to a secret drawer in our bedroom that I'd forbidden Marisol to touch, take up the shirt Jeremy had put in the laundry basket to be washed the night before I shot him. I'd wrap myself in it, press the collar to my face, and breathe his scent in, pretend he was in bed next to me. Wake in the morning and weep silently into the shirt that was empty of my husband, my love. Whose soul had been stolen from me, from himself. And would *we* ever be entirely safe again? Like the woman in Nan's story, I just didn't know.

5

I closed the show. Without Jeremy, there *was* no show. I'd lost my husband and my job in the same instant. I missed Jeremy almost every waking moment, but I missed our show, too. Every evening I missed it like a lost limb. I tried to take stock of my skills, but they weren't much, without magic. I had enough money to float us all for a while, if I was careful, a little breathing space before I had to find work of some kind. Which was convenient, for I didn't feel safe out in the open. I felt eyes on me at the grocery store, at the barn, in crowds, and in nearly empty parking lots with the hot sun beating down on me. I cut my trips outside the house down to the absolutely necessary.

Maybe the girls sensed my terror. Not one of them wanted to return to school. Nathan fell into his old role, staying with us and tutoring them as he had during the happy times we were on the road performing. He was far better at it than I was, and I knew it. I cooked with Marisol, and she put up with my poor attempts at cleaning. Nathan kept the girls busy. None of us wanted to leave the house. We wanted only to be together in some listless configuration of a not-quite family.

Nathan set out jigsaw puzzles on an end of the dining room table, and they became a thread to lead us through the days. Van Gogh's *Sunflowers,* a Landseer Newfoundland. *The Lady of Shalott.*

One day, I stopped in my wanderings to fill in part of John Waterhouse's *Lady.* It had been a month and a day since Jeremy's murder. The strange weather of summer had given way to a dazzling September. There were still no leads on the man I'd come to think of as our Fetch. It was as if he'd never really existed. If it weren't for the gun and Wesley, he might not have been real; he might have been just an ancient story.

Caleigh was at the table, plying her string. Fai was reading to her from *The Wind in the Willows.* Until Jeremy died, Caleigh's favorite books had been about families. *The Five Little Peppers,* the Little House books. Now they gathered dust, and she asked for books with only animal characters. No mothers or fathers. The names of her string patterns had changed, too. Now she made "Sleep in the Afternoon" or "Float in the Pool." The one she made most often was called "Missing Dad." It had a big gap in the middle.

I picked up a puzzle piece, a bit of the Lady's flowing red hair, the color of my own.

"*She left the web, she left the loom, she made three paces through the room. She saw the water lilies bloom . . . the Lady of Shalott.* Tennyson," Grace piped up behind me. Maybe Nathan was managing to get something besides grief to stick in their heads.

Fai looked up from her book. "Mom, do you think it's time for us to leave the web?"

"But when the Lady left the web, the mirror cracked from side to side and she was cursed." Caleigh frowned at the string tangled in her fingers. "She died in her stupid boat. Although I'm not sure why."

"She couldn't ever be part of the world. She could only see it in her mirror," Fai told her, then sighed as if she were the one reflected in the mirror.

That snagged my heart. I didn't want my girls to be like the Lady of Shalott. Neither would their father.

"I think you're right, Fai. It's time to leave the web." It was four o'clock, past the heat of the day, yet with plenty of time till nightfall. "Let's go to the barn. Then we can have dinner at Teriyaki Madness."

Grace whooped and Caleigh leapt up and did a little dance, bumping the table and scattering pieces of the Lady far and wide.

That day, we all realized there might be life after Jeremy's death.

The next morning, Marisol brought a plain manila envelope in with the mail. It had no stamp or return address. It smelled of burning: not cigarette smoke, but sulfurous, like the smoke from an open flame. My nerves leapt wildly as I broke the seal. A sheaf of photos fell into my lap. I opened my lips to cry out, but no sound came. In the photographs, Caleigh carried a water bucket. Grace and Fai cantered their horses in the ring, laughing. Every photograph was of the girls the previous day. And each was scorched by fire. The mirror had cracked, and the curse was upon us.

The Fetch crept through our lives then, like something unseen but deadly: a poisonous snake, our big bad wolf. He photographed us, myself and the girls, even inside the house. Somewhere out there he must have been lurking in the hills surrounding the house, with a camera, a long lens. Daily, somehow unseen, he'd leave the photos where I would be sure to find them. They were always singed, melting to brown ash at the edges. It was as if he knew my fear of fire, my innermost thoughts. As if he knew me from a past I didn't want to think of. The police scoured the hills after the photos began appearing. They didn't find so much as a Twinkie wrapper. Although he left the photos every day, the police found no fingerprints, no stray hair, nothing they could get a DNA sample from.

I'd kept Nan's letter, crumpled but whole. I hadn't answered it. I didn't want to think about that story. But I had to do something. I called her.

Nan has always loathed phones. She usually let the voice mail pick up, but this time she answered on the first ring.

"Nan, I need to come home."

"Yes. You do." I heard the high-pitched keen of a hawk in the background.

"Have you been to see the Hawley houses?" I asked her. "How much of a wreck are they?"

She laughed her old lady laugh, like a nail being wrenched out of a board. "The houses just need a little loving care. They have for many years, you know."

I *did* know. "Maybe we should stay with Mom and Dad."

"No!" Her voice was fierce. "I'll give you Carl Streeter's number. He lives in Hawley Village. Anything you need done, he can see to."

So I called Carl Streeter, and he saw to the basics of running water and hiring a roofer and a company to install the fence I wanted. In ten days' time, the house was ready and we could be bound for Hawley Five Corners. I just had to take care of one more needful thing.

6

I scheduled a free memorial performance at the Bijoux in Jeremy's honor. Most of the magicians on the Strip and many from farther afield signed on to perform. Dan planned the show, assisted by Nathan and Wesley, who'd recovered speedily from his ordeal in an old Westward Ho bathtub.

We went to the theater early that night. Even so, a line of people snaked around the building. The girls wanted to see the exact spot where their father had died. Of course everything had been cleaned, and there was no trace of blood. But as we approached, Caleigh clung to me, hid her face in my sleeve. I heard Grace's sharp intake of breath, and Fai stifled a sob. I reached to take their hands, led them to the urns overflowing with white roses at the edge of the stage. We all wore white: white T-shirts, white jeans. No magician's cape for me that night. I wasn't performing any trick that would require it.

We placed white roses where Jeremy had fallen. Dan turned on the mist machine, and wisps of fog crept around our feet as we made our way toward chairs in the wings. Just then three huge displays lit up, and there Jeremy was, larger than life, his elegant, dexterous self, performing all the tricks we loved best. The girls had helped me choose the videos, but we hadn't seen them writ large, and the girls stopped, stunned, mesmerized by their father, silvery and ghostlike on the screens. At the bottom of each ran the caption "The Maskelyne Mind, 1967–2013." Jeremy's stage name. Forty-six years old. The tragedy of it tore at me again, the uselessness.

"I wish we could stay here forever, watching him," Fai whispered.

I hugged her to me. "So do I, honey."

"But we have to *go*," Grace said fiercely.

Caleigh said, "Shh! Let's just watch."

The audience filed in, everyone encouraged to take a white rose from more big urns at the entrances. The Bijoux was packed to the rafters that night. We sat in the wings until we went on. Detectives and security guards flanked us, the stage, the exits. I scanned the audience, watched the performers with anxious eyes, searched for clues, but found none. The Fetch had to be there, somewhere. Maybe onstage performing, for all I knew. But all the magicians were good friends, and I just couldn't believe any one of them would be involved in Jeremy's murder.

We watched rope tricks and straitjacket escapes and fake beheadings and flying unicycles, all performed under the displays alight with Jeremy's smiling face. Grace and Fai were texting, their fingers flying. Each of them had friends in school, and Grace had a sometime boyfriend named Matt, whose parents were in a Cirque show. I had always trusted my girls to make good decisions, but since the Fetch's haunting, I'd been checking their incoming texts. To my surprise, I found that they texted each other constantly, and almost exclusively. Usually they were right in the same room. I could see they were at it again, texting each other throughout the performance. Caleigh lay across my lap, looping her string, watching her father's face.

When Lance Burton was being hanged and resurrected, Wesley crept up. "Siegfried's speech next. Then you're up." I expected him to creep away again, but he put a bony hand on my shoulder. "It was . . . you were . . . *better* than Devant." It was Wesley's highest compliment, I knew, and my eyes brimmed with tears. "I'm more sorry than I can say that I let you down," he told me. I took his hand. He squeezed mine, and left us.

Siegfried's speech moved the audience to tears. I heard sobs as I led the girls to their marks behind the curtain, and talked them through the trick one final time. So I missed most of his ode to Jeremy, his fallen comrade. The story of his life and his death.

Then Siegfried introduced us, "the magical Maskelyne family," and the curtain opened to thunderous applause. We all bowed from our platform set high above the stage. When the audience settled, I began, "Just over a month ago, my husband was performing a trick called Defying the Bullets." I walked down the stairs to the spot Jeremy had died. "This is where he fell." Some audience members groaned. One man yelled, "I was *here*!"

"Many of you were," I gestured to include them all. "And so was his killer. Someone took my husband from me, and from our children." I pointed to my girls standing square on their marks, their hair flaming under the lights. "And from all of you." I strode to the edge of the stage. I snapped my fingers. "Abracadabra. But one of the cardinal rules of magic is that you can't just make something disappear. You have to bring it back. Now, for my final illusion, on this or any stage." A scrim was lowered behind me, a gauze curtain that blurred the outlines of the girls, but through which their three shadows could still be seen.

My eyes scanned the gleaming gold of the boxes, the swags of velvet curtain, swept up to the catwalks. I gazed out at the audience, my audience. It might be the last time I ever stood before them, at the intersection of stage magic and real magic.

"You have been . . ." My eyes filled again, and for a moment I couldn't speak. The audience erupted, clapping and cheering, throwing their white roses at my feet. I picked one up, held it to my cheek, its petals cool against my burning skin. I signaled for quiet.

"You have been so good to us. You didn't just buy tickets to our shows. You gave us your attention, your wonder, your amazement. It is with a full heart that I say thank you, and goodbye. For we will *not* obey that cardinal rule of magic." I raised the rose high above my head. "We will never be seen again, myself or my girls . . . until my husband's killer is found!" I lowered the rose, and as I did, the images of the girls shimmered, then faded away.

Instead of applauding, the audience held its collective breath, waiting for my next move. I saluted them with that one rose, one last time. I walked down the steps, up the center aisle, among them. They reached out to touch me, they called my name. When I could feel their fingers brush the fabric of my clothes, smell their perfume, their sweat, their belief, I performed my last and finest trick. I vanished.

Hawley Five Corners—October 10, 2013

1

Our plane landed in Boston midday. The city was languid, hushed in the heat of Indian summer. The cabdriver's pace was slow as a dream. The office workers walking to lunch downtown slung jackets over their shoulders, loosened ties. An old ivory haze hung over the city.

We rested at the Park Plaza, our haunt from the days Jeremy and I played Boston, when my Maskelyne and I made orange trees grow before our audience, then picked the perfect golden fruit and tossed it to the crowd. An illusion of both production and of time control. I wished again that I had the gift of true time control, that I could travel back to those days before I smelled the lilacs in the desert, and keep us all safe somehow. Keep my husband alive, walking on the earth next to me.

Time travel was not my forte, though.

The girls were passed out on smooth, cool white sheets after three flights—from Las Vegas to New York to Iceland, then to Boston. The crazy flight pattern had been part of our escape. After the girls had gone through Harry Houdini's trapdoor in the Bijoux, Dan had smuggled us out of the theater during all the uproar over my vanish. Nathan was waiting with a car to drive us all to the airport. I'd wanted to get the girls out of the country, hoping it was less likely the Fetch would follow. Not that I put much faith in airport security, but flying out of the country and back in added another hurdle, and I needed to put as many as I could between him and my girls.

But at the hotel, I was restless. Nathan stayed in the suite with the girls while I went down to the restaurant in the Park Plaza lobby. Boston is not a city of magic, not like Las Vegas, where it reigns supreme, or even L.A. No one came up to my table to murmur, "Your Metamorphosis was the best illusion I've ever seen" while presenting me with a limp napkin to autograph. Although Jeremy and I had appeared on Leno and Letterman, had our own few television specials, performed nightly for months at a time to packed houses, we were not usually recognized outside Las Vegas.

And now no one stared at me because they'd seen me splashed all over the nightly gossip shows and the tabloids after Jeremy died. No one remembered the face of the lady magician who had killed her husband. So I sipped my tea in peace, while a man with a crew cut played Cole Porter songs and sweated onto the piano keys. No one watched me, no one at all. What a difference three thousand miles makes. No police, no magic fans. And no Fetch. I just hoped it would last.

We set out for our new home in the afternoon. Before we'd left, I bought an SUV online, had it delivered to the hotel. I drove it toward the westering sun. As the hours passed the trees became thicker, the air cooler, the houses fewer, the voices of my children more strident.

"Oh, my God! Where are you taking us?" Grace whined

when I turned onto the main street of a classic New England town. HAWLEY VILLAGE, a white sign with stark lettering told us, FOUNDED 1741. She flipped her red hair back. I could see it spark in the rearview mirror, bouncing like Slinkys released. The twins had my fierce curls. Their faces were identical, down to the constellations of freckles that spangled their delicate noses, but it was otherwise easy to tell them apart. Although both were just starting to come out of a Goth phase, Grace was still partial to ripped black jeans and black leather jackets, with black eye paint in swaths up to her eyebrows. Fai, less inclined to denim and makeup, wore long fringy things that made her look as if she'd stepped fresh-faced out of a fairy tale, a milkmaid in mourning. Because they always dressed in black, they'd wanted white for the funeral, white for mourning their father. Now each of them always wore something white, a scarf or a shirt. The black clothes were ceding to white, but their clothes still reflected their personalities, Grace's sleek, Fai's princess inspired.

Caleigh inherited my russet coloring but Jeremy's stick-straight hair, was solid where her sisters were lean as greyhounds. She played her usual never-ending string game, her hands busy leaping from her warm-up patterns—"Cat's Cradle" to "Cup and Saucer"—then to the patterns of her own devising. Her patterns were now called things like "Falling Leaves" and "Maple Candy." "Missing Dad" was still in the rotation, but she wove it a little less frequently. Maybe it was a sign this move was good for us all, even though my heart hurt when I thought how Caleigh was getting used to a world without Jeremy, how we all were.

"Hey, look, a fair!" In spite of her concentration on the string, Caleigh didn't miss much.

A large wooden cutout of a pumpkin proclaimed HARVEST FESTIVAL, OCTOBER 19, 20—FOOD, FUN, MUSIC.

"Hey, it's next weekend! Can we go?" Caleigh was a lover of caramel apples and fried dough, like most ten-year-olds. "Mom, will you take us?"

"I don't want to go to some raggedy-ass fair," Grace sniped.

"Language, Grace." Although I knew that far worse words than *raggedy ass* could, and did, come flying from their mouths.

"Yeah, you didn't hear her *language* at the hotel."

I sighed. "And I'd rather not hear it now, Faith."

"Don't call me that. You know I hate the *thh*. It makes people spit."

I was almost grateful for some grumbling and crankiness, the times my daughters reminded me of their old unguarded selves. We had all been trying too hard, and I could see that Grace and Fai felt the strain of it. Fifteen is a vexing age. All fifteen-year-olds want to grow up faster than they have a right to. Without their father to brace them up, I was afraid for the twins, balanced on that cusp where a child can become a woman overnight. I wished I could wave my magic wand and make everything better. But the magic was gone from our lives, along with Jeremy.

In a strange and horrible way, the Fetch had made us closer. My daughters could have turned away from me after Jeremy died, blamed me as I blamed myself. But now it was all of us against the Fetch, against their father's killer. The sad truth was that not one of us was the same person we had been. Maybe fighting this battle together would get us through to some other side, where we were scarred but still ourselves, still there for each other, still a family. I could hope for that, cling to it while everything in our lives was changing, shifting in the wind like drifts of fallen leaves in the yards of Hawley Village.

I turned off Main Street, past the church, the row of stores that included Pizza by Earl, the Suds & Stuff Laundromat, a drugstore, and Elmer's, the tiny grocery that proclaimed FRESH CURED BACON, DAVE'S EGGS, LAST OF THE SILVER QUEEN from a blackboard on the sidewalk.

"Dad would love this place," Fai said. "It would crack him up."

I had a flash of longing for Jeremy. He *would* laugh, Fai was right. The town was a caricature of New England quaintness, a caricature of itself. But in a moment we were beyond houses, beyond sidewalks and stores. The sharp light caught and flamed in the saffron-colored leaves of maple trees.

I nearly passed the road, had to screech onto it. The girls screamed.

"Mom, it can't be *here*!"

"What, we have to live on a *dirt road*? No, we can't, I'll be *mortified*."

"Aren't there even streetlights?"

"You saw the pictures," Nathan reminded them. Carl Streeter had sent photos, so we knew what we were getting into.

"Yeah, but nobody told us we were gonna be hicks." I felt her kick the back of my seat.

Nathan turned and gave her one of his burning looks. "Save it, Gracie. And if you don't want to be a hick, don't act like one." I just went on driving down the road, which was smooth as a board in spite of the lack of paving. The road dipped down, dappled with sunlight and floating leaves.

"There are so many trees," Fai grumbled.

"Yeah, too many." Grace resumed her complaining. "I don't see why—"

"Here we are." I cut her off, mid-gripe. Drove down another sweep of road, through a tall gate in a high fence, a gate that swung open after some unseen device read the bar code I'd fixed to the windshield. Past the line of huge old sugar maples, past what had once been an active Congregational church, white and imposing, in spite of needing a fresh coat of paint. Past two houses, also white, also peeling paint, old New England farmhouses, one with a rambling porch. Briars and weeds grew up around them all.

The girls just sat for a moment, awed.

"This is it? We're gonna live here? It's almost a whole town."

"Well, it was a town once. A very small town," I amended.

"Does the fence go all the way around?"

I considered the tall fence, the electric wire strung above it, and a luxurious calm washed over me, unknotted muscles I didn't know were clenched. "It sure does."

"Mom," Fai said, "don't you think it's overkill?"

I looked back at my daughters, their fledgling faces. They waited for an answer, unaware of their loveliness, or their fragility in the world. Losing their father had tempered them, but hadn't made them feel any less the invincibility of youth. They believed they would live forever. Always a bad assumption.

"No. I don't think it's overkill."

"It makes me feel like what's-her-name. Snow White." Grace was staring at the cluster of old houses. "Wasn't she the one in the castle with the thorns all around?"

"That was Sleeping Beauty. Snow White had the glass

coffin." Caleigh, closer to the years of bedtime stories, corrected her.

"Yeah, her, Sleeping Beauty."

I recalled the story, the spell cast. If only our problem was a fairy with a grudge.

"Is this where they lived?" Caleigh asked. "The ladies that had your name?"

"Our great-great-great-whatevers," Grace clarified.

I pulled into the drive of the farthest house, the largest, the loveliest. The paint was peeling, like the others. But the grass was mowed, the weeds subdued. And the fanlight over the massive front door was glowing, welcoming us, so at least there was electricity. The windows of the plain, vast Federal house shone bluely in the last of the afternoon light. We were home, in the land I grew up in. The land of the Revelations.

"Yes," I told my daughters. "This is where they lived."

2

The townspeople in Hawley Village knew me as only Reve Dyer, a widow with three girls. Not as the Great Revelation, one half of the Amazing Maskelynes.

I'd used my maiden name for everything, bank accounts, contracts, in my conversations with Carl Streeter; I drilled the girls that they must, too. I doubted that any of the locals were true magic fans. Even if they'd been to Las Vegas, even if they remembered the tragic death of a well-known magician, they probably wouldn't guess who I was. They didn't know why I'd moved to Hawley. And they wouldn't know about my connection to the forest, to the Five Corners. None of them would remember me as a girl. I'd grown up in Williamstown, fifteen miles and a different world away. Only Jolon would remember, and he was long gone.

I might have been the first Dyer woman in over two hundred years to use my husband's name, but I'm also the last in a series of women with the name "Revelation" twining through a few hundred years of the Dyer family. I'd heard tales of them and their magic from the time I could understand speech.

Thanksgiving was a harrowing time for my mother's family, the time of year when the dark settled in and they contemplated the past, sowed it in the fertile ground of their children's imaginations. Hearing the first murmured tales, my uncles and boy cousins would leave the table laughing at their witchy wives and mothers. But not me. I wanted to hear those stories. They were my birthright: I was a Revelation, after all.

I was named, like the others, after the first Revelation in the New World. The great-granddaughter of Mary Dyer, who'd been hanged in Boston on the first day of June in 1660, for her Quaker proselytizing. Mary Dyer's sons and daughters headed to Pennsylvania, where Quakers were better tolerated than in Puritan Massachusetts. That first Revelation's grandparents were among them. But New England roots remained strong. Decades later, when Revelation herself was suspected in the Mount Holly, Pennsylvania, witch scare of 1740, she fled with her family to Massachusetts. To the place that became Hawley Five Corners.

The first Revelation and her family were never seen again in Mount Holly. But Revelation's sister Prophet received a letter the following year, in the spring of 1741. The letter said only, "Come to us. Travell the Massachusetts Western Highway and aske for the Hawley Five Corners as you go. You will finde us here, where we live in safety and peace." Prophet never went, and died that year under mysterious circumstances. There were no other letters, but Revelation's family almost certainly founded the town of Hawley Five Corners, "Hawley" an alternate spelling of their old Pennsylvania town. That is what we knew from the oral history of our family. Why the town had been abandoned didn't figure in the family tales, only Revelation's part in its founding, and the stories of her descendants.

My Nan still owned the houses at Hawley Five Corners, yet had never gone to live in them. But I was bound to Hawley in another way. When I was a young girl, Hawley Five Corners was my own secret town, mine and Jolon's. Jolon Adair was my best friend, then my first love. Every Saturday my parents would drive me to the Adairs' house in East Hawley, and we'd ride their ponies. From the time we were big enough to saddle the ponies ourselves and ride into the forest, the abandoned village at the intersection of five roads had been our dream town. In those years we were growing up, vagueness was acceptable; parents had been lulled into the complacency of believing nothing lurked in wait for their children. We never told where we rode, that we'd eat our picnic lunches in that forsaken place. We grazed our horses among the abandoned houses while we ate our sandwiches, and hawks drifted in lazy circles overhead.

When we were children we were quiet, almost reverent. Years later, we talked and laughed, smoked the cigarettes Jolon stole from his father's pack of Chesterfields, and kissed among the lilies by the church, or on the steps of the white house with the tangled lilacs that would become *my* house. Then we'd ride to Pudding Hollow, or Bozrah Brook, or the long way round Hell's Kitchen. We always ended up back at Hawley Five Corners, just at dusk, with only enough time to ride back and be home for supper.

I had always known the history of the Five Corners was entwined with my own family's. By the time Jolon and I started riding in Hawley Forest, the old stories just seemed like other fairy tales. Over the years, I all but forgot them. All the years our horses loafed and crunched the tall grass, and we laughed too loudly, blowing smoke rings into the fairy air.

The stories came back to me, though, after Jolon was long gone, lost to me. On cool misty evenings when I'd trailered my horse to the forest, ridden too long and too late and arrived at the Five Corners alone. Even when I was cold and sweaty and chilled to the bone, a warmth would blanket me at the Corners. I never felt afraid in the forest. It was my refuge then, so it wasn't really surprising to me that I ended up in Hawley, the place of all places I'd felt safest in. Things do happen for a reason. When Nan's letter came to me, I remembered my childhood rides in the forest, and coming upon that abandoned landscape. I remembered Nan's stories, too, and the satiny edge of the blanket I liked to clutch between my fingers while she told them, and the nightlight, with scenes from Sleeping Beauty revolving in a magic lantern.

Nan was right. I still felt safe at the Five Corners. But the feeling had no basis in solid fact, only old memories and older stories.

As I looked at my girls in the fading light of our first day in Hawley, I hoped I'd done the right thing, reverting to the past, to the Dyer name. Or was I just trading one kind of magic for another?

3

Magic is the oldest art. The first person who learned to control fire was the first magician. Perhaps it is its unimaginable age, its place at the beginning of human history, that ensures there is nothing new in it. Elements of the same tricks and illusions are performed in nearly every magic show, to greater or lesser perfection, with perhaps a new twist every hundred years or so. There is something a little tawdry about magic. It is the magician's finest trick to rise above the dime-store tackiness that infuses our profession.

I'd never been good at it. I still remember the magic show Jolon and I put on when we were ten. I was the magician, he was the assistant. Jolon was always too trusting, let me have my head like his favorite pony. I wore a long dress and a cape made from an old velvet bathrobe of my mother's. I shuffled cards and dropped them, pulled my guinea pig out of the balaclava I'd stitched him into. I would have tried to saw Jolon in half, but for my grandmother who took the saw away from me. Altogether, I was a rotten magician, but I'd always had a soft spot for magic.

My magical inheritance was of another sort, although no less necessary to the success of the Amazing Maskelynes. It began with the Dyer women.

An artful conjurer can set her own body on fire with no visible damage, can cut off her arm without pain, can eat glass or razor blades. All are tricks that must be learned and practiced. But vanishing—and its necessary counterpoint, reappearing—is an art that relies not so much on tricks as on timing. The audience's attention is directed away from the person disappearing. Even the visible vanish is not truly visible. Except in my case. Because my gift is that I really can disappear.

We all have them, all the women in my family, extraordinary gifts. Occasionally, a boy reveals a power, but not often, and none in my generation. One of our Dyer ancestors could play any musical instrument she picked up without benefit of lessons. Another could make a feast from a bit of bread and water. Yet another could summon rain. Sometimes these gifts take years to reveal themselves, and have varying degrees of usefulness. I knew from experience the talents of my living relatives. My Nan is able to tame animals, even the wildest—has had raccoons and flying squirrels for pets. Even a bear cub once. She is a falconer, and trains others to handle birds of prey.

My mother is a healer. She discovered her ability when she was in college and her roommate had a grand mal seizure, which my mother quelled with a touch of her finger. She volunteers at the local hospital, which for many years now has had the highest recovery rate of any in New England. My aunt Gwen will let you know where any lost or misplaced object is. Aunt Viv has a compass in her head, and can tell you right off how to travel to any place at all, even places she has never been. My Caleigh, as I've said, can affect her surroundings with her string games. The twins' gifts have not yet been revealed to them, and I often worry over them. Will their gifts be simple and straightforward, or difficult and sometimes dangerous, like my own?

Disappearing isn't exactly the word for it. It's as if I walk through a curtain, enter the passageway to another world. I sometimes feel that I could go further in, but I never do. I remain in the antechamber of that other world, while I can see, and even take part in, events around me in this world. I stay close, then I return, performing the perfect visible vanish and reappearance.

I moved to Las Vegas when I was twenty, worked as a change girl in a casino, and went to shows every night before my shift. I thought that with my gift, I could surely find a place in that world. I had no skills but my one turn, so I went to the smaller clubs and casinos, looking for someone on the rise. Someone who might be willing to hire me with no obvious experience. One evening I went to see a young magician perform. He asked for a volunteer and I was onstage before I knew it, choosing cards and cutting open lemons to reveal dollar bills with my name written on them. At the end of the show, I slipped out, too shy to approach him. But the next day I walked out the service door of the casino after my shift and there he was, sitting on the wall, making doves appear and releasing them into the bright air. He'd tracked me down.

I couldn't believe my luck. I thought I'd have to do some fast talking to get signed on as a magician's assistant. Not even my wildest imaginings featured a young, handsome magician with a Colin Firth accent falling in love with me. My boyfriends after Jolon had never lasted more than a few months. I wasn't overly confident in the relationship department, but with Jeremy, everything seemed easy, right. So I quit my job and we formed the Amazing Maskelynes. In the beginning, I was relegated to the role of the Three Part Girl, the Girl Levitating. The magician's assistant, the pretty girl in the skimpy costume.

I was still the magician's assistant the first time I revealed my gift to Jeremy. He'd asked me to marry him, and I was stalling, uncertain how to break it to him. I felt it was wrong to conceal it from him before I accepted, and he was committed to my aberration forever.

But then it just happened, without any thought on my part at all. We were working out a trick in which I was to disappear in a sheet of flames. It was a little frightening, although perfectly safe. I was always nervous just before he lit the flame. Fire had always frightened me.

I was in a large box made from metal poles, behind a piece of non-reflective glass. When the fire was lit, a trapdoor opened beneath me and I plummeted down under the stage, jumped up and raced to the back of the house, where I "reappeared." The audience would be distracted by the flames, and we'd worked it out so that it took me only about fifteen seconds to reappear, to walk down the center aisle and rejoin Jeremy.

That day, instead of gritting my teeth, staying put, and dropping down as we'd rehearsed, I stepped away from the flame and right out of the box. I was about to apologize, but I saw that Jeremy was watching for me, timing me. When I looked toward a mirror we used in the next trick, I couldn't see myself. I had disappeared. Jeremy whipped around, looking for me, worry growing in his eyes. I waited, my heart pounding, then reappeared right in front of him. He stared at me with his eyes all big and wild, like a spooked horse. I couldn't help laughing.

"It isn't funny," he scolded me.

I quenched the still-burning flames with my cape, then sat down on the edge of the stage. Jeremy paced beside me.

"I was right here, and you know, I could swear you . . . well, vanished. How? Have you been practicing a bit without telling me?"

I reached for him. "It's no bit, sweetheart. Just come here, and I'll try to explain."

He sat next to me and gazed into my eyes. "This should be interesting."

"Well. I've always been able to do it." And I did it again. He got the spooked horse look, and I reappeared.

"Bloody hell . . . Where *did* you go?"

"I don't really go anywhere. It's just that you can't see me."

"But how . . . I don't . . . arrghh!" He slammed his forehead with the flat of his hand, then pointed an accusing finger at me. "Okay, wait just one minute, miss. Can you start at the beginning, please?"

I took his hand again and stroked it, to settle him. "I know I should have told you before, but I was waiting for the right time. It's kind of hard to understand if you don't *see* it. It's just that in my family, all the women have these . . . gifts. Mine is that I can disappear."

"You can disappear."

"You saw it."

"I did. I *think* I did. But . . . you can't be serious, can you? It's a prank, right? Maybe I deserve it. I can be a wanker, I know."

"Jeremy. Stand up." He did, a little shakily. "Now look at me, and keep looking." I disappeared again, and he startled. I reached for his hand.

He jumped back at my touch. "Bugger and blast!"

"Oh, come on, just walk around me." I took his arm, guided him around. "See, no smoke and mirrors." And I reappeared. He startled again, but was silent, his muscles tensed.

"Jeremy?" I was afraid I'd gone too far.

His eyes softened then. "Well, I would say you gave me a fright, just at first. But do you suppose you could do that again? Any time you like?"

"I know I can."

"So you have a spectacular visible vanish, and we don't need all the claptrap. Darling, why didn't you just tell me?"

"I was afraid you'd think I was . . . I don't know, some kind of monster. Do you still want to marry me, even if I'm a freak of nature?"

"I especially want to marry you, Revelation Dyer, if you're a freak of nature with a perfect visible vanish. Oh, what a posh wife I'll have. How rich we'll be! It will be . . . magic!"

At midsummer, my dad walked me down the aisle of Exeter Cathedral, and I was married to my golden, shining Jeremy. On the same day I became a Maskelyne, I avoided some of the more dismal Maskelyne cousins by disappearing, big pouffy gown and all, in the middle of the garden party at the manor house that John Nevil built from the proceeds of the Original Levitating Girl. I found Jeremy talking to some old school friends, threaded my fingers through his. I led him to an unused guest room, shut the door, and reappeared. He took me in his arms and pulled me onto the bed. "This little trick of yours is useful in many circumstances."

"You don't know the half of it, buddy." I laughed, while he tried to slip his hand into or under that dress, find skin.

"Now I know why they make these huge satin confections.

It's so the groom can't get at the bride until they've actually tied the knot," he grumbled.

His hands inched under the bones of the bodice, nearing my nipple, then just brushing it, teasing it until it was hard. I felt feverish under his fingers. "Mmm . . . that's a lovely kind of torture," I told him.

His eyes were so blue, I felt I was falling into the sea of them. He kissed me then, our first real married kiss, not in public, just ourselves alone, breathing together.

"If you don't take off that alien life-form that calls itself a dress this minute, Mrs. Maskelyne, I swear I'll do something drastic. I'm in a fair way to bursting."

I reached down to feel his burstingness, laughed again. "Well, Mr. Maskelyne, you'll just have to wait. I can't take it off without help. I can't even *pee* without help."

"I'll help you, then."

"You'd just rip it."

"So?"

"So I want to save it for our daughter."

That sobered him. He sat up, stared at me. "You can't mean it?"

"I might. I *think* so."

He just sat for a moment, with that startled horse look he had. Then he leapt up, took my hands, pulled me to my feet, and hurried me outside again.

He stopped to talk to the glitter-rock cover band, and in moments they began the first familiar chords to "Golden Years," and we danced, until long past the late English twilight descended. Jeremy, me, and the first glimmers of the twins inside me, we all danced. He bent his shining blond head down and kissed me, mussing my hair, then smoothing it down again.

"What a perfectly disappearing darling you are, what a Revelation."

So I became the Great Revelation, the disappearing half of the Amazing Maskelynes, and gave up the Dyer name.

Every feat of magic tells a story. Often it's the story of resurrection. Of death and rebirth. We went through it countless times, Jeremy and I. Jeremy, my Maskelyne, my love. He was always there to take my hand, to hold me in his arms when I reappeared, resurrected, while the audience gasped, then cheered. He'd hold out his hand and there I'd be, back from the lobby of that other world. Until the day he died in my arms, and I became a Dyer for the second time, and probably forever.

4

The girls were beguiled by the town.

"Mmm . . . spooky. This place looks like it belongs in a Shirley Jackson story," Grace said.

"Well, I like it. It's cool." Fai popped a car door open.

"I didn't say I didn't *like* it, you dweeb. And stop saying *cool*," Grace commanded. "*No*body says *cool* anymore."

"Are Grand and Gramps and Nan coming?" Caleigh asked.

"You never know about Nan, but Grand and Gramps will be here tomorrow. I thought we'd be too tired to be much fun tonight."

"I'm not tired," Fai informed me. "Hey, is that the barn, behind the house?" She scanned the lawn, the green paddocks, a breach in the woods that surrounded us. "The horses will love all the grass."

"All you think about are horses." Caleigh kicked her door open and jumped out.

"At least I'm not obsessed with *string*."

"Stop, now. Who's going to help me with the bags?" Nathan

had the back hatch open, hefting suitcases and Caleigh's stuffed animal trunk.

"I'll help, let me." Caleigh started pulling things from the back, while Grace and Fai slumped to the house, trying not to be seen and called back to help. I let them go. I lifted the heaviest of the suitcases out of the car, began wheeling it behind me. The twins left the front door open. Caleigh, hauling a heavy duffel bag, staggered then dropped her load, ran back to me. There was a woman standing in the doorway. Gaunt and stiff, she wore a dark housedress, her hair ratcheted behind her head in an unforgiving bun. Grace may have been thinking of Shirley Jackson, but this woman put me in mind instantly of Mrs. Danvers in *Rebecca*.

Caleigh clung to me. "Mommy, there's a lady!"

"Honey, it's just Mrs. Pike. She's going to be our housekeeper. Like Marisol back home."

"But she's nothing like Marisol. She's old. And *really* wrinkly."

"You'll get used to her." I kissed the top of her head, took her hand. It wasn't often I still got to feel like the mother of a young child. Children grow up so fast; even ten-year-olds rarely want to be seen holding their mother's hand. But Caleigh didn't pull away.

"Come on. I'll introduce you."

We trudged up the walk, the stones slanted and uneven, grass growing between them. The suitcase thunked behind me, threatening to topple over.

Mrs. Pike didn't rush out to help us. She raised an arm in greeting, that Yankee wave that I remembered from childhood, the hand unbending, unmoving, as if warning us to stop right there.

"You must be Mrs. Pike." I smiled, held out my hand. She nodded curtly. I'd never actually clapped eyes on her before that moment. She came by way of a recommendation from Carl Streeter, who'd sent me her business card. GOOD HOUSEKEEPER, COOK. REASONABLE RATES. RELIABLE. The essence of brevity. When I called she'd been agreeable enough, except for one strange moment.

"Yut, could do for you weekday mornings."

I told her the date we'd be arriving, that we would want dinner that night, and the address of the house.

"That's at Hawley Five Corners," she told me, as if I didn't know where my own house was. I said that yes, it was, and a long pause hung between us, so long I thought the line had gone dead.

"Mrs. Pike?"

"Hang on, will you?" I heard a mumbled conversation, then Mrs. Pike was back. "I'll have to charge more. Fifty an hour." It was twice her usual rate.

"May I ask why? It's not far from the village."

"Well, the roads are one thing. Dirt roads, wear and tear on the car." But I could sense that there was something else, the other thing that Mrs. Pike wasn't saying, nor would she.

"What's the other thing? You said the roads were *one* reason."

"Did I? The roads is all I meant. It's only that."

I knew I wouldn't get anywhere. "Okay. Fifty is fine."

I could tell by her silence that Mrs. Pike wasn't expecting agreement. She thought I would balk, try someone else. I wanted to be done with the housekeeping question. I could find someone else if she didn't work out, or maybe wouldn't need anyone after the initial clean and spruce-up. "I'll see you, then.

October tenth. We'll be there before dark, but I'd like you to wait for us, so the house is open. It will be more pleasant for my girls if someone's there when we arrive."

"Oh, someone will be there, don't you worry." Mrs. Pike laughed tinnily, a sound like a rusty hinge. It made me uncomfortable, a little shivery. Like she knew something I would have to find out on my own, like she had one up on me.

She seemed normal enough, however, standing in the doorway, greeting us with her thready smile. Just an elderly woman having to make ends meet. Maybe she'd heard about the work being done at the Five Corners, figured I could afford her doubled rate. Nothing strange in that.

"This is my daughter Caleigh." Who had become unaccountably shy, turning her face away and pressing against me. "Grace and Faith were just here. My twins. Maybe you saw them?"

"I saw two others run upstairs. Why I came out." The tinny laugh again. "Thought maybe they didn't belong here."

"I'm sorry if they startled you. They can be oblivious sometimes."

"No, that's all right, then. Just thought . . ." But she didn't say what she thought.

"And this is Nathan Landry. Nathan is the girls' cousin. He tutors them, as well, so they won't be going to school in town."

"Very pleased to meet you, Miz Pike," he said, dropping the bags and taking her hand gently, as if it might break. "I'm sure you have a lovely dinner ready for us." Always the charming southern gentleman, yet moving things along all the same. Nathan, the Renaissance man. I suddenly thought how his many talents would be wasted here, felt a stab of guilt that he'd left his life in the city for us. I hoped it wouldn't have to be for long.

Either not noticing or not caring that Nathan was gay as well as charming, Mrs. Pike smoothed her hair, patted down her dress. "Supper's keeping warm in the oven," she told him. "Pot roast, potatoes, string beans. And there's a white cake for dessert."

"That sure does sound splendid, and we're all famished."

"Guess I'll get along then, leave you to your supper and settling in." She gave Nathan a smile, which faded as she looked back to me. "I'll be by tomorrow morning, missus. Nine sharp." She turned and marched out the door.

"Please call me Reve," I petitioned her retreating back. She kept walking to her car, a Buick so ancient and decrepit I thought it surely had been abandoned in the forest. But the rusted, piebald car started right up, and Mrs. Pike rattled off, the car's taillights glowing in the shadows beneath the many trees.

"Not exactly the Welcome Wagon," Nathan remarked.

"No, but I think I like her. I guess I'm still a Yankee at heart." And she seemed too taciturn to be much of a gossip. We hoisted our bags again, and the house claimed us.

5

No one in town knew anymore when the original part of the house was built, Carl Streeter had told me. But in 1775, when it was owned by the Sears family, a large extension was added. Urbane and his wife, Bethia (née Dyer: She figured in some of Nan's stories), lived there for many years, a well-to-do couple with eight children. Urbane was the first merchant of Hawley, and the progenitor of the Sears clan that populated all corners of these Berkshire hill towns. Urbane Sears came from Gloucester to open the Hawley General Store, now home to the hardware store and Pizza by Earl in the village. Then he married Bethia, and nine years later renovated the house at Hawley Five Corners for his growing family. He opened a second store there near the tavern. Neither building—store nor tavern—exists now. Just old cellar holes a quarter mile down Hunt Road. That was the thumbnail historical sketch Carl gave me, unbidden. He probably had no idea the town's history involved my family. As far as I knew, Nan never made an appearance here, never kept up the houses, just paid the taxes and left them benignly neglected. Carl didn't seem to know that the Five Corners had been in our family one way or another for more than two hundred years. I didn't enlighten him. Our family stories stayed in the family.

When I'd seen the photographs Carl e-mailed, I knew instantly which house was the one to restore for my own family. The lines of the Sears house were still true, the barn large and airy. But the widow's walk was the main draw for me. It was a peculiar addition to a house of that era, a few hundred miles away from the sea. There is no record of why it was there, but since Urbane Sears had come originally from Gloucester, that seemed reason enough. Every other house built in that period in those seaside towns north of Boston had a widow's walk. It was what Urbane was used to, I guessed. And compelling to me. Now I was a widow, after all. So I ignored the rambling King house, the Warriner house with its broad porch. Because as a young girl I had looked up and wondered so many times about the view from that narrow catwalk on the mansard roof. Although Jolon and I had managed to jig the locks of the church and the other houses, we had never been able to break into the Sears house to see that view. And when I'd asked Nan where the key was, she told me to mind my own beeswax.

I remembered coming upon the houses with Jolon the first time we rode his pinto ponies bareback into the forest. It was the summer I turned eight, the very first summer we were allowed to ride on our own. Even then the abandoned village seemed to hold magic, to be a little unearthly, part of another world altogether. Although they'd been deserted for so many years, the houses were not decayed. I'd thought Nan was crazy when she'd urged me to go to Hawley as a place of refuge. When Carl Streeter sent the photos, I expected collapsed roofs and rotting hulls of houses. But they were the same as when I'd first seen them as a child. Untouched by time. It did seem as if the Five Corners was waiting for me.

All the same, everyone around Hawley probably thought *I* was crazy, to move there. The houses were in good shape, considering their age, but they were a far cry from the pristine homes of the other city folk who'd migrated to Hawley Village. They would need a lot of work to rise to that standard, so I was sure all kinds of rumors were flying. That I was the heiress of a steel or soap-producing family, that I'd married an old billionaire who'd finally kicked the bucket. That I'd won the lottery. The possibilities were endless, really. As for the fence, the electronic gate, well, we had to be wealthy to move there in the first place, and wealthy people were often paranoid, as well as crazy, weren't they? But there was no security against ghosts. Mrs. Pike wasn't the only one who reacted strangely to the mention of the Five Corners.

I'd asked Carl Streeter to hire electricians and plumbers, so the house would be marginally habitable when we arrived. But when he'd called Hawley or Plainfield contractors, they'd never called me with the estimates. Carl hemmed and hawed, but finally had to hire from Pittsfield, the nearest city "down the valley," as they say in the hill towns.

Ghosts or not, the house was as ready for us as a hasty few weeks could make it. It had seemed silly to move all our things, so I'd enlisted Mrs. Pike to shop for the basics: some towels and sheets, a few pots and pans, plates and glasses. Carl had also been there to take delivery of the necessary pieces of plain pine furniture I'd bought online, so we had beds set up, a sofa, a kitchen table and chairs, a desk for my office.

Even so, the big house still felt empty and unlived in. It *felt* like it might be haunted. Mrs. Pike had begun cleaning, but the house retained an ancient smell, of old smoke and dry wood. An aura of disuse and abandonment pervaded the very air. Cobwebs still clung to corners, and the walls needed washing. The floors were stained, the windows were dirty. But at least we could use new dishes, sleep in clean beds that first night.

I wanted to thank Carl, and when a big man with white hair and a handlebar moustache stepped out of the kitchen and crushed my hand with his big meaty one, I knew I'd have the chance.

"I came to let Mrs. Pike in, been fiddling with the water heater downstairs when she wasn't happy with the temperature. Good to meet you in person. I'd be glad to show you around, since I'm here."

After he'd taken me over the house, we went out to the barn. It still needed to be cleared of the bits and bobs that had been stored there and never taken out—nothing interesting, only old boards and cans of dried-up paint, some shredded old canvas tarps, and endless bales of musty, decaying hay. I'd have fresh hay delivered before the horses came, but I made a mental note to get the old nasty stuff cleared out, adding it to about a hundred other mental notes. So much needed to be done. But at least we were here. Safe. I crossed my fingers behind my back whenever I thought that word.

"Yut, I remember this old barn." Carl thumped a chestnut beam, and the dust motes flew in the late afternoon light. "I remember the auction, oh, it must of been twenty years after the buildings were abandoned," he told me. "This was in the forties, during the war. I was just a kid. We lived in Lithia then, but I had Hawley cousins. I only moved to Hawley when I married my Brenda, who was a Hawley girl. Anyway, Mother took me to the auction. She bought a pie safe, and other junk. They had the houses open so we could all troop through, pick what we wanted to bid on. So we went in." Carl paused for effect. "And you know, it was like everybody up and left in the middle of some ordinary day. This barn still full of hay, grain still in the mangers, set up for the night feeding. You should of seen it. You'd think over the years some teenagers would figure to use the houses for a hangout. Destroy stuff, torch the furniture for campfires, maybe. But when we went in, it was all just as if it was left maybe a few weeks before. Stuff was dusty, that's about it. Tables still set for dinner, a bed or two still unmade. What wasn't auctioned off was cleared out and hauled to the dump."

Of course, by the time Jolon and I discovered the Five Corners, the buildings were empty. I had always assumed that the abandonment had been gradual, one family dying out, another moving, leaving the houses unclaimed. My family among them, leaving Nan holding the bag eventually. What Carl told me put a different spin on things.

"Why was so much left?" I asked. Carl was closing the barn door. I turned back because he hadn't answered, was still fiddling with the latch. "Carl?"

"Huh?" He finally turned toward me, a little reluctantly, I thought. "Did you ask me something?"

"I was wondering why so much was left. When people moved away, why did they leave their things?" I sensed more story, something I was good at, digging the dirt of the past, digging nuggets of magic or of fact. None of Nan's tales had featured the abandonment of the town. I had always figured it had happened long before she was born.

Carl scuffed his loafered foot at a big shiny beetle on the gravel, smashing it to a slimy pulp. Then he shoved his hands in his pockets, peered up at the blue of the sky. "Well, I couldn't exactly say. Maybe they were in a hurry to get somewhere. To get to a job. Probably moved to cities and lived in small apartments." He looked at me appraisingly, looked away. "Hey, that's some spiffy tow package you got on that 4Runner."

I had no idea why he was trying to distract me, but I was charmed by the mystery. "You'd think they would have sold the furniture before they moved."

"You have horses, right? I'd expect you'll want to think about a real truck if you're going to do any serious towing." His face was shiny with sweat, although the day was drawing in, the air cooling. I didn't bother replying. I knew we were done with the subject of the abandonment of Hawley Five Corners. He wandered over to his own truck, tucked behind the barn. He got in, closed the door, looking sheepish, as if he'd done something wrong and I'd caught him at it. "I'll be sure to get back to you about getting the rest of the junk out of the barn."

"That will be fine, Carl. Just call my cell."

He started the truck, and I waited for him to drive off. Instead, he surprised me. He bent his head out the window toward me, almost whispered, "About the town. It's just stories. Don't mean anything. I wouldn'a opened my fat mouth, but I forgot for a minute you're not from here." He pounded the truck door in farewell, and I waved him off.

6

When I returned to the house, the girls were still running from room to room, exclaiming over all the fireplaces, the white moldings with their deeply carved grapes. The same things I'd loved about the house when I was young myself and peeking through windows.

"Hey, look at this cool fireplace. It has Noah's Ark all around it!" Caleigh crowed.

"No way!" I heard Grace pounding into the parlor. "OMG, she's right. Fai, c'mere!"

"There's giraffes, and a lion . . ."

"Cats and bears, and a monkey!"

"What are those things?"

"Anteaters. See, their long tongues are sticking out," Fai chimed in. "But, you guys, you have to come see this thing in the kitchen. It's a huge iron thing with a horse pulling a sleigh on the side of it . . . oh, I can't describe it, you have to come look."

I heard more pounding feet, then Caleigh saying, "Didn't you all ever see a woodstove before? Even I know what a woodstove looks like."

"That's a *wood*stove? It looks more like the wicked witch's oven. And where'd you ever see one?"

Caleigh answered in her superior ten-year-old voice, "Catalogs."

Nathan entered, bags still in hand. "Will you just drop those," I ordered, and he did.

He took a moment to look around him, then told me, "This house is fabulous."

It was. Our house in Nevada seemed brash by contrast, too new, uncouth. Even in its desolate state, the Hawley house was an aging beauty from another era: elegant, timeless, built before the country was a country at all, when Massachusetts was still a colony and wealth could be measured by the number of windows a house boasted.

"Mom!" Caleigh yelled. "Come look!" I followed her voice to the dining room, large and formal. Even unfurnished, it looked grand. At the end of the room was a mural, painted on the wall. I found the girls clustered before it.

"This is *awe*some." Fai took my hand. Her eyes were glowing.

"It's in bad shape." One of the only things in the house that had really suffered with the years, the paint flaking, patches of dampness spotting it. But I remembered it resplendent with color. Silvery green willows hanging over azure ponds, shining red barns, the white houses standing ghostly among autumn trees that were like plumes of smoke, scarlet and gold and purple. Tiny people rode horses on the hilly roads, stood outside their houses, hung wash. It was Hawley Five Corners, dated 1824. Painted by an itinerant artist whose name had been long lost and forgotten. "Jolon and I used to look through the windows at it."

"Who's Jolon?" Grace demanded, instantly alert to a secret.

How could I explain the complexity of Jolon? "He was my best friend," I hedged. I was on safe ground there. He had been.

"You mean your *boy*friend?" Fai goaded me.

"Maybe."

"What happened to him?"

"He left, a long time ago."

"Like you did."

"Like I did."

"But now you're back. Maybe he is, too."

"I seriously doubt it."

"You could Google him. Or find him on Facebook. Then you'd know." Fai hated to let things go.

"Shut *up*." Grace pounced on her. "Mom doesn't need to find any old stupid boyfriend. You make her sound like some Facebook slut. She isn't even *on* Facebook."

"Well, I guess my virtue is safe, then. That's a relief."

Grace was under the impression—they all were—that I was functionally illiterate when it came to modern technology. The Amazing Maskelynes' website had been kept glossy and exciting by strangers to me, our Facebook page as well. Fai was right, though. It could be that simple. Maybe I would google Jolon. It might dispel my nostalgia to know that he was a bank manager somewhere in Wisconsin, or a sheep farmer in South Dakota. But nothing I imagined seemed right. Nothing real could satisfy me. It was better he stay in the past, where he belonged.

"Hey, what about dinner?" Fai asked suddenly.

"I'll set the table. You girls need to help me find everything," Nathan told them. "We'll eat in half an hour."

I wanted to get to my office, to make more mental notes as I looked it over. It was a room I'd be spending significant amounts of time in.

I had a new job: writing scripts for other magicians, other magic shows. Henry, my agent, suggested it. The money I had seemed like a lot, but with none coming in, it wouldn't last forever. If I was going to support my family, I had to do something. I couldn't perform, probably never would again, but the shows I scripted were moneymakers. I'd never had a flop. It used to be that magic shows were just one trick or illusion after another with no theme, no integrity. All that changed with David Copperfield, Siegfried and Roy, Cirque du Soleil—their spellbinding spectacle shows told intricate stories. And if I brought anything to the Amazing Maskelynes beyond my disappearing act, it was my ability to weave a story.

Writing is a kind of magic. One person sits in a room alone and makes marks on a page that represent the images in her mind. Another person looks at those marks, weeks or months or a hundred years later, and similar images appear in *that* person's mind. Magic. Plays and choreography hold yet another level of magic and meaning: The marks on the page leap to action in another person's body, to be seen by thousands of others. The ability to weave that kind of magic paid well in Las Vegas. Stage magicians were a dime a dozen there, but a show that would run for years—that was gold.

I planned to write them in the third-floor attic of the Sears house, my choice for an office from the photos Carl had e-mailed. It wasn't anything like my old office, a tiny closetlike room in our magic workshop, a warehouse outside of Las Vegas, where Dan and Jeremy and our engineering crew planned and constructed new illusions. My office there was usually crammed with bits and pieces from tricks that were in the works or abandoned. Casts of heads and arms, boxes of discarded wigs or masks. The junk that magic produces. It was also filled with sound drifting in from the warehouse, including the occasional explosion. It was dear to me, the place where I plotted the story lines of our shows. My office in Hawley could never be the same, so I wanted it to be as different as possible. But it held its own magic—the view from the widow's walk.

The way out to it had been sealed for some long-forgotten reason. Perhaps so children like my young self wouldn't climb out and fall three stories. I'd asked Carl to have the French doors stripped of the plywood that had covered them, so I could throw them open and walk out in fine weather. My refuge in the trees, my sanctuary from the real world, which no longer contained any magic for me.

I climbed the wide flight of stairs. What had once been the attic seemed like an attic still; no Ikea desk and chair could change that. But I could polish the chestnut beams so they'd glow in the afternoon light. My desk was set up at the far window, with a view of the treetops. If ever I could write anything, this was a fine place to do it.

The small dish that would give us satellite TV and Internet access was just visible, just the edge of it, from my window. The girls assumed that there was Internet and cell access everywhere in the world. But there was none in the forest, without satellite to bring it.

I set my laptop down, booted it. While I waited for the screen to come up, I went to the antique French doors that looked out to the formerly forbidden widow's walk. I opened one side, and saw myself reflected in the waves and bubbles of old glass, a small woman with wild red hair and a pale face. A widow, walking.

Then I startled. There was another face next to mine in the glass. I gasped and spun around. Across the room from me was a portrait of a woman in nineteenth-century dress. She was young, lovely, her upswept auburn hair framed a pale oval face. A straight nose, classical in its lines. Hazel eyes, calm but with a glint of irony. A slight smile played on her lips. Her gaze revealed culture, intelligence. She was seated in a carved chair, her arm resting on a table covered in a crimson cloth, her finger pointing at the floor. Frothy lace adorned her wrists and slender neck. A delicate pink rose and trailing vine grew by her chair. I walked closer. Her ring—was it a wedding ring?—sparkled, as did her eyes, and the gold chain she wore that pooled at her waist. She had been a wealthy woman. Her dress was black silk. Perhaps she was a young widow. Like me.

I thought that maybe the painting had been marooned in the house, a relic of the past, as the mural downstairs had been. But as I examined it more closely, that seemed less probable. In spite of a patina of fine lines, the painting glowed, shone, as if it had been well cared for. The frame was delicate, richly gold-leafed wood. No dust bloomed on it. I looked into the woman's eyes. She compelled me. She seemed to be watching me, appraising me.

"Who are you?" I asked impulsively, and she looked as if at any moment she might answer. But of course she didn't. She was just a painting. It was strange, though, that I hadn't noticed the portrait just a half hour before, when Carl showed me the house.

I stepped out into the cooling air and breathed it in. I walked along the roofline of the house, looking over my domain, new and old. The steeple of the church, the slate roofs of the empty houses, the tall, protective wall with its comforting electric wire receding into the woods, the massive gate with the computerized entrance. Even with all the beauty surrounding me I felt forlorn. I had to face the fact that here I was, without Jeremy. I'd made a home without him. As hastily thrown together as the Hawley house was, it was our home now. A home we would never share with him. How final it seemed. I realized, though, that something had altered in me. Under the darkening sky, I felt I could breathe for the first time since Jeremy died, that in this place I could live my life and keep what was left of our family safe. Compared to what I'd had, it wasn't much. But it was something.

7

Nathan had uncorked a bottle of wine, and he proposed a toast to happiness in our new home. The girls raised their glasses of sparkling apple cider, giddy in the festive atmosphere Nathan had created with candles and their champagne-like drinks.

"I have a toast to make, too." Fai lifted her glass again. "To Mom's old boyfriend, who I just found!" Her eyes sparkled with delight.

"Whoa. Wait a minute." Grace frowned suspiciously. "How do you know it's him? Mom didn't even tell us his last name."

"Be*cause*," her twin retorted, drawing out her explanation for the slow-witted among us, "Jolon's not a common *first* name. There were a lot of entries for other things, like a site in Ireland selling Bibles, a town in California with a headless ghost."

"Oooh!" Caleigh squealed. "Tell that one!"

"Well, sometime in the 1800s, this guy was driving a wagon with his wife and baby through the town of Jolon, going to claim his land. The Indians warned him the river was too high to cross, but he was dumb and tried it anyway. His wife's head got chopped off, and she haunted the town forever after, looking for her head."

"Cool!" Caleigh had a consuming love of ghost stories.

"But I found Mom's old Jolon, too. It's got to be him, or else he's a performance artist that looks about sixteen in Seattle, or he had a sex change and is a lady realtor in Texas. There were only three actual people with that first name."

"Well, where is he then?" My skin stung, hot all over, like a sudden fever had engulfed me.

"You have to guess!"

Nathan, looking up from spooning Mrs. Pike's pot roast, told Fai, "No need to torture your mother, *chère*."

"Oh, all right, then. He's here. In Hawley. He's the chief of police!"

"You were right," Grace begrudged her. "He came back. Not that we care. We don't need him."

I hoped she was right. I hoped we wouldn't need to have anything to do with the police in Hawley.

"Is Mom okay?" Caleigh was staring at me.

"Hey, Mom. You look pale."

I felt pale. I felt like all the blood had drained from my body. I looked down at my laden plate, picked up my fork. "Nothing dinner won't cure," I asserted, pushing away thoughts of Jolon. I was the mom. It was up to me to keep on, always, in the midst of any storm, in the real world or in my own heart. We bent over our plates to do justice to Mrs. Pike's pot roast.

After dinner and a ferocious game of Scrabble, I made the girls turn in early. They clamored for a Revelation story, so I told them about our ancestor who had spied for the patriots during the Revolutionary War. Her power was reading minds. After the story, I settled them, kissed them all good night, and went to my room. I paged through a new cookbook. I like reading cookbooks before bed. They're soothing, innocuous. Nothing troubling in a cookbook. But I couldn't concentrate on the recipe for polenta soufflé with mushroom cream sauce I'd turned to. Our big day, our candlelit dinner with the night and the forest pressing in around us, had not tired me. The yaw and pitch of my memories, and the discovery of Jolon's return, unsettled me. I gave up on sleep, went to my office, and sat at the desk. Right by the phone was a Hawley telephone directory with a picture of the historical society on the cover. I opened it to the first page. There it was in black and white: "Chief of Police, Jolon Adair," and a phone number. My hand went to the phone without my consent. I snatched it back. It was thirty years too late to call. I'd keep the past in the past. I slapped the town directory shut, went out to the widow's walk. I paced its length, heard an owl calling for its mate. I thought about that more recent past that had made me into a widow, walking. I thought of Jeremy, in those few moments before I pulled the trigger, juggling bright things for the last time. Barely two months ago. I shook my head, tried to clear the image. It never did me any good to remember that night. What happens in Vegas stays in Vegas. I thought of the shirt that still held my husband's scent, the first thing I'd unpacked. I'd had enough memories for one day, enough pain. I went to bed, where I dreamt of Jeremy anyway. I dreamt of being with him in the golden sunlight of a long western afternoon, where I had thought we'd live forever, together. It wasn't a nightmare, but good dreams can be bad, too. They are almost worse than the nightmares, their fleet moments of hope always shattered by waking.

Caleigh's Vision: Nightlight

Caleigh minded the move to Hawley much less than her sisters, because of her string. It was always with her. Plain white, woven, hard string that slipped through her hands easily, yet took form quickly and held its shape, the lines crisp. She liked yarn less, even with all the colors. It didn't slide as well into the forms she required. For every pattern had a different reaction and interaction with the world. She had to be precise and careful.

That is what he'd told her, the magician who had given it to her, years ago, when she was only five. The magician was not a close friend of her parents, but she knew him. So when she saw him in the playground at the park she went to sometimes with her friends and their mothers, she was not afraid. She went about her business, which was hanging from the monkey bars. She was a pro at monkey bars. So why she should suddenly lose her grip and begin to fall, she couldn't think. She had that heart-stopping feeling for only an instant, and then was caught up by the magician, the not-quite friend. He set her down and brushed her off. "A good thing I was near, Miss Caleigh," he told her. "That might have been a nasty tumble." His smile transfixed her, made her think of Siegfried and Roy's tigers, for some reason. "You remember me, don't you?" he asked her, his very white teeth gleaming.

She nodded. She did remember him. She'd seen him at the magic award shows her parents sometimes took them to. He was tall, taller than her father, with coal black hair. Even though he was older than her dad, he was very handsome, like the prince in the fairy tales. He wore his magic cape, though it was hot outside, and his tuxedo. That didn't seem so strange to Caleigh, a child of magicians. Maybe he'd just come from his matinee show, and hadn't bothered to change. It happened. Everyone around Las Vegas was used to seeing performers out in the normal world wearing costumes of some kind.

More troubling was his breath, sweet like candy. And his eyes. They seemed extremely old and keenly watching, as if he were the wolf come to eat her up. But only for a minute, then he laughed and held out a shining length of string. "This," he said, "is for you!" As he threaded his long fingers through it, wove and twirled it, it turned into a white rabbit made of string. Caleigh could see its long ears poking up. Then he said a strange word, like a magic word, *"I-undias!"* And a real, fuzzy white rabbit hopped up through the grass and nibbled at her sneaker.

"How did you do that?"

"It's easy," the magician told her. "You were born to do it, too." He wove the white string through her fingers. His hands made her own feel fiery when he touched her, but then a pattern emerged. It was a butterfly, and yes, a blue butterfly came from out of the sky and landed on her shoulder. "You can see it isn't difficult at all. Just practice, hone your patterns, and make sure you're careful to only summon what fits wherever you happen to be. That's the rule." She was staring at the butterfly with its azure wings. She couldn't quite believe that she had summoned it. Maybe it was a trick the man was playing on her. She looked into his old eyes again, the string slack in her fingers. "Oh, it's real enough," he assured her. "But let it be our secret. You needn't tell anyone, even your lovely mother, that I gave you this string. Its magic could fade the more people know about it. That's the way magic works. You know that, don't you, Caleigh?"

"Yes," she told him. Her mind felt heavy, her tongue slow. She thought she might fall into his dark, deep eyes. "I know that." Then she saw a flash of red behind him. It seemed to release his hold on her. Her friend Sharon's mother walked toward them, her red shirt fluttering in the breeze. When Caleigh looked back, both the man and the rabbit were gone.

"Where did he go?" she asked Sharon's mom.

"Who, sweetheart?" She smoothed Caleigh's hair, wove it through her fingers.

"The man." Then she suddenly remembered the man's magic name. Setekh the Magnificent. But she wasn't supposed to tell it. Sharon's mom scanned the playground for strange men.

"Just a man who had a white rabbit," Caleigh told her.

"Oh, a magical friend of yours?"

Caleigh nodded. She guessed that about summed it up.

"Well, don't worry about him." Sharon's mom seemed relieved. "Come and have a snack with the other girls." And Caleigh went, trailing her string.

For the most part, she followed the rules, but when she was younger, she liked to confound the universe by calling forth lightning in February, moose in the city. Once she had perfected the patterns, she could change things, summon things. Some patterns took longer to perfect than others, especially ones that affected living things. When she was six, the moose she'd conjured onto the Las Vegas Strip was killed by a car while it was ambling by her parents' theater, and she realized the power that was in her hands. She felt terrible, promised herself she'd be more careful. Since then, Caleigh tried to weave her patterns in accordance with the elements and the geography, as the magician, Setekh, had told her. Sometimes she felt the fiery feeling he had stirred up in her fingers, but it no longer troubled her. She thought of him fondly. After all, he had given her the string, her most precious possession.

But Caleigh was worried that her ability to summon with string hadn't followed her to Hawley. The first night, she fell asleep as soon as her head hit the pillow, before she had a chance to find out. She woke in a room bathed in moonlight. Her string was beneath her pillow. She pulled it out, lay in bed, and tried a simple pattern, one she'd worked many times before. "Nightlight," she called it, and when it was formed, it looked like a flashlight beam. At first, she couldn't see the pattern in the darkness, but as her fingers worked, a faint glow began to creep from the corners, sliding up the wall to encase her in the bed. Caleigh boxed out the corners of the pattern, then said "Stay," as she might to her dog if she had one (why hadn't she ever thought to summon a dog for herself?). She dropped the string. The light remained. "Well, that's all right then," she said to no one in particular. She sighed and closed her eyes, but her fingers still worked on the string, as if she were telling herself a bedtime story. Thinking of that, she wanted her book. She was reading *At the Back of the North Wind*, but she'd forgotten it in all the excitement of getting to Hawley, had left it in her mother's book bag, the one from the Petroglyph National Monument, where they'd gone the year before. She thought she'd seen Nathan carry the bag upstairs.

She listened hard, but didn't hear anyone stirring. She thought it must be very late. She'd just run upstairs quick to get her book. Moonlight streamed into the hall from the window on the landing. She didn't really need the nightlight, but it preceded her anyway, reminding her again of an obedient little dog. She climbed the stairs to the third floor quietly, her bare feet gliding on the smooth wood. The moonlight splashed small pools and intricate, lacy shadows in her path. The house was so still around her that she could hear her own breathing. If she had been a fearful child, she would have been afraid then.

Caleigh walked into her mother's office and spied the Petroglyph bag, leaning against the desk. She shone her night-light inside the bag. Just as she placed a hand on her book she felt someone watching her, but still she was not afraid, only curious. She spun around quickly, shone her nightlight at the watcher. It was a lady, in a painting from another time. The lady looked nice. She looked smart and very kind. She looked as if she was just about to ask or tell something important. Washed in moonlight and nightlight, Caleigh could see that the lady's hand was pointing downward. All that blue, milky light shone on a slight crack in the wall just below the lady's pointing finger. In the crevice, Caleigh saw a flash of red and gold.

She put down *At the Back of the North Wind* and slid her fingers over the wall. It was smooth and unbroken. The crack in it was gone. She shrugged her shoulders, scooped up her book, and ran on tiptoe back to her room.

Caleigh jumped into bed, pulled the covers over her head, and started reading by the nightlight, which had scooted in under the blanket with her. As soon as she started reading the part of the story about the fairies who lived in the woods, her eyes grew heavy. She dropped the book and slept.

Behind her eyes, in her dreams, a room popped up, a room that she knew to be the dining room below her. Only it was changed. The ceiling was low, and plants hung from the rafters upside down. Herbs, she decided, like her grandmother grew.

A girl about her age walked into the room, carrying a metal pail. She dumped it into a wooden trough. She wore a long dress that touched the toes of her thick brown boots, and a white hat with sides like wings. Caleigh couldn't see her face at first. A woman walked in then, way too old to be the girl's mother. Maybe her grandmother. She wore a long brown dress as well, but only a delicate lace cap perched on her gray hair. She asked the girl, "Be the cows in the hollow?"

"They are."

The girl took a big wooden spoon and had a drink from the trough, then handed the spoon to the woman, who shook her head. "Is your father down plowing still?"

"I brought him water."

"Then rest, girl, and I'll show you a thing you'll need fore long." The woman moved to the big brick fireplace that took up half of a wall. It was where the Noah's Ark fireplace was now. The woman looked toward the door, pried out one brick, then another. She reached her hand into the space she'd made in the wall and pulled out a book with a faded red leather cover, gold writing. It looked very old. The woman stroked its pages.

"Tell no one of this. Keep this to your own breast. Soon you'll be the woman of this house."

"I cannot . . ."

"You know how it must be." The woman spoke sharply. "I am old. I have lived beyond my years. You must know how to use your power. You will be the next to write in this Book. You will be the Keeper of the Book, Revelation."

Caleigh's eyes flew open. The girl, the woman, and the room spun, then were whisked away, just like when she closed a document on her computer.

Revelation. The old-timey girl had the same name as her mother. She was one of them.

8

My eyes flew open. I sat up, but nothing seemed familiar, the dark shapes of furniture in the wrong places; even the dusty air seemed wrong. Then I remembered. We were in Hawley. The setting moon shone bright through the curtainless window, and its steady light calmed me. I remembered my dreams of Jeremy, then a weird pastiche of nightmare. I'd been in the theater, trying to practice a trick. The trick was called Book of Life, and it was one I'd never done. To perform the trick, I held a red leather book open before me, and in it I could see scenes from the past. People from other times lived their lives in it, were children, crawled then walked, learned to ride, work sums, tend fires. Courting couples were in the book. Battles and babies and treks through great forests and deserts were there, too. The trick was that every scene in the book must spring onto the stage, take its turn under the lights. I couldn't make it happen, though. I couldn't concentrate because a man's voice was in my head, saying, "I'll find you, my pretty one. I'll have you yet. I'll find you, always and forever."

I rose from my solitary bed, but I kept hearing the voice:

"I'll have you yet." The phrase echoed in my head. It troubled me. I knew it from somewhere. I went to the drawer that held Jeremy's shirt, wrapped it around me, and slept soundly.

Caleigh's Vision: Missing Dad

Caleigh felt feverish and infinitely thirsty, like she could drink an ocean. She thought about getting up, getting a drink, maybe going to tell her mother of her dream, but her muscles were limp as overcooked spaghetti. To comfort herself, she wove the "Missing Dad" pattern, and there he was, sitting on a rock by the ocean near their house in Ireland. She wanted him to hold her, pet her hair as he always used to do, tell her, "Poor, poor. Poor Caleigh," until she felt better. But she couldn't get to him. She could only watch while he looked out at the ocean. Even just seeing him comforted her, though, and soon she fell into a second deep sleep. By morning, she'd forgotten all about her adventures in the night. Her dreams had faded as dreams tend to do, until darkness falls again.

Hawley Village—October 19, 2013

1

We spent the next week getting settled. The twins fussed over their rooms, painting walls and rearranging their furniture and clothing. Caleigh read and ate apples from the trees out in the yard, crunching and turning pages loudly while we all worked. My mom, dad, and Nathan had all been enjoined into domestic service, and every day they helped me scrub floors, knock down cobwebs, load hay into the barn. The heat persisted, the air thick and hazy. Sweat pearled on our skin at the least exertion. But the morning of the fair dawned cooler, and with that jewel-edged clarity October days have only in New England.

I made myself coffee and poured it into a thick mug to take up to my office. I gazed out the French doors at the sun, listened to the birdsong. The heat hadn't stopped the transformation of the foliage. We were poised at the turn of the season. The winds and sleet and cold could come any time, but that day the glow of the trees was still like palpable light. Scarlet and salmon, and fleshy gold-veined green they shone, although soon enough the leaves would fall and dry and blow away, leaving only skeletal branches reaching like bones into the sky.

But that day was golden, like the David Bowie song we danced to at our wedding, the one Jeremy used to sing to me. Our first time away together had been to London, to visit his parents. We'd seen Bowie's *Sound + Vision* concert at the Docklands. "Golden Years" was Jeremy's favorite song. He'd often pop up and startle me, croon it tunelessly in my ear. One of his little jokes I told myself I'd never miss. And now I was crying in my coffee, wishing I could hear him sing it one more time.

I had a flash of memory. It was a Monday, our very last Monday together. The one day of the week completely devoted to smoothing out kinks in our current show and developing new tricks for the next we were planning. The theater was dark Monday nights, and Jeremy and I often stayed late at the workshop, got takeout. It was also one of the only times we could be completely alone.

I was in my office, puzzling over an awkward transition in the *Mascherari* script when I heard Dan call, "See you tomorrow," and the big overhead door slam and lock. I pushed back my chair and began working the knots out of my neck. Then I felt Jeremy's hands grip my shoulders, gently coaxing my muscles. "*That* feels good."

"How about this?" He breathed the question into my ear as he slid his hands down the length of me, to rest at my waist. He kissed me then, just at the base of my collarbone. I could smell the oniony scent of flash powder on him. It was like an aphrodisiac to me, that smell. I took his face in my hands, kissed him deep. I loved the view of his known face when I kissed him, its planes and arcs. I never closed my eyes, but always looked into his, elementally blue as sky or water. He pulled me to him, carried me to the couch I kept there for those late nights. Jeremy wasn't tall, but he had the kind of strength that came from using his whole body for his work, the strength acrobats or jockeys have.

His hands, clever from card and coin tricks, unbuttoned me as he went. "It's a minor miracle to me that you are still a featherweight after three children, Mrs. Maskelyne." I laughed. When his mouth settled on my breast, his hand slipped into the wetness between my legs. My laugh turned to a hum of pleasure at the magic our bodies always seemed to find together.

My hands reached for him and hit glass. The old window didn't shatter, in spite of its bubbles and fissures, but there I was, back in Hawley. A glaze of tears shone on my face reflected in the window, and I felt the sting of freshened pain, the wound Jeremy's death made opening again.

But then I heard Caleigh's heavy feet pounding the stairs. I steeled myself to go and make breakfast. By the time I'd wiped my eyes and got down to the kitchen, Caleigh was slamming cabinet doors, complaining in the whiny little girl voice I was trying to break her of.

"Why can't we get some *fun* cereal?"

"Because it's full of sugar, and you're ready to jump out of your skin now. How about scrambled eggs?"

"With cheese?"

"You know it." I felt another stab of grief as I remembered the last meal Jeremy ever made for her, Caleigh's green eggs and ham. She never asked for it now. Maybe someday she'd make it for her own children, tell them how her father had invented it for her. I hoped so. There were so many lasts, and I couldn't help but replay them all, my mind stuck on rewind. I knew it was the same for the girls. We all carried him with us in different ways, the loss still so fresh we hadn't found any ease in bearing it.

I started assembling pans and ingredients, pushing aside my brooding thoughts while Caleigh formed and re-formed patterns with her string.

"I wish we could have breakfast at the fair. I bet they have good doughnuts."

"I bet they do. But we're not meeting Grand and Gramps there until eleven."

"We could go early."

"We could, but then we'd be there for hours and hours."

"That would be great. Hey, will Gramps take us for a ride in the cool car?" My father's not-quite retirement from the Williams College faculty had freed up enough time for him to restore an ancient Packard convertible. All the girls loved it. I could see the wheels of the car Caleigh was shaping in string.

"I bet he will."

She tucked into her eggs, and after she finished, she threw herself into my lap. She was dressed in her favorite bright green Hello Kitty T-shirt and a plaid skirt. At least we'd be able to find her in a crowd.

"Mom, I've been having some weird dreams. Well, not really dreams. More like, I don't know . . . like something that happened a long time ago, and I can see it."

A thin shiver ran through me. The strange dreams I'd been having over the past week shuffled around in my mind like a pack of cards. "Well, do they upset you?"

"Not really. They just seem so real."

"What happens in the dreams?"

"A girl is there, in long dresses. Her mom, too, sometimes. Or her grandmother. They do stuff. Cook things, or clean. And there's a book—a book the girl has but she doesn't really want it."

The book with red leather covers pursued me in my dreams, too. Sometimes I'd be trying to perform the trick called Book of Life, sometimes I dreamed of a woman who was supposed to keep the book safe. The woman would shift and change; sometimes she would be the woman in the painting, but often others would take her place. An old woman, or a woman with red hair like my own. Many of the dreams would begin with the ever-changing woman writing in the book with a quill pen. Then she'd startle at a noise, close the book up, run to hide it. Some nights she buried it in the earth. Some nights she hid it behind a loose brick in a wall. But the next night, it would appear again.

Caleigh looked up at me, searched my face, as if she knew about my dreams that echoed hers. "And Mom? The girl has your name."

I held her tighter, kissed her cheek. Wondered what it meant, that the Revelations were in our dreams. I felt them close, surrounding us in this house. The woman in the painting might have been a Revelation, for all I knew. Was some kind of relation, probably. It still troubled me that I hadn't remembered seeing it the first time I went through the house, with Carl Streeter. I'd thought about calling him to ask if the painting had always been there. But he'd think I was a nut-cake.

"Well, sweetheart, your dreams may be flashes of what happened here, many years ago. You know your string games are a kind of magic you can do, and divining things that happened in the past could be another part of your gift."

"Yeah, sometimes it starts when I'm making a pattern. Or when I'm reading."

"I don't think it's anything to worry about at all."

"So it's not weird?"

"No, I don't think it's weird. But you know, sometimes it's

good to write down your dreams. Then they don't bother you as much. Can you do that?"

"I guess I can." She paused, then said, "Daddy helps, too. I see him, Mom, when I make the 'Missing Dad' pattern." I hugged her close, breathing in her fresh, milky smell. She pinched the skin of my knuckle. It amused her that it stayed in a ridge, didn't snap right back like hers. Her face had lost its troubled look. "*Now* can I go wake up Grace and Fai?" One of Caleigh's favorite pastimes was leaping onto her sisters' beds and bouncing them until they got up.

"Sweetheart, we don't have to leave for a while yet. Let them sleep. If you don't they'll be cranky. Then none of us will be pleased with you, you know."

"Oh, all right," Caleigh sighed. "But what will I *do*?"

"Last I knew Nathan was outside. You could go and bother him."

"I think I'll just read." She slid off my lap, plucked an oatmeal cookie from the jar, then darted out, the door banging behind her.

I crumbled uneaten toast between my fingers, wondered what our twinned Revelation dreams meant. Although I felt better behind my high fence, I didn't want to risk the lives of my children on it alone, or on my own unconfirmed feelings of safety, or old family legends. We sure hadn't been safe in Las Vegas. But would we be any safer in Hawley? I had fled in desperation, but I'd had a lot of time to think in the past week while washing old panes of mottled glass and hacking at weeds. I realized that there were just too many unanswered questions. Why had Nan been so adamant we come here to Five Corners? And how had she known about the Fetch? Before I even had much of a clue myself, she had *known*.

I'd taken the girls to visit her just after we'd arrived, but she'd kept us busy, made sure we were all swirled up with her hawks and helping the girls fly them. Tiny and implacable, she'd commanded and coaxed the girls all morning, her long silver braid swinging as she gestured at them. When she'd gone in the house to supervise snacks, I followed her, caught her in the hall, asked her what she meant when she sent the note.

"An old woman's fancy, maybe . . . no need to dissect it, Reve. You're here now and that's what matters."

"But why were you so insistent? And how did you know about the Fetch? Our Fetch? I never told anyone." I took hold of her bird-wing arm, thin as a stick. Nan tisked at me, just as one of her birds might, and shook me off. She was shrunken with age now, but still strong with ropy muscle from handling hawks and cleaning mews every day of her long life.

"Don't look for more trouble, Revelation," she told me. "You have enough." And she strode into the kitchen, commanding her housekeeper to hurry with lunch.

The connection of the distant past with what was happening now had been tugging at the periphery of my consciousness, and my dreams kept stirring it all up again. And now Caleigh's. I sighed, yanked my hair back until my scalp hurt, determined to pull all the weirdness out of my brain.

Miss May, our goat, bleated desultorily just outside the kitchen door and brought me back to the present. She was missing the horses. As soon as I knew where we were bound for, I'd had them shipped to a farm in Vermont. Even before I had any idea how I would get my family away. The horses had been bred and raised in the West, with its dearth of trees, and I knew they'd need time to get used to the heavy foliage of New England, the shadows it cast, the drifts of leaves. Even a well-trained horse will spook at things it's unaccustomed to. It would have been stupid to uproot us all to ensure the safety of my children, then let the twins crack their heads open in a needless fall. It was a risk to even bring the horses, since the Fetch could track their route as well as ours, but I reasoned that I couldn't take everything from Grace and Fai. Or myself. So I'd written up false bills of sale, trying to cover their tracks, too.

I'd shipped Miss May with the horses, but as soon as the owner of the farm learned we were on the East Coast, she insisted on sending the goat down to us before the horses were due back. She informed me that Miss May had wreaked more havoc than any horse she'd ever trained. I chalked up her complaints to goat ignorance. If Miss May didn't get what she expected, when she expected it, she'd let you know. For instance, she was usually quiet for most of the morning as long as she had a treat after breakfast. So when I opened the door armed with an oatmeal cookie, Miss May trotted up, her dark coat shining like a Hollywood starlet's mink. She took the cookie I offered gently, then ran off, her white tail twinkling at me.

I nudged a cookie out of the jar for myself, picked up my mug, and headed back upstairs. Caleigh's noise had brought me down to the kitchen before I could check my e-mail.

When I got to the office, I turned on the computer, and the usual morning spam greeted me. Offers to update my wardrobe, my body, my car. Nothing crucial, so I logged off, went out to the widow's walk. Something shone metallic in the white steeple of the church across the common. A breeze came up, and I heard a faint sound, a resonance, almost like singing. I whirled, thinking the sound came from the portrait behind me. But the woman's smiling face was as serene as ever. Then I heard it again, that singing, from the other direction, soft on the autumn air. A scream snagged in my throat. But the scream became a laugh. What I'd heard was only the church bell, glinting in the sun, sounding in the wind. I laughed at myself until I felt better. We wouldn't start living in fear again that day. It was only slightly haunted Hawley, stuck a few hundred years in the past, that lurked here.

I went down to wake my sleepy twins. We'd go to the fair and pretend, at least, to be a normal family. I thought again of Jeremy's favorite song, and hoped for a golden day.

2

Main Street teemed with cars and people. The town hall was a hive of Girl Scouts and farmers. The Ladies Benevolent Society hawked warm apple pie, spicy chili, fried dough with maple cream. The common overflowed, a bluegrass band played, and children clambered over hay bales or threw balls into buckets for lime green yo-yos or purple bears.

I drove down the street, looking for a place to park. I was still slightly panicked being out in a sea of strangers. But I'd promised the girls. And there hadn't been any trace of the Fetch in our wake.

"There it is!" Fai shouted in my ear. Dad's Packard, parked in the church lot, was hard to miss—spring green, long and low-slung. I parked next to the Suds & Stuff Laundromat, and the girls leapt from the car.

"All right now, let's stay together until we find them," I called, to no avail. Grace and Fai were already halfway up the block, their hair bright halos in the sun.

"It's okay, they know we're meeting in front of Elmer's," Caleigh reassured me. But I held tight to her hand as we made our way through the crowd. The sidewalk was overrun with kids and old people, farmers in feed caps and tourists sporting "Life is good" togs.

"Grand!" Caleigh whooped, racing to her, throwing herself between Grace and Fai to get at my mother. She was dressed in her gardening clothes, red clogs, faded and pilled green Fair Isle sweater, wide-legged chinos. She never cared what she wore, yet somehow managed to emit repose and a spontaneous elegance. She *was* Grand, as the girls called her. Maybe it was her height. Whatever it was, I hadn't inherited it from her. I always felt like a pygmy beside my mother. At least I *had* inherited her greyhound thinness and a wilder version of her stunning hair. Although hers was now threaded with silver, it was as glorious as ever. It shone, a Pre-Raphaelite golden red. She was growing it again, as the twins were, for Locks of Love. She smacked Caleigh on the cheek, then reached for me. I felt her cheek soft as the petals of the roses she grew. But the worry lines on her brow were furrowed.

"Where's Dad?" I asked, after she had embraced me.

"Oh, off looking at some old tractors. You know how he is about machines. He says he'll meet us at the pie stall, oh . . ." She glanced at her watch. "Now, actually. He says he's hungry, but he's already had blueberry cobbler and doughnuts."

"Just like Caleigh. She'll eat her way through the fair. I hope he's prepared to be dragged around to every food opportunity again."

"And to all the crafts," Fai reminded me.

"And the crafts. Don't worry. He's been briefed. Just stay with him, and stay *together*."

My mother and I watched the girls sprint up to the town hall steps. I took her arm. "You look tired, Mom."

She waved that idea away. “Not tired. Just . . . I don’t know, thinking too much.” She hesitated, and a strange look came into her eyes, one I’d been seeing more often, and that worried me. Then it passed like a summer cloud.

“But you! Look at you!” She shed her gracious smile on me. I felt like a committee meeting she was chairing. Ever since we’d moved to Hawley, she’d been distant. She always seemed to be deflecting me. And although she’d been helping me at the Hawley house nearly every day, there had been something subdued about her. Somehow I felt she was holding back, holding out on me. Like Nan. The girls had been helping or hindering us every moment, though, so I hadn’t been able to grill her. Until today.

“*You’ve* been looking better since you moved back,” she told me. “More like yourself, Reve.”

That annoyed me. “How did you expect me to look after my husband was murdered, Mom?”

Her eyes flared with an unreadable emotion—not exactly pain, or shame. Maybe a little of both, mixed in with something elusive. “Oh, honey, I didn’t mean that.” She hugged me. “Let’s just try to enjoy the day. They have good weather for it this year. Poured buckets all last fall, I remember.”

I sighed, decided to let it go for the moment.

We found my dad sitting on the wall outside the town hall, snacking on apple pie topped with a thick slice of cheddar cheese. Grace and Fai were making gagging noises, but he was feeding Caleigh a bite from his fork. Unlike my mother, he always looked as if he had prepared to face the world with care, but something was just a bit off. He forgot to comb his hair, or his vest was buttoned wrong. But then he’d smile and his eyes would crinkle and you’d forget any little flaws, his look bathed you in such kindly warmth. For the fair, he wore a jacket and bow tie, but the tie was crooked and now dusted with powdered sugar, probably from his breakfast doughnut. He almost upset his pie on Caleigh's head when he rose to greet me.

"Sweetheart!" He wrapped me in his arms. "Everything okay?"

I nodded into his tweedy shoulder. "Just . . . watch the girls."

He looked in my eyes, saw enough to know I was still troubled. "Of course I will."

For all his absentminded ways, my father was incredibly observant. So I left him to shepherd the girls around, and my mother and I went off in search of treasure. For Mom, it would be interesting old garden tools; for me, maybe an opportunity to get some answers.

Our first stop was the blueberry cobbler tent. I toyed with the perfectly sweetened blueberries, the crumbly biscuit. My mother commented again on the fine day, all the people who'd turned out. Then I plunged in.

"Remember the stories you all used to tell? About the Revelations."

The fragrance of apples wafted around us. A woman rolled a red wagon full of Macouns by. Mom licked her fork speculatively, leaned back in her chair. "Is that why you moved here? Because of the story of the first Revelation, how she came to Hawley Five Corners?"

"Not really. I probably wouldn't have given Hawley one thought. But Nan . . . she sent me a note, just after Jeremy died. Basically commanding me to come here."

"*Nan* sent you a note?" Her tone was accusing, her eyes filled with hurt.

"Mom, what's the big deal?"

She looked down, scraped at her dish again. The sound of the fork on Styrofoam set my teeth on edge. "Nothing. No big deal. I was just . . . surprised, for a minute."

"I tried to call her yesterday, to invite her to the fair, but you know she never answers that phone. I tried to talk to her when we went there last week, but she wouldn't. Not about why she was insistent we come here. Do you know?"

"Oh, that's just Nan. She loves being mysterious."

My grandmother had always been eccentric. There were the powers and the stories of the Dyer women that preoccupied her. And the falconry. Then about twenty years ago, she'd gotten involved with the Baptist church. She had lived with each of her three daughters in turn when I was a child. But after I left for Nevada she moved back into her family home in Bennington, Vermont. A few months later, the Reverend John Steel insinuated himself. Nan insisted that she had always hated living alone, and that's all she would say. We still had no idea what their relationship was. The Reverend was three decades younger, and pretty strange himself. I'd met him only a few times. Enough to know he was odd. But then, so was my Nan. I always suspected the rift between my mother and Nan had to do with the Reverend, although neither of them would ever talk about it.

"Anyway, in her note, Nan mentioned the story of the Fetch. Do you remember it?"

She closed her eyes. Against the sun? Or maybe against the myth?

"Yes. I remember. That's the one where the father is spirited off by a creature that haunts a family. One of the stranger tales Nan tells. Of course it's one of your father's favorites. It always gave *you* nightmares."

"I've been calling our stalker the Fetch. Thinking of him that way, after Nan's note reminded me of the story. But the note was . . . well, pretty cryptic. I'd love to know the *reason* she's so sure we'll be safe here. It might make me feel better. It can't all be old legends and stories. Or the legends must have some basis, anyway, if she was that certain. She wrote something about history repeating itself. What did she mean?"

My mom looked off into the blue distance of the day, thoughtful. "I really don't have a clue. But Nan has her own way of seeing things. And telling things."

I laughed. "That's for sure. When I asked, she just said not to look for trouble. I need to know more, though, and Nan talks in riddles half the time. She dodges my questions. Maybe because she's so old, maybe she doesn't really remember. But it frustrates me."

"Nan's always been like that. Old age is no excuse. She remembers plenty, but your aunts and I gave up ever trying to get any kind of clarity out of her. You're more persistent."

"You mean stubborn. That's what Nan said, too." I speared a blueberry with my plastic fork. It tasted like the forest. "But, really, the stories are kind of a blur, like fairy tales you read to me when I was a kid. I don't remember all Nan's tall tales. I remember some of them, especially the story of the Fetch, and the one about the first Revelation and the founding of Hawley. I've been having dreams about the Revelations. Caleigh has, too. It's a little . . . I don't know, unsettling, I guess." I mashed another tiny blueberry. "There's a painting, an old portrait in the house. I think the woman in it must be a Dyer. One of the Revelations. Maybe it's the portrait that triggers the dreams. I wanted to ask Nan if she knew anything about it, but I never got that far."

"I don't remember ever seeing a painting of any of the Revelations. Do you know the period?"

"I'd say mid-nineteenth century, by her dress, and her hair. She looks about twenty-five, maybe thirty in the portrait, so she would have been born around 1840 or 1845."

"Well, there was Nan's grandmother," Mom suggested. "Those dates seem about right for her."

"Could she have lived here?"

"I'm not sure. I always *thought* all Nan's family lived in Bennington, from pretty far back. Her grandmother was a Revelation, though. She might have been the last of the family to live in Hawley." The Dyer women had scattered over time, but not so very far. Travel was slower and more costly in the past. Unless you were suspected of being a witch, there wasn't much incentive to leave the town you were born in. A woman might move to the next town over. The one next to that if she met her husband at a barn raising and his family lived twenty or thirty miles away. "Didn't Carl Streeter work on the house? Did you ask him about it?"

"I don't want to rock that boat. He probably doesn't know anything, and . . . well, it's creepy, how everyone in town thinks of the Five Corners. *They* don't think it's safe there at all. They think it's haunted. The day we got here Carl told me a story. Then he got all jittery as if he'd done the wrong thing telling me. About the last people who lived there, and how they just left their possessions and took off all together, all on the same day. No one seems to know where they went. Have you ever heard anything about it?" I asked. "I've been wondering if any of the Dyers lived in Hawley then, if there are any family stories."

"I don't think so. Nan lived with relatives in Bennington after her parents died in the Spanish influenza epidemic. Your aunts and I grew up there. But you knew that. Nan never talked about her childhood much. It was a bad time for her, losing both her parents that way, within days of each other. And some of the family history just got lost. Even Nan's legends are pretty sketchy. She tells bits and pieces. As you said, they're like fairy tales, bedtime stories."

I knew what my mom meant about the loss of history. Any recorded history was more likely to be about the men. Some of the Dyer history was lost because the wives bore different last names than their husbands. Then, after their deaths, they were buried under their husbands' names alone. "Mary, wife of John Smith." A double whammy of lost connections. I'd seen the stones in the old boneyards scattered around, like all New Englanders. If you live in New England you can't spit without hitting a cemetery.

"Mom, have you ever heard of some kind of book, a book that's important in our family? Caleigh and I have been having dreams about a book, too."

My mom's mouth opened, and she made a strangled sound.

"Mom?"

Her eyes went blank, turned dark, like a doll's eyes. She gasped, then her hand shot across the table to grab my wrist. She squeezed it, hard.

"Mom! Are you choking?" I leapt up, but suddenly her hand relaxed its grip, her eyes went back to normal. She smiled at me, then stood up, stretching her arms to the sky. "Well, let's go poke around. See if we can get some information here in town, at the historical society. Maybe we can get a bead on your painting."

Relief flooded me, but I had no idea what I'd just seen. "Shit, Mom. You scared me. *Were* you choking?"

"What?" She looked at me like I had two heads. "How could I choke on blueberry cobbler? You're too stirred up, honey. You're imagining things."

"I am not!" I snapped. "I'm worried about you!"

"Oh, Reve, don't *fuss*."

I fumed as I followed my striding mother as she made her way to the house with the Betsy Ross flag out front. Hawley's historical society was capitalizing on the crowd, selling key chains and old maps on the front porch. I had no idea what we were doing there, and I was cross with Mom, but I sure didn't want to send her into another one of those fits.

A faded older woman sat behind the displays outside the historical society. She was reading an Elmore Leonard book. Unlike the other booths and exhibits, this one was not packed with people. Only one man, obviously from out of town with his polished Docksiders and a camera bobbing against his navy polo-shirted chest, was perusing the offerings.

He left after buying a key chain, left us alone with Hawley's history. My mom plucked up a monograph with a sepia photograph of Hawley Town Hall on its cover. She flipped through it, while I turned the pages of the latest calendar. The faded lady, brought out of the depths of her book, looked up at us.

"Is there anything I can help you with? We only have a few things out for sale. The historical society museum isn't open to the public today, I'm afraid." Her voice dropped to a near-whisper. "We had some theft last year during the fair, some museum items stolen. So we decided it would be better . . ."

"Oh, of course," Mom piped in, using her committee meeting voice. Whatever had happened at the blueberry cobbler tent, she was definitely back to normal now. "The same thing happened in Williamstown, at the parsonage

Christmas tea. Do you know, somebody snuck upstairs and stole a chamber pot?" I stifled my laughter, as the faded lady did not seem amused.

"Well, here it was a file of original Howes Brothers plates," she informed us grimly. "Quite a loss." The Howes Brothers had been itinerant photographers in the late nineteenth and early twentieth centuries. They traveled all the towns of western Massachusetts, photographing families and thousands of structures, houses, barns, and grange halls that have since been torn down or renovated beyond recognition. My mother sent me the Williamstown Savings Bank calendar every year, which always featured Howes Brothers photographs of the old towns and farms. The images were evocative of a kind of life just as vanished as the original settlers.

"How dreadful for you! My daughter and I have always loved the Howes Brothers. I'm Morgan Dyer and this is my daughter. Reve's just moved to town, and was thinking of becoming a historical society friend." I had to admire her skill. The faded lady was eating it up.

"Here's the information, and the form. If you join at the individual or family level, you'll get a Hawley Pudding Contest apron. At the friend level, you'd also get an autographed copy of Howard Stark's history of Hawley. But we don't get too many friends in this economy." I figured I should have the book anyway, and for the $200, maybe I'd get more information from the faded lady. I whipped out my checkbook. I could afford to be a friend, and God knew I needed some, too, even if I had to buy them.

"Where do you live, dear? Are you the ones bought the Hartland place?"

I tore out the check, handed it to her. She studied it for a moment. Maybe it was my imagination, but her pale face seemed to pale even more.

"Hawley Five Corners," she said, and dropped the check I'd given her as if it scorched her hand. We both scrabbled on the floor for it. She captured it, then looked at the amount. "Two hundred dollars! Well. This certainly is generous." She slid my book and apron in a white plastic bag, handed it over. "You sure have your work cut out for you there. Carl Streeter's society treasurer. We've heard quite a bit at the last meeting about your move to the old Sears place."

My mom nudged me. "Carl is the one I give credit to. Without him I would never have been able to find workmen, or get the house ready in time. I moved here with my three daughters after my husband's death . . . so I'm happy to be closer to my parents." As usual, I stumbled a little on the explanation that placed the words *husband* and *death* in the same sentence. My mother flashed her best "what a good daughter" smile. The faded lady was looking on with interest now. She seemed to have regained a little color. "I *am* sorry. It must have been difficult for you. But Carl is a wonder. I'm sure he was a great help. It's due to him we have such a good collection. He scouts the auction catalogs, raises money for acquisitions. Even goes to yard sales at the old houses, hunting for historical treasures."

"Carl told me a little about Five Corners history," I said. "About the auction that took place after the town was abandoned. Do you know if anything from Five Corners made its way to the society's collection? There's a painting in my house, and I was wondering about it. Whether it was painted by anyone local. Whether there might be more by the same artist. It's a portrait, maybe painted in the 1860s." I didn't mention the possible family connection.

The lady faded again. I had to lean in to hear her muffled answer: "The society acquired only a few things from the Five Corners. No paintings, that I know of. And nothing from the auction."

"I wonder why. It seems like it would have been a wonderful opportunity."

"Well, the society didn't have the member base it does now. Then acquisitions were mostly by donation."

"I see. Of course I'd like to find out more about the Five Corners. Does Mr. Stark's book deal with its history, too?"

"Not much. Five Corners was a separate town, though. Not really part of Hawley Village, ever. They had their own store and post office. Even their own church."

"Then the abandonment of the town wasn't recorded in any way? Which families went where, how long the process took?"

The faded lady had not only faded, but turned to a pillar of salt as well. "No," she said at last. "Nothing that's definite. Just that by the midtwenties, they were gone."

"Then there wouldn't be any documents that might shed light on why they left?"

Faded lady took a sip of water from a Poland Spring bottle stashed under the table. "I thought it was the painting you were interested in."

"I'm interested in Five Corners history, in general. Since I'm living there now."

She toyed with her book, ruffling the pages as if she was dying to get back to it. "Well. The Five Corners church may still contain some birth and death records, maybe even church attendance. If no one has taken them, although I can't see why anyone would want to. I don't know where in the church they'd be, but you could look around."

"Yes. I'll do that. I heard the church bell chime a little in the wind this morning, so I know *that's* still there."

If I thought the lady's face was white previously, now she looked like all the blood had been drained from her.

"But . . . you couldn't have. The church bell was one of the few things taken for this town. It was cast in 1759, for the church at Five Corners, but it's in our town hall now." We all looked across the street at the belfry that topped the town hall. It must have been open for the fair. People in bright T-shirts were up there enjoying the view, standing around a big brass bell. "That's it. They only added on the bell tower here after they took the bell from the Five Corners church. It went up in 1928." She gave me an odd look. "I wonder what it was you heard."

Mom took my arm, and pinched me as she did so. "Oh, it must have been music from the fair," she told the faded lady. "Sounds echo off these hills in strange ways, don't they? When the wind is right in the summer I hear music from the Williamstown Common concerts, and my house is two miles away."

"That must be it then." Our lady looked relieved.

"I'm sure it must. Look at the time! We should go, Reve." She propelled me down the steps. "It was lovely to chat!"

Faded lady waved my check in the air. "Thank you again, for becoming a friend!" It almost rhymed.

Mom steered me through a pack of children eating maple cotton candy, spun in foamy clouds bigger than their heads.

"That was interesting. You're right, Reve. She behaved so oddly the moment she realized you lived at the Five Corners."

"Maybe she's just odd to begin with."

"How about Carl Streeter?"

"Everybody's strange here. It must be the water."

"And you didn't tell me about the bell."

"I didn't think much about it, until history lady had a cow."

"Let's go see it. They're letting people up." My mother loves a mystery. Agatha Christie and Dorothy Sayers are her favorite writers.

"All right," I said. "Let's go see the bell."

After climbing the narrow, dark stairway, we came up into brilliant light. The town and the forest were laid out like a bright quilt, the saturated colors of the trees—gold and scarlet, magenta and emerald—scrolled out to the edge of the state and beyond, to the Green Mountains of Vermont. Suddenly a tag of poetry flew into my head. *The woods are lovely, dark, and deep.* I knew it was Robert Frost. I couldn't remember the rest of the poem at all, but the rhythm echoed through me like another pulse.

We crowded around the rail with other sightseers: a pair of teenagers locked in an embrace, the polo-shirted man we'd seen on the historical society porch snapping pictures of the view, his big-haired wife gripping his camera case, a mother holding her young son back, warning him not to climb the railing. After a look at the hills, we stepped back from the crowd and turned to the bell itself. It was cast from bronze that had turned nearly black with age. There was writing just above the lip of the bell, which I pointed out to Mom. All we could see on our side were the words BEHOLD, I AM. My mother read aloud as we walked around the bell again: "'I am he that liveth, and was dead; and behold, I am alive forevermore.'" She paused before the attribution, then read on: "'Revelation 1:18' . . . it's from the book of Revelation. Isn't that strange?"

It might or might not have been strange that a quote from

the book of Revelation was inscribed on the church bell. It might or might not have been a sign that I was in the right place to keep my family alive, if not forevermore, then at least for the usual span. But I wanted to think that it was.

3

We walked out of the sun into the darkness of the stairwell, which was very like a well altogether, and smelled of damp and mouse. I'm used to negotiating the shadowy spaces of theaters, can see in the dark better than most, but I must have taken a false step. I lurched forward, unbalanced. I scrabbled to catch myself, but went down anyway, hitting my elbow, my knee. I braced myself for landing on the hard wooden floor, but when I tumbled into the light, I was caught by steadying hands. I fell against a man's solid chest instead of the floor.

I felt myself blushing an unattractive color, fuchsia, maybe. Why are we so mortified by a stumble, a fall? After a certain age we want to stay on our feet, even though the children we started out as are always with us, always falling, being hurt in one way or another. We just get better at hiding it. But when I looked up at the man who'd rescued me, I knew there was no way to hide anything. Eyes I knew too well met mine.

"Reve!"

I would have fallen farther if he hadn't still been holding me. Jolon. His black hair short now, only a little graying, his lithe boy body filled out to a man's. His face had hardened with his body. Although he smiled at me now, it was a long-lost smile. Maybe one he rarely used.

My mom caught up to us. "Jolon! What a surprise!"

"Ma'am." He stepped back and let me go. Although before he did, he made sure of my steadiness and told me, "You're all right, then." He gave me a heads-up look, nodded. An old familiar gesture. He'd picked me up many times, after all, saved me again and again from my headlong self. I thought suddenly how unlike Jeremy he was. Jeremy who knew never to catch me. Jeremy who knew I could take care of myself, and wanted to, more than almost anything. I'd learned to save myself, and wanted to keep it that way. Even after all that had happened, *that* intrinsic bit of my makeup hadn't changed.

"Are you visiting from away?" Mom was smiling up at him, delighted.

He shook his head. "I live here. I'm just taking a break from flipping burgers at the police- and firemen's food booth. I'm Hawley's police chief now."

"I didn't know that, although *how* I didn't mystifies me." Mom was usually up on all the small-town current events in western Mass and southern Vermont, even if she wasn't steeped in the history of the place.

"I just transferred over from Worcester a few months ago. I've lived back here for years, though. Not far from my parents' old place. The end of South Road, little cabin in the woods."

Mom gave his big hand a squeeze. "I can't say how wonderful it is to see you." She shifted her eyes to me, a questioning glance. I tried to will her to stay. She couldn't be matchmaking, I thought. But it seemed she was. "I should go find your father," she said. "Let you two catch up."

"Mom!" I knew I sounded like the twins, shrill with mother-induced exasperation. I made a vow never to mortify them again.

"Have to make sure he isn't boring the girls to death with lectures on old farm implements!" And she slipped into the crowd around the caramel corn booth.

Jolon turned to me. "Girls? Your daughters? How many?"

"Three. Fifteen-year-old twins and a ten-year-old."

"A lot *has* changed," Jolon said.

"Do you have any?" I realized I knew nothing about him beyond his phone number in the town directory. He was probably married with six kids.

"Children?" He looked toward the line for fried dough with maple cream, the progeny of Hawley clutching sweaty dollar bills. "No. Somehow didn't get around to it. Marriage, kids. Can't say exactly why." His hand went up to the triangle of scar on his right cheek, one he'd carried ever since a sledding accident when we were nine. When I'd goaded him into climbing the biggest hill in town, with a hedge at the bottom that he crashed into, slicing his cheek open. He'd had to have thirteen stitches. I'd plummeted off my sled unscathed. Touching that scar was an old reflex. It meant he was thinking more than he would tell you. At least that's what it used to mean. I reminded myself again how long it had been. That everything was different now. I was different beyond imagining, and so must he be. Then the smile flashed again, and he said, "Walk with me?"

I smiled back, hoped it was a warm smile, not wintry. My smile hadn't been used much lately, either. "I can't refuse my Good Samaritan. Although you left me stranded all those years ago. You never wrote, after that one letter."

"Call me your Not-So-Good Samaritan, then."

We walked out into the sun, away from the crowd to the relative peace behind the town hall. The view was of distant fields, dotted with round bales as tall as he was. Third cutting, last of the season.

"What *did* happen, Jolon? I always wondered." I looked up at him. His silver eyes were turned to the fields, their expression stark, unreadable.

"It's a long story, now, and long ago. But you, Reve." His gaze returned to me, his face softened. "I read about your husband. I'm sorry."

It felt like a slap, that unexpected allusion to Jeremy. Then I remembered how easily Jolon could blow my cover.

"Jolon, I have to ask you something. I'm using my maiden name. I'm a Dyer again. No one here knows who I am, really. Could you just . . . well, go along with that?" I didn't say why.

"Sure I can, Reve." His eyes held so much pure kindness I had to look away. "I wish I could do more. It must have been hell."

This is where I would always shut down. Any time anyone wanted to offer comfort, I'd get all stoic. But with Jolon, I wanted to spill it all, to cry and throw myself at him, to tell him everything I was keeping in. All the rage and fear and pain. I wanted to tell him it still *is* hell, it still is every minute. I wanted to beg him to hold me like he used to until all the hurt went away. But we were grown-ups now. Grown too far apart.

"I should get back to my girls."

"Reve, if you need anything, I'm here." It was a simple enough statement, a common platitude, even. But I hoped like hell I wouldn't need him. Although he was my oldest friend, I couldn't forget the Hawley police emblem on his T-shirt.

"I'm sorry, I just . . . I have to go." I turned and stumbled off to find my family. I'd been without them too long.

Caleigh's Vision: Witch's Broom

The old-time girl came to her at night, and in the daytime when she used her string. Of course Caleigh knew the family stories, knew there had been other Revelations, dozens of them through the generations, probably. She'd tried to poke around the dining room fireplace one time, looking for the girl's red book, thinking that if she found it the dreams and visions would stop, but Mrs. Pike came in to dust and Caleigh fled. Mrs. Pike scared her more than any ghost. She reminded Caleigh of the witch in "Hansel and Gretel," just waiting to pop her and her sisters into the woodstove.

It was this unfortunate connection that prompted a more troubling and strange visitation from the past. "Witch's Broom" was an old and easy string pattern, not one of her intricate inventions. It was the first she'd ever learned. She hardly used it anymore; there was no reason. She'd been concentrating on designing a pattern she called "Skipping Rope Girl," trying to draw a friend into her new Hawley world. She was still working it out during the fair. She was sitting on a stone wall in the sun with her grandfather and sisters, watching the pony pull and occasionally dipping into a cone of maple cotton candy Gramps had bought for them all to share. Then she happened to spot Mrs. Pike across the road, riding a bike, of all things. One of the old-fashioned kind without gears, and a basket on the handlebars. "Duh-nuh, duh-nuh, duh-nuh-nuh," Caleigh sang under her breath. *The Wizard of Oz* was her favorite movie. She must have unconsciously slipped her string into a "Witch's Broom," for when she next looked down, she saw the fan of the broom and the loop of the handle taut between her fingers.

The world seemed to get all slow then. There was a strange humming in her ears, and her eyes went blurry. When she could focus again, she was still sitting on the same stone wall, but everything else around her had changed. Her grandfather was no longer next to her enjoying his cotton candy. Her sisters were gone, too. The paved road had turned to dirt. The huge maples that lined the road had dwindled to sticks. Most of the houses were gone, turned into tall stacks of loose hay dotting the rolling, stubbly fields. The houses that remained were smaller, meaner, unpainted. But the town hall was there, big and white and imposing among all the tiny houses. There were people crowding around the common. There still seemed to be a fair or something happening, but instead of T-shirts and jeans with baseball caps, the women wore long, dark skirts and those white hats with wings. The men wore wool pants and light blue shirts. Some wore long jackets. It was like a uniform. Caleigh tried not to move, to be noticed. She didn't know if she could be seen, but she hoped not. She was wearing her green Hello Kitty shirt, which looked good in the twenty-first century, but she didn't think it would go over wherever, or *when*ever, she was.

She tried to figure out what was going on. There was a kind of stage where the pony pull had been. It had a wooden plank on it, like a picnic table on its side, with holes cut out in it. A man walked up to the plank, followed by two other men holding the arms of a woman. Caleigh couldn't be sure, but she seemed like a younger version of the old woman of the dreams. The woman's hair was fuller, red and shiny as a sheet of copper, a little like Caleigh's own hair. But her eyes seemed the same. The men stepped away, and Caleigh could see the woman's hands were tied.

The man on the stage spoke, loudly enough so everyone could hear. "Ya been accused of hexing Josiah Tompkins and his mule, Bethia Dyer." The woman's last name made Caleigh gasp. It was her mother's family name, the name they all used now.

A skinny, crotchety old man piped up from the crowd. "And that's the truth, Deacon Taylor! I rode my good mule past her house not two weeks ago. She spooked my mule so's I fell on the ground and caught a cast in my knee. Had to be away from my fields a week, now I canna get the mule to plow or ride at all."

"Had you any witnesses?" the man called Deacon Taylor asked from the stage.

"What have I the need? She be the evil one. *She* need the witnesses. Remember, she spelled Eliza Chook's girl, who had the pox after Bethia taught her her letters."

There were murmurs in the crowd, and a woman yelled, "And she an't right from it yet!" All heads turned toward a fat woman with double chins. "That's right! This girl hexed my little one, sure enough. Martha were still too poorly to come today, or she'd be here with me. Her father had to stay to mind her."

By the time they all turned back to the stage, the red-haired woman was gone. She'd escaped somehow, in spite of bound hands and two men standing beside her. A gasp rose up from the crowd, and Josiah Tompkins ran to the platform, looked under it every which way. Caleigh forgot herself and laughed out loud. He was like a chicken scurrying for food. "She's gone and vanished!" he exclaimed. "Another spell!" The crowd buzzed.

A big man strode up onto the stage. "Rubbish," he said.

Deacon Taylor stepped toward him. "Now, Urbane Sears, I don't know how the girl was spirited away, but we're tryin' to—"

The big man laughed then, but to Caleigh it sounded harsh and bitter. "You can try all you want. You'll not be trying it on my Bethia." He turned to the crowd. "I won't let you country fools break my marriage to this girl, or my family, or my store. I'll close up and move back east, and you can trade down to Northampton if any of you put a hand on her again. Or set your tongues going. There's no such creatures as witches. Get that into your thick pates. I won't abide this." He stomped his way down the stairs, where the woman joined him, her hands free now.

Urbane Sears led her away. The crowd parted for them. Just then, it seemed to Caleigh that everything started fading at the edges, breaking up and rearranging itself. First the stage faded, then the crowd, then suddenly the magician Setekh appeared riding Mrs. Pike's bicycle, and said, "I'll get you, my pretty." Then even he faded and Caleigh was back at the fair with her grandfather and sisters, the ponies straining against the weight on the stone boat. The sun on her face was hot, and she was sleepy. She wondered what had really happened, then lay down on the wall, propping her head on her arms and having a little nap for herself. Her grandfather gently placed his cap over her face to shield her from the sun. He let her sleep.

4

The horses arrived while we were at the fair. I'd planned it as a surprise for the girls. Grace and Fai had been mopey, longing for their horses. And even though Caleigh didn't like riding, she'd grown up around horses, liked to pet and groom them, and spoil them with treats. We all loved the barn smells, the velvety horse noses, the sounds of the big animals crunching grain and whickering softly to us.

When we pulled in the gate, Nathan was feeding them apples, and three lovely heads swiveled toward the car.

"The horses!" Grace shrieked. All three girls had been telling me about their time at the fair, fizzing with excitement. Caleigh was bragging about everything she'd eaten. Grace and Fai were all googly-eyed over a boy they'd met, a cute boy who told them about the old tavern and the ghosts that haunted it near the Five Corners. But all thoughts of the fair flew out of their heads at the sight of our horses.

"Stop! Let us out!" Caleigh had already flung the car door open. I hit the brakes and they all catapulted out of the car. They slowed as they neared the fence. They'd been taught early and well never to run around horses. Each girl shimmied through the fence and flung her arms around the neck of her favorite.

I climbed through the fence last and my own horse, Zar, left Caleigh to rub his face against me. As usual, I planted my feet and leaned into him so he wouldn't knock me flat with that heavy, bony head. I ran my hands over the soft chestnut coat that had begun growing out for the coming winter. I could feel the muscles in his neck flex, and he groaned with pleasure when I scratched under his mane. It was a comfort to breathe in his horsey smell of wild garlic and sweat. I'd missed the horses as much as the girls.

"Mom, I think Rikka put on some weight." Fai's gray horse, Rikka, thin and lithe, was a fine-boned twelve-year-old mare, narrower than the two geldings.

"I think it's just the hair," Grace said. "They're all so furry." Her horse, Brio, black as a cloudy night sky, deserted her when Rikka reached her head to nudge him in the butt. Brio was the tallest and youngest at ten, but Rikka was boss of the pasture. Zar was the elder statesman of the three. Our horses are Arabians, the most elegant of horses and the toughest for the desert riding we love. They had logged hundreds of miles on the trail; in Zar's case, thousands. Zar was eighteen. He'd been with me longer than my children had, longer than Jeremy and I had been married. He'd carried me through both pregnancies, had helped teach all the girls to ride, even Caleigh, who begged off after a year of lessons left her as indifferent to riding as her sisters were passionate about it. "I just like to pet Zar's nose once in a while. That doesn't make me National Velvet," she'd famously said when she was eight.

"I suppose all you horse-crazy girls will settle down now you've got your children back," Nathan teased.

"Hey, coz." Grace sidled up to him. "Why don't you ever ride with us?"

Fai piped in, "Because riding is one thing we do better than him." All three girls collapsed into gales of laughter.

Nathan just shook his head. "You guessed the secret! You're too good. You all just laugh at me."

It was true. Nathan could ride well enough, but the twins were naturals.

"I hope you don't mind going out with only your old mother tomorrow. I want to show you the trails I rode when I was your age."

Grace snickered. "Aren't they all grown over by now?"

"Yeah." Fai butted me with her shoulder. "I bet all the brambles and things have grown up around them, and trolls live under the bridges, and the princess has been asleep for a thousand years."

"Oh, come on, your mother's not that old," Nathan came to my defense. "She was just a little girl when the spell was cast."

"Hey! Say I don't have an evil spell cast on me!" I pinched him.

"Owww! All right, all right. No evil spell, a nice one." He rubbed his arm, grinning. "Okay?"

"Okay."

The girls paid no attention to us. Grace perched on the fence with Caleigh, helping her braid Zar's mane. Fai, her face furrowed with care, plucked a burr out of Rikka's tail. For that moment, we almost seemed like a family again, almost complete, almost whole. But then I remembered it was a fragile illusion, one that could tumble like a house of cards.

"Why can't we ride today?" Fai broke into my cheerless thoughts.

"Yeah, let's go for a ride!" Grace urged.

I scanned the sky. "I don't think so. By the time we tack up, it'll be too late to go far. And the horses had a long trailer ride already today."

"We could take a short ride! They won't care. They'd love it!"

"I know your short rides," Nathan told them. "They never last less than three hours. And your mom hasn't done a lick of work all day. How do you expect her to keep supporting you all?"

"Then can't you come with us? We won't make fun of you!"

"Please?"

I put the brakes on. "Nathan hung around here most of the day just to meet the trailer for us. Now he's taking the rest of the day for himself."

"Then we can go alone."

"No!" The word shot out of both my mouth and Nathan's. "You girls listen to me. Caleigh, too," I commanded. "Turn around and look at me, right now."

It wasn't often that I became really stern. The girls had their eyes on me like rabbits transfixed by the glare of headlights.

"None of you, not one of you, not two of you, not all together, may leave this property without either Nathan or me. That means you never ride, you never even walk out those gates without an adult present. Never. This is very important."

Grace shot me a sulky look. "Why did we move, then? If everything's the same. I thought we were supposed to be okay here."

I put my arm around her. "We weren't riding at all back home," I reminded her. "So this is better, isn't it?"

She tried to shrug me off. "I'm tired of this. It isn't fair. Isn't it enough that the Fetch killed Dad? Aren't we punished enough? I don't understand why they can't just *stop* him."

Fai said, "Because, you bonehead, nobody can find out who he is. He's really good at hiding. Like the Unabomber or something."

I hugged Grace, felt her bony girl shoulders resist me. "It will get better, honey, I promise. We just have to be good at hiding, too, until he makes a mistake and is caught. I know this is hard on you, but I just don't know what else to do to try to keep us safe." Grace fumed silently at me, her arms folded, implacable. "Honey, I'm doing everything I *can* do." She looked away, but not before her eyes softened.

"Okay?" I asked her.

"Okay. I guess."

"Good." I needed to get us back to the ordinary weave of the day, back from the edge of fear and sorrow. "I know . . . let's get out some maps. We'll plan a ride for tomorrow."

"Is the forest on Google Maps?" Fai wanted to know. "Can we find it on our phones?"

"You probably can here at the house, but remember, cell phones won't work in the forest."

"Hey, can we go to that haunted tavern?" Grace pleaded.

"Sure," I told her, glad to have found a distraction for them. I thought, too, that I'd be lucky to trade a few ghosts for the real man who plagued us.

Faice Off

Grace and Fai's texts, October 19, 2013:

Fai: We r the winners . . .

Grace: Of the word!

Fai: U mean world.

Grace: My thumb slipped.

Fai: Anyway.

Anyway . . . do u think Faice is a good name?

It combines both our names, and we can alter it for different shows. U know . . . Faice of America, Faice of Love, Faice of an Angel.

Don't know about that last one.

Faice of Doom, then.

We r plenty chuffed.

As Dad wd say.

As Dad wd say.

We feel him in our hands when we do the coin tricks . . .

The card tricks . . .

When no 1 sees, but us.

Like now.

Does he take over our hands to make magic, do u think?

Our whole selves.

Our *whole selves . . .*

Its like he left us with these pieces of himself.

But not the rest.

No. Not the rest.

It's hard not to blame . . .

Blame mom?

Yeah, but that would be wrong.

She pulled the trigger.

She didn't mean to . . .

Yur right. It would be wrong to blame her . . .

Shit if we started blaming, we would never stop.

We'd blame Caleigh.
We'd blame Nathan.
Blame Mrs. Pike. Yeah let's blam HER . . .
Yeah, let's BLAM her!
U know what I mean . . . blame . . .
Blame the sky.
Blame the grass.
The leaves on the trees.
The stones.
Ourselves . . .
But we are the winners . . .
We ARE the winners
No time for losers, cause we are the winners.
Of the world.
The word.
The wold.
Not a word . . .
Yes, it is.
What does it mean then?
A hilly forest.
Like here.
Like here.
We are the winners . . .
Of the WOLD.
But we'll go home.
Yes.
Soon.
Yes.
Make it happen.
It will be . . . magic.

Suspension

Moody Spring Road—October 20, 2013

1

The next day all three girls were up early. The twins were already dressed in their breeches and boots at breakfast. Planning a morning ride was the one sure way to get them up before ten on a Sunday. I was ready as well, except for changing from my slippers to boots and half-chaps. It's strange how you can get used to anything. I was almost feeling normal after our day at the fair. Almost happy to be going riding with my girls, as if nothing bad had happened, was happening. But I knew at the back, in the primitive part of the brain where fear is stored, that this skim of happiness was just illusion. Smoke and mirrors.

"What are you going to do today, Caleigh?" Grace was in a mellow, pre-ride mood, disposed to be kind to her little sister.

Caleigh shrugged. She was still in her *Wizard of Oz* pajamas. Scarecrows and Tin Men and Cowardly Lions cavorted through the poisonous poppy field. Dorothy and Toto were already down for the count. "I don't know," she mumbled through her granola. "Nathan said he'd take me . . . back to the fair. Or to Gramps and Grand's. I haven't made up my mind . . . what I want to do."

"Sweetheart, don't talk with your mouth full, you look like a cow," Nathan told her, flipping pages of his Sunday paper.

That finished the girls, and breakfast. Grace spewed oatmeal onto the tablecloth, Fai spouted milk out her nose. Both her sisters shrieked with laughter as Caleigh mooed at them, knocking her half-full orange juice glass to the floor.

Nathan sprang from the table, sweeping his paper to safety. "Reve, what should we do about these creatures? Do you think any boarding school would have them?"

"Probably not." I had my section of the paper safely tucked to my chest.

"That's too bad. Well, I think I'll have a quiet read on the porch." He swept off, his bathrobe flapping around his pajamaed legs. Caleigh skipped after him. "Nathan, call Grand first. I decided I want to go there and see the giant pumpkin!" That was another of my father's retirement projects. His giant pumpkin had won a prize at the Tri-County Fair, and now he was coddling it so the girls could carve it for Halloween.

"Mom." Fai wiped the milk from her face. "We're ready. We'll tack up Zar for you, okay?"

"Great. Give me a few minutes, and I'll be out." The girls bolted to the door.

"Hey! Dishes." They clomped back, tumbled bowls and spoons in the sink, sloshed a little water and soap around while they grumbled about not having a dishwasher. I wiped their messes off the table and sponged the floor. "And don't go running just yet."

When the kitchen was almost orderly, I led them to the closet in the mudroom.

"Here, take these with you." I handed them blaze orange vests, walkie-talkies to put in their pockets.

"What are these for?"

"What *are* they?"

"So the hunters won't shoot us. It's the start of deer season."

"You mean they're going to shoot Bambi?"

"They're going to try. It's bow, not shotgun season yet, so it's not as dangerous. They aren't supposed to hunt on Sundays, but I want you to get in the habit of wearing them."

"Yeah, but what kind of cell phones are these? They're weird."

"That's because they're not cell phones, they're walkie-talkies. Remember, we don't get signal much beyond the gate."

Grace thunked her head with her hand. "I keep forgetting. That's just . . ." I could tell she was searching for an acceptable word, settled for "*countrified*."

I ignored her protests. "So, I want you to have these with you anytime we go out. We'll all carry them, in case we get separated. Nathan will have his turned on while he's here, in case . . ." I looked at my lovely daughters holding the unfamiliar equipment they'd need to live this woods life, and I wondered again if I'd done the right thing. But I said nothing. What was there to say?

"All right, go tack up." They raced out to the barn while I pulled on boots and chaps.

Nathan had a small apartment in an ell that had been a nineteenth-century add-on to the back of the house. Two rooms, a tiny galley kitchen, a bathroom. A porch that hung over what used to be a terraced flower bed, now tangled with overgrown Michaelmas daisies and egg-yolk yellow chrysanthemums. And nettles. Lots of nettles. I added another mental note to my impossible list as I knocked on his door.

Nathan answered, walkie-talkie in hand. "I'll keep this with me until Caleigh and I leave. We won't be gone long. When will you be back?"

"I'd say four hours. But give us an extra half hour before you come looking. You have the map?"

"Not only that, I took the 4Runner out early and drove your route. So I'll know right where you'll be."

"That was above and beyond the call of duty."

"It was a good idea. There sure is a lot of forest out there."

"Four thousand acres. One of the largest protected forests in the state."

"I don't know if that's a good or bad thing."

"You know, Nathan, neither do I."

I headed out to the barn. I loved its lines, its huge hayloft and the cupola to allow air circulation when the barn was full of hay. It was a faded red, the classic color of New England barns, and sunflowers bloomed along the wall beside the big slider doors. It remained unseasonably warm for October. Pink phlox and flame-orange daylilies still rioted away in the old flower beds. The sun shone bright and eerily warm over New England.

I could see the silhouettes of horses and girls in the shadows of the barn. Maybe I didn't love Grace and Fai any more when they were around the horses, but I did love watching my daughters burnish their horses' coats, making certain their bridles were adjusted perfectly, that their saddle pads were flat. All the twins' sloppy ways were transformed by horses. They were careful and thoughtful and moved with a dignity that always took my breath away. The beauty of wild things shone from them when they were riding, when we had a canter and they flew before me, in seamless motion with their beloved horses.

I leaned in the doorway, at that moment feeling

extraordinarily lucky. Lucky to have our girls. Lucky to have kept them safe.

Fai called me out of my reverie. "Mom! Get your helmet on! We've been waiting for you *forever*!"

I meekly took the helmet she handed me, tucked my hair under it as best I could, snapped the chin guard. Grace led Zar out to me. I stroked his head, looked into his eyes. They were dark with an unusual green tint, almost like my own and Caleigh's. The twins had their father's deep blue eyes.

Zar attempted his head-rub greeting, which I fended off because of the bridle. I took the reins, stepped into the stirrup, and threw a leg over. Zar shifted his weight to accommodate me, and we found our center of balance. I hadn't realized how much I'd missed that feeling—that coming together of weight and purpose—over the past months we were horseless.

The girls led Rikka and Brio out. They mounted, and our horses stepped lightly forward. Zar tossed his head with joy. Brio snorted, then reached back to wipe his nose on Grace's knee. It was a trick of his that always made her laugh.

"He'd never make a show horse," I told her, not for the first time.

"Phhh!" Fai snorted, too. "Could you see Brio in an equitation class, wiping green snot all over Gracie's breeches? Or worse, wiping his nose on the judge!"

"I don't guess we'll ever go *in* an equitation class, so I'm not fussed."

My girls weren't into the show scene. Like my own childhood self, they'd rather be on the trails.

"So what's the place we're going to?" Fai asked. "I keep forgetting its name." We'd pored over maps the night before, decided on a loop.

"Moody Spring. Most of the trail runs by a stream. It's very pretty."

"But next time we're going to the tavern, right? The haunted one."

"We could go today, except that you decided on the cemetery, and that's in the other direction."

"Okay, okay."

At the top of the drive I flashed a key card at the unseen electronic eye. The gate swung open and we rode out into forest.

The way we'd chosen dipped us down the wide stretch of Middle Road. It was the longest road in the forest, starting in a golden-arched beech and birch wood, then descending into pines and past a beaver pond. The road leveled out there, covered with soft drifts of pine needles. We had a long trot to the corner of Cemetery Road, and by the time I pulled Zar up, I'd realized that although he was in fine shape, I wasn't. I knew I'd regret the months I hadn't ridden and was already thinking of a soak in a hot bath. But the girls were not fazed.

"Let's canter up the hill!" Grace led the charge, and the horses rolled into a fast canter, blowing and snorting, happy to be given their heads. At the top of the hill, the old graveyard loomed, with its headstones like rows of prehistoric teeth. We pulled the horses up and walked them through the rusty propped-open gate.

Fai threw herself off Rikka and walked her among the stones, reading to us. "'Elijah King. 1792 to 1884.' Hey, he was over ninety years old. And his wife, Abigail. She was ninety-*five*! But they had a baby and it must have died. It just says 'King infant.'"

Grace had hopped off. "Hey, Mom, listen to this one. 'Lavinia Hall. 1829 to 1878. Planted in the Realms of Rest.' Like she's a petunia or something."

I had done this same thing with Jolon all those years ago, reading and exclaiming and laughing over the headstones. I remembered one with an open Bible on top, carved from stone. I found it. " 'Elizabeth Pool. Improve in the Present and Prepare to Die,' " I told the girls.

"That's pretty gruesome." Fai was petting a stone lamb.

"Trust Mom to find the creepy ones."

That had been what Jolon said, too, that I liked the darkest epitaphs best. Probably I did. It was unsettling, how often I'd been thinking of him. His memory haunted me here, ghostly, and I didn't know what to do about his present self, over at the Hawley police station filing reports, or trolling the roads for speeders. I still felt a connection to him. That first loss dredged up by all the recent ones, maybe. I tried to shake off those thoughts. I'd hardly considered him in years. Why start again now? He had his own life, as I had mine. It wasn't likely we'd meet very often.

"Hey, listen," Grace called. "This girl was just a little older than us. She was only sixteen. We'll be sixteen soon. 'So Fades My Last Remaining Flower.' That's spooky, too."

A cloud passed over the sun. The lace of leaves above us faded from a glowing bright lime color. A flat grayness fell over the cemetery. The birds stopped singing, and suddenly I smelled the familiar and troubling scent of lilacs. In a moment it was gone again.

"I feel shivery all of a sudden," Fai complained.

"Jolon and I spent hours here." *The woods are lovely, dark, and deep*. "We even had picnics. We can go now, though. If you want."

Another line of the elusive Robert Frost poem came to me. *But I have promises to keep*. Why couldn't I get that poem out of my head? And what were the rest of the words? I couldn't think of them.

"You had picnics right on the graves? Mom, that's *disgusting*."

"Our mom, the sicko." They both laughed, and the mood lifted.

"Hey, did you ever call Jolon?" Fai asked me.

"I did run into him at the fair." Literally.

"And?" Grace pumped me for information, suspicion glinting in her eyes.

"And nothing much. We talked for a few minutes. That's all."

"What do you mean, 'That's all'? What's he like now? Is he fat and bald? I bet he's fat and bald."

"No. Neither. He's . . . the same, I guess. And different."

"You have to describe things better than that if you're going to write scripts for other people, Mom," Fai pointed out.

I thought about Jolon, how I could best describe him if I had to write him down. Synapses sparked in my brain, and I was thrust back into distant memory.

2

I lay under the irises in my mother's garden. The shimmering blooms, the sword-shaped leaves enclosed me, the scent like heaven drifted in the air. I was six years old, tracing out animals in the big puffy clouds of June. A dog's head, barking and snarling, an elephant raising its trunk. I laughed at the elephant, then heard a rustling at my feet, saw the leaves shift. I lay very still, thinking it might be a snake. Not that I was afraid of snakes, only curious to see the diamond head and flicking tongue. But instead of a snake, a boy's head peered through the foliage. A head with shining long black hair.

"Who are you?" I demanded.

"Shhh!" The boy slithered up on his belly, very like the snake I had thought he was, and clamped a hand over my mouth. "There's an owl just above us. A barred owl," he whispered urgently. "You'll scare it away."

I looked up and saw something big and brownly gray on a branch. It didn't look alive. Then it swiveled its head and gazed down at us with disapproving golden eyes. It shook itself, unfolded sweeps of wings. With a flap and a puff of warm air, it plunged through the trees and was gone.

The boy rolled onto his back. "Now you've done it."

I scrambled up. "I didn't mean to. I didn't do anything but ask who you are."

"The owl thought you meant to ask *it*. They don't like to tell. Keep themselves to themselves."

I absorbed that news about owls, then said, "Well, now you might as well tell me your name. Unless you don't like to tell, either."

"Jolon."

"Jolon what?"

"Jolon the groundskeeper's son. And see, I've got a mind to keep after that owl."

An only child, I was lonely. I had a mind to keep after the boy. But I didn't tell him that. Instead I said, "I'm Reve Dyer and I'm six. And I know where there's snapping turtles." That began our adventures.

Jolon's father worked at planting and weeding and shoveling on the college grounds. A tall man with a deep voice, cigarette always clamped between his lips. I often saw him from a distance, from my perch on the garden wall overlooking the college. When he saw me on the grounds with my dad, he always pulled pretty things out of his pocket for me—a tiny bird's nest, a piece of pink quartz, a jay's feather. Jolon's mother stayed at home, in their little house on the edge of the forest. When he wasn't in school, Jolon stayed with her and all their animals until the summer we met, when three days a week she had a new job baking scones and muffins and breads at the tea shop in town. Then Jolon accompanied his father and roamed the streets and fields and woods around the campus.

On that first midsummer morning we went to the pond at the bottom of the garden, where we splashed somberly, looking warily for snappers, finding only a big wrinkly box turtle and armies of delicate green frogs. Jolon didn't think them any replacement for the owl, but when I asked him to come to lunch, he shrugged and followed me when I ran up the hill to the house.

I thumped onto the porch, leaving black footprints. Jolon stopped in the yard. The screen door banged behind me, and I turned.

"Well, come on," I called through the screen. "Don't you want to?"

He looked down at his legs, caked with mud, dripping pond water.

"Come *on*." And he did.

Before he met me, Jolon spent most of his time alone, too, following birds to their nests, tracking foxes and other wild creatures. When he came upon me in the garden that day, though, things changed. As soon as he got to the campus, he'd kick off his sneakers, crawl through a culvert, skin his knee, and fight his way through brambles—always arriving at my house in a dire state of disrepair. He never would knock on the door. Instead he stood in the garden, out of sight of the house. All he had to do was think of me, he said, and I would always then skim around the wall in a flowered cotton dress, shining like a bright penny, only for him.

"Hey," I'd say, and tap him, touch his arm, then run from him, not looking back. To the meadow, the snack bar, to the sculpture garden, or the ice cream parlor at the edge of the campus. And he would follow, hanging back until I'd reached the morning's destination. He'd help me pick flowers for a crown, take the hot dog or the pistachio double scoop I offered. Mostly, we did not speak. Mostly, we knew everything we needed to without speaking, as if we were young animals playing together.

Jolon lived on the border of Hawley Forest, with his parents and fairy-tale goats and pinto ponies, one red and white, one gold and white. The first horses I'd ever ridden, bouncing on their backs while Jolon laughed. The riding was like flying. It was our magic.

We grew up together, inseparable. By the time we were ten, we knew we'd be married. We talked about where we'd live, what the names of our children would be, names from the books we loved. Aladdin and Crusoe, Lucy and Aravis. But when we were adolescents, the cough that troubled his father became worse. It turned out to be lung cancer, advanced and so virulent he was dead in three months. After that, everything seemed to fall apart, in the slow-motion drift that accompanies sudden disaster.

Jolon gripped my hand all through his father's wake and funeral, as if he'd never let me go, as if I could save him from a sea of grief that would drown him. We were both thirteen, the years overlapping. Soon he would be fourteen and pass me again. Although I knew he was sad, knew to tread lightly, I was certain nothing had really changed.

Two months later, just before the Fourth with its extravagance of sparklers and corn on the cob and staying up way past our bedtimes, Jolon came over for a tenting sleepover. Nan's idea, to give him a respite from his mother's stony sadness. I overheard my parents and Nan talking. "They're getting older," my dad said. "It might not be such a great idea."

"Are you afraid for your daughter's virtue?" asked Nan. "She's just a child."

"But children grow up so suddenly now, Mother," my own mother said.

"Are you telling me she could have a baby?"

My mother hadn't been squeamish about telling me the facts of life, but this embarrassed me. I felt myself turning lobster red, even though I was hidden in the coat closet I'd whisked myself into when I realized they were talking about Jolon and me.

"No. Not yet. But maybe it's better that at least they don't have sleepovers anymore."

"Oh, that's ridiculous. The boy's just lost his father. They're together every day, anyway. You can't stop a moving train, is what I say."

Then the talk turned to Jolon's mother. How she might go to her sister in Fitchburg for a while, or stay and work for the college, cooking in the student center, but no one really knew. She spoke so rarely. When Nan had stopped by their house to ask about the sleepover, she'd merely nodded. Nodded and walked away into another room.

So Jolon rode over on his bike, with his tent and his flashlight bound behind him, and a sack of wild strawberries he'd picked. Nan helped us set up the tent on the porch, in the mosquito-filled late afternoon, as the sky roiled and darkened above us.

At dusk, Nan brought us ham sandwiches and iced tea just as the first drops started to fall. Thunder rolled over us slowly, lingering like church bells on a Sunday morning. The sky turned the color of the crayon in the box I used to mispronounce "violent." And violent is what it seemed to me, purple-gray and threatening. I didn't want to admit I was afraid in front of Jolon, who was calmly making bird and rabbit shadows on the tent walls. Lightning streaked white hot, made spangles behind my eyelids, and that decided me.

"Nan!" I yelled. Jolon flashed me his what-a-baby look, but I called until I heard the whoosh of wings that accompanied my Nan everywhere, then the thump of one of her hawks landing on the porch railing. My grandmother thrust her head between the flaps of the tent, her eyes keen, her braid swinging like a pendulum.

"Climb in and tell us a story."

Jolon scrutinized me as if he could smell my fear, then said, "Yeah, Mrs. Dyer. Good night for a story. Tell us a scary one." Nan was a terrific storyteller, and he knew it. I'd heard most of her stories, maybe all of them. I'd heard all the Revelation stories, and knew they were reserved for family. That night I thought Nan would tell "The Hook," or "Spanish Tom," one of her scary non-family stories. The thunder cracked and boomed in our chests. She placed the flashlight under her chin. Her bony, disembodied face, just like mine but with wrinkles and spots, was thrown into harsh relief. "A long, long time ago, a family lived in Mount Holly, Pennsylvania," she began and I gasped, dropped my sandwich. No one outside the family, not ever, was told the story of the first Revelation.

"What is it, Reve? You've heard this all before."

"But . . ."

"We're entertaining your guest, young Jolon, here." Nan gave me a stern look, one she usually saved for misbehaving hawks. "As I was saying. They lived in Mount Holly. A mother, a father, and two daughters, twins with long, long hair. They owned a spread of land by a river, grew turnips and corn and winter wheat. Planted a row of heady lilacs before the cabin, which bloomed from spring until autumn. Their cows were penny red and milk white, maiden white. The girls wore white everywhere, even when they dug in the garden. The mother grew herbs, dyed her own clothes a heavenly blue never before seen in Mount Holly. When she was asked which plants she used for her dyes, especially that color like sky, she just smiled. Only the father made his way in the world with forthrightness, selling his cheese and grain, meeting the other men in the tavern of an evening. He, at least, was liked generally. But it wasn't enough to save them."

A ragged bolt of lightning cracked above our heads, slashing through the darkened sky. Nan's hawk flapped and cried its alarm. It was her Swainson's hawk, I could tell by the long, piercing *kree*. Suddenly rain sluiced down in silvery curtains beyond the porch rail.

"Good thing you set up here rather than the lawn. Now, how about some tea for a parched old lady?"

Jolon handed the Thermos cap over. His hand shook, just a little. Nan drank the tea down, poured more. "Go ahead, eat your sandwiches." Jolon looked at me. I shook my head, knowing Nan would tell in her own way. But Jolon said, "Ma'am? Aren't you going to tell the rest?"

She pointed the flashlight at her own chin again, and grinned ghastly. "Just creating a little suspense, my dears. Well, the townspeople took against that family, wouldn't buy the father's grain. Wouldn't buy the red-and-white calves. Just shook their heads when he asked them why. The mother took to making little dolls and flower wreaths to sell, but no one bought them when she set up her stall at the market. People crossed to the other side of the street to avoid them. Even the daughters, lovely girls of sixteen, were shunned. After a bit, bad things began to happen in the town. The aldermen got gout and stomachaches and inexplicable fevers. Their children became sickly. One child, a comely golden-haired boy, disappeared without a trace after going out to bring the cows home. Now, maybe these things would have happened anyway, but everyone whispered that the woman was a witch and had cast a spell over the town. So, they put their heads together and decided to set fire to her family's house, then drive them away, if they happened to survive.

"That night, the men who'd drawn the short straws waited in the forest until the father had checked his livestock for the last time, and the last candle had been extinguished. They waited still, until they heard the father's snores. Then they crept up to the house. They lit their torches made from straw soaked in bear grease, threw them in the windows, and ran back to the forest edge, to watch and wait.

"They did their work well. That little cabin burned to the ground, and not a soul was seen leaving it. Not a sound of distress was heard, nothing but the terrified bellowing of the cows. The men said the witch and her family must have been stupefied by smoke while they slept and died before they had a conscious thought. They hoped it was so. After all, they were decent men, not wanting to cause undue suffering, especially the minister, who'd drawn one of the short straws himself.

"Then a strange thing happened. In the next days, when the fire finally stopped smoldering, when the townsfolk went to examine the devastation they'd wrought, they found blackened pots, beds and chairs turned to charcoal, which disintegrated at a touch. A scorched tea tin. Even the carcasses of those red-and-white cows, burnt up in the shed attached to the house. But they found no human remains. Not a bone or a tooth. As if they'd fled unseen, all that strange family. Of course, they knew it must not be so. The men had waited the night through and had seen not one soul escape. There were only embers and charred sticks left. Except the lilacs, which bloomed on, which had refused to burn.

"Not a trace was ever found of the family, dead or alive, in that part of the world. Everywhere they went, though, the townspeople smelled not scorched flesh, but lilacs. Where the cabin stood, the lilacs bloomed all the year through. Even today, in the forest that grew up around the ashes of the cabin, those lilacs never cease to bloom, and the scent of them perfumes the air, even in the dead of winter."

Nan turned off the flashlight, and the tent was filled with the pink and golden light of sunset. The storm had passed. The birds were singing, their last chorus of the waning day.

"That was some story, Mrs. Dyer."

"If you want more, you'll have to wait till true dark, now. I'll tell you some Poe tales, next time." Nan kneeled and unzipped the tent flap. Jolon grabbed her arm. "But what became of them, that family? Where did they go?"

"Where do you think they went?"

I hesitated, then answered, "They came to Hawley Forest."

Nan laughed, smoothed my hair. "You ought to know."

"How could *she* know?" Jolon piped in, caught between fascination and skepticism.

"She bears the name of the woman, the first of the Revelations."

Jolon seemed dissatisfied with this answer. "But she wasn't *there*."

Nan studied him appraisingly. "Suffice it to say there's more to your friend than meets the eye. Just like her forebears. Best you know now." She turned and crawled out of our tent. The tang of the lemony-scented soap she used hung in the air.

Jolon looked at me, but I just shrugged, passed him a bag of gummy worms. He bit the head off a yellow one. I started wrapping them around my wrists, where they stuck, like snakes biting their tails. Then we played badminton in the wet grass until we couldn't see the shuttlecock anymore. We played gin rummy in the tent, cozy with lanterns dispelling the deep dark around us, and that's the last thing I remember until I woke when I felt eyes on me. Jolon's. His eyes reflected the moon as he studied me. His face was inches above mine, his cheek smooth as a plum, his brow furrowed. "I don't know why," he said. And his mouth pressed against mine. Soft as berries, sure as if he'd been kissing me forever, all our lives, and always would.

3

The sun came out. My daughters and I rode on to Moody Spring, then looped around toward home. I didn't smell the lilacs again, and I tried to put it from me. I tried to put any further thoughts of Jolon from me, too. I felt the weight of every act that had brought me to that moment, balanced on the verge of something large and mysterious and frightening. If Jolon had stayed in Hawley, I wouldn't have met Jeremy at all, wouldn't have my three precious girls. But if we hadn't met, Jeremy would still be alive. Then I couldn't help but think that I was being unfaithful to Jeremy, just remembering that first kiss. Jeremy was under the ground, with a gravestone over him. My Jeremy. The twists of fate had worked their spell on me, for sure. As we rode, though, the magic of the forest lulled me, banished my gloomy musings. Grace and Fai were happy and smiling, their sunny, excited faces shining.

When we rode up to the barn, Caleigh ran out to meet us. She helped us untack and bathe the horses, bubbling over with news about the big pumpkin and the Chinese restaurant where they'd had lunch. "What did your fortunes say?" Fai wanted to know.

"Mine was good. It said I'll be lucky in money matters. But Gramps's was funny. Funny strange, not funny ha-ha. Something about what is dearest to him would be lost. Weird, right?"

I didn't want to think about fortunes. Neither the past nor the future seemed important that day. We had an early dinner, then played a noisy game of Bananagrams. No one mentioned the headstones, or my father's not-funny fortune, or Jolon. It was a fine day, without distressing dreams or strange discoveries. I wanted the spell to remain unbroken, wanted there to be many more days like this.

Hawley Bog—October 23, 2013

1

It was the first real day of reckoning for my daughters. I left them huddled over textbooks with Nathan, in the schoolroom he'd set up for them. Life had to get back to normal sometime. As normal as life without Jeremy could be.

Mrs. Pike arrived in her rusty chariot, and was busy scouring inside the kitchen woodstove when I walked by in my riding clothes.

"Off riding, missus?" It was the first time she'd spoken to me unbidden.

"Only to Hawley Bog and back." It was also the first day I wasn't cleaning or cooking right beside her. I thought she might resent it, and I resented her for her resentment. Even if it was only in my own mind. "Then I have to get to work. Upstairs, in my office." I wasn't going to apologize for the work I had always done. "I'll be back in an hour."

"Hey, I'm just askin'. But you want to be careful in those woods."

"I've known Hawley Forest since I was a girl. You don't have to worry I'll get lost."

"It was worried about what you'd *find*, I was."

"And what might that be?" Her cryptic insinuations unnerved me.

She rose creakily, pulled off her stained rubber gloves one by one. They looked like they came from a crime scene, red with rust rather than blood. "Hunting season, you know. Got to be careful."

"It's only bow now. I'm not fussed. I have blaze orange everything, anyway. As you can see."

She put the gloves down, smoothed back her pewter hair. "Well. You know best, missus."

"My name is Reve," I snapped. "Call me by it. Or 'Mrs. Dyer,' if you absolutely have to."

She nodded impassively. "All right, missus."

I slammed the screen door on my way out.

I saddled Zar and headed toward the gate, past the buildings that once comprised the town center of Hawley Five Corners. The Warriner house, the King house, then the church across the wide street that was my driveway. Except for the strange abandonment of the town, no notable events had taken place here, no Revolutionary War battles, not even any dinosaur tracks or ancient Indian villages discovered. No famous person had grown up in the shadows of these trees. Quiet lives had been lived here.

I knew a little of the history of the buildings, courtesy of Carl Streeter's e-mail missives about the town. The Warriner house was once the schoolhouse for the town, had a stark center, two up two down. But then, as was often the case in New England, the house was added on to as families grew. Ethan Warriner bought the schoolhouse from the town when the South Hawley schoolhouse was built, added on a rambling connector to his blacksmith shop so he wouldn't have to go out in the rain and snow, and the deep porch, covered with wisteria vine.

Next came the King house, a tall saltbox that might or might not have been a stop on the Underground Railroad. It also had the distinction of carrying the rumor that a murder had taken place there, a wife poisoning her husband. But it was never proved, and Ida King lived on into old age, dying in 1843 and joining her husband on Cemetery Road, never having remarried. I felt a certain kinship with Ida, had looked for her during our visit to the boneyard the previous day, but hadn't found her gravestone.

It seemed strange to think that less than a hundred years before, this had been the center of a bustling little town. There had been stores and a tavern nearby. Children had played here, young people had courted, carving their names in trees that bore the scars of their old love to this day. People had lived and worked and died here. Then something had happened, that was clear. But what? Was it only because it was abandoned, left empty for so long? Maybe there was a real basis for Carl Streeter's and Mrs. Pike's insinuations that the town was haunted, but I didn't feel anything amiss. I felt only the weight of history. The church might hold answers, as the historical society woman had implied, but that was for another day. My Nan might, as well, but there was no guarantee she'd ever tell me. I'd just have to be happy with what I could glean on my own. I rode out the gate, making sure it swung closed behind me. What happens in Hawley stays in Hawley.

The weather was almost sultry. I put Zar into a gentle but ground-covering trot. There had been an old mill on the road to Hawley Bog, and the cracked stone foundations stood by the rushing stream that ran from the bog and mirrored Middle Road. The trail branched off, and the stream coursed beneath it. A mist rose before me there, hanging over the water. I turned Zar up the Bog Trail, a steep and winding track, deep with small loose stones. When the rains came in April, the water would run over the trail, making it another streambed, but now the path was dry and skittery. Zar picked his way carefully. Mist hung like a curtain around us. Near the top it wisped and thinned. Then when the stream widened again, it became almost solid, a gray quilt of murk. I heard a tinkling of bells and Zar jumped under me, braced his front legs, ready to spin around and run to safety if required. I saw forms then, not the two-legged forms of human hunters I expected, but swaying four-legged ones.

A herd of red-and-white cows appeared out of the mist, tossing their wide heads and lowing. The white of them was milky, translucent, very clean. Their red patches seemed bright in spite of the dusky light. Some wore brass bells around their necks, sounding sweet and muted in the air. They were coming straight for us, then swerved and made a run at the bank edging the road. They cleared it with no problem, like grand prix jumpers, like cows jumping over the moon. Then they melted into the forest again, the bells sounding fainter and fainter. A good thing, because if there's one thing Zar does make a fuss about, it's a cow. He trembled beneath me, and when we went on, he sidestepped by the bank the cows had jumped. I stroked his sweat-lathered neck. "It's only cows, kiddo." I looked back and wondered, though. What were cows doing in the forest? There had been maybe seven or eight. I hadn't precisely counted; they seemed to flow together and apart with such fluidity they were like a school of big fish. Did some farmer let them out to eat mast in the forest once the grass had gone? But then they were so clean. And there was still good grass, to the horses' delight. I added the stray cattle to my growing list of mysteries.

The hill up to the bog was steep and shaley. Stones rattled behind us as Zar's hooves ground in for purchase. I leaned forward over his withers. We'd just gained the top of the rise when I heard voices. Men's voices. Maybe they were coming for the cows. I rode around a sharp bend, nearly stumbled into a circle of men standing near three pickup trucks parked in the road. Ten or twelve men. Again, the mist seemed to befuddle me. I thought they might be hunters—almost without exception they sported orange caps. But they had none of the other paraphernalia of hunting. No bows, no camouflage jackets or pants. I saw no six-packs or liquor bottles, either, and I was grateful for that. Most were in coveralls, some in jeans and T-shirts. They stared at me as I came on. Not one smiled. A few touched their cap visors. An older man, with a face brown and wrinkled as a walnut, said, "Mornin'."

I nodded, suddenly feeling apprehensive. Zar felt it, too, and tensed. I knew he was longing to bolt back down the hill to home. I tucked two more fingers over the reins to steady him, made fists with my hands. We would go on.

The men saw my intention, but did not make way for me. I cleared my throat and asked, "Are you here for the cows? I just saw them go hurtling into the woods, about fifty feet back."

The wizened man stared at me as if I'd lost my mind. "Cows?" Before I could respond, a fat man in a Red Sox T-shirt said, "Bill Scott used to fence near here, but didn't let his cows wander round the bog."

"Yut. But that was years ago, when you was a kid," said the walnut man.

"Bill Scott's in the nursin' home now down Northampton. Don't keep no cows no more," a man with black hair told him.

"Maybe them cows she talks about is the ghost herd. . . ."

"Shut your trap, Mike," the black-haired man told the fat one.

"I'm Reve Dyer," I told them. "I just moved to the Five Corners."

They all looked away. The black-haired man spat. Even though they seemed to want me gone, they did not move to let me by. The walnut-faced man spoke. "We know who you are, missus. And we know where you live."

"She don't know, does she?" the fat man semi-whispered.

"Better she don't," the walnut-faced man replied.

"Better I don't know what?"

"The old town at the Five Corners, how . . ." began the fat man. He stopped when the black-haired man shot him a look.

"You mean when the town disappeared?" I asked. "I'd heard something about that. Maybe you all know more, can tell me."

They fell silent again. The fat man shuffled and kicked a rock.

"Never mind, missus," the walnut-faced man called. "You're all right. You just go on with your ride, now."

They parted then like the Red Sea, let me pass, touched two fingers to visors again, watched me ride on.

2

I looped around the bog, saw no more men or cows. When I got home, I checked in on Nathan and the girls, who were involved in a spirited debate about Greenpeace. I went upstairs to try to do some of my own work, but the encounter with the men in the forest troubled me. There were secrets in Hawley, past and present, that I wasn't privy to, secrets I wanted to know. Maybe I could find something in the book I'd gotten at the fair that would shed some light on the past of Hawley Five Corners.

I went to the bookshelf, pulled out the Hawley history. At first it seemed like any small-town history, beginning with the founding of the town by a man named Everett Rice and his brothers in 1771. The name *Hawley* was thought to be in honor of Joseph Hawley of Northampton, a famed legislator. There was no mention that Revelation had settled here in the 1740s, named the town after Mount Holly. Revelation's part in the founding of the town was buried by time, and the fact that she was only a woman. But there were oddities about the book, written by one Howard Stark, in 1932. Mr. Stark was a religious man, who liked to sprinkle Bible quotes throughout his text.

Even though he never once mentioned my ancestor, every quote was from the book of Revelation. They were not attributed, but when I consulted my Bible concordance, it was always Revelation. Mr. Stark had used the quotes as epigraphs to every chapter. Among them was "I know your works, your toil and your patient endurance." It was as if my ancestor Revelation's history was hidden, but he couldn't altogether suppress her influence.

I found some interesting facts. The first slave in Hawley was white, a Frenchman captured during the French and Indian War. But there was precious little about the Five Corners. Just a passing reference to the tavern, and one tale about the disappearance of a young man during the Civil War.

After an hour, I gave up reading and went to my laptop for an e-mail check before I turned to my work on the script. I scrolled past e-mails from Restoration Hardware, Bed, Bath & Beyond. Nothing urgent. But then a smiley face in a subject line caught my eye. An address I didn't recognize, eyeforaneye@aol.com. I was tempted to hit the delete button. But something compelled me, a faint premonition, maybe. When I opened it, there were only two lines: "It doesn't matter where you are. I'll find you, disappeared or not." And a photograph. Of Maggie. Maggie dead, her eyes glazed, staring and empty.

I'd had a sickening déjà vu feeling since Jeremy's death. I'd been trying to believe it was just coincidence, desperate to push away the nightmarish memories that the scorched photos of my family sent shivering through me. But what happens in Vegas doesn't always start in Vegas. I knew now, beyond a doubt, that the Fetch had haunted me before.

I felt a flood of panic. Memory surged over me like the crash of icy sea water.

3

It is impossible to make sense of some things that happen. In my line of work, this is easy to forget. The magician must be in control of every moment. And offstage, most events from the mundane to the remarkable have some identifiable reason for their occurrence. Even my vanish seems normal to me now, easy, just a part of who I am. But there are times in our lives so bizarre that the rational mind cannot account for them. I'd experienced it years before I met Jeremy, before I turned my life to magic. When I was in college, when a girl named Maggie Hamilton had been my friend. I always hoped to be able to make sense of what happened to Maggie, but the facts were intractable, stubbornly impenetrable.

It started when I was a freshman in college. I was a faculty brat at Williams. I saw Maggie in the dining hall our first day. A black girl dressed all in denim and plaid with a smiley-face cap perched on her head. She drummed a knife on a metal folding chair for attention, then stood right up on it and announced that she was having a record sale in her room. Duke Ellington, Afro-Cuban jazz, Beatles, the Go-Go's, Roxy Music. I was mesmerized by her. I tried to imagine myself being as bold as she was, as much of a performer. I guess I wanted to be her. Why she chose me as her friend is still a mystery to me.

I went to her sale, sat on the floor, and watched her bargain among all the milk crates stuffed with albums. I stayed to the end, reading her books: *The Wizard of Oz*, Petrarch, Emma Goldman, Zora Neale Hurston. Her taste in books was as eclectic as her taste in music. The cool kids bought up the retro and popular records. Maggie counted her money after they had all gone. I wasn't even registered on her consciousness, sitting in the corner. I may even have disappeared. I still wasn't completely in control of the disappearing in those days, and it sometimes happened without my realizing. Maybe it happened that day in Maggie's room.

"Hey," I said, and startled her.

She whirled to face me. "Oh, man, you scared the shit out of me!" She narrowed her eyes. "Hey, what?"

"Why are you selling your records? You must like music. Or did you inherit them or something?"

She shrugged. "Not that it's any of your business, but I need money for books. You know how much a biology textbook costs? I'm dumb broke after buying books for *one class*. And I haven't got enough yet for them all. Your friends got no taste, left the jazz." Two milk crates were full, merely picked over, a few albums scattered on the industrial gray rug of Maggie's dorm room.

"Those are the ones I want," I told her.

"You like jazz?" She sounded skeptical.

"I'll find out."

"I'm no pity case, little white girl."

"I like the covers." I did. Watercolors of Havana, beautiful black women in shimmering evening dresses, flowers in their hair. "Didn't you ever buy a book because you liked the cover and it turned out to be the best book you ever read, changed your life?" She smiled then. Took my money and helped me haul the records to my house. She stayed for dinner. From that day, we were inseparable. I liked the jazz, but it didn't change my life. Maggie did.

One day in early spring, as we sat in my mother's garden after dinner, Maggie told me she wouldn't be back for sophomore year, that she was transferring to the huge state college in Amherst.

"What? What are you talking about?"

She pulled apart a dark red tulip that had drooped to the grass. "I don't feel right here. You know I don't. There are too many rich kids, kids who wouldn't think of going to a state college. No one in my family ever even *went* to college before, and here I am among the children of the rich and famous. It's too . . . I don't know. Jarring, I guess."

"But that's all the more reason for you to stay! You got a scholarship because you worked hard, you're smart. You belong here more than all the ones whose families went here for generations. You belong here more than I do, that's for sure."

"Come on, Reve. You know what I'm talking about. I'm not here just because I'm smart. I'm here because I'm black. And I don't want to be some poster child for smart black people, the popular minority."

I could say that didn't matter, but she'd just huff and tell me I was naive. So I said, "You're not the only one."

She looked at me appraisingly, her eyes narrowed. "I thought so. You can't even say the word. Yeah, there are other *black* kids here. Their parents are surgeons, or performers. Oh, and there's that guy who's some kind of African prince. They went to prep schools. As in, they are *prepared* to live in this fishbowl. I fit in real good, as my mom's a hairdresser, and my father made and lost millions at the dog track. Mostly lost."

"Maggie, that's not fair. You're not being fair to yourself."

"At Bay State, there'll be about ten thousand kids from what the powers that be call 'the inner cities.'" She made quotation marks in the air. "Loads from Springfield, kids I went to high school with. They'll know who I am."

That stung. "Are you saying I don't?"

She got up, dropped the mangled tulip, and put her hand on my shoulder. "I'm saying nobody could have a better friend. I'm saying you are my good friend, and I don't want this to be the end of our friendship. But I've got to go. Or I'll feel like I'm on the edge of screaming, all four years. And I know my good friend Reve wouldn't want me to feel that way."

I took her hand off my shoulder, held it, examined her palm. "Of course I wouldn't want that. . . . It's just, I'll miss you. You're the best friend I've had for . . . well, for a long time."

"You can come visit. It's not that far."

So I did visit. I went most weekends, for a Saturday-night party or Sunday brunch. Bay State was only an hour away from Williams, but it was another world. As Maggie said, there were many kids from her hometown. There were kids from Japan and Bangladesh, too, from every corner of the globe. And Maggie seemed to know them all. She started getting more politically involved. We went to the peace vigils on the Amherst town common, to the protests against military research at the university. We did the usual things politically aware kids might do. We thought the worst that could happen was that we might get arrested, have to call our parents to bail us out, then go on blithely with our lives.

One day, we were sitting out under a willow by the pond, studying. Nobody was around, just a couple of boys throwing a Frisbee, their shouts and laughter a distant background chorus. It was March and the trees were still bare. Just on the cusp of spring, just barely warm enough to hang around outside wearing only sweatshirts. There had been more activity by the pond, but the clouds had spread a cold gray quilt over us, and rain threatened.

"Let's head back to your apartment. I'm freezing." I pulled my hood up over my hair, tucking in all the wild strands I could. Maggie looked at me, her brow furrowed in a way that I knew meant she'd been mulling something over for a while.

"What?" I asked her. "You might as well tell me. I know, you hate my leg warmers." She didn't laugh, and she usually would have. My leg warmers were a running joke. I was wearing new ones, bright pink, over my jeans. "They *are* stupid, but it's cold!" I waited—not even a smile.

She looked down at the book she hadn't been reading. "Shit. I hate this. I wouldn't bring it up, it's your own thing, but . . . it might be important."

"Just tell me already."

"If you say no, it's all right."

"Maggie!"

"Okay, okay." She took a breath, then plunged us into something that would change our lives forever. "The disappearing thing you do . . . can you do it whenever you want? Say, if you wanted to sneak into a place?"

I must have startled, because she put a hand out to steady me.

I shook it off. "You didn't *tell* anyone, did you?" I demanded. Hot fury, blended with fear, surged through me.

"Of course I wouldn't tell anybody. Do you think I'm stupid? They'd put me away if I started telling people about my friend, the girl with hot pink leg warmers *and* superpowers."

I was able to hide the disappearing from most people. My mom and my Nan had schooled me. One of my regular lessons was Disappearing and Reappearing 101. But I hadn't learned to control it every moment. With most people I could pass it off as a trick of the light, or laugh away any little glitch in timing. I couldn't hide anything from Maggie, though. It didn't seem to bother her, but I felt vulnerable nevertheless. Outside my family, the only other person who'd known had been Jolon. And that was long before, in childhood, when we believed miracles were common.

"Hey, it's okay—"

"Don't tell me it's not bizarre, Maggie. You know it is."

"All right, Reve, so you're a freak. But it's not so noticeable; you have to be looking for it to really see it." She made it sound like acne. Sometimes it felt that way, like a blot upon me. My mom tried to reassure me. It would never be an easy power, she conceded, but it would be useful, like all the gifts the Dyer women possessed. In the turbulent years of young adulthood, I found it hard to believe her. Never more than at that moment, when I thought my best friend might have betrayed my secret.

"Reve." Maggie touched my arm, and I pulled back again. "You believe me, don't you?"

"If you say you haven't told anyone, I believe you. Of course I do. Only it makes me feel . . . strange." I curled my arms around my body, tucked my head deeper into my hood. I wanted to disappear right then.

"I'm sorry I have to hassle you about it, but I need to know. Reve, *can* you do it whenever you want?"

"Why? Why is that important?"

She glanced around. Even the Frisbee players had given up on the day. The sky was the color of battleships.

"You know military researchers are working down in the tunnels." There was a network of tunnels below the quad, constructed in the 1950s during the Cold War. The tunnels were made to access bomb shelters. Everyone knew it; it was college legend. There was always gossip and speculation about what went on down there, what the tunnels were like, but few people had ever been in them, past or present.

"I don't know, I guess I'd heard that. So?"

"So. If you wanted to, you could . . . do your disappearing act and get in there, see what's happening—"

"We don't even know how to *get* to the tunnels."

"Actually, we do. Leon's been in there. He does work study for a couple profs in the science department. A few months ago, they had him and some other kids down there cleaning. He says there are whole buildings underground, a mirror image of the quad buildings, connected by the tunnels. Not much was in them when he first started working there, but then guys started bringing in boatloads of stuff—desks and lab equipment, mostly. One day, he gets there and there's a locked gate, right in the tunnel entrance. No warning or explanation. All of a sudden there's this big-ass gate up and he can't get in. He goes to Professor Allen, who tells him he's been reassigned to cleaning the rat cages, not to go down to the tunnels anymore. By the way, no need to mention the gate to anybody, either. But Leon told Eli. Then Eli got snagged by some men in black while he was scoping it out."

"Men in black?"

"You know, guys who work for government agencies."

"What, like the FBI?"

"FBI, CIA, Defense Department, who knows? Scary dudes."

"So what happened?"

"They grilled him for a while, then they let him go."

"Okay, so how am I supposed to get past that gate?"

"There's a key card system. Like some hotels have now? You could disappear, wait until someone comes with a key card, and sneak behind them when they go in. Scope it out, check their records, maybe. See what's really going on." I could feel her excitement. "Reve, you could make a difference. No one knows what they're doing. They could be working on something really evil, like a biological warfare agent. Who knows, they might get around to testing it on us, on the communities around here. Or it might get out, by accident. We could blow it all to hell, expose them, make it stop, before it goes Project Blue."

I'd read *The Stand*. Maggie had lent it to me. I was convinced the scenario really could happen, just as she was. A super flu created in a military research station let loose, causing a pandemic. I guess I was as altruistic as any dumb kid, as ready to take on the role of superhero, especially since I *did* have a superpower, as Maggie pointed out. There was also the pure desire to please her, to live up to her righteousness. And my aunts, my Nan, my mom all used their powers, used them in real ways. Wasn't this my chance to do the same? I saw my destiny in Maggie's face, in her smile when I promised her yes, I'd go down into the earth.

4

I forced myself to save the Fetch's e-mail. I forced myself to rise and go out to the widow's walk, gulp the clean air. I gripped the rail hard, until my hands ached. All those years not knowing Maggie's fate weighed on me, like a stone on my heart, always there. But this new knowledge came with a price.

After things went wrong with Maggie's plan, after she had disappeared more thoroughly than I ever had, I left. Left college, left the Northeast. Nothing made sense to me anymore, except the need to get away. So I went to Las Vegas. The city was the capital of illusion: What better place to conceal true magic? I could use my gift there without putting anyone else in jeopardy. I could camouflage it in that city of magic and loss, like nowhere else on earth.

But magic has its price. Maggie had paid the price for urging me to use my magic. I could only speculate that Jeremy had, too. Now I was in a place where the magic of my ancestors had taken root. Would that magic, converging with my own, harm or protect us?

I thought of calling the Las Vegas police, but then tried to imagine what I'd say. How could a twenty-year-old photo of a missing girl have anything to do with my own husband's death, with someone stalking us now? There wasn't any solid evidence the episodes were connected, only this one e-mail. I certainly couldn't tell the cops about my ability to disappear. But there *was* someone I could talk to.

I found the Hawley town directory, punched in a number. A woman's voice answered, a cranky woman's voice. "Hawley Police Department, Myrna speakin'. Whadda ya want?"

"May I speak to Chief Adair?"

"Who's callin'?"

"My name's Reve Dyer."

"Uh-huh."

"Is he there?"

"What's this about, exactly?" She wasn't letting me off the hook.

"It's . . . personal. The chief and I are old friends." Great. Now the whole town would be talking about us. "I mean, it's not a police matter." That wasn't exactly true, but I had no intention of divulging anything to this surly woman. Certainly not the more mysterious elements of my dilemma.

"I can't give out his cell number, just like that."

"Then he's not there?"

"Well, I guess I can tell you he's not."

God, I was getting tired of these Yankees and their reticence. You had to wring even simple scraps of information from them. "Could you tell me where he is?"

"I could."

There was a long pause, while we waited each other out and I thought maybe she'd hung up after all. But then she caved. "Gone over to Lithia this mornin'. Had a meeting with the new chief there. Bill Streeter." This part of the world was filled with Streeters. Bill was no doubt some third or fourth cousin of Carl's.

"At the Lithia police station?"

"Well. Probly not." Myrna sounded perkier. "Since they're buildin' a new one now, and the temporary station's in the old apple barn. That's what we still call it, though it hasn't had any apples stored in it for years. Still smells of rotten apples. And it *is* coldish of a mornin' so you might just find them at the Creamery."

"That's on the corner of Main and Route 9 in Lithia, isn't it?"

"Always has been. You could look for Jolon there."

"I will. Thank you, Myrna."

"And, missus? Could you ask him to bring back some a them mocha scones?"

"Thanks, Myrna. I'll make sure he does."

I checked in on Nathan and the girls, now wrangling over the 2004 presidential election. I decided I could safely leave them for an hour or so, told Nathan where I'd be, and headed out to find Jolon.

It was only a fifteen-minute drive to Lithia, through some of the prettiest farm country imaginable. In Plainfield, one of the towns Edith Wharton might have based Ethan Frome's town of Starkfield on, I realized I'd been feeling as isolated as Ethan Frome myself. Just getting out of the house, away from the Fetch's menacing e-mail, did me good. Bright tunnels of blazing maples lined the road; the fields were golden with sunflowers and late hay.

There was indeed a Hawley police cruiser outside the

Creamery. I rolled into the potholed parking lot, then saw a vision that stopped my breath. Two little girls were sitting on the store steps, playing with paper dolls. One was pale with hair the color of rust; the other's burnished brown skin reminded me of coffee with lots of cream. It could have been Maggie's head and mine, bent together over a game, had we known each other as kids. Had we been that lucky. The brown girl looked up and smiled at me. I gave her a little wave, but it made my heart ache to look into her laughing eyes.

The brew of sound and scent nearly knocked me over when I opened the door. It was a small store, but so much was crammed in it—a bakery and deli counter, grocery shelves spilling over with every organic and locally grown or made product imaginable. The air was pungent with scents of spices and roasting meat and strong coffee. The seating area by the big windows was crowded with people talking and eating, from men in business suits to dreadlocked women in hemp dresses. Kids played tag around the tables, up the aisles, shrieking with glee.

I spied Jolon in a corner, sitting with two other men. He seemed, in his uniform, very official. A wave of shyness washed over me. Surely my headlong rush to talk to him about the Fetch was ill-conceived. I should have waited. I should have thought before I leapt. Why *did* I always want to leap? Fools rush in.

I was turning to slink back out the door and bolt when he looked up. That craggy, seldom used smile came over his face when he looked at me. He said something to his companions. Then he rose and made his way over, skirting running children and deli girls bearing trays laden with sandwiches and soups.

"Hey, Reve, what're you doing this side of the hill?" He

took my arm, steered me toward the coffee station. "Let me buy you a cuppa."

I glanced back at his companions. Both were in their thirties, boys in blue. Both leered at us. "Aren't you busy?"

He ignored the stares we were getting. "Nah. We were just finishing up. Bill and Bob just got their lunches." I nodded to them faintly as he saluted Bill and Bob. The B boys. They went back to wolfing sandwiches.

"Did you have lunch?"

"Lunch?" I echoed stupidly, as if I had never heard of the meal.

Jolon grinned. "You know. What you eat between breakfast and dinner. The food's good here, if you want soup or . . . Hey, Reve, what's wrong?"

"It's . . . it's just that . . ." I had no idea what to say next. It was hot in there, and there was too much noise and too many people. "Look, I really need to talk to you."

"You came here to find me?" I nodded, and he flushed. Or maybe I imagined it. It *was* hot in there. "Myrna told you where I was? Usually she won't budge. You'd think the security of the nation depended on her silence."

"It was the possibility of mocha scones that did it. She wanted me to tell you to bring some back."

"You always did have great powers of persuasion."

At the mention of my powers, a kind of vertigo swept over me. I leaned against the counter to steady myself. Jolon touched my arm, his face growing serious. His touch made me feel weaker.

"I'll send Bob back with the cruiser. You can give me a ride to Hawley and we can talk." Without waiting for me to answer, he returned to his table, talked briefly with the B boys, paid for two mocha scones for Myrna, tucked the white bag in his jacket pocket. Then he turned back to me. "Let me at least get you something to drink. They have passable coffee here. Or would you rather tea?"

"Tea," I croaked. "Please."

In a few minutes he returned and handed me a cup filled with fragrant liquid. "You're in luck. This stuff isn't for the teeming masses."

"You know your way around." I took a sip, and the tea's smoky tang shored me up.

"I'm pretty much a regular. But then, everyone is. Peri manages the place, keeps stashes of our favorites on hand. My vice, decent tea. There's a tea shop down in Hamp. They mix some up special for me, call it Hawley Forest blend." I almost dropped the cup. Then remembered he lived in the forest, after all. I realized he was trying to calm me. Talking softly, not moving too fast. He steered me out the door, into the autumn-scented air. Almost immediately, he was beset by the two girls on the porch. "Hey, Jolon, when can we have a ride in the cruiser?" "Will you turn the siren on?"

"Okay, you two, calm down. Ms. Dyer here will think we have no manners." The two girls regarded me solemnly.

"Is she the lady from Five Corners? My mom said she had red hair, kind of like mine. But hers is curlier." The grapevine had clearly been busy.

"Like I said, manners." He put a finger to his lips. "Reve, meet two young ladies of Lithia town, Bridget Granger Sears and Tilda Delaney." I wondered how Bridget was related to the Hawley Searses, and perhaps to me, to the Dyers, way back. Her eyes were green as sea glass, like my own. But it would take a genealogist to parse it out.

"Where's your mom, Bridget?" Jolon asked her.

"The liberry. Gave us money for ice creams."

Tilda, the brown girl, spoke up. "But, Bridge, we forgot. We were s'posed to go right back."

Jolon gave them a stern look. "I suggest you go ahead, then. Don't want your mother to worry."

"She can see us right from the window by her desk."

"Even so."

Bridget looked crestfallen, but brightened when Jolon reached in his pocket, gave them each a Cow Tale.

"Gee, thanks, Jolon!"

Just then the wind picked up, and their paper dolls went fluttering to the pavement. They scrambled, and Jolon and I bent to help pick them up. They weren't Fancy Nancy dolls, as I'd thought at first. They were fairies, blue and green and pink, with delicate wings. When they were all safely tucked back into their tin, the girls ran off toward the stone library.

Jolon led me to the unoccupied picnic tables by the road, weathered gray hulls that creaked when we sat on the benches. I sipped my tea, noticed more layers of flavor, smoky yet sweet, even a little flowery. It tasted like the forest smelled.

"Good tea."

"You didn't come here to talk about tea. Tell me what's wrong, Reve."

"Oh, Jolon." I put my head in my hands, rubbed at my temples, tried to coax the fear that lodged in my body into words. "I don't know where to start. . . ."

"The beginning is always a good place." His words were abrupt, but his voice was gentle. I thought of all the secrets we'd shared so long ago. This was only one more. And I had no one else to help me.

"The beginning seems so far away. Do you remember my Nan's stories?"

"As far back as that?"

Maybe he wouldn't believe me, after all, but I didn't have much choice. "I needed to get out of Las Vegas. It was because of Nan and her stories that I came back here." I took a breath, plunged on. "The short version is that the man who killed my husband is stalking us. I just . . . I don't . . ." I could feel tears welling, stopping up the words.

"Reve, you should have told me sooner." He reached for me again, and I let him. I let his hand brush mine, caress it softly. I remembered the baby wren we found once. He'd stroked the tiny thing so delicately, it was more like his mind alone was touching the bird's, willing it to live. It had.

I took a breath, tamped the tears back down. I struggled to answer Jolon calmly, to *be* calm. "He's not anywhere close by. I don't *think* he is yet. But I got an e-mail from him this morning. Saying he'll find us, no matter what."

"And you have no idea who he might be?"

"None. I just call him the Fetch." Jolon studied my face, his eyes seeking more answers. "You remember Nan's story of the Fetch?"

"The stealer of souls? Yeah, I remember that one. Guaranteed to terrify an eight-year-old. But if you're right about your husband's murder, this guy's real, not just a specter."

"He's real, all right."

"Do the Las Vegas police know?"

I nodded. "But they think . . . Well, they still think I had something to do with Jeremy's murder. Although they also know that whoever he is, the Fetch isn't just a figment of my imagination. He was sending photos, of me, of the girls . . ."

The rest of the story just spilled out. "That's why we moved. I thought maybe he wouldn't be able to find us. That he'd just leave us alone."

"Shit, Reve." He folded my hand in his then, but in a moment let go and scrubbed his hair back. I could see him shift into cop mode, but it was all right. He'd been my friend first, and his touch had reminded me. "Okay—first thing is, I need to see that e-mail. And those photos."

"Can I forward the e-mail to you? The Las Vegas police have the photos. I don't want the girls to know. You don't have kids, but . . ."

"I understand. I won't come to the house. I can get copies of the photos from the LVPD, and their reports. Just forward the e-mail, like you said."

The Lithia church bells chimed the hour.

"I need to get back, Jolon."

We got in the car, and I drove out of the parking lot toward Hawley. The day was still beautiful, the leaves striking in the pearly autumn light. But it was all blurred at the edges to me, blunted by nerves. The man beside me had to know more if he was going to help me, more than the police in Las Vegas had, more than anyone else probably could.

"Jolon. There's something else I need to tell you. I think all this may have to do with my . . . ability. You know what I mean."

"I do. I remember, Reve. I remember everything." I knew he did. And I knew I was safe with him, at least in that moment. So when he said, "Tell me why you think that," I did. I told him the story of Maggie.

5

Two nights after my conversation with Maggie by the pond at Bay State, I drove back to Amherst. I left my car in town and met her outside the old Stockbridge horse barn. It was eerie in the moonlight. Bats swooped around our heads. We went into the barn, stood under its chestnut beams. It had been all but abandoned when the university bought a new barn to house their equestrian program. The few horses that remained seemed restless, although they knew us from past visits bearing apples. Three Morgan mares and Teddy the old Paint gelding shifted in their stalls, snorted and pawed.

"I've got nothing for them," I whispered.

"I didn't think of it . . ."

I went to the stall that held a few bales, threw them each a flake. "We *are* using their barn." Teddy blew into his hay, then settled. I walked back to Maggie's silhouette. The mares remained watchful. Their breath in the cool air wreathed around us. Maggie was silent, and I felt a tremor of fear that unsettled me. "Did you find out where the gate is?" I asked. Maybe she hadn't, and we could go home.

"Yeah. Right under the barn."

"Where the manure pile is?"

"Can you think of better camouflage? There's an opening. It's hard to see, but at the same time, you could drive a truck through it. You'll find it. I'll be here when you come out. You won't have to wait long. They do most of their work at night, just like Leon told me. I was up here last night and from Eve's stall window, I could see them. They come and go till sunrise. It should be fine, with you disappeared and all."

I prayed it *would* be fine. I couldn't back out now. "What exactly am I looking for?"

"We don't know. Not really. Anything that might be a clue to what happens down there, what they're working on."

I sucked in a breath. "All right. Here goes." I started toward the manure pile. Before I turned the corner, I glanced back. I could see Maggie petting Eve's nose. I knew that she could no longer see me. No one could.

When I got to the lower level of the barn, I stepped under a low tree limb, and there it was. A wide opening beneath the barn, hidden by trees and the manure pile. I ducked into it. There was no light at all, so I felt my way along a cement wall. The wall went down and kept going down. Soon enough, the entrance was just a moonlit gap as big as my fist. I crept slowly, and in another minute felt the wire mesh of a gate. I pressed against the wall and waited.

It seemed like forever. I slid down the damp wall, rested my elbows on my knees and tried to be patient. I hoped no one would come. I hoped it was all made up, only another one of the many legends that flourished around campus, only another tall tale. Just as I was drifting into a doze, I saw the pinpoint of a flashlight at the tunnel entrance. I jerked to my feet. The light danced and bobbed, and a man walked up to the gate. He shone the flashlight at a panel, swiped a card, the gate opened, and he went through. I stepped behind him, my heart thudding, glad I'd worn my Adidas, like silence on my feet. The man paused just inside the gate, looked around. I was only inches from him. He could have stepped on me. But people trust their eyes more than their other senses, and he saw nothing when he swung the flashlight beam. So he went on, with me padding softly after him.

Only a dozen steps and he came to a door with another panel, where he swiped his card again. When the door opened, a blaze of light hit me. Blinded, I almost didn't make it in, but I managed to squeeze through as the door swung shut. The man continued down a hallway lined with windows. People sat at desks and typed, or drank coffee, or were busy looking through file drawers. Maggie was right: It was just like the administration buildings aboveground. Everyone was dressed casually, in jeans and sweaters. I didn't see any lab coats.

I decided to keep following my guy. He'd taken off a trench coat, draped it over one arm, and I could see that, unlike the others, he was wearing a suit. Maybe he was more senior, would go deeper into the labyrinth. He strode down another hallway, then into an office that was identical to all the others I'd seen. Another suited man was there. He was sitting at a desk but had his feet up, reading a Tom Clancy paperback. He only gave a lazy wave when my guy entered. I hung in the doorway and listened.

"Hey, Lupo. What's goin' down?"

My guy, Lupo, answered, "Dunno, Andy. Another quiet night with the lab rats?"

"Yeah. Guess so."

"Boss been in?"

"Yeah. He's somewhere. In some big-shot meeting." Andy rose from his chair, cracked his knuckles, yawned. "S'pose I'll head out. Busy day tomorrow."

"You back here?"

"Nah, detail in town the next few days. Glad to be done with the graveyard shift for a while. Boring as hell. And it gives me the heebie-jeebies. I'd rather be tailing the kids. Who the hell knows what they're doing down here? Could blow us all up."

"Yeah. You never know," Lupo agreed. "Me, I'm happy not knowing. Your problem is you read too much. Those books put ideas in your head."

"Maybe you're right." Andy stuck the book in a drawer, hitched up his pants, and saluted Lupo, who planted himself in the chair, took up a file from the desktop.

"Anything else in the hopper?"

"Same old." Andy smoothed his rumpled jacket. Then he lifted something out of the desk drawer. "Good one," he told Lupo as he snicked the gun into a holster under his arm.

"Yeah. You, too."

I stepped aside for Andy and took a shaky breath, concentrating hard on staying unseen. The gun made me break out in a sweat. The guys in the suits must be FBI. Or something. The men in black, Maggie had called them. Whoever they were, getting shot was not on my agenda. But I hadn't really found anything out, except that these guys were serious about whatever secrets they were protecting, even if they had no idea what the secrets were. Figuring I'd get nowhere hanging around Lupo at his desk, I walked to the end of the hall, turned a corner, and went back to the area where the non-suits were working. I hoped they didn't have guns.

I wandered around gaping at all the desk jockeys. I tried to read their work over their shoulders, but what I read didn't make any sense to me, only graphs and numbers.

Then I saw the flash of a lab coat. I followed the coat to another hallway. The lab coat was worn by an older woman with graying hair in a ponytail that swung as she walked. She was heading for a green door that said LEVEL 6 CLEARANCE. I caught right up to her, so close I could hear her rubber-soled shoes squelch softly on the linoleum floor. She swiped her card; I whisked in after her.

It was like another world behind that door, although I still can't describe what I saw there with any precision. The room was vast. It seemed as if there was no end to it. There were more men and women in lab coats, working at stations with microscopes and petri dishes. There were big tanks and vats filled with who knew what. Wires and pipes ran every which way above and around me. Compressors thunked and whooshed. I slunk around for a while, watching one scientist and then another work. But I realized soon enough that even if I watched and listened all night I hadn't the knowledge to interpret what was happening. All I really knew was that something big was going on. At that moment, though, I was more bored than frightened. Maybe I was just too young to understand the potential consequences of what I was seeing, and the corresponding price I would pay if I were caught spying.

Eventually I decided I'd had enough for one night, and was heading for the door to wait for the next opening, when my eye caught movement in a recessed corner. Two scientists—a man and a woman—were standing before a glass wall, looking into a small room. One held something like a television remote. I looked in. The narrow room was even more brightly lit than the lab. It held only a chair, with a man sitting in it. The chair was made of wooden four-by-fours, dwarfing the man, who seemed caught in the web of rubber tubing he was struggling against. His bare arms and legs were bound with it, and the skin that showed looked red and raw from his struggles to free himself. He was leaping and jerking, as far as the tubing would allow.

A scream burned in my throat but I choked it back. I stood frozen, as captive as the man I couldn't drag my eyes from. His face was covered with a black cloth, but I could see the metal cap on his head, and the singed white hair and scorch marks on his scalp. The black cloth across his face moved like a curtain in a powerful wind, sucked into the hole that must have been his mouth, then blown out again by what could only be screams. But there was no sound outside the glass window. That was almost the worst of it. The soundless screams of the electrified man, who seemed unable to get away, even by dying. Minutes must have ticked by, while the scientist with the remote pushed the button for more electric current, and still the man did not die. Just screamed and screamed in that awful silent way.

Then one of the scientists turned suddenly and walked right into me—walked into my disappeared self. She fell on the floor at my feet. Somehow I had the sense not to reach to help her up, but I must have lost control and reappeared for an instant.

She saw me and screamed. Like I was worse than the frightful experiment being conducted in that glass room.

"Dr. Harmon? Are you okay?" Men and women in white coats swirled around me while I concentrated on disappearing again, and staying that way.

"She . . . she . . . There's a girl!" Dr. Harmon pointed to where I'd been, but I was invisible again. I tried to calm my ragged breathing while I waited for someone to open the door so I could slip out, escape.

"Call Security! Call the boss! There's a student in here!"

"Where?"

"I saw her, too!" another white coat called. "She has to be here somewhere."

Drumming feet sounded outside the door, and then pounding. One of the scientists had the presence of mind to swipe his key card to open the door. I rushed out into a cluster of men wearing suits, Lupo and three or four others. Men with guns. I slammed into one with the full force of my weight before I could stop. I caromed off him and ran, but then he was after me. I had no idea whether I was disappeared or not—I was too frightened. I looked back, and his eyes bored into me. Bluest of eyes, ice blue. A big man, but graceful. He leapt, and caught me. Panicked, I fought like a fish on a hook, and like a hooked fish would have stayed caught, but Lupo tripped and fell into the man with the ice eyes, toppling him. I felt his hands on me slipping. I gave one heave and I was away, running as hard as I could, safe in my invisibility again.

I ran, didn't look back until I was past Lupo's office, at the door to the outside. There were alarms going off, people running everywhere, but I pressed myself against the wall and waited, focused on quieting my hammering heart. What had I gotten myself into? I stayed frozen, terrified to risk another run-in. There must have been a lockdown. No one came near the door for more than an hour. It was hard to stay invisible all that time, and to keep from going further into that parallel world I always sensed floating near me whenever I disappeared. I was afraid of being found out, but I was more fearful of the absolute cipher that world held. So I kept it up, balancing just out of sight. It was well after midnight when a whistling office worker finally keyed the door, and I tore out.

When I reached the barn, breathless, Maggie sprang to her feet. "Where the hell were—"

I clamped my hand over her mouth. "Shhh! Don't talk! Come on!"

I made her run all the way back to her apartment. She brewed tea that I gulped down, not minding that it scalded me. I told her all of it—the offices, the lab, the men with guns. And the horrible man in the chair, whose face I never saw. Who I might identify by only one thing. The tattoo of a thick blue snake winding around his wrist and up his arm. From that day on, for years after, that blue snake would twist through my dreams, a recurring nightmare.

"Shit," Maggie whispered when I was done telling, slumped with fatigue and the aftereffects of terror. "What are we going to do now?"

I had no answer for her.

About a month later, just before the summer, I felt something alter in Maggie. She changed in some indefinable way. We didn't see each other much, only met off campus, away from Amherst, and she didn't seem to be as present when we did. Her eyes were constantly shifting, as if she were looking for someone. She got quiet and moody. Then one morning, she called me in a panic.

"Reve, you've got to come. You've got to get me out of here!"

I heard traffic noises through the phone. "Where are you? What's wrong?"

"I'm at the Sunoco station on Pleasant. But I can't stay here."

"What happened? Maggie—"

"Please, Reve, just come. I'll wait for you at Classé. If I'm not there, I'll be outside Barsies. If I'm not there . . . I don't know." Her voice was edgy, pleading. That, more than anything, terrified me.

"I'll come right now."

"Borrow someone else's car. Is Lisa on campus? Take hers."

"But—"

"Reve, damn it, just do it! Please. Really, don't take your truck, or your parents' car."

Her panic was contagious, compelling. "Wait for me," I said.

I screeched up to Classé Café, leapt out of Lisa's monster Impala, and tripped. A man in a white shirt with a camera around his neck caught me.

"Whoa, there. Where you going so fast?" One of the FBI guys, I was sure. Maybe he'd even been in the tunnels. I had kept away from Amherst since that night—was scared stiff I'd be recognized, although I still thought the only one who'd gotten a good clear look at me was the man with the ice eyes, and this was not him.

I pulled away, said, "Thanks" over my shoulder, and ran into the crowded café. Maggie was nowhere to be seen. I checked the bathroom, then ran back to the car. Camera man was gone.

I drove to Barselotti's. Just as I pulled up to the curb, Maggie threw the door open, jumped in, and snapped, "Drive, just drive, until I figure this out."

"Mom said to bring you home."

"No. Not there. They can't find out where you live."

"Shit. What happened?"

"I'll tell you everything, Reve. I promise. Just drive around. Drive somewhere there's traffic."

I took Route 9 toward Northampton. We drove past the malls and the bucolic farms, and Maggie told her story.

"Right after you went down in the tunnels, I started feeling like someone was following me. I didn't tell you, I didn't want to scare you. I don't know, at first I thought it was just me being paranoid. But I was nervous about them, FBI, DOD, whoever they are. Eli's Freedom of Information Act files were broken into last month. Then stuff started happening to me."

"What kind of stuff?" My mouth was dry. I felt feverish. Maybe I was entrenched in a nightmare, unable to wake up.

"First, I started thinking . . . no, *knowing*, I was being followed. Then I was in the Campus Center, writing in my journal. I left it on the chair and went to get some water from the fountain, which was, like, three feet away. When I went back, it was gone."

"Are you sure it didn't just fall?"

"Unless it fell into some black hole, yeah, I'm sure. I looked all around for it. And if somebody wanted to steal something, my whole backpack was right there, with my wallet and everything. I swear my back was turned for all of five seconds."

I took a deep breath, tried to be rational, tried to stop my hands from trembling on the steering wheel. "Okay, so what if somebody did take it? Maybe some hoser just needed paper."

"That's not the only thing. Last night I went to the gym. When I got back my apartment was torn up. I'm scared, Reve. *You* should be scared."

I almost slammed into the car in front of me. "Oh, shit! Did you write anything about the underground lab?"

"That's the weird part. There was nothing much in the journal. Just stuff about my little life. Classes and parties and rallies. You know. I would never put anything in writing about what you saw. Or that either of us were there at all."

"Maybe they were looking for information about other people. Maybe Eli."

"What do I know about him, more than anybody else? It's not like he's my boyfriend or anything. No, they're suddenly all hot on me, for some reason. Maybe there was something in Eli's files. I changed everybody's names in my journal, too, just in case."

"What? Why? What made you do that, if you weren't writing anything much? Were you writing in code, too?" It was all starting to seem too much like a James Bond movie.

Maggie glared at me. "Stop the car. I'll get out."

"Don't be stupid!"

I could feel her gaze burning my face. "All right. Turn around. Let's go back."

"Why?"

"Just go to the center of town and park this beast. There's something you need to see."

We walked around the Amherst common, down Main Street. Every now and then, Maggie would give an almost imperceptible nod, whisper, "There." I'd look and see a conservatively dressed man or woman, always alone. But they all had the same look, as if the emotion had been squeezed out, made them pale and nondescript. I couldn't ID one two minutes after I'd seen them, they looked so generic. And there were lots of them. They were like a swarm. Even after the tunnels, I had no idea there would be so many.

"Maybe they had a sale on white shirts and dark ties at Sears."

Maggie laughed for the first time that day. I tried to keep it going. "Maybe they're Mormons," I suggested.

"Well, that I could believe, except that lady over there has a camera and is taking pictures of us." And there she was, less than ten feet away, a pinched woman with no-color hair holding a camera up to her face, pointing it at us. I whipped around to see if she could be taking a photo of something else. There was only the street, with blowing paper and telephone wires. A shiver of foreboding ran through me, chilling me on that warm day. I heard the shutter click and didn't stop to think. I started walking toward the woman, but she turned and walked briskly away. "Ma'am?" I called. She walked faster. I ran. "Ma'am!" I called louder. She didn't turn. When I caught her by a white sleeve, she had to face me. Her lips twitched, as if she was trying to remember how to smile. "Yes?"

"You took a photo of me and my friend. Why?"

She managed to push the corners of her lips further up her face. "Why would I do that, dear? I don't know you."

"Then what did you photograph?"

"I've been to the Emily Dickinson house. So interesting."

"I mean now, just a minute ago."

She shook her head. "I haven't taken a photograph since I left the tour. I'm sorry, but you're mistaken."

A jolt of terror rocked me. It took all the control I had not to disappear. Here I was, on a perfect spring day, in the middle of a public place I knew well, talking with a mild-looking woman who almost certainly had no intention of hurting me, at least in any physical way. But I felt my certainty about everything I thought I knew spiral away. Maybe she was right. Maybe I was crazy. I turned to Maggie for confirmation, but she was tying her sneaker, looking down so I couldn't see her face. I turned back and the woman was gone. I looked up and down the street. The relief I felt made me dizzy.

"Forget it." Maggie put a hand on my arm. "She's not going to give you any straight answers."

"She said she didn't take a photo. And I almost believe her. It's scary."

"I heard." Maggie said it wearily. Her face was drawn. I noticed then how thin she'd gotten, how her clothes hung on her. "I've tried to corner them, too, ask them what they want from me. They always deny everything. But they're always on me. Everywhere I go. They're starting to make me believe I really am nuts. Except I know I'm not. And now you know, too."

"Yeah, I know." And I did. I finally knew what Maggie had been going through, alone. These men and women who looked like Mormons or office workers were able to spread fear like a virus. It was a fear worse than I'd felt in the tunnels, a fear for my own sanity, for Maggie's. It was still pulsing through me. I had to sit on a bench in front of the town hall. I tried to think rationally. "Look, they can't link you to anything. Not really. Maybe they'll just stop after a while."

"Yeah, well, I can't just wait around for that to happen. I think they actually *could* make me crazy. That they're *trying* to."

I took Maggie's hand, squeezed it. "What can we do?"

She tugged her hand away. "I don't know. But I'm scared they'll find out who you are, that it was you down there." She looked away. "And they might make me crazy enough to tell them. Shit, Reve, I'm the one that got you into this mess in the first place, and now—well, I might just be getting you into worse trouble."

"I guess we should have thought about that before we let that woman take our picture."

"What were we going to do? Smash her camera? Like that wouldn't attract attention. Anyway, I don't think pictures matter so much. I have a reason. I'll show you. Then you have to make sure no one follows you home. Although that may not be a problem, either."

"What do you mean?"

"It has to do with the disappearing. But now I have to disappear, too."

Maggie's studio apartment was tiny, and when I'd been in it before, it was always neat and orderly. Maggie's taste ran to the spartan—a futon that was always made up the moment she rose, a standing lamp, a glass coffee table with a teapot and never more than one book on it. The bookshelves were only cement blocks and slats of wood, the books arranged alphabetically. But that day, the books were scattered everywhere, pages torn. Shards of the glass coffee table glittered on the floor. The teapot was cracked. The sweats and flannel shirts Maggie favored lay with outstretched arms, the dresser itself on its side, drawers smashed. Flour spattered the floor of the closet-sized kitchen, the refrigerator door swung open, and ketchup dripped like blood. It would have shocked me if I hadn't been so numbed by what had just happened in town. I could see tears starting down Maggie's face. I put my arms around her. "Oh, Mags, I'm so sorry . . ."

She pulled away, wiped her eyes with her sleeve. "Yeah, me, too. But I've got to get out of here. I called my cousin in New York. I can stay there for the summer."

Her suitcase had been kicked into a corner. It had a foot-long gash in its side. "Guess I'm going in style." She got a big black garbage bag from the kitchen and filled it with clothing, books, soap, and a toothbrush.

She took a long look at the room. "I liked it here. You know, it was the first time I ever lived alone." Fresh tears welled in her eyes.

"You'll be back."

"I don't know, Reve. I wish . . ." But she didn't say what her wish was. I could tell she didn't think it would come true.

I drove her to the bus station, waited with her for the bus driver to board everyone heading to New York. He stuffed Maggie's garbage bag far into the storage bay under the bus. I gave Maggie a long hug, felt her bones through her clothes. I held her, breathing her in, denim and Teaberry gum, then tucked five twenties in her jacket pocket. "Call me when you get there. Don't forget."

"Thanks, Reve. I'm sorry I got you into this. I'm sorry for everything." She turned away, then turned back. She pulled a crumpled envelope from her day pack. "I almost forgot. I'm going to leave these with you. They're photos someone took, like today, and sent to me. No return address. They seem normal, but . . . you'll see. I don't think anyone is going to find out it was you down in the lab, as long as you stay away. I don't think you should worry. And don't worry about me now, either. I'll be fine." She nodded, then tipped her baseball cap at me. It was the same dark blue cap with a smiley face on it she'd worn the first day I met her.

I waited until the bus rolled away, straining for a last look at Maggie's face through the window. I knew she wouldn't be fine. I knew I should have got on that bus with her. I'm still not sure why I didn't.

6

I kept the envelope Maggie had given me that day she got on the bus. I still had it, carried it through every move. My only keepsake of that time, of Maggie. It contained photographs of her, at the Big Indian shop on Route 2, in front of the Longview Tower in Greenfield, the places we'd met after I'd infiltrated the tunnels. She was clearly talking to someone. Only the person she was talking to hadn't been captured by the camera's eye. I should have been right next to her in each photograph. It was me she'd been talking to. I was in every one of those photos, only I was in them disappeared.

My parents went to the police with me when Maggie failed to call me, when I'd talked to her worried mom, the cousin she was supposed to be staying with who told us she'd never showed up in New York. The police, whose investigation into the harassment of a couple of troublemaking college girls was cursory at best. Because Maggie was seen at the protests. Because I had been there, too. And because Maggie was black, I was sure. We were told that lots of college kids run away, and she was undoubtedly one of them. Her grades were falling, she'd been acting strangely, she was paranoid and distrustful. There was no evidence anyone but Maggie had been in her apartment when it was ransacked. The detective assigned to her case implied that she had done it herself, to attract attention. That was the sum of his report.

I knew better. I knew Maggie was terrified, with good cause. And now I knew that what had happened to her had something to do with me, with my power. That the Fetch had killed her all those years ago, as he'd killed Jeremy. And it was my fault. Jeremy's death and Maggie's resonated, bookmarking my life. I'd as good as pulled the trigger on them both.

I told Jolon the story as briefly and sparingly as I could. I told him almost everything, even the part about me being disappeared in the photos. But for the first time since I'd met him I kept something from him. I didn't tell him about the tortured man in the tunnels. I thought it would be more believable that way, but I was fearful, too. Fearful of what might happen if I told even Jolon. That it would seem much bigger then, and more terrifying. After Maggie, I'd never told anyone, even Jeremy. It was our secret, mine and dead Maggie's. Ours and the Fetch's.

Jolon was silent after I finished speaking.

"Do you believe me? I know it sounds strange and . . . kind of crazy."

"I believe you. I always have. Why stop now?" He sighed, looked out the window at Hawley Forest, where we were by then. "As for being strange, well . . . it is." He skipped over the crazy part. "If you're right about it being the same guy, and it sounds like it could be, this has been going on for a very long time." Neither of us then had any idea *how* long.

Pizza by Earl—October 24, 2013

1

Jolon called me the next morning. The Fetch's e-mail had been sent from a new Yahoo account set up at a public library in St. George, Utah, the previous day. St. George was about two hours from our Henderson house. The library patron had been a man named David Tolland, who had a Provo, Utah, address. He was otherwise unremarkable, the librarian told them. No one remembered him. He had also been dead for eleven years. A fake ID. Another dead end.

"One thing I'll tell you. Knowing what you've already been through, you and the girls should have protection."

"Meaning?"

"A bodyguard. Maybe a couple."

I laughed when he said it, but I mulled it over. After a day of trying to work, but mostly just spent stewing and checking my e-mail or the girls every ten minutes, I thought it would be good to get us all out of the house.

Most nights at Pizza by Earl are slow. A middle-aged couple sat side by side in one of the green Naugahyde booths watching *Who Wants to Be a Millionaire*. Smoke lay bluely over their heads, clouding the television. A few men huddled in the corner of the bar over beers. No one looked up as we walked in except the waitress, who snapped her gum at us. Earl could be seen flinging dough behind the hatch. A puffy-eyed busboy slung beer mugs into a dishwasher. A sign by the cash register was turned to PLEASE SEAT YOURSELF, so we all wandered over to the booths. Nathan and I scooched into one. The girls slumped into the one behind us, and immediately started poring over the tabletop jukebox selections.

The seats were cracked where they weren't duct taped, but there were real flowers in vases on all the tables, and along the marble counter. Pink and red carnations wafted their spicy scent as we sat down. We picked menus out of a wire rack that advertised BUDWEISER—THE KING OF BEERS. The specials were handwritten in marker and slid into the plastic menu cover: Chicken parmigiana dinner with choice of ziti or spaghetti. Cajun catfish with rice pilaf and green beans, and something cryptically titled "roast beast feast." The dessert of the day, apart from the usual apple, cherry, blueberry, banana cream, and chocolate cream pies, was Grape-Nut pudding. Grape-Nut pudding was Fai's strange favorite. She always ordered it when we went to Mustang Sally's Diner back home. Which we hadn't done in a very long time. Would Hawley turn out to be just another stop on our trajectory of flight? I felt a catch in my throat at the thought. Nathan, sitting across from me, narrowed his eyes. "Is this going to be okay, Reve? We can go home."

I twirled the heavy glass ashtray on the table. I wished I still smoked. "I'll be all right."

The gum-snapping waitress came over for our order, poured waters, sloshed some onto the table. She looked nervous, her face flushed. "My dad says you're the lady from over Five

Corners. Said to tell you we hope you're getting settled in." She said it all in a rush, her face growing redder. She was not much older than Grace and Fai. I felt exposed, felt my own face redden. I was tired of being a curiosity. Why hadn't I fled to a big city, where no one cared enough to gossip about their neighbors? Nathan, ever ready to rescue a social situation, told her, "I'll have the roast beast. Does it come with a salad?"

While we waited for our food, I listened to the girls debate the merits of various singers, the décor, what they might order for dessert. I lost the thread of their conversation, twirled my straw in my iced tea, and snuck glances at the four men in the shadows near the bar. Two of them seemed familiar. I wondered if they had been part of the strange assembly in the forest the previous day.

The door chimed and more of the forest men walked in. I was certain about *them*. Walnut man and Mike, the fat man. The walnut-faced man made a beeline for the bar, but Mike looked around, saw me, and froze. Then he tipped his feed cap at me before he, too, scuttled to the bar.

I remembered a thing Maggie used to say. That if you wanted to know something, it was better to just ask. Even if you were 99 percent sure you wouldn't get an answer, there was always that 1 percent variable, and usually the odds were better than you thought. Especially if you surprised the truth out of a person.

I said to Nathan, "I'll just be a minute," and slid out of the booth. The waitress pointed to the signs that said GULLS and BUOYS, but I walked right by them, and planted myself at the bar. The men looked at me, looked away.

"I thought you all might like a drink. On me." I dug in my bag for my wallet, dropped a fifty on the bar. "That should cover a few rounds. I'll have a Sam Adams, too," I told the bartender. His head was shaved, polished as if he'd rubbed it to its high sheen with a bar rag. He sported a tribal tattoo on his arm that reminded me of a crown of thorns, with USMC in the center. A marine, then. He wordlessly plunked a bottle down in front of me, slid five Buds down the bar for my new friends.

I raised the bottle, tipped it toward them, said, "Cheers," and took a swig.

Mike was busy peeling the label off his sweaty bottle. The walnut-faced man gave a quick nod in acknowledgment, but didn't look at me. Then a tall guy from the other end of the bar got up, tugged at his jeans, took up his cane, and made his way over. The age spots on his face were the color of tea. He held out his hand. I didn't recognize him from the woods.

"I saw you on TV once. You and your husband. Your magic act was the bee's knees. I'm sorry about . . ." He shook his head, and what hair he had left floated like cotton.

"We're all sorry. And we hope it don't start again at Five Corners. Hope you're all safe there."

"Christ sake, Hank!" the walnut man exploded. "*She* don't . . ."

"She don't what, Len? She got a right, it's her kids."

Hank nodded toward our booths. Fai and Caleigh, their heads bowed, were absorbed by the puzzles on their place mats. Grace was blowing bubbles with her straw in time to "I'll Never Get Out of This World Alive." Hank turned back to me. "Don't mind these guys, missy. They got their heads stuck up their keisters so far they can see out their own mouths."

Hank surprised a laugh out of me, the first real laugh I'd had in a long time. It felt good to laugh. Normal. "Well, Hank, I have no idea what you're talking about, but you sure have a way with words."

"Why, I'm talking about the disappearances at Hawley Five Corners in the twenties."

The smile froze on my face.

"You know," he went on. "The six young girls. And then the whole church congregation just up and vanished one Sunday morning. You must've heard that story?"

I thought back on the conversation I'd had with Carl Streeter, about the abandonment of Hawley Five Corners. He hadn't said anything about children disappearing first. Girls.

"Aw, Hank, you know that's just an old legend—" Len piped in.

"No, I don't know any such thing. Just because nobody here ever talks about it don't mean it's not true." A couple of the men in the corner had swiveled around on their bar stools and were staring at him now. I saw that one of them was the black-haired man from the forest. Hank did have a voice that carried, but I didn't think they were staring because of that.

"Well, I believe it. That forest is haunted, especially the Five Corners. I was just a boy then, six years old. But we knew what happened, all right. We knew that the girls were disappearing. Fall of '23. Why, the search for Lucy Bell went on for months, even before what happened in the church that next spring. You can't tell me that everyone who lived in Hawley Five Corners decided to move out all on the same day. And it was a warm fall when it started then, too, just like now. I *remember*. And there's a few others that do, as well. Only they won't speak of it. Rather it was forgotten. Dead and buried. Len's one of those, miss. Ma'am. But I'd sure hate for anything to happen to those girls." He nodded again in my daughters' direction. They were intent on choosing more songs, Fai's hand flipping the cards that listed music from a past they had only heard of. Elvis and Johnny Cash just distant echoes to them.

Hank rested his bony hand on my shoulder. I tried not to flinch. "You know . . ." He shot a look to the men in the corner, then whispered, "One of them came back. Hannah Sears did. Gone two months. And then one day just walked on out of the forest. Couldn't even say where she'd been. Thought it was the same day she'd gone out blackberry picking down by the old tavern. She came back still carrying her basket of berries, even though it was December. Those berries were a wonder."

"Hank, will you just shut it?" the man with the black hair snapped. "He's old, he believes all that hoo-ha. Ghosts and vanishing towns. Don't pay him no mind."

"Remy, she *saw* the ghost herd!" the fat man said.

"Mike, you can just shut your big yap, too. Shit. I'm surrounded by old men and fools." Remy went back to his beer.

Hank jabbed painfully at my arm. His mottled, moony face was alight with urgency. "He wasn't there. I *was*."

I pulled away as gently as I could. "I think my food is here. It was . . . good to meet you, Hank." I took my once-sipped beer back to our table.

On the way home, while the girls were quiet, digesting their roast beast feast, I thought about the disappearing town story. It was probably just a ghostly legend parents scared their children with to prevent them from straying into the forest. But the disappearances Hank had mentioned, the girls he knew disappearing, his hope that "it" wouldn't start again—it all pointed to something more real, and more troubling. His fear for my own girls frightened me. And Hank's story had another layer of doubt and mystery that he probably wasn't aware of: its connection to my own family's past. My grandmother's name, before she went back to just plain Hannah Dyer, had been Hannah Dyer Sears. Hannah Sears, like the girl who disappeared, then reappeared, in Hawley Five Corners ninety years ago.

2

I couldn't call Nan, not that late, even though it would serve her right for keeping me in the dark, as surely she had done. I got up, put on a robe, and went up to my office. I sat across from the portrait of the mystery woman and mulled. It seemed like all I could do in the middle of the night was to pray, although I wasn't exactly a believer. I didn't even know *how* to pray. The closest I could come was to shut off the light, close my eyes, and say to whoever or whatever might be listening, "Please help me out of this mess. Please keep my girls safe. Please let me do the right thing."

No great flash of insight hit me. I opened my eyes. Moonlight suffused the office, weaving ghostly patterns through the room. The mystery woman gazed down at me from her portrait. Moonlight, crisp as a spotlight, shone on her pointing hand. I got up for a closer look.

The wall below her, with its chair rail painted green, had seemed smooth and unblemished, but now, when I looked again, I saw what she seemed to be pointing at: a crack in the wainscoting. I dropped to my knees, slipped my hand into the shadowed breach. I pulled at it, and a small door concealed in the wall dropped open.

Something thunked to the floor. I shivered, a deep shiver that started at my spine, radiated out to my skin. A book had fallen at my knees. It was covered with worn crimson leather and there was printing in gold on it: *The Hawley Book of the Dead*. The book from my dreams.

I closed the small door. I could see it was cleverly hinged—impossible to detect, except on certain moonlit nights. I took up the book. It seemed light for its size, and inexplicably warm, as if it had been beamed in from a sunny meadow on a summer afternoon. I carried it to my chair and opened it. The fragrance of lilacs hit me like a truck. And another smell beneath that one, a metallic scent I couldn't identify for a moment. Then it came to me. The book also smelled of blood.

I didn't need any more mysteries, and I almost closed it right up again, but something made me begin turning the pages. They were thick, like woven linen, and at first glance, completely blank. I riffled through them, and near the very end, ink began to shimmer onto the page, form words. I could read them in the moonlight. Then after a few words, I didn't need to read at all. I could see everything the book described. More than that, I could feel the story the words told unfurl inside my head.

> A man sat at the entrance to a shallow cave in a sandstone ridge. He looked down on a house, sometimes raising binoculars to his sunburnt face. For days, all there had been for him to do was think. He ate PowerBars and thought. He thought while the heat dried his lips, made his tongue stick to the roof of his mouth between sips of

warm water hauled from town. He thought while the stars, huge and almost menacing in their clarity, wheeled above him every night in the frost-lapped desert. His thoughts began in one cankered, corrosive track, then shifted to a place of bright desire. Revenge, then redemption.

But this night was different. There was something in the air, something old that didn't belong in the desert. The man turned toward the East. He inhaled the ghostly scent of a New England flower, a faint breath on the air. It made him think of the old days, before he'd been caught in this web of hatred and vengeance seeking. It reminded him of his mother's garden in Massachusetts. It reminded him that the woman he sought was from the East. And in that moment, he knew where she had gone. She had gone home.

I woke from my trance, gasping and struggling. The man in my vision was hiding out in a cave above our house in Nevada. He was a man I knew. Our Fetch was the ice-eyed man who'd pursued me in the tunnels.

Caleigh's Vision: Turkish Delight

Caleigh woke, shivering. She had been having a dream of the magician, Setekh. It was a dream of a real memory. She was in the Bijoux, her parents' theater, soon after she'd gotten her string, during a party they'd hosted after the World Magic Awards.

Caleigh had been with her sisters in a little cubby behind the stage where they often hid, watching all the performers arriving, many still in costume, coming right from their shows. Criss

Angel looked normal except for big sunglasses. Siegfried was there without Roy. Their friend Penn was still dressed in his tuxedo and the bright red socks he wore for their show, carrying Teller's head around on a platter, making the showgirls laugh. The Maskelyne sisters didn't know what he was saying, but he always made them giggle, too.

"Hey, Caleigh." Grace jabbed her with her elbow. "Get us some crab cakes, okay?" The buffet was set up on the stage right below them.

"Why can't you go?"

"It'll just be boring down there." Grace nudged Caleigh with the toe of her light-up sneaker. "It's all grown-ups. Go on. You know you want to."

"And bring some for me." Fai flopped down on the rug. Having watched enough, she went back to reading Lemony Snicket.

"You guys are just lazy."

"But you're the littlest, can get between people and snag stuff easier," Fai observed without looking up from her book.

Grace pushed with her sneaker again. "And don't forget cake."

Caleigh *was* hungry. Even though they'd had dinner with Marisol at the usual time, it was late now, maybe even after midnight. She liked staying up past her bedtime. And she liked being in the theater when there wasn't a show. Even with so many people down in the house, it was all dark and mysterious backstage. She could hear the buzz of talk and laughter out front as she skipped along behind the scrim.

Then she saw someone up ahead. A shadow moved in the dusky light spilling from her mom's dressing room doorway. She stopped. "Mom?" But she'd just seen her mom, all glittery in a long silver dress at the back of the house, greeting new arrivals. "Wesley?"

But it wasn't Wesley, either. A tall man emerged from the shadows. The light blazed behind him, so Caleigh couldn't see his face. She heard the swish of tuxedo tails as the man came toward her. She didn't know why she felt afraid, in her parents' own theater that she knew as well as her own home, but she did. She was frozen, as if something was keeping her from running away, into the light and the crowd to safety. She took a big breath, in case she had to scream. Then the man spoke. "Caleigh. My little friend. Fancy you being allowed to stay up so late." She unfroze and heaved the big breath out. It was only Setekh the Magnificent.

"You scared me."

"I didn't mean to, my dear."

She wanted to ask him what he was doing in her mother's dressing room, but when Setekh bent to her level, so they were eye to eye, his candy-cane breath soothed her. So close, his face was beautiful, as striking as a lion's or an eagle's. "But where is your string?" he asked her.

She reached into the pocket of her overalls and produced it. Even though he had given it to her months before, it was still bright white. It glimmered even in the darkness, almost as if it had its own interior light.

"Show me how you're doing, would you?"

Caleigh looped her string through her fingers, making the white rabbit pattern, and soon a little white bunny with pink eyes came hopping from behind an abandoned shoji screen.

"Very good!" He scooped the bunny up, stroked its ears flat. The creature looked frightened, and squirmed in his hands. Caleigh reached for it, felt its soft fur, its small heart beating wildly. Setekh let go of the bunny. Caleigh scrabbled at thin air, trying to catch the poor thing, but the magician just clapped his hands together, said, *"I-undias!"* And the bunny was nowhere to be seen.

"Now I think you must be hungry, Miss Caleigh."

"Where did it go?"

"It doesn't matter." Setekh's voice was low, soothing. It lulled her. He reached into his pocket and brought out a beautiful red satin box. He opened the box, and the scents of roses and oranges, peppermint hot chocolate and lemon meringue pie perfumed the air around them. Pieces of glowing candy tempted her, layered on velvet, as plush as a rose petal, as lovely as the moon. "This," he told her, "is for you!"

She wanted to eat it all then, but she thought of her sisters, as hungry as she was.

"What is it?"

"Why, it's Turkish delight. And it's all yours. Eat up!"

She reached in and took a piece. She chose a lush mauve square that carried the scent of violets. It felt heavy in her hand, and warm, as if it had just been made fresh, just for her. She was about to take a bite of the heavenly candy when she heard Fai's voice call, "Hey, Caleigh, what's taking so long?" Then Grace chimed in, "We're *starving.*" She turned to see the lights of her sisters' sneakers twinkling as they ran toward her. The piece of candy she held disappeared in a flash, as if she'd never held it. She spun around to see that Setekh was gone, too.

"Come *on.*" Grace grabbed her by her overall straps. "What're you just standing here for?" And she dragged Caleigh back to the real world, back to the noisy party, and crab dip and chocolate cake. But no Setekh, no Turkish delight. It might have been her imagination, but when Caleigh looked at her hands, they were dusted with sugar so fine and light it glowed. It could have come from the moon, after all.

The dream disturbed her, and made her hungry, too. She'd forgotten all about that Turkish delight over the years, but now she longed for it. She held her breath and listened to the house sounds. She could hear her sisters rustling their sheets, running and sighing in their sleep. She listened for her mom, and heard her soft footsteps on the third floor above. She was in her office. Caleigh slid her string, still the brightest white after all these years, from under her pillow. She made a box pattern and tried to fill it with the candy she craved, but the closest she could get were Russell Stover chocolates. She set them aside for her sisters. Then she tried again, and in the string box she'd made, lo and behold, was one perfect piece of moon-colored Turkish delight. She popped it into her mouth before it could vanish. It melted on her tongue into all her favorite flavors, lemon giving way to chocolate, creamy brie giving way to honey. As the candy melted away, she found she was very tired. She put her heavy head on the pillow and slept, and dreamed again.

The next morning, no trace of these dreams remained, except for the ghostly taste of honey in her mouth.

The Perpetual Tag Sale—October 25, 2013

1

I would have thought that finding the book was a dream, but there it was on my night table. *The Hawley Book of the Dead*. I hesitated, then reached for it. The small red leather book felt colder than it had the night before, and no lilac scent wafted from it, only a clean, meadowy smell. I opened it, expecting to find the closely written words I'd seen the night before.

All the pages were blank.

So much for the vision. It *must* have been a dream.

But I couldn't lose the panicky feeling I'd had when I saw the man in the desert. The Fetch. Even if it was a dream, it seemed somehow right that he'd been in the tunnels, too, had almost caught me there more than twenty years before. Dream or no, I pondered all the strands and webs of incident that might bind us while I fruitlessly checked my e-mail, woke the girls, fed the animals, and wondered what fresh strangeness this day would bring.

I didn't have to wonder long. I was raking up loose hay, my last barn chore, when I saw a man walking down the driveway. I looked to the gate and it was closed tight, but there he was, striding toward me. My mouth went dry. I called to him, "Stop right there!" I ran for the pitchfork resting against the barn wall, then brandished it at him, while random thoughts flew through my mind. How did he get in? More to the point, what if he had a gun? Why *hadn't* I hired a bodyguard? Was it really worse to have guns around my girls than have an intruder shoot us now?

The man held out his hands, showing they were empty of weapons.

"Your Nan sent me. I come not to harm you, but to keep you from harm."

Only then did I recognize the falconer's costume, the breeks, the leather gloves. Falcon Eddy. Still dusty and unkempt, still looking like he'd come walking across deserts and over mountains. His hair resembled a bird's nest. I kept the pitchfork raised. "How did you get through the gate?"

He laughed, a booming sound that startled me. I dropped the pitchfork, then scrabbled for it.

"Well now, dearie, we have our ways. But I'll let your Nan tell you, or no. What matters now is that I'm here to keep you safe."

I let the tines of the pitchfork rest on the ground, but kept a grip on the handle. I might need it yet. "Just . . . just stay where you are." I pulled my cell phone from a back pocket, punched Nan's number. Her phone rang and rang. Eventually the machine picked up. Nan's quavery recorded voice said, "For the Bennington School of Falconry, press one. For the Reverend Steel, press two, for the home of Hannah Dyer, press three. If this is Revelation, and Falcon Eddy has appeared, he's what you asked for. Make him feel at home."

I pushed "end," stuffed the phone back in my pocket.

Appeared. I supposed that was the word for it. I gave Falcon Eddy a dubious look. "Okay. Just tell me this. How exactly *are* you going to protect us?"

He laughed again, then reached behind him. In one hand, he held a wooden bow. The other hand held an arrow. It was my turn to laugh. "Look, the man who killed my husband is coming for us. And I somehow doubt his weapons are as outdated as yours. I think you mean well, but I just don't see bows and arrows being much help."

I didn't see him release the arrow. I didn't even see him string the bow. I only heard what I thought was a mosquito whine by my ear. I reached up to slap it away.

Falcon Eddy kept up a steady grin while he walked around me, giving the pitchfork a wide berth. He walked to the barn, and calmly pulled an arrow out of the wood. An arrow that skewered the baseball cap I'd been wearing. He'd somehow shot it right off my head. I touched my scalp, my ears, expecting blood. There was none. "But, I didn't . . . how did you . . ."

"Don't worry yourself, now. You have your magic. I have mine."

I showed Falcon Eddy the grounds, then brought him into the house. I still wasn't sure about him, but after his bow-and-arrow display, I was willing to take him on trial. The kitchen was fragrant with freshly brewed coffee, which thankfully camouflaged the whiff of falcon mews that trailed after Eddy. Mrs. Pike was nowhere in sight. I thought maybe she was starting to exhibit a Yankee version of the treasure-like qualities that characterized Marisol back home. Mrs. Pike had never before made coffee for us without prompting. I poured some for Falcon Eddy and myself.

As we sat at the kitchen table with our steaming mugs, the outside doorknob rattled. I leapt up.

"Hellooo," a man's voice called. Falcon Eddy threw open the door, seized a tiny white-suited man by the collar, and dragged him into the kitchen.

"Don't hurt me, oh, please don't! It's only old Reverend Steel come to pray with you, ease your pain! A man of the Lord doing his duty!"

"How'd you get in the gate?" Eddy demanded.

"The estimable Mrs. Pike opened the floodgates. A fine Christian lady."

I was not happy with Mrs. Pike.

"I've come to lift your burden. Prayer is the answer!" His spit hit me on the upper lip. I wiped it away.

"Oh, it's you, is it?" Falcon Eddy seemed to know him, but still held a fistful of the Reverend's collar in his grasp.

The Reverend swept off his hat, one I imagined had been kicking around on the floor of the shiny new white Cadillac I could now see parked just beyond the open door. An old straw hat for impressing his followers with his meekness. "The Reverend John Steel at your service. From the Bennington First Baptist Church. Well known to Revelation, as she can tell you, you . . . oaf! Could you bring yourself to unhand me?"

I nodded to Eddy. Eddy turned the Reverend around and gave him a long, questioning look before dropping him. Then he frisked the Reverend thoroughly, with more loud protests from the little man.

The Reverend Steel was a Baptist from the South, come to bring salvation to the heathen of Vermont. From Nan's reports, the Bennington First Baptist Church had recruited him twenty years before, and he had won over the dour Yankees. Quite a feat, I had to give him credit, especially considering his lack of good looks. A handsome face often was the leverage needed to sway church ladies of all stripes, in my limited experience, and the Reverend didn't have it.

He was maybe sixty, his longish white hair thin and streaked yellow. His face was pink, his ears were pink, even his eyes had a pink cast to them, like a white rabbit's. He was not a true albino; his pupils had a rheumy brown tinge to them, and his hair had once been blond, but his pinkness had an unsettling effect. As did his size. He had tiny hands and feet, was shorter than I am. The word that came to my mind, not often applied to men, was *petite.*

I had no real reason to dislike him, but I did. I saw him infrequently, maybe five or six times in the years he'd been living in Nan's house, and each time he made me uneasy. I always felt as if I'd seen him somewhere, in some other context. I could never name it, but I couldn't help thinking it wasn't a good one.

"I suppose I should invite you in. Although technically, you are in."

The Reverend burst into fresh exaltations. "The Lord is good, the Lord is great, He'll protect your sweet daughters, never you fear! Unless they're meant to be safe with Him in His heaven, the lambs."

"Balls," I told him. "What have you done with Nan?" I didn't see any point in mincing words.

The Reverend tugged a handkerchief from his vest pocket with a flourish, and swiped at his brow. "Well, I have to say, I take umbrage at your tone. I haven't *done* anything with your grandmother; she's at home with a cold. She's a fragile little lady now, and we don't want to risk pneumonia."

I gritted my teeth. "Fragile, my foot. Nan caught cold

teaching falconry to fools in a thunderstorm. I know all about it; my mother told me. Why aren't you home with her, anyway, if you think she's so fragile? Nan didn't tell me anything about your coming today."

"She and I spoke only this morning of the possibility of my visiting you, praying with you for the safety of your girls."

"At the moment, praying isn't high on my list of things to do. But since you're here you may as well sit down. I suppose you'd like some coffee."

"Well, now, that would be most welcome."

Mrs. Pike had undoubtedly been skulking behind the pantry door, for she bustled in then, greeted the Reverend, and brought out a freshly made cake. She did a double take when she saw Falcon Eddy, but she didn't comment on his presence. I could see I'd been set up. She poured the Reverend's cup of coffee, and I noticed she didn't ask before she poured cream and spooned sugar. Just the way he liked it. I remembered she was a denizen of the Hawley Baptist Church, and that the Reverend sometimes took over when their preacher went on vacation. So Mrs. Pike had some truck with him. She cut two enormous slabs of cake. Chocolate with creamy frosting, the Reverend's favorite, I surmised. She set plates down before the Reverend and me, giving Eddy a few nods toward the door as she did so. Eddy did not budge. Mrs. Pike huffed disapprovingly, but decided there was nothing further she could do to oust the intruder, and sidled toward the door.

"Thank you kindly, Jerusha," the Reverend called after her. I nearly spilled coffee down my shirt. I had no idea Mrs. Pike's first name was anything but what I'd written on her checks: plain Jeri Pike.

The Reverend looked longingly at the cake, but before he

wielded his fork, he told me, "Actually, I'm here for another reason altogether. Although, of course, I was hoping to pray with you as well." He skewed his eyes at Eddy. "Perhaps we could have some privacy?" Eddy stayed where he was, humming a little tune under his breath, cleaning his fingernails with a knife.

"I don't think that's really necessary." I didn't relish a private audience with the Reverend. "Reverend Steel, this is Falcon Eddy. I have no idea what his last name is, but he claims Nan sent him." The Reverend rolled his eyes, and Falcon Eddy looked up from his grooming to glare at the tiny man. "Although it seems as if you two are already acquainted. Look, I didn't get much sleep, and I'm too cranky for small talk, so let's cut to the chase. Does Nan even know you're here?" I asked the Reverend.

"Not only does she know. She sent me." He dug into his cake then, took a big mouthful, and chewed complacently.

"All right. I'll take the bait. Why did she send you?"

He paused to wipe icing from his lips before answering. "Some things are best left alone, I find. But if they make an appearance, they must be dealt with."

"Stop talking in riddles."

"You made a discovery last night. Unearthed something—an object that, well, shall we say, had a certain *impact*."

"You mean the old book I found? How did you know about that?"

He took a sharp breath, looked pained. "My dear, I really must insist this . . . man . . . leave us."

"Okay, okay. Eddy, it's all right."

He rose slowly, picked up his coffee cup. "I'll be right outside if you need me."

As soon as Falcon Eddy closed the door, I pounced on the

Reverend. "What about the book? What do you know about it? How did you know I found it?"

"All your questions will be answered in due course." He paused to take another bite. He chewed wolfishly, swallowed, then told me, "The Book belonged at one time to your grandmother. She still has a . . . connection to it." He said the word *book* as if it should have quotation marks around it.

"Why haven't I ever heard about this book, if it's so special?"

His head swiveled, reminding me of a snake's. "Shhh! It's not something we shout about!"

" 'We,' Kemosabe? Since when are *you* privy to our family secrets?"

"Since a very long time ago indeed. So don't get huffy. Your grandmother wishes to speak to you. Not by phone. Come to us for tea today at four. That's my message to you. And don't use the Book until then. It's not just any book. It's *the* Book."

Had the Reverend changed? His skin seemed almost translucent. That jogged some faint fragment of memory, but it again eluded me. The next moment he was just a tiny, wizened, nearly albino man again.

"Well, you don't have to worry. I could have sworn it had writing in it last night, but now it's blank."

"You can't just open it up and read it willy-nilly, dear. You can't command the Book. It commands you." He smiled infuriatingly. Then he took another bite of cake. "As Jesus is our Savior, this is divine."

"Since you know so much about our family, you must know that the first Revelation settled here in Hawley Five Corners. Was the book hers, originally? Is that how it got here?"

He flashed me a quick look, then lifted his fork again.

"It's amazing to me that you can be interested in peripheral matters when your daughters are at risk. And it hasn't been long since your husband's unfortunate accident. Admirable, really. You must be an exceptionally strong woman. The strength of Judith."

I closed my eyes. A memory flashed: Grace and Fai as babies, clean and fresh in sprig-patterned onesies, their skin soft as flower petals, sleeping on our bed, nestled like peas. Then Caleigh, just days ago, digging in the dirt, helping me plant tulip bulbs, her grin wide as she patted the damp earth.

"I have my reasons for being interested," I told him. "You're just trying to distract me with your accusations. You know more, but you won't say. And *everything* I do right now is to keep my daughters safe."

"The best way is to trust in the Lord," the Reverend let me know. "When we're done with Mrs. Pike's excellent cake, perhaps you'll pray with me."

"Perhaps. But the book, Reverend. Did Nan leave it here, hide it here for some reason?"

"You *are* persistent, Revelation. I can't tell you anything more about the Book. I'm merely the messenger." The Reverend dabbed at the corners of his mouth with his napkin. When he put the napkin down, he reached for my hand. I expected him to begin praying over me, and bit back more harsh words. But what he said next wasn't a prayer. "My dear, some things should not be dredged up again. Follow a righteous path, for your own sake and that of your beautiful girls." His pink eyes were locked on me. Again he reminded me of a snake. I certainly felt like a small animal transfixed.

He paused, licked his thin pink lips. "I would hate to think that it may have started again." It was the same thing Hank had said the night before. Almost the same words.

"What? What do you think has started again?" But he just shook his head, wincing as if he was in pain. He took another gulp of coffee. He smiled at me, stood, and took up his hat.

"Well, this was truly lovely. But now, I must go. Parish duties call." He threw open the door, crashing into Falcon Eddy in his haste. He leapt back, spun toward me again. "Don't forget. Tea. Four o'clock."

2

Falcon Eddy refused a shower and still smelled of hawk guano when we found Nathan and the girls clustered around a small table in the parlor. Fai had discovered a Ouija board on a shelf in her closet, and they'd all become obsessed with it. I didn't know how it counted as a learning experience, but knowing Nathan, he was probably feeding them tidbits about Henry and William James and how their belief in ghosts and spirits informed their writing.

"This is Falcon Eddy," I told them. "He's . . . he's a friend of Nan's who will be staying with us for a while. To help keep us safe."

"Cool." Fai was the first to look up from the planchette. For all her gentleness, she was shrewd—would size people up with her wide blue eyes without their suspecting. "Where are your birds?" she asked him. "Although I *could* just ask the board."

"Home where they belong, I hope. My brothers are taking care of the buggers."

I winced.

"Hey, you talk like our dad," Caleigh observed. "Are you

from England?" She sounded so hopeful, wistful for her father. My heart lurched.

"From the isles, a longish time back."

"Which isles?" Grace wanted to know.

"Why, the only isles worth being from. The Scilly Isles."

Grace narrowed her eyes. "Islands can't be silly," she declared.

I groaned. "I guess it's time for a geography lesson." I'd spoken before I thought, and a blush suffused Grace's face, the white skin beneath her freckles crimsoned. Almost proud of her ignorance sometimes, at other times she could be unexpectedly sensitive. I felt like the worst mother in the world. I placed a hand on her shoulder, but she shrugged it off.

The planchette began to fly over the Ouija board from letter to letter: *S-C-I-L-L-Y*. "I'm not moving it!" Fai shrieked, staring at her fingers perched on the speeding planchette. "I *swear*. This thing is *so cool*!"

Grace's blush deepened. "So there's a 'C' in it. Big deal," she snapped.

"Och, girlie," said Falcon Eddy. "Many and many make that same mistake! Why, even the queen of England misspells the name, I know that for a fact."

They all laughed, Falcon Eddy the loudest.

I was starting to like him.

"You're nervous as a cat," Mrs. Pike remarked later as she was sweeping under my feet in the kitchen. I'd had it out with Mrs. Pike, instructing her never to open the gate, for anyone, even her friend the Reverend. Neither of us was happy with the other.

"I'm just fine. No thanks to you," I grumbled. She put down her broom and left me to my worries. She was right, though. I *was* nervous after both Eddy and the Reverend breached our gates. My nerves were too jangly to work in my office. I sat at the kitchen table with my laptop, so I could be within hailing distance of the girls.

Just as I was powering up, Fai came in, poured herself a glass of juice, and sat down next to me at the table.

"I'm surprised you left your planchette."

She tucked her hair behind her ears. "Mmmm. Well, it told me something weird."

"What did it tell you, honey?" I didn't know what to say about Ouija boards. I remember Jolon and I scaring ourselves with one, one particular summer. Then we lost interest; it was relegated to the basement and never seen again. But while we were caught up with it, we believed in it completely.

"I asked it when we'd get our powers, Grace and me."

"So did it tell you that you never would? You look so serious."

Her blue eyes scanned me. "*Mom*. That's because I *am* serious. The Ouija board said *two* dates. First it said 2011. And that can't be right. That was two years ago! Then it said 2015."

"Maybe it was confused. Maybe 2011 was the answer to a different question."

She thought for a minute, then said, "Okay. That makes sense." But she remained pensive.

"Something's still troubling you, honey. Tell me."

"It's too long to wait!" Fai burst out. "We'll be seventeen in 2015! We'll be *old*."

I touched her face, tried to smooth the furrows from her forehead. "You know you can't control that. The powers just come when they come. Grand didn't get hers until she was around that age. It's all right."

She took my hand, whispered, "But it's not. We're in danger, all of us. I want to help! I want to *do* something!" Tears filled her eyes, brimmed, and dropped down to her freckled cheeks.

"Oh, honey!" I held her to me, stroked her thin back. "Was it what I said about Falcon Eddy? Having him here is just a . . . a precaution Nan thought of. It doesn't mean we think there's—"

"It's not *that*!" Fai sobbed.

What was it then? I'd kept the Fetch's e-mail from the girls, but had Fai overheard something, guessed something? Even if not, she was the most intuitive of anyone in the family. Maybe she'd sensed my distress, even though I'd tried to bury it when I was with them. Then I thought of my conversation with Hank at Pizza Earl's. Maybe she *had* overheard us, although she seemed involved with the jukebox as much as Grace and Caleigh.

"Did you hear anything that upset you, Fai?"

She sniffled, wiped her face on my shirt. "No, Mom." She raised her face. Her eyes were red from crying, but clear of any terrible knowledge. "I just want to help, in case something . . . in case the Fetch finds us."

"Sweetheart, it's going to be all right. We haven't heard a peep from him since we came here. He's probably given up." I smiled, though I knew I was lying through my teeth.

"Now, get back to your game. And remember, it *is* a game. No piece of plastic can tell you your future."

She kissed my cheek, even though I knew she thought she was too grown up for such demonstrations. "Thanks, Mom." So she left me to my work, and my musing.

*

I had begun a script for one of our colleagues, Setekh the Magnificent, which at that point I called *Rosabelle, Believe*. It was a fanciful re-creation of a Houdini séance, with Setekh playing Houdini come back from the dead. It took advantage of Setekh's innate creepiness, so it wasn't really a far cry from my haunted-New-England-themed shows like *The Devil's Dance*, or even *Mascherari*, the intricate Venetian Carnevale show, our last.

But I knew *Rosabelle* was far from my best work. It didn't help that although I'd seen him around for years, I never liked Setekh. He made me uneasy. He'd been touring in Europe at the time of Jeremy's death, and well after. I was glad he wasn't there to perform at the memorial show. I kept reminding myself that I didn't have to like him to write for him.

After I'd fiddled with the script as long as I could bear, I powered down my laptop in frustration. I noticed the book of Hawley history I'd gotten at the fair on the counter where I'd left it. I picked it up, started reading. Maybe I'd discover more about the Five Corners, the Dyer family, clues that might lead me to knowledge about the disappearances, about Nan's Sears connections, anything at all. But my reading was again as fruitless as my work on the script.

When Mrs. Pike had gone, Nathan came in to tell me that the girls were in the barn showing the horses off to Falcon Eddy.

"You know, I do feel better that he's here," I told him. "Fai, at least, is still feeling unsafe." I told him what she'd said.

"I guess having him around doesn't hurt. What I want to know is, how did he *get* here?"

"Nan sent for him. Other than that, I couldn't say. He seems okay. Do you think he's okay?"

"Your Nan wouldn't steer you wrong."

“Ha. I’m not so sure. . . . Nathan, I just wish I knew what to *do*.”

“You’re already doing everything you can do.”

He always told the truth, Nathan did. But maybe he trusted me too much. I was more like a second mother to him, after all. I searched his face. There were few signs of Jeremy, but they were there in his high forehead, the sweep of his light hair. I felt tears welling, threatening to drown me. “Oh, Nathan. I *miss* him.”

“I know.” He put an arm around me, patted me. “But he wouldn’t be doing anything different, *chère*. And he believed in you.”

“I wish I knew . . . I don’t know, just *more*. Where the Fetch is. What really happened here, why everyone is worried it will happen again.”

“Did you find anything in this?” He ruffled the pages of the Hawley history. I wiped at my eyes, even though the tears hadn’t come, a preventive measure.

“Nothing interesting. Nothing about what happened in 1924.”

“That guy Hank said it all started in the fall the year before, didn’t he? It seems strange that there wouldn’t be anything in here about Hawley Five Corners. Was it just these few houses?”

“No, a hundred people or so lived here. At the Five Corners and scattered around the hollow. There was a store and a tavern. And there were quite a few farms, judging by the foundations and stone walls.”

“What happened to the houses, then? They didn’t all just fall in on themselves since 1924. These didn’t, after all.”

It was a good question. “Maybe Nan will know. If she *did* live here.”

"Do you really think she might have?"

"I don't know. I don't know if this is a wild-goose chase. But . . ." I hesitated.

"But what?"

"I'm not sure. It's just a feeling. Maybe of disturbing something. . . . You know, the woman Mom and I met at the historical society said there might be records in the church. Births and deaths, anyway. I've been meaning to go over, look around."

"Hard to believe no one's found them. Brought them to light, for the historical society. You'd think they'd like to have them in the collection."

"You'd think. But after the town was abandoned, except for the big auction they had, no one disturbed this place for years. When I rode here as a kid, everything seemed so . . . untouched. No beer bottles or cigarette butts. We never once saw a soul when we came here, Jolon and I. We went all through the buildings, except this house. We somehow could never break into it. We never found anything in the church. But we weren't looking."

"So let's look now."

I didn't need convincing.

The church was dazzling white, its upright spire reaching to a sky so pristine it looked scrubbed. I unlocked the double door with the big brass key labeled "Church" that I'd found on a hook in our kitchen. I'd been in the church as a child, and I'd given it a cursory looking over just after we'd moved, but it still seemed nothing more than a plain, nearly square room. The varnished pews were narrow and carved of oak, the seats covered with split cushions. I ran a hand over the fabric, dull red silk, and my fingers came away smeared with a bloom of dust. I wiped it on my jeans and went to stand at the pulpit with Nathan.

"There's not much to it. It has a certain grace, though. It's elegant, with those tall windows and all the whiteness." I looked up at the arch of ceiling, pressed tin, painted white. There were small white crosses at each corner above our heads.

"Where would any records be kept? There's not even a vestry."

I lifted each hinged window seat by the altar and saw only stacks of ancient hymnals. Then I rummaged in the one small cubby of the stained pine pulpit, came up with a chewed Blackwing pencil and a child's tiny prayer book bound in shredding white leather. *The Little Book of Prayer* was stamped in gold on the cover. I ruffled the pages. Nothing fell out. I opened the book. My throat closed up. The name *Dyer* seemed to leap from the page. *Hannah Dyer Sears* was written in faded ink on the flyleaf. Hannah Dyer Sears, my grandmother. My Nan.

"Nathan," I whispered. He was examining a long-handled wicker basket leaned up against the altar. It must have been used for collections. He turned and saw my face. "Reve, honey, you're all pale."

"Look at this. It was definitely Nan's. She lived with us, and she never said. In all her stories, she never mentioned she'd *lived* in Hawley. Even when she knew Jolon and I rode here. Even when I moved to Hawley Five Corners. When she *sent* me here. Why not tell me?"

"Well, now you can ask her."

3

Nathan drove us north toward the Vermont border. Falcon Eddy sat in front to talk with him about medieval archery, while I squashed into the back with the girls. Caleigh was half on my lap, getting heavier by the minute. Just as we were crossing the state border, she squirmed and yelled, "Hold it, coz! Pull over!"

We all looked to where she was pointing. A huge yard sale blanketed the stubbly hay fields around us. It seemed to spread out to the horizon. Junk of all kinds tempted the traveler, piled on tables, spilling over into the vestiges of grass. On display were headboards and cribs, mirrors and luster jugs, mountains of plates and bowls, heaps of children's clothes, an enormous fiberglass rooster, and three Easy-Bake Ovens, that I could count. I'd never seen anything like it.

Nathan stopped next to the handwritten sign that let us know we had stopped at

The Perpetual Tag Sale
Open 24 Hours, 7 Days a Week
See a Treasure, Make an Offer
No Reasonable Offer Refused

There was no house in sight. The only sign of life was a very old man with a long white beard sitting in a bentwood rocker. A resplendent brass cash register was positioned on a Chippendale table before him.

"Howdy, folks. Welcome to the Perpetual Tag Sale," he chirped at us as we piled out of the car. "Look around and find your heart's desire. No reasonable offer refused, just like the sign says."

Caleigh and the girls scattered, while I called after them, "Be quick like bunnies. We only have a few minutes!"

"Oh, missus," the old man chuckled, "don't ya know ya can't rush the Perpetual Tag Sale? Take your time! But don't worry, it won't make ya late for wherever you're needin' to be."

"So you're really open all the time?" Nathan asked.

The man nodded, his snowy beard wagging like Miss May's. "Ever day, 24/7, including major holidays. Always here, always open. Whenever ya need us, here we are. But look around! Sure you'll find a treasure!"

Caleigh was already in raptures over an Easy-Bake Oven, a vintage turquoise one, complete with countless pans and rolling pins. "I always wanted one of these!" she gushed. Grace and Fai were one row over, pulling silky scarves out of a battered trunk. I walked down the first lane, convinced I wouldn't find anything I needed or wanted among the dizzying array of cuckoo clocks, mixing bowls, and lava lamps. But I was wrong. My eye was drawn to a bejeweled scabbard resting against a massive cabinet television from the 1970s. The scabbard looked tremendously old, like something a Knight of the Round Table might carry. It shone gold, was etched with symbols and designs, and encrusted with what looked like, but couldn't possibly be, emeralds and diamonds. Not at the Perpetual Tag Sale. All the same, I hefted it. It was weighty, but seemed right in my hands. I pulled out the sword, and its golden surface reflected parabolas of light. It stopped my breath, it was so beautiful.

"That looks real."

I wheeled, swinging the sword before me. Nathan jumped back. "Hey, be careful with that thing!"

"You startled me." I sunk the tip of the sword into the earth. The blade had come within an inch of Nathan's chest.

I sheathed it in its scabbard. The imitation gemstones on it sparkled like the genuine article. "It can't be real. Just a good reproduction."

Nathan reached for it, examined it closely. He finally shook his head. "It's real, all right, crazy as that sounds. It could have come right out of the Royal Armouries' collection, or the Met Museum's." He had to be right, with his vast knowledge of old armaments. "They have one like this . . . but this one's in even better condition." He pulled the sword out again, and the sun caught the blade. Dust motes danced around it in lacy patterns. I felt a shifting inside me, as if the world was slowing down around us. "And instead of plain iron or bronze, this one looks like gold-plated silver. If you buy it, we can add it to the Bijoux collection. It's pretty incredible." We did have a good collection of antique swords of all periods, curated by Nathan, often used in our shows. But I had put magic behind me.

"Nathan, what's it doing here?"

"Who knows? But I say, don't let it get away." He squinted

at the small white tag fluttering from the sword hilt. "Hmph. Ten dollars. Now that's a *steal.*"

"Ha, ha."

Minutes later we were on the road again, the sword stashed in the back alongside a bag of miscellaneous junk that the twins had chosen, and Caleigh's Easy-Bake Oven.

4

Nan's house was the oldest in Bennington. A low-slung Cape, with tiny windows that lined the upper story, like the windows of a doll's house. It was not painted the conventional white or barn red of most New England village houses, but instead boasted ancient stained chestnut planks. The roof was shingled with mossy slate. Altogether it had an air of age, and the kind of spookiness one might expect from a dwelling that had housed generations, witnessed any number of births and deaths within its walls. A wooden sign, white with black lettering, hung from a post and proclaimed it THE PHINEAS COBB HOUSE, 1755.

Nathan parked in the gravel drive. Falcon Eddy went directly to the back of the house, where the mews was. I toted the bag with the basket of fancy teas I'd brought from home. Superstitiously, I felt I could not come empty-handed. The girls raced up the walk.

Caleigh smacked the brass clapper that hung next to the front door, and it was thrown open almost instantly by a gaunt woman with hair the rusty color of old iron, bound tightly around her head like a crown. Nan's housekeeper, Willy. "Come in," she croaked in a sepulchral tone, more suited to a wake than afternoon tea. She wore the same kind of flowered housedress that Mrs. Pike usually donned for her work, with an embroidered apron tied around her thick waist. She stepped aside and indicated a door off the hall, then seemed to melt away. We walked into a long, bright room, a parlor, kitchen, and dining room combined, with an immense fireplace, the bricks blackened with age and use. A fire snapped on the hearth, and Nan rose from a tall-backed chair to greet us. She looked tiny even in this house with its low ceilings and doors, but her presence filled the room.

Caleigh ran to her. "Hey, Nan, guess what?" In her excitement, she tripped and nearly fell, but Nan caught her, righted her. Caleigh, unfussed, went on with her story. "We stopped at a tag sale, the biggest one ever! Look what I got!" She clutched her twee rolling pins and spatulas. "They came with a toy oven, but Mom wouldn't let me bring it in!"

"Well! That's quite a greeting." She hugged Caleigh then, kissed her cheek. I suddenly noticed that Caleigh was almost as tall as Nan, now. "And what did my young ladies purchase?" She turned to Grace and Fai, who had puppets on their hands and were jabbing at each other with them, giggling in the doorway.

"I'm Lamb Chop. A plesh-ah, I'm shoo-ah." Grace did a passable imitation of the girlie sheep from the Bronx. When she held the puppet up to her face, we could see that her eye makeup and Lamb Chop's were nearly identical.

Fai opened her fox's mouth wide and made it chomp on Lamb Chop's neck. "Hey!" Grace squealed. "That hurts!"

Nan's sudden laughter was like the caw of one of her hawks. The twins sidled up to Nan for her kisses like quick bites.

Nan pecked at my cheek next. "It's good of you to come, Reve." She seemed to have forgotten that she'd summoned me. "Jackie doesn't usually join me for tea, since he's called away by parish duties." *Jackie* was the improbable diminutive that Nan used for the Reverend John Steel. "I would have come to you, except for the bronchitis."

I'd suspected the Reverend of exaggerating her symptoms, but her voice *was* raspy and thin. And she did seem paler, more fragile than when I'd seen her last, only weeks before. I hated to think that she was failing. In so many ways she was still the same, with her one long silver braid, her flannel shirts, her sharp eyes.

I sat next to her on a very upright Queen Anne sofa, restless. I wanted to leap right in and pummel information out of her, about the book, about her youth spent in Hawley. But I knew that she always had to be in control of a story. If I rushed her, she might not tell me anything after all. The girls sprawled on the faded Oriental carpet near Nan, continuing to spar with their puppets, while Caleigh perched on the arm of her chair. Nathan chose a rocker by the fire. There were numerous small tables in the room, the wood polished and gleaming, every table set with a vase of flowers: pink carnations and red-edged white roses, deep blue monkshood and huge sprawling yellow chrysanthemums like fireworks. The flowers were reflected in a big sideboard mirror and also in gleaming silver and crystal ornaments. The room was always beautifully kept, in spite of frequent visits by Nan's birds of prey. That day, a barn owl gazed at us from its perch by a window. It was so still it might have been stuffed, but I knew from experience that it wasn't.

"I see you admire my room, young man," Nan told Nathan, and I remembered he'd gone to run errands in town the last time we'd visited. He hadn't yet seen her in her natural environment. "We eat our meals in here as well. The other rooms are so poky, and I like space around me. I apologize for the heat. The fire is necessary for my old bones. We have a fire most days. These old houses are always on the cool side. Ah, here's our tea."

Willy returned, triumphantly bearing a huge silver tea tray. She set the laden tray on a table near Nan, who hefted the big silver teapot with practiced ease and poured out. Nathan leapt up to help her, but she waved him away. "I'm a strong old bird, never fear, young man." The owl puffed up and chipped at her. Nathan twitched, and his eyes widened with surprise, but otherwise he kept his composure. "Caleigh, I will ask you to hand the tea, and the cake."

"Okay!" Caleigh carefully ferried the fragrant steaming cups, and the plates bearing slices of poppy-seed cake. We all concentrated on our tea, until Nan broke the silence.

"I'm pleased you're here, Nathan," Nan told him. "It must be comforting for our Revelation to have you with her."

I cut her a look. "Yes, I'm grateful Nathan's here. I need my family around me now." I placed the emphasis on the word *family*. "So I don't know if sending Falcon Eddy was really—"

"Are you girls finished?" Nan interrupted me. They had wolfed their tea and cake, and were busy with their hand puppet fights again, while Caleigh slapped at them with a tiny spatula. "Why don't you all run out to the mews?"

Fai jumped up, nearly upsetting Nan's big tray. "Can we take Gillie out?" Gillie was the Swainson's hawk Nan used to start falconers.

"Sure, now," her great-grandmother told her. "But use the gloves. And don't forget her jesses!"

They were gone in a flash, headed for the mews, a long, barred enclosure surrounded by wire fencing where the hawks sunned themselves.

"Nathan, why don't you go along with them?" Nan asked. Finally ready to talk, it was clear she wanted a tête-à-tête. But I wanted a witness.

"I'd like Nathan to stay. He knows . . . well, almost everything."

Nan's gaze flickered over me. Then she nodded. "Of course, you can't be too careful." Nan went on. "Not with a Fetch after you. After all, the evils of this world are great. But you need to be concerned with the worlds beyond, as well. I don't think young Nathan knows as much about our . . . history?

"He knows enough," I told her. He knew about the powers of the Dyer women. He'd grown up with my vanish, and Caleigh's string magic.

Nan huffed. "More tea, I think, though. Nathan, would you be a love and pour us another cup?" He did. I took a sip, looked up, and Nathan was no longer sitting across from me. His fragile porcelain cup was balanced on the arm of his chair, but he was gone. I choked on my tea. Nan rose from her chair to pound me on the back.

"Wh . . . wh . . . what did you *do* with him?" I managed to stammer out.

"He's perfectly safe. He's just out back by the mews with the girls and Falcon Eddy, having a look at the hawks. He'll come in after we've done, won't remember how he got out there." Nan seemed taller and more vibrant, more like herself.

I looked toward the mews, and Nathan *was* there. "What the hell is going on? How did you do that?"

"I think you know how, my dear." Nan sat next to me on the

sofa and put her arm around me. Her sharp lemon scent enveloped us. "Let's slow down, shall we. Now. You found the Book, or it found you." Could she be right? Could the book have found me with more deep magic? When she spoke of it, it was in the same way the Reverend had spoken of it, as if she thought it was the only book in the world.

"Yes," I told her. "I found this." I lifted *The Hawley Book of the Dead* out of my Petroglyph bag, and the meadowy wildflower fragrance swirled around us, competing with Nan's bitter lemon scent. "I also found your prayer book in the Hawley Five Corners church. I never knew you lived in Hawley. Why didn't you tell me? Did this book belong to you, too? The Reverend said so."

Her eyes were fixed on the book. Some emotion I couldn't read flickered in them. "It did, once. Now it belongs to you."

I felt my anger building, and my confusion. "You don't seem happy about it. If you wanted to keep it, why didn't you? And why didn't you tell me all this before?"

"It's not that simple. I *didn't* want to keep it, but I never meant for you to find it. I wanted to hide it so completely it would *never* be found again. But I should have known it would turn up, come to you, eventually." She reached for my hand.

I pulled away from her. "Nan, why did you want us to come to Hawley? I need to know anything that might help us. You need to tell me what's going on!"

Nan got up, poked the fire, took the book from me, stroked its soft cover. She sat across from me again, with the book in her lap. "Now this has happened, now you've found the Book, it *is* time for you to know. I wish you could have avoided it, passed through your life without this knowledge."

"Nan, you're scaring me."

She nodded slowly. "You should be scared." Her gaze fell to *The Hawley Book of the Dead*. She gripped it tightly now, and the blue veins in her weathered hands looked as if they'd burst through the skin. "It's a Book of instruction in magical powers. It also possesses magical powers itself. Very compelling magical powers. It decides when, and how, its owner may use it."

"But how can it belong to *me*? I didn't even know it existed!"

"It can only be possessed by a Revelation. And you're the next."

"But you said it was yours. You're not a Revelation."

Could I be imagining that her silver hair had darkened to pewter, that her hands, holding the book, were no longer clenched with arthritis?

"It's a long story. One that I hoped never to have to tell. I wished to forget all about it. What do you know about Hawley?"

"The only thing *I* know is that the first Revelation is supposed to have lived there. You lived there, too, but in all the stories, all my life, you never mentioned it. I had to be told by some old farmer. *And* I find out that children disappeared from the Five Corners. Young girls! Everyone's saying that they hope 'it' hasn't started again! What the hell does that mean? The locals are convinced the town is haunted. You insisted we move there because it was safe. Sorry, but it doesn't seem very safe, after all."

"And you need to seek safety, after your encounters with the Fetch."

"How did you *know* about him?"

"That hardly matters."

"But it does, Nan. Everything matters now! The Fetch sent me an e-mail. He killed my friend Maggie. And I had . . ." I hesitated over my dream or vision of the Fetch in the desert.

"Anyway, he's looking for us. He won't give up. He'll find us here, too! And what the hell does he *want* anyway?"

"Don't get overwrought now, that won't help."

"You sent the Reverend for me, so I assumed you knew the most about that book, about everything. That you'd just for once *tell* me!" I glared at her.

She reached for me then. She touched my cheek, while keeping one hand on the book. She seemed different. More like the Nan I remembered, the powerful, frustratingly independent yet kind woman I grew up with. And her hair *was* darker, dark red mixed with gray, as it had been when I was a child. Is that why I felt like a child again?

"Nan, I don't know what I'm supposed to do now. You should know, if anyone does. What am I supposed to *do*? How can I keep my girls safe? You have to tell me . . ." I felt the sting of tears building again.

She looked at me penetratingly, with eyes that now shone bright. "I understand your torment, more than you think, my dear." She glanced down at the book, then went on. "It is because of Hawley Forest that I'm alive to tell you this, Revelation. Once, like you, I loved nothing better than being in the woods. We'd play out there, my friends and I, the day long. Childhood was good then. Until young girls began disappearing." Nan's hair had darkened more in the late afternoon light, a pure auburn, not a thread of silver. I wasn't imagining it. She was getting younger.

"It began in Pudding Hollow, at the Bell farm. Lucy—Lucy Bell—disappeared. Just after she'd turned twelve, in September. We'd had a rain and Lucy's mother sent her out to the woods to look for mushrooms. She never returned. Her family searched through the night, her father and mother and brothers. By dawn, they sent for the police. They brought in searchers from as far as Worcester. But Lucy Bell was never found. In the strange and blistering heat of that fall, every few weeks another girl went missing. All from Hawley Five Corners, and the farms around. Until there were six gone. Then, it just stopped. No more children disappeared. The town was scarred, though. It still is." An ember leapt from the crackling fire, but she didn't move.

"But in 1923, you were there . . ."

"In 1923, I was eight years old. I lived in the Sears house at Hawley Five Corners. Your own house, now. I lived with my aunt and uncle. My parents were dead, from what we called the Spanish flu. Influenza. It claimed many lives, the great epidemic of 1918. So I was an orphan, an only child. Went to live with my Sears kin. Then, after they'd disappeared in the church that day with all the others, I stayed with a friend for a time, then went to the relatives here in Bennington. To this house."

"They disappeared in the church? How?"

Nan's eyes fell to the book she still held in her lap. Her fingers, smooth and strong now, gripped it fiercely, as if she wanted to tear it, rend it. Her voice, when it came, dipped and pitched with emotion. "I was with my friend, Vienna Warriner. She lived in Hawley Village, not at the Five Corners. She used to come to play with her cousins in the Warriner house, and that's how we met. We were best friends. It was March, and it had been her birthday the day before. March sixth. Her parents, as a treat, took us down to Springfield, to the circus. It was a big trip, even in Vienna's father's new Ford car. We stayed overnight, in a hotel. Red velvet and gold tassels everywhere. We were as excited as magpies, Vienna and I.

"They brought me home the next day, the seventh of

March." Was I imagining it, or did her voice tremble? "But no one was there. Not one person was to be found at any of the houses." She looked into my eyes, and hers were filled with tears. But her face was smooth and fresh as Caleigh's. I was stunned, too shocked to exclaim.

"It was late afternoon." She spoke again in her new young voice. "But no one was preparing a meal, no children were playing. Not even the newest Sears baby, my cousin Luke, was in his cradle for his afternoon nap. Things had been left half done. In the Warriner house, we found a roast in the oven that Vienna's aunt Ruth had put in before church. Burnt to a crisp, the cookstove cold as could be. In the church itself, we found hats and coats in the pews, the minister's Bible open on the pulpit. But no people, none at all. Then we drove to the Pooles', which was the nearest farmhouse to Hawley Five Corners. No one there, another burnt roast in the oven. All that afternoon we drove, found not one soul in those houses and farms. And no one ever did."

Her small supple fingers traced the gold letters that spelled *The Hawley Book of the Dead*. "You asked how it could have happened. It's what everyone wanted to know. How a town could just disappear. It was like one of those fairy tales that makes you shiver in your bed at night, thinking and thinking on it."

"Nan, I need to know," I said quietly. "And I think you want to tell me."

She stared at me, her eyes bright and her cheeks rosy as a girl's in the slanted light. Then she nodded.

"All hope of their return died as the year went on, but no one ever stepped forward and put in a claim for the houses, not one relative. No one wanted those houses. No one even came to take any of the furniture, the tools, the farm equipment, the books, the clothing. Feared it might be enchanted, I suppose. That's how it all came to me, the only survivor. Years later, I auctioned off the contents of the houses at the Five Corners, and the state took over the surrounding land, knocked down the houses to make the state forest. Then it seemed everyone became skittish even talking about it. It was something children were *told* not to talk about. Most everyone in Hawley Village had lost family members. My own aunt. Her husband. My cousins. All of them gone. It was a great blow. From that day, very few would go into the forest alone, or near the houses. And it's continued up to the very present. But it began with the girls disappearing in the fall. First Lucy Bell, then Aggie Green. My cousin, Liza Sears. Maria Hall, then Anna Sewall. That was it. All within a few months. By December it seemed to be over. But it wasn't."

There were holes in her story, and I had to know more.

"Wait. I need you to tell me the truth. At Pizza by Earl last night some guy named Hank insisted that he knew you then, that *you* disappeared, too. And you said *six* children disappeared. Nan, you have to tell me what really happened."

"I was getting to that." Once again she reached for my hand. I looked down and suppressed a gasp. Her hand was smooth, unwrinkled. "Hank was right. I was the sixth."

"Where did you go? Were you kidnapped?"

"I don't *know*, truly. I didn't remember, even then. I disappeared in October. It was December when I returned."

"Where did you *think* you'd been?" I didn't believe her. It probably showed.

She shook her head, bemused. "It had been a warm fall. No, it was more than that—hot, unnatural. So warm we were still in our cotton dresses. But the day I came out of the woods was frigid. I was wearing the same blue cotton dress. Not a stain on it. And the berries in my basket were still fresh and warm. I went home to the Sears house, dragging my feet, afraid I'd be scolded. After Lucy's disappearance, we were supposed to stay close to home. I didn't understand the fuss made over me, or why my aunt refused to make a pie with those berries. I hadn't the slightest suspicion I'd been gone for two months. As far as I knew, I'd just been picking berries all afternoon."

I struggled to take this in.

"I wanted to tell you before you even thought to move here," she went on. "When I wrote you that note. But you needed to come to this . . . knowledge . . . in your own way. I wanted you to be able to draw on the magic of the forest, but . . ." She took a breath, went on. "You found the Book. I knew I couldn't wait any longer to tell you."

"Then what happened? After you came back?"

She rose to drop a small log on the fire. "When I came out of the woods after being gone so long, not even knowing where I'd been, I was afraid. Not of the forest. I was afraid of the townspeople. Of my own Sears relations. Their Liza had been taken, after all. When I returned after those two months gone, they began to treat me differently. When it seemed clear none of the others from Five Corners would be found, none of them would reappear as I did, I was shunned. My aunt made me sleep in an outbuilding, away from my cousins."

Her childish voice brimmed with loneliness so deep my heart ached for her. "They believed I had something to do with it. Even though it was irrational, they thought it. I felt safer in Hawley Village, with my friend Vienna. None of their children went missing. When the townspeople were spirited away, and I went to stay with Vienna and her family, I was relieved. Then I was happiest of all to leave Hawley altogether, go to Vermont to live with my relatives here."

"What about the kidnapped children?" I asked, gentler than I had been with her before. "And all the townspeople? What *happened* in the church that day?"

"That's what I've never told anyone." She stroked the book's cover then, as if it were one of her hawks. She watched the flames curl greedily around the log, then went on. "It was because of me that those children were kidnapped. Because of me that they died. Whoever that man was, he was looking for me, looking for this Book. He was a Fetch, seeking me. As surely as your Fetch is seeking you now. For some reason, my Fetch gave up hunting me that December, and I returned. But when people in the town—my own relatives—turned on me, began to call me a witch, well . . . when the town disappeared that day, I did it."

"What do you mean?"

"I took this Book with me when I left Five Corners and went to the circus with Vienna's family. I pretended that it was just another book I was reading. I didn't want to risk anyone finding it, for sure then they'd think it was evidence I *was* a witch. But the Book . . . Well, that Sunday morning, I woke in Springfield, in different surroundings, and I wished never to have to go back to live among the people of Hawley Five Corners. I wished with all my might. Then I opened the Book. On its pages I saw the church, the people I knew. I heard the hymns being sung. Then I saw every person, each and every one, break up and scatter. It was as if they were made of paper that was being torn to pieces. All the people of Hawley Five Corners, scattered on the wind." A tear glittered on her cheek. I stroked her hand again, smoother even than it had been, and smaller. A young hand, the hand of an eight-year-old girl.

"I felt horrible, for years. I still do, when I think of it. That I could make a whole town just . . . vanish. I've never told anyone before this. I wanted to forget all about it. My great sin."

"Nan, it wasn't your fault! I had a vision when I opened the book, and I know *I* had nothing to do with that."

"Oh, it was my fault, girl. When I went into that empty church the very day we returned, there was my prayer book, right there on the lectern. All the Revelation passages looked as if they were written in fire. They *blazed*."

"Someone must have marked the passages—"

She shook her head. "No. It was a sign that I'd used my power, even without completely knowing it, to wish them all away, every last one of them, all the people who had hurt me. I left the prayer book in the church. I buried *The Hawley Book of the Dead*. I never used my power on any living being again until I learned how to control it completely."

I knew the answer, but asked anyway. "Your real power isn't taming animals, then?"

She shook her head. "That? Just a skill I cultivated. No. My 'real' power is my ability to transport objects to other places."

"Objects, and also people."

"Anything. Or anyone."

"And *The Hawley Book of the Dead*? Why did you have it? You said it could only be used by the Revelations."

"I *was* a Revelation. Long ago. When my parents died, and I was taken in by my Sears relatives, they changed my name to Hannah. They thought *Revelation* was too odd a name. My aunt had always feared my mother's power, shunned her. And she was right. Certainly it was *my* power that destroyed her family. For no matter what I was called, I still had the power that went with my original name. As you do now."

I remembered something. "You said you buried this book?"

"Behind the church. In consecrated ground. I hoped that might make a difference. That was why I was surprised you found it. That you would dig it up, that you would know where to find it."

"But, Nan, I didn't dig it up. I didn't even find it in the churchyard, or the church. It was behind a panel in the wall of my office. There's a painting there, of a woman I think might have been a Revelation. Mom and I thought it might be your grandmother. Her finger is pointing toward the panel."

Nan nodded. "My grandmother. There was a portrait, painted just after her husband died. But I have no idea how the Book got there. I know *I* buried it. But it found you somehow."

Could I ignore this as fancy? Could I ignore it all? Not when my Nan had changed to a child before my eyes. "So how do I use the book?" I gestured at the red volume, its gold title glimmering in the shadows of her lap. "Can I find the Fetch with it? Keep him away?"

"No! That's what you need to know, most of all. Never use the Book! Don't use it, ever, for any reason! My mother gave it to me when she was on her deathbed. All she had time to say to me was that the Book would tell me what I most needed to know. It's all the guidance I ever had, and all I can pass on to you. That and some old stories. My mother got sick so suddenly, and was taken so quickly, before she could teach me how to properly use the Book. I was only four years old. I was afraid of it, never even opened it until . . . well. I've told you enough about that. But when it has been in your charge, you'll feel its influence. That's how I knew you had found it, or it had found you. It's yours, now." She held out the book to me. I almost refused to touch it. But I did, and when I did, I felt a wave of something powerful, a storm assaulting my body.

Nan bent forward and gripped my hand, stared into my eyes. I could see hers turning, clouding. Her face had again assumed the wrinkles and furrows of the old. "Reve, be *careful.* I never would have told you any of this, had the Book not come to you. I wanted you to be safe here, as I was safe. I prayed the Book would remain hidden. No one anymore knows its secrets. It is not something to use lightly. It's like our powers. They can save our lives, when we cultivate them in the right ways. But the Book . . . I can't teach or tell you how to use it. I myself never learned. Remember this, remember all I have told you. The Book is powerful. It is also . . . dangerous. And your Fetch? I had a Fetch after me, too. Someone found me all those years ago in Hawley, as he's now trying to find *you.* It's the Book he wants, and your ability to use it. He's looking for you because you are the Keeper. He wants to control you, and the Book through you."

"Then Jeremy *did* die because of me."

"You can't think of it that way. Some things it's best to ascribe to fate. It was only fate that my mother died before she could teach me, and I could pass the knowledge to you. How to hide the Book, and how to use it to your advantage. Not to have it control you. If you know how to use it, it can be a tool of unimaginable power. If you don't, well . . . we can only hope to keep it from someone who might use it for harm. Beyond that, there's nothing I can tell you."

"Isn't there anyone who might help me? If not, why can't I just burn the thing?"

"Don't you think I tried that? The Book can't be destroyed. And there's no one who knows enough to use it properly. Not anymore. I wish to God you weren't alone with this, but the fact is that you are. All I can do is provide you with someone to guard you, keep you safe."

"You mean Falcon Eddy?"

She nodded. Her hair was pure silver again, shining in the firelight.

"I knew you needed someone to protect your family. It couldn't be an outsider, so I sent for him. He's been a friend to me for a very long time, and a fine protector in times of need. And remember, Hawley Forest is not negligible. It protected *me*." I heard Nathan's step in the hall and dropped the book hastily into the Petroglyph bag.

Nathan walked in. "Your birds are beautiful, Mrs. Dyer. I was transfixed by your hawks. For some reason, I kept thinking of the seraphim around the throne of Christ. It was almost like some kind of waking dream." The girls trooped in after him, threw themselves on chairs and sofas, breaking any spell there might have been.

Maybe my whole conversation with Nan had been some kind of dream. She had shrunk into her old lady self again. Her skin was thin and powdery, her hair wisping silver around her head.

"As the Bard says, there are more things in heaven and under earth than are dreamt of," she said, so softly I had to lean forward to hear her. "I'm quite tired, though. I tire easily in the afternoons now. I am sorely in need of my nap."

"We'll let you rest, then. Thank you, Nan." Although I

wasn't sure thanks were in order. I wasn't sure of much. I squeezed her hand and felt the frail bones beneath the papery skin.

"You must come again when I'm over this wretched cold. It was so good to see you girls, with all your spirit, and that Danann hair." Her eyes closed. I took a flowered afghan from a chair, and covered her gently. Nathan stirred the fire so it blazed, put another log on, and made certain the screen was secure. Then we left Nan to her dreams.

"She misquoted Shakespeare, you know," Fai remarked as we were walking toward the car. Falcon Eddy leaned against it. He was smoking a pipe. The smoke from it tanged the air.

Nathan nodded. "'There are more things in heaven and earth, Horatio, than are dreamt of in your philosophy.' *Hamlet*, somewhere in the first act."

"She said *under* earth. I wonder if she meant to misquote it."

"She's one sharp old lady."

"Hey, what did she mean about our hair?" Fai asked, her bright tangled hair glowing in the sunset. "Dannon, she called it. Like the yogurt?"

"That's just gross!" Grace exclaimed.

"I wish I knew half of what she meant." But I felt something dredged up from the past, something I'd heard once, or seen. Like a bottle washed up from the bottom of the sea floor. A bottle with an urgent message in it.

We rode through the stunning light of late afternoon, the shadows stark and the white painted houses luminous, my head full of story. The disappeared children, the disappeared town, my grandmother all those years ago, the townspeople's conviction she was a witch. A dangerous belief in New England. I felt alive, as if I were getting close to something, something large and immensely powerful. A fairy tale like a rushing train. Would it somehow carry my girls to safety?

As we were passing into Massachusetts, Caleigh cried, "Hey! Stop! It's gone!"

"What's gone?" Fai looked up from her book. Grace was curled in the corner, asleep.

"The Perpetual Tag Sale!"

The field just on the border where the Perpetual Tag Sale had been was thick with tall, dried cornstalks. There were no tables, no piles of junk, no sign, no old man. Only rows and rows of corn waiting to be mown down for silage.

"Are you sure it was here?"

We sat in silence for a moment before Falcon Eddy said, "It was here."

"Then where did it go? There was so much junk, that old guy couldn't have moved it all," Fai observed.

"As old as the mist, and older by two," Falcon Eddy told her.

"What's that supposed to mean?"

"You'll never plow a field by turning it over in your mind, missy."

"Falcon Eddy, do you ever talk plain English?" Caleigh wanted to know.

I could see him smile through his beard in the rearview mirror. "When it's warranted, I do."

We stared out into the cornfield, where the Perpetual Tag Sale had been just a few hours before.

"Was it real?" Grace asked softly.

Then Caleigh hit me in the eye with her elbow, climbing over the seat to the back. "My Easy-Bake Oven's still here! *It's* real. Every piece. And the sword's here, too, Mom!"

Falcon Eddy was right. We couldn't go trying to plow this field with our minds. All we could do was chalk it up to more magic in this strange place we found ourselves in.

Faice of the Moon

Fai: Look at the moon.

Grace: Its kind of orange.

Fai: Waxing gibbous.

Grace: Wha?

Fai: That's the phase its in.

Show off. What you think of weird falcon man?

Hes ok.

What u think of weird tag sale?

I like my fox. And at least we got out of the house. But I dont think it was really there.

What u mean?

Like, it was another world.

Dumbface.

You mean Dumbfaice.

No. Dumb Fai. No "ce." Dumb u. How could it be another world?

It was there, then it was gone.

It wasnt where we thought it was.

We didnt think it was there. We knew it was.

So it disappeared?

Mom disappears. Where does she go?

Not to Perpetual Tag Sale.

I mean she goes to the same place the tag sale came from.

Wha?

Like a parallel world.

Like a shift in the time/space continuum?
Yeah. Like that.
Oh. Why she not tell us?
Maybe she doesn't go all the way?
If she didnt go all the way, we wdnt be here.
Ha ha.

5

I headed straight to my office when we got home. Something was almost on the surface. What was it I half remembered? I reached for my laptop.

First I typed in "Perpetual Tag Sale." For all I knew, it was a movable feast, and there would be listings for it in the local papers. But I got nowhere fast. The closest link was to an article about a tag sale ordinance to stop people from holding permanent tag sales. But that was in Palmer, Massachusetts. Eighty miles from the Vermont border.

Then I typed in "dannon" and got the yogurt, nothing else. "Danen" yielded a wedding photographer, a gospel singer, and a garden. I typed in "danann," and an old familiar name from my childhood came up. Tuatha De Danann. I should have remembered. Wikipedia told me they were *a race of people in Irish mythology . . . the fifth group to settle Ireland, conquering the island from the Fir Bolg . . . thought to derive from the pre-Christian deities of Ireland*. I remembered how among Nan's other stories was the story of the Tuatha De Danann, how they ruled Ireland, how they had four treasures they'd brought with them over the seas, the Stone, the Cauldron, the Spear, and the Sword. The sword. I thought of the sword I'd bought at the Perpetual Tag Sale. What Nathan had said about it. But it couldn't be. It was just a coincidence. The Tuatha De Danann had been forced underground by the Milesians centuries ago. Or, in reality, had probably just died out. But the Dyer women were supposed to be descended from them. That must have been what Nan meant when she remarked on the girls' Danann hair. And misquoted Shakespeare. Under earth, she had said. The Tuatha De Danann went under the earth. To a place called Tir na nÓg, I remembered from Nan's stories. A land parallel to the real world.

It seemed crazy that Nan could have been out there, in the forest but in some parallel world. That it had happened to her. But who was I to say what was crazy? The Perpetual Tag Sale had landed us with hand puppets, an Easy-Bake Oven, and a pre-Christian sword, then vanished. The entire population of Hawley Five Corners was supposed to have vanished. I had a magic power, after all, and now I had a magic book, too.

I picked up *The Hawley Book of the Dead*, and its soft leather was warm like skin. Nan had warned me not to use it, but just then it seemed I couldn't help myself. The scent of wildflowers wafted up. "The book holds magic dark and deep. . . ."

I picked up a pen and curled up in my favorite chair. *The Hawley Book of the Dead* lay open on my lap. It had been blank every time I looked into it that day. But this time when I riffled through it, the book was filled with writing, page after page, in different hands, different inks. I tried to focus on one page, but my eyes felt so heavy, I couldn't seem to keep them open. I turned to the first blank page and began writing, my eyes closed, without any thought that I was doing anything dangerous, without any thought at all. Then it seemed I no longer had any idea what I was writing. The words flowed from my pen onto the old paper. It felt like they were coming up through the earth, up my body and through my heart like blood pumping. It wasn't like writing. It was like *knowing*.

Rigel Voss had been named after a star. And a star he was, all through the military schools his parents sent him to, his Navy SEAL father eager for him to excel. He did, and graduated first in his class at Annapolis. He served with distinction and no apparent physical or psychic injury in Vietnam, went to Yale for graduate studies in behavioral psychology, then to Quantico. He joined the FBI in 1977, one of the best and brightest. Then, on a clear spring day in 1989, when the buds were just sprouting an extravagance of silky young leaves in Amherst, Massachusetts, Rigel Voss met his nemesis, and his charmed life dissolved as surely as if some fissure had opened up to swallow him.

He'd been in charge of an operation at the university there, a huge undertaking involving scores of agents. Like other schools in the Northeast, the university had been besieged by student protests against the military research conducted on campus. Bay State hosted a program that even he was not allowed full access to. It was a black project, and it was big, whatever it was. The security was state-of-the-art. The choice of the university had to do with many factors, its setting far enough from major urban areas, yet close enough to the Boston–New York–Washington triangle to attract top scientists. But perhaps the greatest draw was the intricate network of tunnels beneath the quad. There was an entire underground campus that few knew about. And that appealed greatly to the military. It also appealed to the student protesters, who'd managed to infiltrate it on two occasions, had found out perhaps more than the FBI agents would ever know about the project, and were only lying in wait to uncover more.

He'd been at a meeting in the complex beneath the ground when the most serious breach happened, the breach of Level 6, where even he had no clearance. When he and his agents had been buzzed in, he'd come face-to-face with something so terrifying he still turned his mind from it in a panic whenever he thought of it. He'd also nearly caught the red-haired girl who'd been the perpetrator of the breach. He'd caught her, had hold of her. Then she vanished, right before his eyes, and he'd been so startled he had let her slip away. Abracadabra.

Voss had agents spying on the protesters, ransacking their scummy student apartments, gaslighting the weaker ones. A few had cracked and told their stories. To expendable agents, who would then be reassigned. Voss rarely appeared on the campus in daylight, and never involved himself directly. But for weeks after the breach, no one saw the red-haired girl, and he was getting desperate. He had to know who she was.

Then, his agents started reporting a strange phenomenon. They'd found a black girl who was involved in the protests. They'd photographed a red-haired girl with her, more than once, they insisted, but the red-haired girl appeared in none of the photos. Furious, Voss thought it was a joke his agents were playing on him. But so insistent were they that he broke his own rule. He tailed the black girl himself. He was beginning to suspect the two girls of being the ringleaders, the most elusive of all.

Voss followed the black girl when she borrowed a car, and drove to Greenfield. She stopped at the Indian junk store on Route 2. The red-haired girl stood waiting. His red-haired girl. The two girls talked at the warped, ketchup-stained picnic tables outside. Voss took thirty-six photographs of them, an entire roll, just to be certain. He followed the white Dodge truck when they parted, an easy ride up Route 2. But near Shelburne Falls, something happened. That's the only way he could describe it to himself later. He'd followed hundreds of suspects and never had anything like it occurred. He must have looked away for a moment, gotten distracted by something he couldn't quite remember, and the white truck that had been a few hundred feet ahead of him was gone. Worse than that, he couldn't even remember the license plate. He drove into the village of Shelburne Falls, scoped out the streets, even walked across the Bridge of Flowers, then down to the Potholes, but the red-haired girl had vanished again. Abracadabra.

He developed the photos himself in a darkroom at the FBI field office in Springfield. He watched intently as exposure after exposure cleared in the wash. He hung each carefully, sat in the red light waiting for them to dry. When they were, he pulled them down, filed them in his briefcase, and left the darkroom.

No one noticed anything amiss with Rigel Voss,

Special Agent-in-Charge, Counterterrorism Division. His dark suit hung as elegantly as ever from his lithe frame. His silver-blond hair was as perfectly in place. His hand did not shake as he waved to the security guards at the door. Yet he was shaken beyond anything he remembered. No memory of rice paddy warfare held as much terror for him as those photographs he'd taken. The red-haired girl had laughed and chatted, swung her glowing hair out of her eyes as he'd snapped photos of her with his tiny camera. Now every glossy paper square revealed budding trees and tepees, Maggie Hamilton talking away, apparently to no one.

In the photographs, the red-haired girl was gone.

Later, he tried to ignore the sniggering as he walked through the federal building, past agents who had only weeks before respected or feared him. Now they whispered, smiled, shook their heads. He made his way to Assistant Director Hunter's office, staring past the sneering faces. He hadn't been prepared for how fast he'd been turned into a laughingstock. Him. Voss. He'd always been deferred to, his good opinion sought. Not anymore. Not after the series of fiascoes all involving the red-haired girl. It wasn't in his nature to adapt to this. It wasn't possible.

Hunter's secretary, a young woman with good bones and bad skin, who had always before tried to engage him with her very blue eyes, now merely waved him in, hid a smile. Her name was Cinda, he remembered. Cinda, cinders, ashes to ashes. Maybe he *was* crazy.

Hunter clearly thought so. But, Voss had to admit,

Hunter tried to salvage what he could of Voss's career. Did not relish losing SAC Voss. He had the file on his desk, Voss's latest report, like lines of black ants marching across the page, the photographs fanned. Voss glanced, then glanced away. In the photos, Maggie Hamilton still talked and laughed to the air beside her, no red-haired girl, no one at all near her.

"So this is it?"

"Yes, sir."

"You don't want to change your report?"

"I can't, sir."

Hunter raked a hand over the photos, which skidded to the floor. "Damn it, what kind of game are you playing? You know this means I have to send you for psych testing, take you off the roster. You've been at the university for, what? Almost two years, directing that operation. Now it all goes up in smoke, because you say you saw a red-haired girl, first in the tunnels, and now in these photos. That she's got to be there, even though the photo lab says she's not. Does that seem even remotely possible, Voss? An entire operation will be discredited, and I will lose one of my best SACs, because of this crap. Because of some disappearing mystery girl only you can see. Does that seem right to you?"

"I'm sorry, sir. I'm only telling it as I saw it. And I wasn't the only one who saw her. Agents Rivera and Lindley said the same about photos they took. The girl was there. And Lupo. Lupo saw her on Level 6 that night. Two of the scientists did, as well."

"Yeah. And now they all deny ever seeing her. Swear that one of the scientists fell and hit her head, got hysterical, caused a panic for nothing. No student was ever on Level 6." Lying scum, Voss thought, looking down at his feet, at the stained brown carpet, not wanting Hunter to see his rage. But Hunter wasn't responsible. Nor were the cowardly scum Rivera and Lindley. Not really.

"Look. We've been over it and over it. Now the only thing I can do is take you off active duty and send you for testing. In the end, you'll be demoted. I can't protect you. Not from crazy, I can't. Your judgment will always be in question. No matter what the shrinks say. You'll never rise to SAC again. Back to wiretaps, if you're not canned altogether. Jesus, Voss, if you don't care about saving yourself, you have a wife and a kid on the way to think about."

"I know that." Voss reached into his pocket, pulled out an envelope. "I'm tendering my resignation."

"Don't be an ass, Rigel."

Voss shook his head. It felt as if it were filled with bees. Yes, he must be crazy. Better to admit it straightaway. "I don't have a choice."

"Of course you do." Hunter leaned into Voss's face. His breath was sour. "Just do this. Tell me it was a joke. Stupid, maybe, but not crazy. What the hell's so difficult about that? Look, I don't care if you see ghosts. I don't care if you see elves dancing around the campus. As long as you don't file reports about it. You're a fine SAC. You have a good career ahead of you. Stop screwing around!"

Rigel Voss tossed the envelope on the desk. It fell on his report, the last he would file as an FBI agent.

"Voss, get your ass back here!" He heard a fist slam on Hunter's desk as he resolutely closed the door. Resolutely walked down the hallways of his past, out the revolving doors into an unknown future.

He didn't really mean to harm Maggie Hamilton. Not at all. Just follow her, look for her red-haired friend. Talk to them, that's it. Find out about the infiltration of Level 6, the photographs, how it was done. The red-haired girl must be the key. She must be the one behind all the unrest, the demonstrations. It must be her. Why else would her identity be so hidden, fading her even in photographs? It must be some trick she knew, that Maggie knew. He'd find them, find the answer. Go back to Hunter, be reinstated. It would be simple.

The first time he drove to Maggie's apartment there were no lights on in the big Victorian. It was dusk, a beautiful spring evening. All the students like bright moths on the common, playing Frisbee, grabbing a burrito from La Veracruzana, studying in Classé Café over endless cups of coffee. Or in the Tower library, looking out from their carrels over the farmland, tobacco barns, and sunset over the pastoral valley that held the university like a cupped palm. It didn't seem like an evening for plotting the overthrow of the administration, longing for the blood of research scientists, or firebombing secret tunnels. The future of biowarfare was safe on such a night.

He parked along the stretch of Amity Street where the large houses had been divided into warrens for students. Strode to her house and around the back, pulled on gloves, lifted a low window, and climbed into the apartment. Such snooping had been beneath him for years, but he found it easy, and interesting. The fading light showed enough of Maggie's one room: one bed with an Indian spread in pink and green, one desk with a book of poetry and a typewriter, and one locked drawer. A cement block and board bookshelf, a file cabinet, also locked. Voss broke the desk drawer, yanked out bills, a blank notebook. He flipped through the book on the desk, then pulled one book after another from the shelves, shook them out, tossed them. One heavy dictionary landed on the glass coffee table, cracking it in half. The file cabinet was flimsy; it was easy to break the lock with his pocket tools. He took what files looked promising (Letters, Financial Aid, Bank), threw the rest (Electric, Heat, Term Papers) on the pile of books. He looked for phone records but didn't find them. Didn't see a phone at all. He went through the kitchen cabinets methodically, dumped flour, sugar, rifled through the refrigerator. Then he slipped out the window, closed it after him, walked to his car in less than full dark, the street hushed. He saw no one. It had taken him twelve and a half minutes to go through this girl's life, take what he wanted. The next day, he took the girl herself.

It was that day, April 23, 1989, that started Voss down a trail of funhouse mirrors: the end of his family, then obsession and ignominy and menial jobs. After long years of fruitless searching, he had found the red-haired girl, now a woman. It had taken him more than twenty years.

On November 10, 2012, he was working in a warehouse outside Minneapolis, where remaindered books and DVDs waiting to be shipped were stored. He cared only for books about history, neutral books about times past, about wars and presidents. He didn't even own a TV. He might never have come across her, but in that warehouse, he was moving pallets of books and noticed a cover photo. A red-haired woman with a crow perched on her arm, and a smiling blond man, dressed in a tuxedo. Voss jumped off his forklift and sliced the ribbon of yellow plastic binding the books to the pallet. He grabbed one and read the jacket, stared at the photos. Then he pocketed the book and walked out of the warehouse without even shutting down the forklift. That was the day his hunt began in earnest.

6

"Dearie?" I opened an eye. I was lying on the floor of my office. There, but disappeared. Falcon Eddy had come up to check on me. *The Hawley Book of the Dead* lay open beside me. Finally I believed in its power. I had to.

I closed the Book, slid it under the desk. I reappeared, and Falcon Eddy jumped.

"Well, that gave me a bit of a turn. Are you right enough?"

"I'm okay," I told him.

"Did you hit your head? You look . . ."

"Never mind that now. What time is it? Actually, what day is it?"

Now Eddy looked truly worried. "Um, it's Wednesday?" The same day. At least I hadn't lost any time. Maybe it was all just a dream. But I didn't think so. I was reaching for my phone.

I was expecting Myrna's cranky voice, but Jolon answered on one ring.

"Adair."

"Jolon, it's Reve. Listen. I know who he is."

"Reve, are you okay?"

"Yes, yes—Jolon, his name is Rigel Voss."

Voss. Not "Boss" as I'd assumed all those years ago in Frankenstein's lab, when the ice-eyed agent had almost caught me in the tunnels. Voss was my Fetch.

Jolon called me again, an hour later, an hour I spent pacing the widow's walk, then going out to feed the horses. The girls were helping Nathan get our late supper ready.

"Jolon. Did you find him? Voss?"

He hesitated, then told me, "It didn't check out. He couldn't be your Fetch."

I wasn't expecting that. "Why?"

"Rigel Voss died twenty-four years ago. He might have had something to do with your friend's disappearance. As a matter of fact, it's almost certain he did. You were right. He was in the FBI, heading up the investigation at Bay State. He resigned from the bureau just before your friend, Maggie, left school and vanished. They never got to question him, though, because he disappeared, too. Then in the fall of '90, a body was found, washed up on the coast of Nova Scotia. It was him."

"I don't believe it." Jolon was silent. I could tell he wasn't used to being challenged about his police work, but I didn't care. "How did they know?"

He huffed, "Still stubborn, I can see. I guess it doesn't hurt that you should know. The body *was* decomposed. No discernible fingerprints. But the dental records were a match."

"I still don't believe it."

"He's dead, Reve. And if you won't tell me *how* you know his name, or something tangible like where exactly he might be, I can't do much. The fact remains that for nearly twenty-five years, there's been no trace of a man named Rigel Voss. If you're right, and he did manage to fake his death, for whatever reason, he's someone else now. It's damned difficult to fake your death, though. Not like on TV. I'd let that one go."

"Thanks for checking it out, anyway." I had no intention of letting it go; I just didn't know what to do about it yet. No matter what Jolon told me, I knew Rigel Voss was my soul stealer, my Fetch.

Vanish

Poverty Road—October 26, 2013

1

It began in such an ordinary way. Nathan called my cell phone that morning. He had a fever and a sore throat that made him feel like he was swallowing knives. I told him to stay in his ell, go back to bed. We'd probably all end up sick, but I could hope. I nearly tripped over Falcon Eddy when I stepped out of my room. I had no idea if or when he slept, but he must have showered. Instead of falcons, he smelled of Old Spice and wet grass.

"Come down for some coffee, Eddy."

I wasn't sure what I could say. Ask him to be extra vigilant because of something I saw in a magic Book? I made it simple.

"I have reason to believe that the man who killed my husband is on his way here. I know Nan told you the circumstances. Jolon . . . Chief Adair, is working on it. The girls don't know, and I want it to stay that way as long as possible. I don't want them to be afraid in their own home, ever again. I need you to help me with that."

He nodded and said, "Fair enough. You've done a good job making this place secure, now it's on my watch. I've activated the outdoor security cameras, and I'll be monitoring them at night, as well as doing spot checks on entrances and exits. During the day, I'll be in the house, near the girls, and still be watching the cameras outside on the grounds from my phone. You'll need to let me know when you'll have any guests besides Mrs. Pike. Don't want to be surprised, like we were by the Reverend."

Eddy had suddenly switched from his usual hokey, homespun self, to all business. Maybe Nan had been right about him. Strange as he was, he seemed to know what he was doing. "Where exactly do you come from, Eddy?"

"Here and there. Been years in the desert. But that doesn't mean I've my head in the sand, now." And his laugh echoed through the house. We heard Caleigh's pounding feet hit the floor a moment later. "Now we're for it. But one last thing, before we're descended on. Leaving the property will be more complicated. You should let me know well beforehand, so I can be prepared for eventualities."

Suddenly it seemed real, when he said that. I hated that we'd need to be "prepared for eventualities" just to take a ride to my parents' house. But the alternative was much worse. The alternative was what had happened to Jeremy. I took a deep breath. "All right. That sounds fine."

I waited for Caleigh, and she came with me to the barn to feed. When we returned to the house, she sat at the kitchen table, engrossed in her string, weaving a pattern I didn't know the name of. "What's that one?"

"It's 'Get Well Soon.' It's for Nathan. Hey, can we have the day off from lessons?" Falcon Eddy melted away.

"Not this time, sweetheart. You've had a lot of time off in the past few weeks."

"But I could go to Grand's."

"I'm sorry, honey. You need to do your schoolwork. Grand can't be entertaining you every minute." I kissed the top of her head as I set down her granola. I certainly wasn't going to tell her about the protocols a drive to Grand's would now require.

She wriggled away. "Yeah, well, what about you? I'm really mad at you. You spent all Sunday riding with Grace and Fai. You always do fun things with them, not just boring schoolwork. You never have time for *me*!" She stuck out her tongue and stormed off, trailing her string.

I poured more coffee, not too worried about Caleigh's tantrum. As soon as I got them all going on some task, she'd come around, Caleigh of the naturally sunny temperament. The twins were still in bed. I thought I'd better rouse them and get everyone settled before Mrs. Pike arrived.

The twins have always had their own rooms, but they migrate together to sleep. Each room has two beds to accommodate this habit. I checked Grace's room and saw only the usual clutter she produced and empty beds. Fai's room, next to Grace's, held them.

The shades were drawn, but the bright autumn sun made its way around them and fell in slabs and strips of light on the gleaming wood floor, illuminating the walls covered with horse posters. Fai's room, unlike her sister's, was neat; the books stayed on the shelves and the clothes in the closet, rather than heaped in piles on the floor. Fai was curled up on one bed, Grace spread-eagled and openmouthed on the other. Their sleeping faces were uncannily alike, with the same sprawl of red-gold curls on white pillows, the delicate spread of nutmeg freckles across each straight nose, their eyebrows bending at the same angle like birds' wings. My heart melted at the sight of the two perfect creatures that had somehow come from Jeremy and me.

The translucence of their skin, as if they were formed from porcelain, nearly fractured me with pride and love. And with fear, for they were vulnerable as foals with a coyote in the pasture.

All the same, I had to get them up, and they never woke easily. I wished Caleigh wasn't having a snit, for her attacks on the sleeping pair always got them moving. I sat on Fai's bed, touched her arm. "Rise and shine, honey." She moaned and flopped over. I went to Grace's bed. "Gracie, time to wake up." She sat straight up, said, "No!" and fell back again, still apparently asleep. I decided it was time for more drastic measures, went over to Fai's stereo, pushed the power button, pushed CD 1, and turned up the volume. Bruce Springsteen's voice blasted out of the speakers, advising us that there was a "Tenth Avenue Freeze-Out." Grace woke with a roar. Fai sat up and clapped her hands over her ears. Clarence Clemons and Roy Bittan were having a sax and keyboard duel when I hit the stop button. "Sorry, but Nathan's sick. Mrs. Pike will be here soon, and I need you all in the study so you're not in her way."

Fai got up mechanically and plodded to her dresser, tugged a sweatshirt over her panda pajamas. Grace rubbed her eyes. "How *long* will he be sick? It's no fun having to teach our own selves."

"I suppose he'll be as sick as he needs to be for as long as it takes him to get better. That's usually the way it works. And what am I, chopped liver?"

"You aren't as good a teacher as our coz. He makes stuff *fun*."

"Thanks. But since you think so highly of him, you might be just a little more concerned about his well-being than your own at the moment."

"Oh, yeah. What's he sick with? Nothing bad, I hope."

"Since you ask, it's probably just a cold. He should be better in a few days."

"Days?"

"Days. So until he's recovered, I'll get you going, but you both have to be a little proactive about your work, and Caleigh's. You'd better run down and get breakfast."

She scowled at me. "At least you could blast something more mellow to wake us up. Like Enya or something, if it has to be music from *your* generation."

"You're the one stole my Springsteen collection, honey. Now suffer."

Fai giggled, and started out to the hall. Grace sprang out of bed, "Hey, wait for me." I snagged the back of her skimpy baby dolls. "Go put something on over that, at least. You'll freeze."

"And the falcon guy might be shocked, I *know*. But he lives with us now. He's just supposed to protect us, not oogle us."

"It's still no reason to have your business hanging out in front of him. And it's 'ogle.' *And* he's not just 'the falcon guy,' he has a name."

She threw a robe over her shoulders, and as she whisked her hair from the collar, a faint whiff of perfume rose from her. I grabbed her arm. "Do you smell that?"

"Huh? Smell what?"

I sniffed again, and it was gone. "Nothing. I hope it's nothing."

But I knew what I'd smelled. Not as strong as the lilac scent on the day Jeremy died. It was like the ghost of lilacs, if there could be such a thing. Which there probably couldn't.

2

Nathan had written out a schedule for the girls, some reading assignments, math problems, and a game of Dead Presidents, a board game he had assembled with question cards and dice, a little like Trivial Pursuit with questions about the Civil War, the robber barons, and of course, dead presidents. I tried to work a little on my script while the girls did their reading, but their shufflings and foot tappings and pencil chewing were distracting. We worked on the math problems after lunch. I am not at my finest when doing anything beyond adding and subtracting, and soon we were all frustrated. It was clear that math was a no-go until Nathan was back. At that point I thought it might be safe to go up to my office for a check on *The Hawley Book of the Dead*. Maybe I'd have another Rigel Voss vision and discover exactly where he was. Then I'd call Jolon, they'd pick up Voss, and the nightmare would be over. If only it could be so easy. I left Falcon Eddy in the study with the girls. After a quick check on the sleeping Nathan, I went upstairs.

The Book was still there under the desk, where I'd left it after my Voss vision. It still felt as warm as a summer meadow.

When I opened it, though, it wasn't the usual meadow scent that hit me. It was the warning smell of lilacs. I closed it up again, almost ran down the stairs to check on the girls. Then remembered Falcon Eddy's cell, and punched in the number. He told me all was well.

"Everything is fine," I told myself. "Everything is normal." I sat at the desk and opened the Book again. This time the scent of lilacs was so strong that I was dizzy from it. I tried to close the Book, but couldn't. I started falling into it. I reached out both hands to steady myself, grabbed not the smooth wood of the desk, but twining green tendrils, with thorns that were ripping my hands. I looked and the windows were choked with growing vines, climbing past the widow's walk railing, through the French doors, into my office. They surrounded me, until all I could see were depths of green, then . . .

> Rigel Voss drove the green-tunneled roads of the forest, a forged hunting license pinned to his jacket, a bow for deer hunting in the back. He'd stopped a number of times, climbed out of the SUV he'd rented earlier that day with a fake ID, threw the bow and a backpack over his shoulder, and slunk through the brush. Once to explore an old mill near a bog. Once to travel along a high wall, recently constructed. The last time to follow two girls on horseback, in the late afternoon light, at the corner of South and Poverty roads. One girl rode a gray horse, the other black. The girls both had red hair, looked alike. Even from a distance (and Voss maintained a goodly distance, even in his excitement not wanting to be betrayed by crackling brush), he could tell they were twins. The girls he was looking for. When

they veered from the road, up a bank and onto a smaller trail, Rigel Voss followed. It didn't matter so much if they heard him once they were off the road. It would take only a few seconds to aim and shoot the small darts from one of the two tranquilizer guns he also carried in a belt holster. He'd shoot the horses first, with big doses of fast-acting tranquilizer, then he'd have a moment to switch guns for the girls, who would be confused by their horses' strange behavior. They wouldn't realize what had happened right away, because of the silencer. The camouflage he wore assured him that even if he was heard, he wouldn't be seen. If all went well, and he planned that it would, horses and girls would be in the land of nod before they knew what had happened. He would walk back to his rented SUV, drive a short distance to the deserted stretch of road, drag the girls out of the woods and place them in the back, gently bound, for their long ride.

Then he would finally have a way to bargain with the woman who had ruined his life. Now that she had red-haired daughters who would be at his mercy. He would have what he wanted, and what he wanted was knowledge. After he got it, he'd kill the girls as quickly and painlessly as he could. But their mother wouldn't know that. He would send her doctored photographs, and she would think they'd gone tortured, bleeding. Those images would stay with her forever. Her life would be as dead as his own, finally. She'd have to live on after everything that mattered to her was destroyed.

He walked quickly along the road, then headed down the trail. He could see the girls on the narrow path, booted legs gently thumping their horses' sides, reins slack. He could hear their merry voices, catch the words.

"Dale said . . ."

"Was that his name, was it Dale or Cale?"

"Kale's a vegetable, you moron."

"Cale with a *C*. It's a name, too. Anyway, it should be near here."

Then silence, but for birdsong and the muffled sound of horse hooves on the sandy path. Voss padded along the edge of the trail, where the pine needles were thickest. He lost sight of them as the trail wound through dense trees, and his heart quickened. Then he heard one say, "Is that where it was?" The other replied, "Sweet." Then a little laughing shriek, and a thick roar like a distant plane, or like thunder. Tree branches tossed in a big gust of wind, whipping Voss's face. He looked up, a shiver going through him. The sky was deep blue, cloudless, without stain. His cheek stung from the lashing branches, but he barely noticed.

He continued creeping up the path, at each turn expecting to see the horses, hear the girls. He saw nothing but scarlet and golden-green leaves lighting the dusk of the path, heard nothing at all. Even the birds were silent. Nothing stirred.

He palmed the gun in his left holster, stroked its cold grip. The one loaded for the horses. His breathing grew shallow.

3

I came up from the vision gasping, struggling against the deep green wall of vines and thorns. But there were no vines, only my office, bathed in dusky light. "Shit!" I must have fallen asleep. I must have slept for hours. My hands were throbbing. When I examined them, they were scabby, the blood congealed as if I had done battle with real thorns. *Something* had happened in the time I slept or had my delusions. I leapt up and ran downstairs. I found Caleigh asleep on the couch with a book tucked under her chin. Falcon Eddy was gone, and there was no sign of the twins. No twins in the kitchen making snacks. No twins in their rooms. I called Nathan's cell, but he told me in a headachy voice that they hadn't been to visit him.

My heart was pounding in my chest. One key card for the gate was missing from the hook by the door. I ran outside: Their horses were gone. I ran back to the house and woke Caleigh. Nathan came out of his apartment in his bathrobe, clutching a tissue box.

"They weren't in the barn?"

"No. Neither were their horses."

"And where's Falcon Eddy?" I grilled Caleigh. "Did he go with them?"

"I don't know where they all went," Caleigh protested.

"Why didn't you call me when they left you? You know I don't want them to ride alone."

"Oh, Mom," Caleigh sighed, "I fell asleep. Anyway, they'd *kill* me if I told on them all the time."

"They wouldn't kill you. They'd just make life unpleasant for a day or two." I strode to the mudroom. "Don't you have any idea where they might have gone?"

She popped her head around the door. "You don't have to yell." I gave her the mad mother glare. "They'll kill me anyway. But. When they went into the kitchen to get us snacks, they were talking about that old tavern. They were whispering. So I wouldn't hear. But I did. The tavern where that boy they met at the fair said there were ghosts."

"Thank you for telling me. Thank you for having sonar." It was one of the few times I was glad of Caleigh's unnerving superhuman hearing.

I yanked orange vests out of the closet. The girls hadn't bothered to take theirs. Horses could sometimes look like deer in the gloaming. Which it was getting to be. The girls hadn't bothered with the walkie-talkies, either. They probably had their cell phones, which wouldn't work a quarter mile into the hollow. I punched in their numbers, and heard their phones ringing from the study. Tried Falcon Eddy's phone, which rang and rang. What did I really know about him? He could be Voss's partner in crime, for all I knew.

I reached for my riding boots, pulled them on. I grabbed my saddle pack, which contained horse treats, a map and a flashlight, a hoof pick, and vet wrap. Again, I noticed the girls had left theirs. They would never have been so careless in Nevada. What they *had* taken was their water packs. The one thing they probably wouldn't need, but no one riding the desert around Las Vegas would be without water for even fifteen minutes. Old habits die hard, but I resisted the pull to take mine. I'd probably be gone less than an hour. I hoped. I gave Caleigh a quick kiss on her round cheek, said, "I'm going to find them. I'll be home soon. Here, take this." I gave her the other walkie-talkie. "And listen to Nathan," who looked on, his face gray with illness and worry.

I was already halfway out the door when Caleigh ran and stuck herself to my legs like a burr. "Be careful, Mom."

I smoothed her penny hair. "Don't you worry, sweetheart. Mothers are always all right. We have to be." I kissed her, then ran out to the barn, pulled Zar from his grass paddock, and threw my saddle on a surprised horse.

"Don't give me that blinky look. We have to find the girls." He snorted as I adjusted the bridle, cinched the girth, and swung up. "Let's go find your friends."

4

I gave Zar his head. He might find them from the sheer horsey desire to be with the herd. At the end of the drive he swung down South Road at the Five Corners, heading toward the tavern site. I didn't warm him up as usual, but pushed him into a fast trot.

"Stupid, stupid, stupid," I kept repeating under my breath. I blamed myself for leaving the girls alone even for one minute. I knew I was panicking but couldn't stop, slow myself down, stop my hands from trembling. I nearly dropped the reins. I felt Zar's muscles tense along with my tension. He rolled into a canter, without my asking, as if he could read my mind. It was one of the reasons I hadn't taken the truck. I told myself it would be easier to look for the girls on the smaller trails on horseback, that sudden headlights might frighten their horses, but really, I wanted a companion in my search, the reassurance of another breathing creature as I plummeted through the woods. I tried not to think, not to feel, but it was Jeremy I really wanted.

The road was an arrow shot through the darkening canyon of trees, straight and ghostly white at dusk. It seemed to go on forever. My eyes began to ache from focusing to its end point among the trees, seeking without finding the forms of two horses, two girls. My head ached from willing them to appear. Something large and winged swooped over the road and I flinched, but Zar kept up his steady canter, his legs flying out over the ground. He slowed as we neared the old tavern road, grown over with tall grass. There was a disturbance, a flattening there. Some large animal had passed, or perhaps two. Surely it had been the girls and their horses. Zar seemed to think so. He plunged down the track, and I began calling for them. Bracken scratched at me, caught on my jeans. The darkness was closing around us, the trees loomed. I called their names as Zar pushed on, setting each hoof carefully on the narrow, rocky scrabble of the trail.

We came to the tavern cellar hole, a black pit opening up at the end of the track. I pulled the flashlight from Zar's saddlebag and jumped off.

I shone the beam all down and around the rock enclosure, where nothing but weeds and fallen leaves lay. "Fai? Grace?" I called, while I aimed my flashlight into the woods, into crevices in the rocks, over the ground, searching for something, anything that might mean they were near. Suddenly the light picked up a clue, flecks of hay glistening from a mound of horse droppings that looked damp and fresh. Zar snuffed it, snorted, and shook his head, as if to tell me he didn't know how to continue our search. But the fresh manure wasn't what I smelled. I smelled lilacs.

A chill shivered up my back. I searched and called all up and down the tavern track and Poverty Road as night fell and the lilac scent pursued me. I called for the twins, listening for something besides my own voice in the tangle of trees. Finally, the thought that Caleigh would be worried made me turn Zar toward home. By the time I reached the gate, I had convinced myself that they were back at the house eating junk. A dark so complete had fallen that Zar had to find his way home without any guidance from me. Surely, the twins had, too.

But the barn, still blazing with light as I'd left it, was empty of their horses. I even looked over the tops of the stalls in case they were lying down, tuckered from their ride. All I saw was undisturbed bedding. I knew the horses weren't out in the paddocks. They would have called to Zar as we came down the drive. But maybe they'd been benighted at some house on the main road, had already called home. I threw Zar's saddle in a heap, secured him in his stall, and ran to the house.

Caleigh and Nathan were playing cards at the kitchen table, the phones and the walkie-talkie between them. They looked expectantly at me when I raced through the door. Caleigh smiled wide. "You found them, didn't you? I told Nathan you wouldn't come home without them—" She saw my face and the light in her eyes dimmed. She looked down, resumed her shuffling.

The kitchen door slammed, and I spun around, ready to scold the twins as they walked in as if nothing was wrong, as if they hadn't scared us half to death. But it was Falcon Eddy, trailing vines, bleeding from deep gashes that tracked over his hands and face like roads on a map.

"Are they here? Have they come home?"

I shook my head.

He wiped the blood that was seeping into his left eye. "I saw them leave, but was bound by these dratted vines." He pulled at one wrapped around his barrel chest.

I remembered my dream, of thorny vines climbing, twining

through the window and into my office. "Vines here? In the house?"

"I was sitting right over there, and thick green vines grew up around me in an instant. Before I knew it they had me wrapped tight as a tick. My face, as well, and I couldn't speak a word. The girls just walked out the door as if they didn't see me."

I looked at my hands, covered with scratches. I couldn't call him a liar. I'd seen the thorny vines, too, felt their effects. "And then?"

"I struggled free, went upstairs to find you. You were wrapped in the vines, too. I couldn't wake you. Couldn't wake Caleigh, nor Nathan. Tried to use my cell to call for help, but the thing didn't work. None of them did. So I went off to find them." He sighed. "Don't know yet if I did right. But while I was tracking them, I saw a man from a far bit away, called to him had he seen two girls riding. He was fiddling with something in the back of his car. When he heard me, he raised a gun. So I shot my bow. Winged him in the shoulder, thought that would be enough to give him pause." He swiped at another trickle of blood. "Only, it didn't. He pulled out the arrow, leapt into the car, and was away."

I could barely breathe. "Were they . . . were they in the car?"

"Dearie, I'm just not sure. I'm not as fast as I used to be, but I ran and leapt onto the bumper, held fast to the roof rack. But the windows were tinted, full black. I pounded, listened for any sound. Tried to climb onto the roof, so I could get to the driver. He turned onto a dry streambed, blasted over the gullies. Lost my hold, got dragged the better part of a mile before I was jounced off altogether. So. I don't *know*. Got the license plate, but that doesn't seem like much at all." He shook his head. "I did go back to the spot where I'd shot the bugger, looked for the horses, more sign of girls. Saw nothing. Hoped they'd be here."

I'd started shaking as Falcon Eddy told his story. I reached for my phone, but it slipped from my hand. Nathan picked it up. I could see he was punching in 911.

Caleigh said, "I know. I'll deal them in, then they have to come back soon."

"That's a wonderful idea, honey," I said, trying for a steady voice. "You and Nathan go on playing, after he makes this phone call. Then you can have pickle and pimento." Caleigh did not look up, even at the mention of her favorite sandwich meat. She was concentrating fiercely on bringing her sisters back to play their poker hands. But we would need stronger magic than that to bring them home.

5

Jolon wasn't in uniform, and I was grateful for that, grateful for his tan chamois shirt, frayed at the cuffs, his worn jeans. He seemed like an old friend come to help us, not Hawley's police chief. But two young women followed him, to collect "evidence" in Grace's and Fai's rooms. The word itself seemed cruel. More cruel still that my girls' lives might be evidence of some crime, that other hands would touch things that were precious to them. Fai's troll collection, Grace's laptop with both Marilyn Manson and daisy stickers covering it. I felt how exposed they were, not only out in the night, not only to Rigel Voss, but in their own home. I felt like throwing up.

I gave Jolon photographs of the twins, a video of them at our last endurance ride. He faxed the photographs to the state police, the environmental police. I gave him their cell phones, which I'd already checked for photos or contacts or messages that might lead me to them. I'd read the recent texts, to their friends and to each other. I kept thinking that if we were in the real world they'd have taken their phones, and they would have been trackable now. But there the phones were, like pink and green sores I kept picking at.

Jolon brought me to the kitchen, closed the door. Falcon Eddy was there at the table, looking haggard and crestfallen. Jolon questioned Eddy first. He only raised an eyebrow at the mention of the vines.

He sent Eddy to talk to the sketch artist who'd just arrived, then made a series of calls. He ordered roadblocks set up, told us police in all the surrounding states were now looking for the car. The man Eddy had shot would be caught soon.

"You're bleeding, Reve." He took my hand. It *was* still bleeding, my palm pierced like a stigmata. I told him about the climbing vines that I'd thought were a dream.

"Do you believe what Eddy told us?"

"Crazy sounding or not, I know something of Falcon Eddy. Your Nan trusts him. She called me before she sent him to you."

That was news to me. "Why didn't she tell *me*? Why didn't *you* tell me? The guy just shows up here, and I'm supposed to just trust him? What if he kidnapped the girls himself?"

"I don't think so. He's . . . well, let's just say I'd be inclined to believe him. Most of his story, anyway. That he shot at the guy and hit him. Don't know I'd go so far as to put it all down to enchantment, the way he seems to. But we'll have a composite sketch soon."

We heard the search helicopter that Jolon had called in whupping above us. There wasn't much else to be done while night covered the forest, he explained, and evidence there needed to be preserved. The helicopters carried infrared detection gear that would sense heat. Horses were big enough that the sensors would pick them up if they were in the forest. They hadn't yet. And the horses hadn't returned riderless, so the twins were probably out of the forest, riding on the roads. They had to be. Any other possibility didn't bear thinking about. The drone of the helicopter gave me a weird sense of vertigo, and of time standing still.

"I'll have to ask you a lot of questions now, Reve," Jolon said. "And some will be pretty personal."

I stopped at a window, saw my own reflection in the glass, hair snarled, hands clenched around my elbows, holding everything in. My hope that some small accident had stranded the girls—a lost horseshoe, a minor puncture wound—was fading fast. "I can't help thinking about them out there in the dark, hurt or frightened or—"

"Reve," Jolon cut in, his voice gentle. "I need you to talk this through with me. That's how you can help them now."

I nodded. I tried to drive the sick, lurching feeling back where it came from.

"First of all, do you have any reason to believe the twins would take off without telling anyone?"

"No. That's not something they'd do."

"Did they want to move here? Didn't they miss their school, their friends?" He hesitated, just for a beat. "Could they have run away?"

"That just isn't like them. They'd think of their horses first. They have nothing with them but some water. They didn't take their packs. No grain for the horses, nothing even to tether them for the night. And they're too smart to think they could ride back to Nevada. If they meant to leave, they would have taken one of my credit cards, booked a flight, got on a train or bus. But they didn't. Every credit card, my cash, my bank card, are all accounted for. I checked my wallet, believe me."

Jolon wrote something, clicked his pen some more. "Okay. Let's table the running-away possibility. I know your husband died earlier this year. Are you single now?"

I must have looked at him like he had two heads.

"I'm sorry." His eyes turned down to his forms again before he asked, "Was your husband the girls' father?"

"God, yes!"

"Reve, I'm just trying to ascertain if there's anyone who might have reason to kidnap them. I have to be frank. For the girls' sake."

I had to sit down. I slumped into the chair farthest from Jolon. "I know that. No, I don't have a fiancé, a boyfriend, a lover. I work at home now, have no friends here, don't know anyone but you. The girls are tutored at home. Nathan tutors them. He's also their cousin, and lived with us for years. They have no boyfriends here, either, that I know of. I don't know anyone who'd want to . . . to do anything to harm them. Except Rigel Voss."

"Reve," he said my name again in a patient, calming voice that if anything, ratcheted up my terror. "I think we need to keep operating on the information that Rigel Voss is dead."

I glared at him. "All right, have it your way. The Fetch, then. Call him whatever you want, Jolon. Whoever he is, I know he's here. I know he's found us!"

I suddenly remembered that Caleigh was still up, playing board games now with Nathan, plying her string as she did so. She didn't need to know any of this, and she was probably listening in with her acute hearing. She would have to be questioned, as well. But that would be for the morning, when a child advocate would come out, Jolon had told me. A child advocate.

I got up and shut the kitchen door. I poured myself some coffee, gulped it. The black coffee was too hot; it scalded my mouth.

"As soon as I heard from you, I called the Las Vegas PD again," Jolon told me. "Just to see if they could tell me anything more. But they couldn't."

"Somehow that doesn't surprise me."

Jolon had also contacted the few bed-and-breakfasts and private campgrounds in the area. He even found the ranger who patrolled the state forest campground, playing darts at Pizza by Earl. The B and Bs had only families staying. It was late in the season for the state campground to have many takers, even with the warm weather. One single male, a bow hunter, had taken a cabin at Candy Cane Park two days before. Jolon sent two officers to the park, but they came up with nothing. They ran the guy's New York plates, the car registered to an Abel Carmichael, a retired roofer from Syracuse, married, two grown sons. Nothing out of the ordinary, but they slunk up to the window for a closer look. The curtain was cracked, the guy watching TV, alone. They knocked on the door, showed their badges, asked him a few questions. Carmichael was just a guy from New York State hoping to bag a deer.

"Why didn't they search his cabin?"

"No probable cause," Jolon said. "We can't haul in every stranger."

"Jolon, I know the Fetch is in Hawley. Let's cut the crap."

"Okay. Whoever he is, he might be in Hawley. Let's go with that. Have you received any more threats since that e-mail you forwarded to me?"

"No. Only that one e-mail, saying he would find me. Us."

"You know the stalker's a male?"

"Speculating." I sucked in more coffee. It smelled the way I imagined brimstone might. "Look, I know the detectives assigned to the case didn't believe me. Did they tell you they think I planned Jeremy's murder?"

"Not in so many words. Anyway, I like to form my own opinions." He looked at me in the deep way I knew so well, solemn, seeking, as if he might be reading my soul. "I know a lot has changed, but I know you, Reve. You didn't plan your husband's death, or the twins' disappearance. Magician or not. Just so you know where I stand, and we can move on. I believe in your stalker. I believe he could have found you. I may not believe he's who you think he is, but what I do need is some concrete evidence, something I can get a handle on, so we can find your girls. Until we know, let's hope they're just a little lost. Okay?"

He was right, of course he was. "Okay."

"Now I'd like to take a look at the barn, and get a brush or saddle pad that has the horses' scent, just in case we need to bring in tracking dogs in the morning."

I nodded, took a ragged breath.

"I'll go out first at dawn," Jolon said. "I have some experience tracking. The tracks will be all muddied up if we send dogs out first." He saw my look. "I trained in Maine with a Native American Jesuit priest who's one of the best trackers in the country. I went to police academy, and then worked in Worcester County. I still kept my hand in as a consultant to the state police as a tracker. Eventually, they hired me on full-time, to lead search and rescue in eastern Mass. A few months ago, the police chief job came up in Hawley. So here I am. The state cops would ordinarily be in charge, but I was asked to head up this search, since I have the experience and know the forest so well." He narrowed his eyes at me. "Reve, is it a problem that I'm the one in charge of the investigation?"

I looked into his clear eyes and lied outright. "Not at all." Although I knew it would be. A problem for me, but more so for him. I knew he would never rest until my girls were found. That's how it had always been with us. Jolon would do anything for me. That was the way he loved me. He still did. That was in his eyes, too. I wanted to warn him, I wanted to tell him how dangerous I was to anyone who loved me, how anyone without a death wish should just stay away from me. But my girls needed him and I was silent.

The hall clock tolled midnight. We waited in silence for the twelve deep tones to sound, like the extinguishing of hope. Grace and Fai had been gone nine hours.

6

Caleigh was curled up on the sofa, fast asleep. Nathan dozed near her.

I went up to my office. I went for the Book. I walked right by the mirror across from my desk. I didn't look directly in it. I knew I looked like hell. The mirror had been downstairs when Jolon and I were children. We had peered through the windows into its silver plane, speckled with age. The mirror made us look like ghost children. Now, my eye caught the edge of it, and I had to look again. I didn't see myself at all, just the reflection of black sky, and the portrait of my great-great-grandmother.

Then I saw a flash of light that seemed to come from the mirror. The sky reflection wavered and broke, giving way to a woman with chestnut hair, holding a sword before her. She had the face of the woman in the portrait, only younger, more implacable. It didn't seem like a reflection. The mirror looked like a doorway to another world altogether.

I leapt up, and my chair flew across the room on its casters. The mirror quivered, then reflected only blackness again. I felt my scalp contract, all the hair standing up on it. My legs collapsed like someone had cut my strings, and I fell against the desk, then to the floor. "Shit, shit!" I'd turned my ankle during my fall. "Stupid mirror! Great. This place *is* haunted." I sat rubbing my ankle, swearing under my breath, then propped myself in my desk chair. My ancestor gazed at me calmly from the boundaries of her frame. "What are *you* looking at?" Her placid eyes were not at all like those of the warrior woman who'd shone in the mirror.

Seriously shaken, I picked up *The Hawley Book of the Dead*, held it. I thought of Jeremy. My own dead. I wanted him with a physical ache. I felt guilty when I didn't think of him. It had been only two months, and I was beginning to forget things, little things. I wanted to remember everything, not lose one memory. How he tied the rope for the trick called Magic Knot. How he shaved, which cheek he began with. How he'd coat his food with pepper and make us all sneeze. How he held me hard. Not as if I was some fairy princess, but as if he trusted that I was solid in the world, would never break. I desperately wanted him with me now, to help me out of this horror story.

My hands slipped the Book open. I smelled not lilacs this time, but Jeremy. The nutmeg smell of his skin. I began to feel light-headed, then dizzy, as if I were falling down a tunnel of light. I fell and fell, but kept hold of the Book. When I landed, it wasn't the past I saw. I saw Kilcoole Beach, that strand ringing the flat and shining Irish Sea. I was standing on the gorse-lined path from our house on the Sea Road, the old stone house built by Jeremy's grandfather for his Irish wife. She could look out at the changing skies over the sea, and walk to it when she liked. It was a walk we took nearly every day we were there, Jeremy and I, leaving the damp-walled house, the peat fire banked for our return, the walk to the seawall and beyond.

It was not like a dream or a memory; it was not like anything but reality, with the terns keening above me, the wind in my face. I headed toward the beach, walking slowly, expecting something, my heart pounding in my chest, echoing the rush of waves that lapped the sand. At the end of our path, I turned to the south, and the seawall was before me. Only a tumble of rocks really, separating the beach from the grassy hummocks of marshland, and the railroad tracks that ran like a scar by the sea.

There, where he'd come every summer since he was a boy, Jeremy sat looking out toward England. His bright hair shone against the pearly sky. He wore his dreadful old speckled mackintosh, his surety against the Irish rain.

I stood paralyzed, until he turned to me and smiled. As if he'd been expecting me. "You'd might as well have a chat, since you've come all this way, love." He patted the rock next to him. I walked toward him, but I was afraid to speak, afraid to touch him, terrified that at any moment he'd vanish. "Don't worry." He took my hand. He wove his fingers through mine, and they felt blessedly real. I threw my arms around him then, felt his solid presence in that world, at least. My tears, bottled up for so long, let go like the dam had burst. I wept against his shoulder.

"I thought you were dead!" I wailed into his musty rubber coat. That smell convinced me like nothing else that in this dimension at least he was as real as I.

He stroked my hair, said, "But I *am* dead." I looked up into his eyes then. They were full of love, and something else, a longing. "I am dead, I am real, and this is a place we can meet. While you need me."

"Jeremy . . . I'll always need you. . . . But you don't know . . . oh, Jeremy. The twins are gone, and I don't know what I'm doing. What will I do, Jeremy? What should I do?"

"Shh, shh." He pulled me closer, and I thought I could feel his heart beating. I thought if I could stay there forever I'd be happy. Then he said, "But you won't be, you know. Not without our girls."

"You can read my mind?"

He laughed. "In a certain way, I suppose I can. You know, if I could go back with you, I'd be the greatest mentalist who ever lived."

"Then come with me . . . help me!"

"That's not the way it works, love. I only wish."

I pulled away enough to look into his eyes again, trying to take him all in while I could. His arching eyebrows, the planes of his face, so dear to me, almost forgotten in the months since I'd held him in my arms while he died.

"But what *you* can do is look around you, take stock."

"Do you know where they are? Are they . . ." I couldn't say the word.

"Dead, like me? I'll tell you what I know."

He took my hand again. His was warm, and comfort seemed to flow from it. "What I know is this. You can bring them back, and only you. Don't be afraid to use the tools you've been given. Don't be afraid at all, and you'll be all right. You're brave, you know. Think of yourself doing Without a Net. How you always had the courage to take that plunge. Trust yourself."

He paused, then said, "And trust Jolon. Let him help you. He's a good man." I didn't call him on it, didn't ask how he knew about Jolon at all, or what he was like, since they'd never met. "He's smart, too. Smarter than me, obviously." I opened my mouth to protest, but Jeremy stopped me.

"Sshh. He's smarter than me, as I'm dead and he's not. Simple logic, you know. But I'm with you, too." He put his hand over my heart. "In here." He raised that hand to touch my brow. "And here. We're together, Reve. Don't doubt it. You have the strength of both of us now, love. And the magic. Double magic. The magic you were born with, and the magic that I've taught you. Remember . . ."

Kilcoole Beach started fading, and Jeremy, too. I reached to hold him, stretched to kiss him. Our lips met and I felt that liquid rush of tenderness only the kisses of the well and truly married hold. Then he was gone.

I looked up and it was still dark. The moon had risen over the hill. I was in Hawley again, in my office, alone. It seemed impossible that Jeremy was not still with me. Whatever visions the Book gave, they seemed so real. He seemed so *real*. Even thoughts of the musty mackintosh made me want to weep and never stop.

Then I heard the hall clock chime again, three sepulchral notes. Twelve hours, now. I tried to shake off my misery, take stock, as Jeremy had told me to. So I could bring our girls back, from wherever they might be.

I'd waited to call my parents, but by seven o'clock I couldn't bear it anymore.

"Reve, what's wrong?" Panic edged my dad's voice when he answered the phone. I never called that early.

"Daddy . . ." I think the last time I had called him that I was ten. "You have to come. Grace and Fai . . ."

"Oh, God, what happened?"

"They're . . . just gone." I felt as if I was choking on the words. "They went out for a ride, alone. They left around three yesterday. They haven't come home yet." Sixteen hours. Now I had internalized the hall clock, and I felt the time, could sense to a fraction of a second how long they'd been gone. "Dad, the police are here."

There was silence for a moment. It seemed like the longest silence in the history of the world.

"We'll come right away. You could have called us anytime, sweetheart. We would have come right over to be there with you."

"I hoped they'd be back by now. You know . . ." I couldn't go on. I realized that I'd been clinging to the hope that my dad would somehow make it all better, laugh and tell me I'd had a bad dream, that the twins were surely there, sleeping soundly in their beds. I felt the tears coming, the tightness in my chest, but I couldn't break down. Jeremy was right. I would need all my strength for this. I wiped my face, drank some stale water from a glass on the desk.

"And Caleigh?"

"Convinced they'll be home any minute. Sleeping on the couch now."

"Have you told the police about your stalker?"

"They already knew. Jolon's the police chief here now. But they might have to involve the FBI. If they decide it's a kidnapping case. I can't help but think of Maggie. After that . . ."

My father's voice tensed. "I know, Reve." He did know. "But let's just concentrate on what's in front of us, right now. I'll wake your mother and we'll be there soon. I'm sure they'll be back before we get there."

"If only they could be. Oh, Dad, I'm so . . . just . . . *sorry*!"

"Sweetheart, it's not your fault."

Why didn't I believe that?

The evidence team had done its work. The house was still full of police, detectives, and surveillance people setting up recording devices, in case the Fetch called. Most of them were downstairs, so I went up.

My head was full of snot like thick cotton batting, my body stiff from sitting most of the night, answering questions. I felt very old—I had to pull myself up by the banister one step at a time. I paused at the first landing. Grace's room was before me, with its bubblegum pink walls. Her room in Henderson had been black. Not long before, Grace had wanted black everything, including her black horse Brio. Just before the move, a resurgence of girl bands from the '80s had caught the twins' attention, and Blondie, the Go-Go's, and Katrina and the Waves replaced Marilyn Manson. Their colors changed from black to pinks and greens almost overnight.

I went into Fai's room, with walls the color of lime pulp. I fell on the bed, breathed in their scents of watermelon lip gloss and Bed Head Shampoo. The pillow fragrant with the lives of Grace and Fai. I buried my face in it and wept.

7

The early light shimmered grayly, gave everything a dullness that reflected my state of mind. I sat at the kitchen table clutching the phone. I had set up my laptop there, so I could monitor e-mails as well. Only twice had "1 new" popped up on the screen: one from Setekh the Magnificent's publicist, one from a car dealer. I didn't respond to either.

I made more coffee, then dragged myself out to the barn to feed. The gates were open, the drive full of police cars. I took a deep breath, then opened the kitchen screen door. Miss May trotted over, hoping for a handout. I scratched the nubs where her horns used to be. Zar was pacing the fence, lonely for his friends. I dished out his grain and vitamins, poured the sweet-smelling mixture into his feed tub. Maybe the best thing about having animals is that even when everything falls apart, they still need to be fed, turned out, given fresh water. So you know the world goes on around you, somehow. I threw my arm over Zar's neck, smelled his good horsey smell. "We'll go out later to look for the girls if they're not back," I promised him, and myself.

As I left the barn, I saw Jolon walking down the drive. He wore scruffy clothes, a scruffy five o'clock shadow bloomed on his pale, drawn face. I couldn't reconcile this tall, graying, deliberate man with my wiry black-haired Jolon, who'd been so fleet of thought and motion. His hat was tipped over his face, shading his eyes from me. But he brought the same wonderful smell he'd always had, like apples and salt and cut pine. That smell overwhelmed the clean soap smell he'd had the night before, and the horsey smell of my boots. It soothed me in spite of myself, made my tight muscles relax. I realized that I'd been holding my breath.

"Jolon." I held out my hand for him, and he took it in both of his as if it might break. His hands were warm. He looked in my eyes and it was as if he could still read me, would know everything about me. Even after all the years apart. I thought the next minute he might fold me in his arms.

I pulled my hand away. I braced myself against the onslaught of feeling, closed myself off from wanting that human touch. I had killed my beloved husband, lost my girls. What right did I have to be comforted? Something inside me hardened like cement setting.

"You didn't find them."

"No. I found their trail, and yours, judging from your size and that horse's feet. Their tracks went to the old tavern site, then . . . well, they stopped."

"My daughters are missing—maybe kidnapped, maybe worse. Why the hell aren't you out *looking* for them instead of . . . of standing here telling me you can't *find* them?"

I realized I was yelling, that my hands were clenched in fists. It felt good to finally be able to blame someone for something.

Jolon touched my shoulder lightly, as if I were a horse he was gentling. He said nothing.

I turned away, balled up my hands in my pockets so they wouldn't shake. "What happens next?"

"We're sending the dogs out now."

"I'm coming with you. My parents will be here any minute. They'll stay with Caleigh."

He shook his head. "You need to be here, too. In case the twins come back."

"I can't just do nothing. I'll go crazy. I want to ride out, look for them." I saw his questioning gaze. "You don't need to worry, I won't get lost. I still remember every deer path."

He smiled bleakly. "I don't doubt it. Just wait until the search teams go out. We have fifty or so AmeriCorps workers from around the state coming in, as well as more search-and-rescue units. They should be here within the hour. I'd feel better if you waited. So you'll be within hailing distance of people."

I sighed, let out the bad air that had been building in my chest. "I'm sorry I snapped at you," I told him. "I guess I'm just . . . I don't know, maybe a little crazy."

"Don't worry about it. Every parent is when their child goes missing."

Two men were installing a trap and trace on our phone lines. Others combed the wall around the property, the other buildings. Jolon returned, his phone was ringing constantly, and he barked orders into it. The search was in full swing.

My parents arrived, followed by the child advocate, a grandmotherly older woman. After they'd talked, Caleigh declared she was very nice, and gave her a bottle cap necklace. Apparently, Caleigh had told her only what she'd told me. And that Grace and Fai hadn't wanted to leave Nevada, but were kind of liking it here. That she really missed her dad, and Grace and Fai did, too, but they didn't blame me. They blamed the Fetch; the man who'd been stalking them. Caleigh's only complaint about me was that I made her study geography.

My mother and I went up to my room to watch the news on TV.

"I tried to call Nan before, but it just rang and rang. I'd hate for her to find out this way. I'll try her again."

"You didn't tell her? That's funny," my mom said. "She called this morning, just after you did. She knew. We assumed you'd told her."

"Huh. No. I didn't." We looked at each other, wondering over the mystery of Nan. "Maybe Falcon Eddy told her."

"Maybe." Falcon Eddy had gone out to search with Jolon at first light. He must have known he wasn't exactly in my good graces, no matter what Nan or Jolon thought about him. He'd been the last person to see my girls, and hadn't been able to keep them home.

Just then, the news segment of *Good Morning America* came on, and there we were, looking like the happy family we had once been. There were the photos I'd given Jolon of the girls on their horses, then portraits of their faces in close-up, the caption reading: "Missing Daughters of Las Vegas Magician Revelation Maskelyne. Second Tragedy to Befall the Amazing Maskelynes."

Jolon came in to watch. He said, "You'll have to decide whether you want to give interviews. There have already been calls from all the networks." He pointed to Kelly and Michael, now cracking eggs with a celebrity chef after the solemnity of our story. "*Sixty Minutes*, *Dateline*, you name it, all left messages."

"Not *Dateline*, please. Too much tear-jerking." Mom, sitting next to me, her arm encircling me, put in her two cents.

I hated the thought of it. I already felt so exposed. Although I was one of the rock-star magicians, just a little below David Copperfield on the magic-celebrity continuum, it was still much quieter than being a real rock star. The occasional television interview or charity appearance was what I was accustomed to. I wasn't used to my family being splashed all over the news, rather than *The World Magic Awards*. Even the news circus around Jeremy's death hadn't affected me much, not really. I'd been numb, insulated by my shock and grief. This was different.

"You want my advice? You should do some interviews," Jolon told me. "Soon." Then he said something that reverberated in my head. "Time is not their friend."

Nineteen hours, my internal clock said. I knew he was right.

I called Henry, asked him to set up interviews. He knew about the twins, but had put off reporters until he heard from me. I made certain that Caleigh was settled in with my parents, then I tacked up and went out on Zar. It was startling how the forest had changed in one day. I rode out the open gate and realized that we'd been shielded from most of the traffic and chaos the search involved. Looking down the drive earlier I'd glimpsed only a few evidence-team workers scouring our side of the fence, two police cars, and the state police van with the phone tracing equipment. But as soon as I turned down Hunt Road, I saw one of the checkpoints Jolon mentioned. It was manned by four paramilitary guys toting rifles, surrounded by Jeeps and trucks, and about twenty other men and women dressed in bright orange.

They all stepped back, some giving me a solemn wave as I rode by. I had no idea what the etiquette was for something like this, so I just touched the visor of my helmet in a kind of civilian's salute and rode past. It seemed that every step Zar took, the out-of-body feeling I'd been struggling with began to lift. When we made the turn past the clump of searchers, and all I could see before me for a moment was a bright blaze of incarnadine trees, I could finally breathe through the wedge of panic lodged in my chest.

I rode until the moon came up, until I could barely see anymore. Then I turned my horse toward home. The searchers had thinned with nightfall. I had ridden to the very edge of the forest. Suddenly, I saw a glint of moonlight bounce off metal, a moving shape. My heart thudded and skipped. Then the shape resolved itself into a man on a bike riding through the woods, but not on any trail I remembered. It was probably just a search team member, although I hadn't noticed any on bikes. He saw me, pedaled faster. He was coming right toward me. Before I could turn Zar and race off, I felt something wing by me. The man on the bike screamed and fell.

Falcon Eddy jogged out of the woods to where the biker lay moaning. "Here, the woods are closed, ya bugger." He reached, pulled out an arrow that had been lodged somewhere, and the man screamed again. "Aaaathhh! You're killing me!"

"Not a bit of it," Falcon Eddy said. Zar was fidgeting, wanting to run, but I held him where he was, mesmerized by the scene before me.

"Eddy?" I called. "What's going on? Who is that? Is he hurt?"

Eddy lifted another glinting object for me to see. "Bugger here's got a camera. A reporter." The man moaned. "Ah, you're never hurt, I just grazed you. Come on, man, lep up and pedal out the way you come."

The man rose shakily, picked up his bike. "I want my camera."

Eddy threw it into a tree. We all heard the crunch when it hit. "What camera?"

"You're nuts. I'm calling the police."

"Can't call anyone till you're well out of the forest."

"You . . . you . . ."

"Go on now. I'm sick of the sight of ya." Eddy raised his bow. The man got up on his bike and pedaled as if his life depended on it. Maybe it did.

Eddy sheathed his arrow. "All right now, dearie?"

"You've been following me all day."

He nodded.

"Are you sure he isn't really hurt?"

"He was barely bleeding!"

"Thanks, Eddy."

"I'm sorry I couldn't bring your girls back to you."

I remembered the phantom vines growing up so swiftly through the windows, then tearing at their thorny stems until my hands bled. It wasn't Eddy's fault the twins had gone. Whatever had happened in reality, it *seemed* as if we had all been enchanted the day the girls disappeared. I looked off after the man pedaling his bicycle, a dark speck against the white of moonlit road.

"I know," I told him. "But let's get home. Maybe they'll be back now." I said it only to comfort myself. I didn't really believe it. The forest around us was too dark. Too full of threats we couldn't know about.

Hell's Kitchen Road—October 28, 2013

1

I've never trusted clocks. Time is an illusion, as fickle as a magic trick. The principle of time control was a necessary part of our spectacles. One that we revived from John Nevil's repertoire was The Orange Tree. The audience would see at first only a large planter on the stage. I'd talk about the illusion of time, the possibility of controlling it, slowing it to a crawl, speeding it up. Jeremy, beside me, threw bright balls into the air and suspended them. He walked a few steps away, drank some water, with the balls stopped in midair. Then he stepped back and resumed his juggling, speeding up the tosses to a breakneck pitch. While the audience was fixed on him, from the planter an orange tree would begin to sprout, to leaf out, flower, and bear fruit, while he juggled so swiftly the audience could see only the blur of objects. When he finally stopped, he tucked the balls in his pocket and helped me toss the golden fruit out to the audience.

Time seemed to go something like that after the girls disappeared. Sometimes it seemed to run me over with haste and fury; other times I felt suspended in it like a fly caught in a spider's web. The clocks never told the time as I knew it. I woke the next day as if from the dead, my hair plastered to my face, my neck sweaty, clothing binding my limbs. I was wedged in a chair in the parlor, a blanket that someone must have draped over me covering my knees. Caleigh's voice drifted in from the kitchen, along with the smell of bacon cooking, so I knew it must be morning. But without the clue of bacon, it might have been any time at all. Only my internal hall clock told me the right time, every ticking second an agony. It was forty-one hours my girls had been gone.

The morning brought no fresh news, no sign of the girls. Or Rigel Voss. In spite of hundreds of searchers still pushing through laurel and raspberry canes and hobblebush, four thousand acres of state land. The helicopter still whined at night above us with its infrared cameras, finding nothing, no spots of red that might be girls or horses.

After a long day being Skyped in to answer all the questions the talking heads asked, after the news cameras had been packed up, I checked in on Caleigh, playing Monopoly with my parents. Officer Bob lingered in the doorway. I went up to my office. Knowing we were so surrounded eased my worry for Caleigh, at least a little. Every chance I got I'd run up to look into *The Hawley Book of the Dead*, but since my visit with Jeremy on Kilcoole Beach, the Book had shown me only blank pages. That morning was no different. I rifled through every page, examining each for any stray blot of ink. There was nothing. I tried to write in the Book again, to see if that brought anything on, but some force wouldn't allow my pen to touch the page. I slammed it closed, finally, threw it at the wall in frustration. "Stupid, stupid Book! Why won't you show me where the girls are? You're useless." And I stalked out.

I found Falcon Eddy in the kitchen, waxing a bowstring.

"I'm going out," I told him. "There's no need to follow me. There are so many searchers in the forest, I'll be fine."

He didn't look up from his work. "There were searchers in the forest yesterday, dearie. What would you have done had I not been there to shoot at daft bicycle bugger?"

"I was on Zar, I would have just galloped away. Look, I want you to stay *here*. You need to protect Caleigh, not me."

He raised his bow, held it up to his keen eye, inspected it for warping. "We shall see what we shall see," he told me. "You'll find me where I'm most needed."

"What does that mean?"

"It means what I say."

I gave up on Eddy's cryptic talk, and stalked out to the barn. He made no move to follow me.

Clumps of searchers colonized the woods like mushrooms, poring over every inch of ground. What could I hope to accomplish with only a mother's intuition and faith? I didn't know, but I needed to exhaust myself trying. Yellow leaves spangled the path and the air as I rode alone, near the turnoff for Hell's Kitchen Road. A sudden flutter made me whip my head around. I saw two riders, their horses' heads dipped to drink from the stream on the opposite bank, on the other side of the road. I could see their faces clear. Grace and Fai.

I flung myself off Zar's back and ran into the stream to get to them. My tongue froze in my mouth when I tried to call their names. The instant my boots hit the slick stones of the stream I slipped, my right boot filled with water, and I scrabbled to save myself. In that split second everything changed. I could feel the air shifting. I looked again, and the twins were gone. My tongue unfroze and I called and called to them as I leapt the rest of the way across. When I got to the trees on the other side, I felt a blast of scorching air, as if something big had rushed by me. I crashed through it, through the brush, a branch whipping across my cheek, branding it. "Grace! Fai!" I saw nothing. Only trees and more trees and leaves swirling in golden gusts around me. I ran blindly, crashing loudly through the underbrush, scaring up birds. When a hand caught me, pulled me to a halt, I fell to my knees. I looked up and saw it was Jolon.

"Are you all right?" He searched my face, scanning my cuts and bruises. I nodded, unable to answer. He helped me up.

When I felt like I could talk again, I told him, "I'm all right, I'm all right, but I thought I saw . . . I thought I saw Grace and Fai on their horses. Did you see them?"

"I only saw you jump off your horse and run into the forest."

"You didn't see anyone on the other side of the stream?"

"No." He hesitated, then said, "There was no one there."

"You're sure?"

He nodded, his eyes flooding with concern. His hands still held me, steadied me. I wanted to get up on my horse and ride, but I was shaking too much to even hold my reins. I wanted to bolt, to be in motion, but all I could do was try to breathe, stop my teeth from chattering with shock and cold.

"Let me go! I have to find them."

"Reve, they weren't *there*. I know you want to believe, but—"

"You can't stop me!" I shrugged away from Jolon's grip, began walking back to Zar, who was cropping grass. Jolon walked beside me, matching his strides to mine. It sent me back to the time before everything was lost.

Maybe he was trying to get back to that place, too, but the boy I knew was buried deep inside the man he was now. Then he surprised me. He said, "Do you remember when we used to ride here? Your hair then, it was the color of this stream. Chestnut. With golden lights. Just like the pony you used to ride. Her name was Maeve." And I felt the irresistible pull of our childhood, as if we were both trying to get back there, to some magical place, where nothing bad could happen. "Maeve, the fairy queen. You remember?"

I did remember. I leaned against the nearest tree, spent. I had hoped so much to have found my girls. But Jolon hadn't seen them. He of all people would have, with his keen senses. Had it been only a mirage, brought on by panic, loss of sleep, too much caffeine? Anguish spilled over me then, the old mixing with the new, loss upon loss. "I thought of you, you know," I told Jolon. "For years I wondered where you were. I wished you'd kept writing to me."

"This isn't the time to talk of it. It was a long time ago."

I stared into his silvery eyes. "Tell me while I catch my breath. Tell me what happened."

Some old emotion tensed the muscles in his face. Something he thought he'd put away for good, maybe. Here I was, dredging it up again.

"It's not a pretty story."

"I don't want a pretty story. Tell me. Jolon, just . . . help me think of something else."

He leaned into my tree, shoved his hands in the pockets of his jeans. "My mother, she was . . . not herself after my dad died. I think she was scared, on her own. I tried to help her, tried to be the man of the family, but what did I know? I was only a kid. Anyway, she just one day said to pack a bag. She'd sold the horses already. She hadn't told me, but she sold the house, too."

He'd come to find me that day. Rode his bike through the summer heat so hard the sweat soaked his shirt, and mine when he'd held me, kissed me for the last time, told me he'd write. That he'd never forget me.

"I didn't even know where we were going. I didn't mean to lose you. I wanted to come back, but she needed me. I thought she needed me. But then . . . that fall, she skipped out. She left while I was on a weekend camping trip with the Brothers."

"What brothers? Where were you?"

"This one man my mother was seeing was a pipe fitter. We moved up to Maine with him for a job. Portland. Lived in one cold-water flat after another. I wrote you that once, then . . . well, you'd know and what could you do?"

I put a hand on his arm, surprising in its dense solidity, like a stone arm. He didn't step away. I watched his eyes, shifting like the sky, darken to the color of a bruise.

"So," he continued, "one weekend, the pipe fitter says, 'Those good Jesuit Brothers are taking kids from the neighborhood on a camping trip. Why shouldn't the boy go?' I didn't want to, I felt something was wrong with it, said I wouldn't. The pipe fitter cuffed my ear and told me, 'You're going.' So, I went. When the Brothers dropped me off at home, the latest cold-water flat was empty. Not a stick of furniture, no sign of my mother or the pipe fitter."

I wanted to hold him then. I felt how it had been with us. I wanted to sink into the magic of that memory for comfort, mine or his or it didn't matter which. Then I realized I'd bitten my lip so hard it bled. I tasted iron in my mouth, and knew how stupid I was being. Maybe I'd longed for Jolon once. But it was better if he didn't think of that, if I didn't.

"I was lucky, really." He broke in on my tangle of thoughts. "It would have been a sadder story had I gone with them."

"Didn't you have anyone to take you in? My parents would have, if they'd known."

"The Brothers kept me. Taught me this, taught me everything I know. I was raised by the Jesuit wolves of Maine." His wintry smile flickered. "Ah, Reve, it's been over and done a long time."

But I had to know one thing more. "Why did you come back here? Why not stay in Maine?"

He turned his head, so I couldn't see his eyes. "I guess because this was home to me. The only home I ever had. With a family. With a friend. You were home to me."

For some reason I couldn't name, I felt a rush of relief. We'd been friends first, for years, after all. Jolon was, could be, a friend. It didn't have to be complicated.

"That's good to know," I told him.

I thought I'd better leave it at that. I lifted Zar's reins from where they'd fallen in the grassy verge of the stream, put my foot in the stirrup, and jumped myself into the saddle. Because friend or no, old love or no, it didn't matter. He hadn't seen my girls, didn't know where they were. My vision of them still seemed so real, but it had to be just in my head, my heart, my hoping. We had to keep on searching. Our side trip to the past was over.

"Thank you for telling me." I scanned the road, the woods again. "Now I need to go."

I rode out. After a few steps, something made me turn back. But Jolon had already melted into the forest. He didn't reveal himself again.

2

I searched every little footpath and streambed at that end of Middle Road, where it dips neatly into Charlemont, hits Route 8. I saw nothing more remarkable than falling leaves and flecks of pink aster in the weeds by the roadside, and the usual scattered cadre of men and women in fatigues or blaze orange. Some nodded at me when I passed, stopped to talk for a moment, but not one told me they'd found anything, seen anything. Jolon, too, had seen nothing. My sighting of the girls was just a hallucination, then. Blame it on a fevered imagination.

It took me over an hour to trot home, and it was nearly dark when I returned. Dad had been looking out for me, came to me in the barn and untacked Zar when I fell off and sat on a hay bale, watching while he gave my horse a sponge bath, threw a sheet over him, fed him a good supper.

"Anything happen while I was gone?" I asked. I hadn't told him about seeing the phantom girls, but Dad was pretending distraction, playing the absentminded professor. I'd learned to see through it. He had something he wanted to conceal as well.

"Went to Savoy."

Savoy was only forest, dotted with a few Tyvek houses.

"Why?"

"We got a call this afternoon. Hunters found the carcass of a horse. On Savoy mountain. That's why they wanted me there. To see if I could make anything of it, since they couldn't reach you."

"What color was the horse?" My heart raced then, as I hoped wildly for *bay* or *dun*. Not gray, not black. Oh, please.

"Black. What they can tell. The body's been damaged by predators. Not much but bones and some skin left, really."

"Could that have happened in two days?"

"They seem to think it's possible. A pack of coyotes had been at it. Have to wait for the lab results."

"The tattoo isn't there? The microchip?" All our horses had identifying tattoos and had been chipped when I bought them.

"No tattoo left. And they couldn't find a chip. But in the state of decomposition, they had to take it in to tell much."

"Maybe I should see it . . ."

"There's so little left. You don't need that, Reve. They'll try to match DNA samples from Brio's hair."

"They didn't find anything else? Anything that could mean the girls had been there?"

"Not yet. They're broadening the search, though, to Savoy and Plainfield."

"Are they moving out of Hawley, then?"

"Tomorrow, Jolon says."

Probably only the phone men in the van would remain. But even they had moved outside the gates, so we couldn't see them. The next day, we'd be more exposed, more vulnerable. The internal clock chimed fifty-two hours.

3

That night there were no helicopters circling the forest. It was eerily quiet. My parents went home, to get some real rest. Two police cars remained at the gate, courtesy of Jolon.

Mrs. Pike left us beef stew, fresh baked bread, a green bean casserole. It was a heavy meal for the strange, almost sickly warm weather. But it was autumn and Mrs. Pike's Yankee notions of meal planning didn't bend to the weather, only the seasons. I sat down to dinner, for Caleigh's sake if not my own. Mrs. Pike had cooked and cleaned as if nothing unusual was happening, shooing policemen and -women aside with her vacuum when need be. When I asked her to please not talk to the reporters hanging around the forest entrances, she'd just snorted and said, "I'd run 'em down before talking to that pack of jackals."

Caleigh still seemed strangely untroubled. Maybe she was trying to convince herself it was all fine and that the twins would be back any minute. Her eyes were clear of worry, she slept soundly, ate all the food placed before her, played her usual games. She was even talking about plans for Halloween in a few days, what we would do if Grace and Fai were back, what we would do if they weren't. I tried to be glad that she seemed so unaffected, but it was eerie, too. At nine, I tucked her in on the couch, and in moments she was asleep and dreaming.

Caleigh's Vision: Fires in the Night

Caleigh was dreaming of the past. Shreds she'd picked up from the string, here and there. The great fire that burned the Hawley Inn to the ground, where Earl's and the hardware store now sat, was started when a monkey from a traveling circus pushed over a lantern. The building was lost but the monkey was saved.

The string also told her of the naming of Hell's Kitchen Road, the strange name she'd asked her Gramps about when they saw the sign at the edge of the forest. He didn't know, but the string did. Now it seemed normal that the string told her the past, as well as turned the future for her.

Hell's Kitchen Road had been called North Road until the summer of 1883. Edith Miniter, a teenage girl dressed in a long, pretty ruffled dress, was with her friend Evanore Beebe, walking along the road. They'd come from Wilbraham, sixty miles away, to visit Evanore's Warriner cousins for the summer. They were picking berries and didn't notice how dark it was getting, until they saw lights in the trees. They dropped their baskets and ran for home, feeling strange heat and a presence near them. The next morning, berries and baskets were gone without trace. Folks said the devil and his minions made pies in Hell's Kitchen that night, having scared the berries right away from Edith and Evanore.

But Caleigh saw more. She saw a woman with fiery hair streaming, snakes on her wrists, gathering the baskets, the berries, placing one between her lips, sweet juice running, staining them red. Then she saw children leading cows down the road, red-and-white cows. Behind the cows, she saw her sisters and their horses. They rode right up to the woman, who told them, "Take these berries, plucked for us. We'll make pies now."

Caleigh spoke in her sleep. Her mother walked by, heard her say, "Fairy pies, all right."

4

After Caleigh was asleep, I climbed the stairs to my office. *The Hawley Book of the Dead* was still sprawled on the floor where I'd thrown it. I picked it up, smoothed its blank pages. Why had it stopped yielding to me, when I was so desperate for knowledge? Why couldn't I command it better? If that Book could be a tool to find my girls, then I would learn it, I would find a way to make it bend to my will, never mind Nan's warning me not to do so. I shook it, tried to make it give up its secrets. That didn't work.

I thought back to the times it *had* worked. In each instance, I'd been in a kind of trance. I'd come at the Book sideways, not head-on. The way a good horseman approaches a horse. Maybe I could cultivate that state again. Rage and panic didn't seem to get me anywhere.

I sat with the Book on my lap and idly picked up a deck of Gypsy Witch cards that Caleigh had left on my desk. She liked to use them for every card game and would announce the message on the cards she was dealt, taking the risk that her opponents might recognize the card and guess her hand. But somehow, none of us could keep it in our heads that "Children signify friendly disposition" meant the queen of diamonds, or that "The cat indicates flattery" and also the eight of hearts.

I shuffled the deck and made one card leap and spin. It had been a long time since I'd practiced my sleight of hand. The cards felt thick in my hands, not supple and quick as they used to. I picked up the card, which had landed facedown after its leap. The queen of spades. Its message, for some reason best known to Mlle. Le Normand, supposed creator of Gypsy Witch cards, was that of "Amor." A sign that someone was thinking of you with great love and longing. I flipped the card back into the deck. Thought of Jolon, pushed the thought back. Made another card jump, hoping for something benign. The cat, with its flat face for flattery, maybe. But up jumped the jack of hearts: the book, which presages the solution of a mystery, affecting one for the better. I could only hope that one would come true. I pulled another card from the deck. The mountains. "The presence of a mighty enemy," I read on the face of the card, just as mountains loomed up toward me, jagged, unlike any mountains in New England. And suddenly I seemed to be flying over them, over red rock formations that looked fantastical and eerie. On a high ridge I saw a figure in a tuxedo with long tails. A magician, his wand raised toward the east. His stance seemed familiar, his brilliant black hair. But his face was a blur, hidden from me by the velocity of my flight. My brain felt like a fire trapped in my skull. Fire. The Valley of Fire. *That* was where the magician was, the Valley of Fire, east of Las Vegas. We'd ridden there plenty of times. I recognized the landscape, the red rock hullocks and arches. My body shuddered. Whatever kept me airborne failed. My heart plunged, and I heard the magician shout a word, a magic word. Something came rushing at me then, white with dark marks. It was *The Hawley Book of the Dead*, and I fell into its thick pages.

Rigel Voss once had a wife. Alice, an old-fashioned name. They'd met in a Laundromat. He had gone out to do some shopping, left his clothes in a dryer. When he returned, she was folding them. Not as well as he would have, but still. He felt something stirring, a seed husk cracking inside him. His mother had died when he was in college, and no one had taken care of his basic needs since.

"Come have a coffee with me. Just around the corner. I'd like to thank you," he said to the top of her golden head. Her small hands were still smoothing his shirts. When she tipped her face up and smiled, a flash of dimples, and freckles, and very white skin, he realized how young she must be. Just a kid. Doing laundry for her mother, maybe. He regretted asking her for coffee. She'd think he was some kind of sicko. "But your mother probably expects you home."

She laughed. A rasp of a laugh, like a handsaw cutting through pine. "My mother lives in Florida. Nobody expects me home. I know I look about twelve, but I'm on the right side of twenty, old enough for a guy to ask me out." Her voice was unexpected, deep and sultry. He watched her walk away from him, her long pale hair cut straight across, separated like stems of flowers down her back. She wore cutoff jeans, a white camisole, practically nothing. Moving as if she might be a dancer, graceful, slow, her feet in daisyed flip-flops turned in delicately. She stopped at the glass door, her reflection ghostly. She turned back to him. "You coming?"

They sat drinking coffee from thick mugs while Rigel Voss fell in love. He realized that the girl wasn't pretty. Her face was a little asymmetrical, one side turned up more than the other. Then there were the freckles; her hazel eyes were more the color of a toad than either gold or green. But he liked her smallness, the deep voice that cracked when she laughed. Her old-timey name seemed sweet to him.

Alice worked in a grocery store, counted money, took night classes in French. They went to Paris for their honeymoon, just before he was assigned to Amherst. She called him her secret agent man. She teased him, when no one else ever had. She was eight months' pregnant when the disappearing girl ruined them. He still missed her every day, still woke up sweating and parched most nights from his Alice nightmares. He woke from one that morning in a cabin at Candy Cane Park. But if he played his cards right, the red-haired woman, that Revelation, would give him his Alice back. No more nightmares, only golden days with her again.

He decided to stop in the town on his way out to the highway, back to the next phase of his plan. He'd not been to Hawley Village and knew it was a risk, as they'd be alerted, suspicious of strangers. But he had shaved the beard that the arrow man had seen him with. Even if they had a composite, he looked different enough. He'd ditched the SUV in Pittsfield, snagged another car, changed the plates, and had a fresh new identity before the cops even knew to look for him. He was Abel Carmichael, retired roofer. What he'd told the cops when they'd questioned him. It was easy enough, after all the years of being a nowhere man. He'd been prepared. People believed what was right in front of them. So he stopped in Pizza by Earl for coffee, a three-egg breakfast. He sat at the counter, let the conversation swirl around him. It was all about the girls, as he knew it would be.

"What time they go missing?" asked a twenty-something man in a Green Day T-shirt.

"Around supper time day before yesterday. Been all over the news. Where you been, Sam?"

Sam shrugged. "Nowhere special. Just didn't pay my cable bill."

"Well, I hope they find them soon." The waitress, a very thin woman with upswept dyed yellow hair, poured Rigel Voss his coffee as she spoke, then swung around to take the order of a man in plaid flannel. "For their own sake, and mine, too. That helicopter woke me up in the night. I thought they found a pot field. You want the steak?"

"Yeah. And two over, Paula. I think they run away. How else could girls on horses just disappear?"

"If they run away, they'd a found 'em by now." An older man in carpenter coveralls weighed in. "Where could they go on horses?"

Voss thought he'd better seem curious. "The daughters of that lady magician? I heard it on the news up at Candy Cane Park. Been hunting in Hawley Forest." He didn't mention the cops' visit to him.

"Well, you won't be hunting there no more till those girls are found. Got the whole forest in an uproar, not letting hunters in, even."

"Yeah, I heard that. So what happened? Anybody know more than was on the news?"

"I bet they ditched the horses, then went out to the highway and hitchhiked," the flannel-shirted man said.

The carpenter said portentously, "Naw. It wasn't that. Horses would've run home. Boy, it doesn't look good. Jolon didn't find much to speak of, he said. Ran into him at the hardware." They all fell silent.

"Didn't find nothing?" Paula held her coffeepot poised.

"Not so he'd say."

"Well, that's what I woulda done if I was running away. Hitchhiked, like Scott said." This from a young woman with teased hair and long green nails, placing four large coffees in a cardboard tray.

"Aw, Gina, who'd cut our hair if you run away?" The carpenter put an arm around the girl, which she slapped at. "Ray, you old fool. Don't paw at me." But she was trying to suppress a smile. "I don't think it's funny. That poor woman. I can't imagine how she feels. I remember seeing her in Vegas, too. She put on a great show."

The flannel-shirted man turned to her, said in mock surprise, "Hey, when did you go to Vegas? I can't remember the last time I didn't see you here in the morning for your coffee buzz."

She raised her small pointy chin. "Shows how much you know. I've been plenty of places. To Vegas twice.

The Grand Canyon. Even England. I stayed in a castle there, too. . . ."

"Oh, yeah. Like you're some kinda Cinderella. Didn't find your prince, though, didja?" She swatted at him, too.

"Anyway, it doesn't matter who she is. I just feel bad for the mother."

"Doesn't hurt that she's famous," Scott said.

Paula, brushing her resplendently clean pink uniform with a napkin, said, "Oh, honey, we all feel bad for her." She cut the men a look. "Even if she *is* famous. It doesn't matter. When you lose a child, doesn't matter who you are. I think you guys ought to be helping search, instead of jawing here."

"When they makes it known they want volunteers, I'll sign up. But Jolon, I expect, knows what he's doing."

"None better." Paula reached the coffeepot over Rigel Voss's cup. "This bollixes up the hunting for you, though. Where you from?"

Voss looked up. "From over New York State. I've only been here a couple days."

"Didn't get nothing?"

"Nah. Shame about those girls." He held his hand over the cup. "And too bad about the hunting. But I should be getting back, anyway. My wife wants to get the kitchen remodel finished before we start for Florida this year. Go to the Keys for the winter." A few well-chosen facts to make him seem innocuous, normal. It didn't matter that he had no wife, not anymore, had never been to the Florida Keys. "Thought I'd get my deer for the freezer, but maybe the fishing down south will be better than the hunting this year." He stood up, stretched, put a two-dollar tip under his plate. "Sure hope those girls get found." And he slouched out the door, out of Hawley.

5

I came gasping up from the vision, sweating and parched. I struggled to make sense of what I'd seen. Voss had left the forest. Did he have the girls or not? What did he want from me? And what did the magician I'd seen in the Valley of Fire have to do with it all? I tried to think it through. The Book, Nan had said, would tell me what I most needed to know. Why would I need to know about Rigel Voss's Alice?

Then it hit me. The Book could transport me, to the past, to other places in the present. More to the point, the Book could take me to Jeremy. Voss must know about the Book. And believe he could force me to use it. He wanted to be with his wife again. He wanted revenge, but he wanted his Alice more. He could use the twins as a bargaining chip. Voss could have them now—they could be bound and gagged somewhere, like Wesley on the day Jeremy died.

But nothing I'd seen, in the Book or in the solid world, made anything clear. Where in all this tangled web *were* my girls?

Tuatha De Danann—October 29, 2013

1

The next day, the sky was threatening. The unsettled air unsettled me, made my throat constrict. The tears caught there, as usual. *Sixty-three hours,* the internal clock told me. I knew if I did start to cry, I'd never stop. I just wanted my life to be normal. I wanted never to have been born with my magical gifts, or at least never crossed paths with Rigel Voss. If it hadn't been for our long-ago encounter, I'd never have lost Jeremy. The twins would not be missing now. I wanted my family together again. I wanted to have my freedom, no need to hide, to constantly monitor my daughters, to try, then fail, to keep them safe. I wanted more than anything for Jeremy to be alive. I wanted all kinds of impossible things.

Caleigh was still asleep on the parlor sofa. I'd slept in a chair beside her. Nathan was making coffee for us, and Falcon Eddy paced the driveway. I needed to do something. I went out to the barn, grabbed a scythe. I started hacking away at the nettles growing along the fence line, scaring Zar and Miss May. Zar trotted to the other side of the barn; Miss May followed with a cough of disgust.

I felt the sweat pearling on my skin, a fine layer of dust stuck to me. I licked the salt off my upper lip, looked up, and Jolon was there, his smile unsettling me more than the thunderclouds.

"If you gather them to boil, they're the best greens there are. You'll want to wash yourself well after your battle, though." He took the scythe from my hand. "And when you find you're covered with nettle rash, slather yourself with olive oil. Takes out the sting."

I grabbed the wood handle of the scythe right back. I began swinging the blade again, too near Jolon's legs, but he didn't jump. "I don't need anyone telling me what to do about my nettles."

He took hold of the scythe handle again, stilled it. His hand stayed over mine, our fingers entwined. My nerves were pulsing with a riot of fear and crazy fury.

"Reve, you can't bring them back by punishing yourself."

I held the fury, but I longed to burn him with it. Then I sagged and he caught me, kneeling with me on the ground as if we were praying. My head dropped to his shoulder. I fought the tears coming, held on to them, held to him as well until my grip left welts on his arms. He smoothed my sweaty hair, touched my face. I could feel the nettle rash coming out in bursts on the tender skin just above my collarbone. I had a flash of thinking he might kiss me there. It was the last thing I wanted. I sucked in a sob, pushed him away. I balled my hands into fists, pounded his chest. "I'm scared. I'm scared I'll never see them again!"

He tried to put his arms around me, but I fought him. We were still on our knees, like some congregation of two. I held myself away, looked away from his kind eyes. He was an anesthetic to soothe my pain, but I didn't want that. I wanted to feel all the pain, all the anger, let it fuel me.

"I know you can find them!" My voice listed like an old rowboat on a wild sea. "So what are you doing here?" I rose, stumbled, nearly fell, and he caught me again. He was always catching me when I fell, and I resented it. Jeremy let me fall, knew I would be fine. Brave. I batted Jolon's hands away. I started walking but he followed, gripped my arm.

"Reve, listen to me. I can't say I know what you're going through. But I've been all around it. I can tell you you're going to blame yourself, me, everyone. You're going to be depressed, you're going to grieve. You'll lash out, then you'll be sorry. It's all normal. I can tell you that. And it's not me you're angry with, Reve. It's yourself. You have to help me by cutting yourself some slack, whenever you can. Because whatever I do, whatever you do, it's not enough. It won't be enough until your daughters walk through that door."

"When will that be?" I snapped at him. "You have no idea, right?"

"I know one thing: We have to trust each other, Reve. Remember when we were kids and we told each other everything?"

I did. I remembered too well.

"I know there's more happening than you're telling me."

He was right. But how could I tell him about *The Hawley Book of the Dead*, my visions, the crazy stuff Nan had said? I rubbed my face where he'd touched me, swiped at my sweaty forehead again. He took my hand, held it away from my face. "Stop that. You'll get nettle rash in your eyes."

"I don't care."

"I care."

"I don't need you to care about me." I pulled my hand from his, pointed an accusing finger at him. "I need you to care about my girls. You can find them. You can find the Fetch. Rigel Voss. Whatever you say, whatever you've been told about his supposed death, it *is* him. You had your chance to catch him. Now he's gone. He was the guy at Candy Cane Park." I turned and stalked toward the house.

"Reve!"

I spun around. "Do you know how long it's been, Jolon? I do. I know, I *feel* every moment!"

I ran then, wrenched the door open, slammed it after me. I leaned against the hard wood, a solid enough barrier between Jolon and me. I felt like screaming. Instead I kicked the iron pig boot scraper in the mudroom, and the lurch of pain was a relief.

I limped into the kitchen, where I found Caleigh, wide awake, sitting with Nathan and Falcon Eddy. She was working her string and listening to them debate the merits of wooden as opposed to carbon fiber arrows. Falcon Eddy pointed to a note on the table. "Your housekeeper, the redoubtable Mrs. Pike, says she left a casserole in the oven for later. Said she had to go make her granddaughters' costumes for Halloween."

"Halloween?"

"Day after tomorrow, Mom," Caleigh reminded me, her eyes bright with anticipation. "What are we gonna do? Where are we going to trick-or-treat?"

"Oh, honey, I don't know. I just don't." I'd forgotten all about it.

I went to the bathroom, peeled off my clothes and stepped into the warm spray of the shower, trying not to feel anything except the sharp bite of the nettle stings. After I dried off, I changed into jeans and a sweater. My clothes hung on me. I'd probably lost five pounds in the past few days, in spite of Mrs.

Pike's efforts. I had been living on tea and coffee, I realized. At least I was clean.

I heard the *ooga-ooga* of the Packard's horn, along with the first rumblings of thunder, and went downstairs.

Caleigh came running out, hugged my mom. "I brought your Halloween costume, lovey."

"Ooh, my Harry Potter robes?"

"You bet."

She grabbed them and ran. "I'm going to show Nathan and Falcon Eddy!" Caleigh's absence gave me a chance I'd been waiting for.

I led my parents inside, closed the door to the parlor.

"I went to see Nan, just before all this. I meant to talk to you, to tell you both what she said, but . . ."

"Oh, honey." Mom led me to the sofa, sat me down. "What did Nan say?"

I told them her story, how she'd lived in Hawley and thought she'd disappeared the town. And I told them how I'd seen the girls by the stream, how if Nan was right, maybe they were in the forest, still, but somehow hidden.

"Didn't Nan ever tell you this story? About her past in Hawley, the missing children, being spirited away, any of it?"

"She didn't tell me, or your aunts." Mom shook her head, frowning.

Dad pushed his glasses further up his nose, getting settled in for a professorial riff.

My father's field is comparative literature, his own special niche being folk and fairy tales, and their intersection with hedge magic. He made an academic name for himself when he traveled small European towns for five years after graduate school and compiled a collection of folktales that had been buried by time, handed down only orally, and unknown to scholars. Then he came to Williams to teach, met my mother. I always privately thought that it was the fairy-tale quality of my mother's family stories that drew him to her. That, and the Dyer powers. He had his own personal witch. He never did join my uncles in their jokes over the family legends.

"Well. There are many reputedly haunted villages scattered about New England, as well as France and Britain, of course. In Connecticut there's Dudleytown, where something similar supposedly occurred. The town just vanishing. And then Glastenbury, Vermont, and what's called the Bennington Triangle, where up to nine people disappeared in the 1940s and '50s under quite mysterious circumstances. Only two were ever found, and they had no recollection of where they'd been. One man disappeared during a bus trip, not at a stop, but while the bus was en route. The passengers swore to it, as well as the bus driver. But since we've lived here, I've never heard any such local legends about Hawley, nor read anything about it. Have you asked anyone here?"

"Carl Streeter told me about the auction, how the houses all were left with everything still in them. When I asked him more about it, he tried to change the subject. Then one of Nan's contemporaries told me pretty much the same story in Pizza Earl's. And you know I can't get anyone local to work at the house. Except Mrs. Pike, who charges me double her normal rate. It does seem as if people are reluctant to go into the forest, especially near Five Corners. Or even to talk about it."

"Maybe the town itself wants to remain unknown."

I didn't laugh. It didn't seem funny.

Dad went on. "One thing I've come to believe in after all my work on legend and folklore is the spirit of place. Some places on earth, and a surprising number of them, have been centers of evil or of good. They're powerful. Because of events that happened there, or ley lines, or some unknown presence, whether mineral or spiritual. They attract certain happenings, and not just one, but layers of them. In England, Avalon is supposed to be located somewhere near Glastonbury, as Stonehenge is. Many other places that have to do with Grail legend are certainly layered in that way. Temple Church in London, for one. And then certain places are good for certain disciplines. Writing, for instance. In Cummington, just over the hill from Hawley, the same ridge has been home to three national poet laureates over the course of a century, seemingly by pure chance. So the Dyer influence may be particularly strong in Hawley. That could be why Nan thought you'd be safe from the Fetch here."

"But he was *here*. I know he was. And I'm certain he killed Maggie. He wants revenge. For something, something he's convinced is my fault. And, well . . . I saw it all in this book." I pulled out *The Hawley Book of the Dead*. I opened it.

"Even though the pages are blank now, yesterday they weren't. Mom, have you ever seen this?"

She looked stricken. Her eyes were fixed on the Book.

"Mom?"

She rose, her hands clenched so hard her knuckles were white. "I need some water," she said, her voice hoarse. She started toward the kitchen sink, but halfway there, she stopped, and her body shuddered. My dad rushed to her, sat her down again. I remembered the strange kind of fit she'd had at the Hawley fair, when she seemed to be choking. I got a glass and filled it with water for her.

"Here, Mom." She clutched at the glass, drank deeply. Beads

of sweat trickled down her face. She opened her lips, but no sound came.

I turned to my father, frantic. "Dad, what's wrong with her?"

He shook his head, but she fixed her golden eyes on him, her expression pleading.

"P-p-p-p . . ." she stammered, and her hand swiped at his shirt pocket. He pulled a pen from it, took the cap off, and she grasped it. Her eyes raked the room. I ran for the pad of paper near the phone.

She held the pen with both hands and scribbled out the words *tell, tell, tell.*

"Okay, honey," Dad said. "I'll tell what I can."

She squeezed her eyes shut. Nodded once.

My father took the Book from my hands, tried to prize its covers open. It wouldn't budge.

"It's a grimoire, I think," he told me. "Grimoires hold instructions in how to perform magic, sometimes also records of how they've been used, who has used them. Where did you find it?"

"It was hidden in the wall beneath the portrait in my office. Nan said she hid it in Hawley after what happened in 1924. My visions of Voss came from the Book."

I told them how I'd seen Rigel Voss's departure, and his time at Pizza Earl's, as well as the strange vision of the magician. Dad got up and paced while I talked.

"Nan mentioned the Tuatha De Danann. Does that mean anything to you?"

My mom gave a strangled cry. *Tell her, tell her,* she wrote.

Dad gave my mother a quizzical look. "I thought she should know all along, Morgan. Right from the beginning." My mother glared at him. He sighed, turned to me. "Nan never wanted you to know any of this. She made sure your mother wouldn't be able to tell this part of the family history, ever. You can see the result. It's the same with your aunts. Only the approved tales can pass their lips."

Mom slapped the table with her hand, scribbled *just TELL IT!!!*

Dad reached over and stopped her hands. "All of it?"

My mother nodded frantically, made another stifled sound.

"All right." He turned back to me. "You remember Nan's Tuatha De Danann stories from when you were little?"

"They were like fairy tales, bedtime stories. I don't remember much about them."

"Well." He took a breath and plunged on. "Many women in the Dyer family—Mary Dyer, some of the Revelations, and now it seems even your grandmother—have been accused of being witches. It wasn't uncommon in New England, into the last century. Maybe even now, in some places. It's why we don't broadcast this story, why your Nan made it impossible for her daughters to speak of it at all. Why court trouble? The Dyer women have had enough of that over the centuries.

"But I did some research into the origins of the family. Mary Dyer's mother, who was really the first of the Revelations I can trace, was born not in England, but in Ireland. She came from Drogheda, in County Meath."

"Where Newgrange is?" Jeremy and I had gone to Ireland for our honeymoon, and stayed in the Kilcoole house. Newgrange was one of our day trips, to see the underground fortress, the megalithic goddess cult carvings.

"Yes, exactly. Revelation Cullen was her name, but she took the name of Dyer when she immigrated to England and joined the Puritan sect. You see, *Cuilleann* means the holly tree, sacred to the Tuatha De Danann. So the place names, Mt. Holly and Hawley, go back to that, they must. But Dyer, well, Dyer was the name for anyone who could change the color of their skin or cloth or hair. Usually with the help of plant-based dyes. But in this case, maybe she didn't need them."

My mother shot him an impatient glance. "I know, I know. I'm getting ahead of the story. Or behind it." He paused to push his glasses up the bridge of his nose again. "But, yes, my premise is that the girl, Revelation Cullen, descended from the Tuatha De Danann and was a shape-shifter. Her name change might have reflected that power, while hiding her Tuatha De ancestry."

"But weren't the Tuatha De Danann just, well, fairies?" I said with a laugh. Witches, I could just about believe. Shape-shifters and fairies stretched credulity.

"No. That's incorrect. Not fairies," my father insisted. "The Tuatha De Danann were considered an actual historical people until the seventeenth century. They were human, but it was thought that they had supernatural powers. The seventeenth century was a time of witch trials and the war of Protestant and Catholic beliefs. But I think both were really signifiers of the final battle in the war against the goddess cults. The Tuatha De Danann were goddess worshippers. They had blended and intermarried with the Milesians, the first of the modern Irish peoples. Then they were forced further underground, so to speak, to avoid the persecution of those who were different, perhaps those who had powers that seemed superhuman. It's quite possible that Revelation Cullen left Ireland because of persecution by the Catholic Church. That she'd been an accused witch, or was about to be accused."

"So she hid with the Puritans? That doesn't seem very safe, considering."

"It might have been the lesser of two evils at the time. The facts are that a girl named Cullen left County Meath in 1632 and was accepted as a member of a Leicester Puritan congregation, where she was known as Revelation Dyer. She later gave birth to a daughter, Mary Dyer, who immigrated to Boston."

"So you're saying that we're not only witches, but have fairy blood, too."

"Tuatha De Danann blood. They *were* thought of as fairies. But not fairies as we've come to portray them, tiny winged people. They were humans with some strange powers. Like witches. It really all came down to the fact that these women had unusual talents. Passed on through the generations. Right down to you both. To Caleigh. And to Grace and Fai."

"They don't have their powers yet."

"We don't know that."

It was true. "No. I guess we don't." I supposed it was possible, just, that Grace and Fai had come into their powers, whatever they were, then had a hard time controlling them. Whether that was true, or whether Rigel Voss had them, would I ever see them again?

My father continued, "I *know* that you all, descended from Tuatha De Danann as you very well may be, have powers outside the norm. That certain places or situations attract and strengthen those powers, because of your history. The history of your people."

"Places like Hawley Five Corners."

"Certainly Hawley Five Corners. Maybe any place where five roads come together. Crossroads have always been considered magical places, and five roads converging the most mystical. Perhaps Revelation Dyer chose Five Corners as a place to settle because of the convergence."

"Why five? Why not three?"

"Well, three is the number of Christianity. The Holy Trinity. Five has always been considered an especially spiritual number as well. But not in Christian myth. For the Jews there's the Pentateuch, the five books of Moses, then in many non-Christian faiths the five-pointed star, or pentagram, is significant; the fact that goddess-worshipping cultures had a five-season calendar, the perfect fifth on which all Western harmonies are based is also . . ."

"Okay, Dad. I get it. So the power might still be here is what you're saying? To be called upon when needed."

"It's a theory. There's one more thing. The Danann possibility may mean more than you think. You see, it most often seems to kick in when there's danger. When Nan was . . . well, wherever she was for those months, there was a real threat. Children were being kidnapped. She returned only after the danger was past. No more children disappeared after her return, did they?"

"No. I don't think so."

"Then since the girls haven't returned, the danger's still present. Still out there."

"You mean because Voss is still around?"

"Quite possibly."

I thought on that for a moment.

"You know Voss means to do them harm, whether he has them now or finds them before we can. And the Book didn't tell you how far he's gone." My father had a point. "Either way, the girls won't return until the threat is past."

My mother gasped, and her hand flew to her throat. Her

breath was ragged. "If something . . . if something does happen . . . remember what your father's told you. You should remember it, remember *who you are*."

"You mean the Danann blood?" I was still skeptical. "That didn't do Mary Dyer much good. She was hanged, after all."

"She escaped once, went back to England," Dad told us. "She didn't have to return. She chose it. To die for her beliefs."

Mom trembled. She took my face, turned it toward her own. Panic flared in her eyes. "You don't have to die for this. If something happens. Mary Dyer wasn't a Revelation."

"What does that have to do with it?"

"The Revelations have the strongest powers of the Dyers."

"Why did you name *me* Revelation?"

"Nan knew," Mom told me. "She said we should give you the name. It means you have more ability than most to tap into your powers. Powers you may not even know you have until they're needed. Just remember that. *Remember* if ever you . . . well, if you're in trouble. Use whatever gifts you have to protect yourself." Her voice was urgent.

"Okay, okay. I'll remember." How could I forget? She was still inspecting my eyes, as if she was trying to read my future in them.

One thing still puzzled me. "Why can *you* tell me all this, Dad? Why didn't Nan put a . . . a spell on you?"

"That I couldn't say. Maybe she needed a repository of knowledge. For this day."

Mom clutched my hand until it hurt. The golden depths of her eyes held an old terror. "Reve, please, *please* be careful." Her voice was wrought, uneven. "When you first started . . . disappearing . . . you were only two years old. I'd be playing with you, or bathing you, and you would just suddenly be gone.

We were frantic, searching everywhere. We knew what it was, knew that it was your power. But we didn't know where you were, or how to find you. We couldn't exactly call the police." She laughed, a throttled sound. "We could do nothing but keep looking, hoping you'd return. Our greatest fear was that you'd be trapped there somehow, never come back to us. Then we would find you. In a closet or curled under your bed.

"You came back in terrible shape. With raging fevers, infected wounds. Sometimes you had been . . . beaten. You were just a baby!" My mother broke down then, clasping me to her so tightly my breath came in little gasps. "If I hadn't been able to heal you, you would have died. I thought *I'd* die, from panic and grief, and *not knowing*, every time. We began teaching you to curb your power then, but . . . oh, Reve, we came so close to losing you!" She sobbed quietly then, and I held her. It was strangely like comforting myself.

Cemetery Road—October 30, 2013

1

I just wanted my daughters back. I wanted them with me. I wanted their high clear laughter, their quick litheness on horseback, even the maddening teenage slumping they reverted to as soon as their feet hit the ground. I wanted to yell at them for their bad posture, threaten them with yoga classes, as much as I wanted to hold them close. I just wanted another normal day with them.

I tried to stay focused, to keep despair from overtaking me, but when my thoughts turned to ancient races with godlike powers in a land under the ground, that made me feel hopeless, too. Why we no longer want to believe in magic in our real lives is a puzzle, but we don't. The possibility frightens us, makes us retreat into the turtle shells that our rational minds are. We don't like to be spooked, except perhaps on Halloween, which was fast approaching. The night all the evils beyond the rational world are given full reign.

I half-expected Jolon wouldn't be there that morning, after my stupid behavior in the nettles the previous day. But I found him in the barn giving Zar an apple.

"Mea culpa," I told him.

"That's what the Brothers used to say. I always thought it was a slippery way of apologizing. You know, saying it in Latin was almost like absolving themselves. It made the original wrong less real, somehow."

"I'm sorry, then."

"Ah, I didn't mean you. You don't have anything to be sorry for. It was my fault. I pushed you, and I had no right."

"Well, let's just say we're both sorry." I stood next to him, leaning against Zar's stall door. "I guess you'd have told me right off, but is there any news?"

"Not much. We're still in Savoy." Jolon hoisted the full bucket, started carrying it to Zar's stall. I tried to grab it from him, but he calmly lifted the bucket to its hook.

"I can do that," I sniped at him. I made myself take a deep breath. "Okay, I'll try to be civil. Why are you still searching Savoy forest? Do you really think the horse they found might have been Brio?" I held my breath, waiting for his answer.

"It's unlikely, but not all the DNA tests are in. And it's possible the girls rode through to Savoy. It's not far, after all. We'll be searching again in Hawley tomorrow. There are other factors, though." He didn't volunteer what they were.

I could feel my temper flare again. "Oh? Is that so?" I grabbed Zar's halter, led him to the cross ties, and started currying him.

"Yes, it's so," Jolon said. He was weary. Or exasperated. "Reve, you're welcome to bring in a private detective, another tracker. Hell, bring in a damn psychic if you want. But the way the search is being conducted is not the problem."

"Then what *is* the problem?" I snapped, and immediately regretted it. He looked pained, and exhausted, and older. The case of my missing girls was aging him. He sat on a stack of hay bales, ran a hand through his hair and pulled at it, as if he could coax answers out of his head that way.

"Ah, what do I know? I've been in the woods most of my life. I know this part of the world better than anywhere. I've led searches all over New England. But this . . . it's different."

I put the curry comb down on the tack box and went to sit on the bales with him. "So, where does that leave us?" I took another deep breath, forced myself to heave it out. My lungs felt like I'd been holding my breath for days. "Look, I know you're doing the best you can. But you think what? That they've been abducted by aliens?"

He gave me a look, and there was weariness in it, but also a kind of letting go. "To tell you the truth, I'm not sure what I think."

"Jolon, I know the stories about this place. And I'm hearing more, whether I want to or not. Although mostly, no one tells much. I'd forgotten what a closemouthed set you Yankees are."

"You're one. You grew up here, after all."

"And I used to ride in the forest, too, don't forget. There was a strange feeling to it then. You of all people know that. And my family . . . Look, do you want some coffee? Mrs. Pike won't be here for a while."

He checked his watch, nodded. "I ought to be in Savoy soon, but it can wait a little."

I put Zar back in his stall, to Miss May's delight, and Jolon followed me to the house. My mom was still asleep upstairs. My father and Caleigh were consulting the Ouija board in the parlor.

I poured coffee for Jolon and myself. I sat across from him, watched him spoon sugar, stir his coffee, all the time listening as if what I was saying was already known to him, was perfectly normal. "You know some of the stories. My family came here to Hawley early on. Were the first settlers, actually."

"I remember Nan's tales, yeah."

"And now I find out there were . . . disappearances in the fall of 1923. Children in the town. Then in 1924, the whole congregation of Hawley Five Corners, just gone. You know about that, right?"

Jolon nodded slowly. He paused to sip his coffee, then told me, "Most people think the church disappearances didn't really happen. That it was exaggerated over the years, that everyone just moved out."

"Not at Pizza Earl's they don't."

"I wouldn't put too much stock in what Earl and them say. The search for your girls, well, it's got some people stirred up. They're afraid that it maybe could lead to . . . trouble. Stupid, but you know what small towns are like. Mostly people just like to hear themselves talk."

"Not about this," I insisted. "No, everyone has been strangely quiet about the disappearances in the '20s. I wouldn't know anything about it, only something Carl Streeter let slip. Then an old guy named Hank told me about it at Earl's. He also told me a girl named Hannah Sears disappeared, then came back, months later."

"Well, he was around then. He's in his nineties now."

"But, Jolon, my *Nan's* name was Hannah Sears."

"Have you asked her about it?"

"Yes. She says it's true, all of it. And more. But she wouldn't have told me, except for . . ." I wouldn't say anything about the Book, not if I didn't have to. "And Hank." I went on. "It was as if he was telling me something he oughtn't. Carl Streeter tried to pass it off as just some kind of mass migration, everyone moving west all at once. But I know now that's just the story told to strangers, like me."

"Yeah, well."

I waited for some time while he looked down at his boots. This wasn't something that came easily to him, skirting the edge of the supernatural. He finally said, "I didn't know about any of this when we were kids, and I guess you didn't either. It was just an old story then. Lately, though, folks have been dredging it up again. The real story is that children were kidnapped . . . and killed, more than likely. The killer was probably around for a few months, was never caught, then moved on. No bodies were ever found. Then maybe everyone in town did just pack it up and move out, they were so traumatized by what happened."

"Then you don't believe that the forest is haunted? That it's a place that can swallow people up, never to be seen again?"

"I won't say it's not a strange place. But it's a touchy subject. It's still part of the culture here, thinking the forest is haunted. People believe it. So what? People believe a lot of crazy things. The Hawley ghost town is just another story they like to scare themselves with. But at the bottom of it is a real fear. Fear that it could happen again. Almost everyone in town was affected by those murders, then had some relative, some great-grandfather, or great-aunt or -uncle, go off in 1924. It stays in the families. Most people are still a little spooked by it."

"And you?"

"I like facts. That's what I live by. I think all the paranormal stuff is bull."

"I really don't care what they say. The forest can be haunted or not. I just need to find my girls. Where are Grace and Fai? Where the hell are they? Where do we go from here?"

Jolon chose to bring us back to the real world. "Savoy today, like I said. Then a more detailed search here, if we don't find anything. Ten or twenty abreast, covering grids over every inch of Hawley Forest. It's bound to turn up something."

"But searchers have already covered the forest."

"Not like this. Not as many. We'll have more searchers on the ground tomorrow than during the Molly Bish search."

"Molly Bish!" I remembered her, a sixteen-year-old gone missing from her western Massachusetts town. Her body had been discovered years later, just miles from her home.

Jolon winced. "Reve, I didn't mean to make a comparison. This is not the same situation. Your girls have each other, and their horses."

"Which makes it even more strange that they haven't been found."

"We have to face the fact, sooner or later, that they may have run away. Ditched the horses somewhere. Some of their texts—"

"No! I don't want to think that. It's just not who they are."

Jolon stirred the remains of his coffee, silent. "Don't you think it's crossed my mind?" I asked. "Of course I blame myself for Jeremy's death, and for them having to leave all their friends, their home. But I honestly don't think that *they* blame me. Even if they have a right to. *That's* in the texts, too." I felt the sting of tears behind my eyes. Jolon placed a steadying hand on mine. His touch didn't comfort me. I was beyond any feeling at all.

"You know I'll keep doing everything I can. Everything I can think of."

"I know that." And I did. I really did. But it seemed impossible to wait. Some part of me just wanted to sleep through this, hibernate until the twins were back, miraculously found. But I knew it didn't work that way. I had to keep trying, keep searching for them, for the key to this whole mess.

I sighed into my empty coffee mug. "Time to saddle up."

"Shit, Reve. I can't forbid you, but I don't want you riding in the forest alone. There's no one out there today. What about your Fetch?"

"He's gone again. He's not in the forest now. Don't ask me how I know, I just do."

Exasperation and unease warred in his eyes. "All right. Where are you going?"

"Cemetery Road."

"The old King Graveyard."

"And around, and about."

"Reve . . . be *careful.*"

"Being careful isn't getting me anywhere. Maybe it's time to be more careless."

2

Jolon needn't have worried. I didn't run into another soul on the road. Saw no ice-eyed Fetch, no strange men. No mysterious cows. No girls, either. It was a peaceful ride, another gorgeous day to be out if you weren't searching for your missing children. The weather, warm and dry so long into October, seemed unnatural even to a Nevadan. After all, I'd grown up in New England and expected a killing frost by the end of September, the ground to be frozen by early November. But we were nearing the end of October with not so much as a light frost. I rode in a T-shirt, carried a full water pack, stopped Zar at streams to drink often. The leaves were still turning and a few falling, enough so Zar crunched through some trails. But other trails were curiously summer-like, bedded in soft pine needles, some deciduous trees still green overhead. You could chalk it up to global warming, but it seemed even more unnatural than that.

The cemetery that gave the road its name was blazing, dazzling in scarlets and every shade of yellow. It was called the King Graveyard, as it was begun by the King family, but most

Hawley Five Corners families lay there finally as well. There were Searses and Kings and Warriners. I tied Zar to the gate and walked through the graves. The last time I'd been there, Grace and Fai had been with me, laughing and teasing. I remembered the shadow passing over the slanted stones, then the scent of lilacs. Why had it been *there*? Was it my first warning that the twins were in danger?

I concentrated on the headstones. There was Jonas King, whose gravestone was taller than my horse, and boasted of his son's adventures as a missionary in India and Palestine. Jonas King, Jr., was probably buried under some burning sun in a land that was strange to his kin. So this Hawley monument served as his memorial in his hometown, as well as his father's. There was a beautiful headstone with a sleeping fawn carved on it that I remembered from my childhood. But in the hundred or so gravestones that remained, all of which I examined that day, there were none that marked a death in the year 1924, and none after. The boneyard itself bolstered the theory that the town had simply vanished one fine day. Other than that, it told me nothing, and smelled only of freshly mown grass.

I rode out toward Hitchcock Meadow. Just as I got to the meadow pull-off, I heard the sound of a pickup lumbering down Cemetery Road. I trotted Zar behind a lean-to at the edge of the meadow, rested him in the shadows, held my breath. Hoped it wasn't the weird men again.

It was Jolon. He jounced the truck into the pull-off, leapt out. He'd changed out of his uniform of the morning. His black hair needed combing, and his jeans and T-shirt were faded beyond recognizing their original colors. His tracking clothes. A tide of fear washed over me. He was back from Savoy so soon, it must mean something. Probably nothing good.

He made for the trailhead, but then he turned toward me. Of course he could find me. Even if he hadn't been a tracker, he could always find me. I stepped out of the shadows.

"You said you'd be somewhere on Cemetery Road."

"What is it?" My tongue felt thick with dread.

"Just wanted to let you know, it's definitely not your daughter's horse."

I sighed out a long, relieved breath. If that was all, I'd take it.

"It means one less possible bad outcome, anyway," he told me.

The cold crept up the back of my neck again. I shivered. Jolon had seen so many bad outcomes. Had brought them to light.

"I don't know how you do it. I couldn't do what you do."

"But you are."

"Only because I have to. You have a choice. I wish to God I did."

Jolon turned and looked up at the sky, a rich blue. "God doesn't have anything to do with it." He did not turn back to face me. "The Brothers thought they were doing God's work. Tried to make me feel that, too."

"And you don't?"

"I mostly don't allow myself to think or feel, until I find the one I'm looking for." His back was tense, and I knew it cost him an effort to talk about this. He kept looking up at the sky, the trees, as if he thought something he'd lost might be wedged up there.

"Dead or alive." I couldn't help thinking it, speaking it.

He looked at me then, a questioning look, searching for a clue to my state of mind, probably. "Most times, it works out fine, Reve. I find hunters and hikers who just got disoriented in the woods."

Ninety-three hours, the internal clock told me.

Jolon read my thought. "Sometimes it *does* take days. Once I found a girl, seven years old. Went off on her bike while her mother was hanging clothes. One minute she was there, the next, like she fell off the face of the earth. Found her five days later. Halfway up a mountain, lost and scared and cold. But not hurt."

"A happy ending."

"It's why I do it. Not for God. For the happy endings." He sucked in his breath, in that Irish way of affirmation or denigration, according to context. His parents had brought it from their home country, passed it on to him. I was not sure how he meant it, but it was strangely comforting to hear that sound again. It was one of the things that made him himself. Without thinking, I reached for his hand. I felt my own pulse beating with his. Maybe it always had, after all.

"We were too young, then," I said under my breath. Maybe I didn't know I was saying it aloud.

"Too young not to be pulled apart by circumstance." He finished my thought for me, like he used to.

"It's strange how things turned out." My feelings were slithering every which way. I was sad for all the lost years that we might have known each other. And then I had a flash of longing for Jeremy. Wanted desperately to rush home, open the Book for another sighting of him. I wanted Kilcoole Beach, the rustling of stones lapped by small waves, Jeremy's hand in mine rather than Jolon's. That finished it. I pulled my hand away, leapt upon startled Zar's back while he was peacefully cropping grass, put him into a big trot, and rode away with Jolon calling after me.

When I got to the smaller trails off the main road, where I knew Jolon couldn't follow, the tangled skein of regret and self-loathing began to loosen. My feelings for him were like a new shoot off an old, shattered tree stump. But it did no good to think of. It had no place in my life. I wanted to bury it as deeply as Jonas King in his boneyard.

Caleigh's Vision: "The Star"

Caleigh was bored without the presence of her sisters, even though when they were with her she felt as if they used up all the air in the house. Nathan and her Grand and Gramps tried to keep her entertained while her mother searched for her sisters, but there was only so much that could be done, cooped up in the house.

At least she had her string. In Hawley, she'd found her power to conjure with the string was even stronger. She'd had those visions of the past. She'd also made up new patterns: "Fox in the Morning," and the shining red animal slunk across the paddocks, sniffed delicately at the fire pit where Nathan had grilled their supper once. "Bell in the Steeple" and she'd made a bell toll in the church, on the morning of the fair.

She was lying on the couch in the parlor, working on the "Skipping Rope Girl" again. She couldn't seem to perfect the pattern. Conjuring people was harder. But she was getting more adept at using the string to see both the past and the present. She could see her sisters when she wove the "Twins" pattern, just vaguely, in a place that seemed to be under the ground. She thought that wasn't really right, somehow, so she didn't tell anyone yet, even her mother. She kept trying to get it right before she told. It was too important. It comforted her in a strange way.

She sometimes could see the magician Setekh weaving a huge pattern above a stage with clingy silk rope instead of string. She could see her mother in the kitchen, chopping vegetables. She looked up then from the chopping block, distracted, and the knife clattered to the floor. Her mom said "Caleigh?" to the disturbed air around her. Then Caleigh saw Setekh again, weaving his web and laughing.

She suddenly felt very sleepy. She let her "Skipping Rope Girl" slide into the "Star" pattern. "A man is coming," she murmured. Then she fell into a dreamless sleep.

Hell's Kitchen Road—October 30, 2013

1

Mrs. Pike was just pulling out of the driveway when I got back to Hawley. She'd left us another meaty dinner. "Shepherd's pie," she informed me. "From the church supper recipe book."

"Great," I told her. "Perfect." I went in the house to check on Caleigh. I found her stringing on the couch.

"Where is everybody?"

"I told them to leave me alone. I can't have you all hanging over me every minute. I need some privacy."

Falcon Eddy swung his big head around the door to the dining room, gave me a wink.

"Where are Grand and Gramps?" I asked Caleigh.

"Dunno. I think they went over to Nathan's apartment when I told them I wanted them to leave me alone." Her dexterous hands swooped through her string. "Mom."

"What, honey?"

"Now you're doing it."

"Doing what?"

"Not giving me any *space*."

"Okay, okay. I'll be in the kitchen if you need me."

She rolled her eyes. I was almost glad of her snarkiness. At least she wasn't scared.

So I rummaged around the refrigerator, pulled vegetables out of the bin. It seemed like days since Caleigh had eaten a vegetable that hadn't been boiled to death. I pulled a knife out of the block, started chopping and dicing, throwing a salad together. I could at least do that.

The knife slipped, fell to the floor. I thought of Nan, and how she used to say when a knife was dropped, "A man is coming." I called for Caleigh, ran to find her. She was asleep on the couch in the parlor, where I'd left her.

My head seemed too heavy to lift. I slumped onto the couch next to her and fell into a deep sleep. I dreamed about *The Hawley Book of the Dead*. Not in any coherent way, but it was like a red thread through my dreams. I carried it like a baby, rocked it in one dream. In another I kept trying to give it away, but no one would take it. I tried to leave it by the side of a road, but it kept flying back into my hands, like a bird.

2

I woke in the late afternoon. Next to me, Caleigh still slept soundly. The day had become misty and dark with suspended rain. I jumped up, ran out into it, nearly tripped over Falcon Eddy. "Stay with Caleigh," I commanded. I knew something was happening in the forest, something big; I could feel it like damp through my body, chilling my bones. But I didn't call Jolon. I knew where to seek my answers. I bolted up to the office, dug out *The Hawley Book of the Dead*. It wasn't blank this time.

Rigel Voss was all in a tangle. He'd fallen into a cellar hole, crawled through a mass of hobblebush to a cave that must once have been the root cellar of a house. He tried to rest under the damp rock overhang. Tried to breathe shallowly, not the doglike pant he wanted to indulge in. He was somewhere in the Hawley Forest. The handheld GPS he'd carried had sprung from his pocket during one of the belly crawls he'd had to subject himself to, to get away from the guy who'd sniffed him out. Then at some other point, the pocket with his topo maps all protected in ziplock bags tore. It gaped now so his boxers showed, snagged during his headlong gallops and slides, trying to get far enough away. But that wasn't the worst. His gun lay somewhere out in the brush, too.

He'd lost the guy, though. He thought. He hoped. If his senses hadn't been honed, first by his Quantico training, then by years of lying low, he would surely have been caught. It was the smell of the man that had roused Voss's suspicion, set him going. The wind shifted suddenly, and the smell of human came with it. Wood smoke and soap. He knew he himself smelled of sweat and fear to the man he'd never actually seen. Wasn't sure if he'd been seen during the hour or so he was pursued. Smelled, yes, as he'd smelled the man. For all Voss knew, the guy was a hunter, thought he was a deer. That's what he hoped, but he knew better. Hawley Forest had remained closed throughout the search for the missing girls. He himself had hiked in from Plainfield, a long haul. Then, this guy was no average beer-gutted deer hunter. He traveled light, as Voss did. He traveled methodical and sure and eerily quiet. It was only when the moose crashed between them that Voss could make a run for it, run and crawl, run and crawl. For so long his lungs were bursting. The moose followed him. Maddened by flies, or just at the cusp of rutting, something about Voss it didn't like. It tramped and huffed after him, and was faster than Voss thought possible for an animal that size. He could hear it still, stomping and snorting somewhere above him. He'd have to lie low, wait until he could make his next move.

When he'd left Hawley, it had been his plan to vanish for a while, over the state line in Albany. He knew a no-name motel near the Albany airport, where the manager was a guy in an undershirt with ginger hair sprouting from his ears and never spoke, as far as Voss knew. Just took Voss's cash, slid the key card across the counter, went back to watching NASCAR. He was close enough to get back easily, as things developed and he saw his next chance. He watched the TV and scanned the Internet for news.

After a few days, he was getting antsy, just hanging around the room. It was your average low-end old motor court, with a decent bed, a desk, a television, a small fridge and microwave, a Monet haystack on the wall. Voss mostly sat in the breeze from the air conditioner, surfed the Web and television, ate take-out Chinese or ribs delivered from a different place every day so he wouldn't be remembered. He read novels he'd picked up in a Walmart—James Patterson, Clive Cussler, a Stephen King he'd started, but which was spooking him too much. He kept running across coincidences in the book that resonated with his own life. Small things, really. A mention of the Petroglyphs outside Albuquerque, where he and Alice had gone to visit her sister, their only trip besides their honeymoon. The wife in the book used the same perfume Alice liked. He left the book in the lobby for someone else to get creeped out by.

Altogether, the room was fine, though. Restful,

except that it smelled of something sweet and fruity, reminding him of the shampoo Alice used. Often, he would forget for days at a time, then be blindsided by something as innocuous as air freshener, a mention of Petroglyphs. It's funny how our minds work, he thought. It didn't even disturb him anymore, these sudden blasts of remembrance. He looked forward to them. They were all he had left of her.

In his first thirty-six years, Rigel Voss hadn't set a foot wrong. Every move was calculated to yield the best result. But when he'd run across Maggie Hamilton, and through her the disappearing mystery woman, his life had spiraled down to hellish depths. At first, he was certain it could be remedied. He didn't mention it to Alice, eight months' pregnant then, and feeling achy and swollen and hungry all the time. It seemed like whenever he came home, she was spooning something soft into her mouth. Butter pecan ice cream, or chocolate pudding, or tapioca.

They rented the first-floor apartment of a tripledecker in Holyoke then, at the nice end of town where there were real yards and trimmed hedges. Alice liked to sit on the porch high above the street, watch the cars pass, watch the neighbor kids play in their yards, running through sprinklers in the heat. They could even see a small blue patch of the Connecticut River from the porch, and from their bedroom. The yard out back was large and fenced. Perfect for children. The only thing wrong with the place was the steep stone stairway that led to the front door. But as Alice had pointed out when they were apartment hunting, they could always go up the more gradually inclined drive, come in through the kitchen door at the back of the house. All the same, the steps troubled him. He made her promise not to use them at all the last few months of her pregnancy.

Often he would park on the street, dash up those twenty-seven stone steps to the porch and kiss her mouth, sweet from the pudding or ice cream she favored to cool and comfort herself. He couldn't wait to be with her, care for her. Every weekend he cleaned the apartment, then made stews for her, thick and creamy. Even though they'd had a long spell of hot weather, too hot for May, Alice wanted soup. Chewing seemed like too much work in her languid pregnant state. Corn chowder was her favorite, made with fresh corn they'd gotten from a farm stand that last summer. They'd shucked and steamed, sliced the juicy kernels off the ears, and put the corn up in jars one thundery day in September. They'd just found out she was pregnant, their baby not even a gentle swelling between Alice's narrow boy hips. It would be months before she puffed up, couldn't stand all day at the Super Saver, had to take an early leave.

How he loved her. He didn't think it possible, but he loved her even more pregnant. He loved her big belly, her lopsided face and tiny hands, now a little swollen with the heat and the bloating. Her croaky voice asking him, "Honey, will you get me . . ." It was always only a glass of juice, or cool water in a dishpan so she could soak her feet, thickened and painful even though she could put them up all day. But he wished she had asked for more. He would have gotten her anything. Pearls or rubies. A trip to China. The moon and the stars all wrapped up and tied with a golden ribbon. He would have tried, anyway. She asked for only one tough thing, and he did it, at least to the best of his ability.

One day, she was lying on the bed when he came home, instead of reading on the couch. It worried him to see her with her arm curled over her face, the soft underside as vulnerable as a baby rabbit. He went and sat on the bed beside her, smoothed her skin there.

"My darlin' darlin' secret agent man." She rolled onto her side, scissored her legs around his waist. "Now you're trapped, by the fat lady in the circus. If you don't do what she says, she just might crush you."

"Then I guess I'd better do what she says."

She smiled her crooked smile at him. "Sing to me."

"I can't sing, honey. I don't even sing in the shower or the car. Try something easier. I don't know any songs."

"Oh, come on. You're going to have to sing to this baby, you know. Your mama must have sung you some lullaby sometime."

Then he remembered. His father hated when his mother sang baby stuff to him, but there was one song that stuck.

"You'll be sorry!" he teased.

He cleared his throat. "Last night as I lay dreaming of pleasant days gone by . . ." he sang. The first notes were squawks, really, but after his throat got used to singing rather than talking, it flowed better.

My mind was bent on rambling so to Ireland I did fly
I stepped on board a vision, I sailed out with a will
Until I came to anchor at the cross of Spancil Hill.

I paid a flying visit to my first and only love
She's fair as any lily and gentle as a dove
She threw her arms around me, crying "Johnny, I love you still"
She is a farmer's daughter, the pride of Spancil Hill.

Well I dreamt I hugged and kissed her as in the days of yore
She said, "Johnny, you're only joking as many the time before"
The cock crew in the morning, he crew both loud and shrill
And I woke in California, so far from Spancil Hill.

Alice reached up and pulled his head to hers, stared into his eyes. "See. That wasn't so bad, was it?"

But it was bad. A month later she was dead, and he was gone away to a new and terrible life. He never did sing a lullaby to their baby.

After he'd tendered his resignation, Voss went out every day as if he still were heading to work, to the university. He dressed carefully in his good suit, tied his bland tie precisely. He kissed Alice, took the packed lunch she never failed to make for him, leftover grilled chicken legs that he could eat cold, chunky potato salad, homemade chocolate chip cookies. He didn't eat the lunch, he wasn't hungry, but he made sure he threw it away before he got home.

He thought it could all be set right if only he could discover how the trick was accomplished, how the girl had disappeared from the photos, from out of his grip in the research lab. He could bring Hunter evidence that he was not lying, was not crazy. Then he would be reinstated, and Alice would never have to be worried with it all.

At first he thought his good luck had returned. The day after he'd tossed Maggie's apartment, it had been easy to track her, going in the same old loops all Bay State students made. All he had to do was wait in Amherst Center for her to show up. And then, miracle of miracles, the red-haired girl showed up, too. She and Maggie got into a huge old Chevy Impala, fawn colored with a white top, Mass plates 403-XLC. Voss followed them easily all afternoon. They drove down Route 9, then back to Amherst. They walked around, talked to Field Agent Evelyn Wilson, who'd taken their photograph (good luck, Evelyn). They drove to Maggie's apartment, then to the bus station in Springfield. Maggie toted a black garbage bag, got on the bus to New York City. He tried to follow the red-haired girl, but lost her somehow in the not-very-crowded weekday afternoon bus station. He loped out to the car, knowing he'd catch her there, which would be better, after all, than the station. But in place of Chevy Impala 403-XLC was a brand-new navy blue Honda Civic. Voss kicked the tire savagely, then leapt around swearing, his maroon tie swooping and jigging like a new kind of bird.

He ran back to the station, found out Maggie's bus stopped in Hartford, New Haven, and Stamford. Got in his car and drove hell for leather to Hartford. He passed the bus on I-91 just outside Enfield, Connecticut. He thought he glimpsed Maggie's profile. In Hartford, though, she did not leave the bus.

In New Haven, he waited while blue-haired old women and beer-bellied men got off the bus. Maggie was the last off. He'd had time to scope out his options and found the ladies' room was only a few feet from the exit to the parking lot. He'd positioned his car as close to that door as possible. Another bit of good luck was that Maggie went straight to the ladies' and did not linger to buy coffee or a magazine. When she came out, Voss had only to place a firm hand on her neck so the vein popped up, jab the tiny needle in he'd readied beforehand. She slapped her hand to the place as if she'd been stung by a bee, swung around. By the time her eyes met his, they were glazed over. He held her as she fell against him, frog-marched her inert body out to the car, tucked her into the passenger seat, and drove away.

He drove carefully until dark. He finally stopped at a run-down motor court in the Berkshire foothills, with small cabins, poorly lit. Maggie hadn't stirred at all. A good thing, he thought. Then as he unstrapped the seat belt, he knocked her arm from her lap, heard something jingle. He grabbed her wrist, felt the medical alert tag. He placed her hand in her lap very gently, turned the tag so he could see. But some deep part of him already knew. She was allergic to two things. Penicillin and barbiturates. Thiopental, a barbiturate, was the tranquilizer he'd shot her up with. It had been used effectively as a truth serum, and he wanted the truth from her. Now he'd never get it. Her lips were swollen, her neck bulging. He grabbed her wrist again, then her neck, feeling blindly for a pulse. It was too late. Maggie Hamilton was dead. A sick horror washed over him. He knew that nothing would ever be the same. He wished he could turn back time.

But Rigel Voss kept himself moving, knowing what he had to do.

The motel he'd chosen was the kind of place agents used when they wanted there to be no questions asked. He carried Maggie's body into the room, drew the curtains and set up the photos he knew he would need, to coerce the red-haired girl when he found her again, to get her to talk, to tell. Then, at the darkest time of night, he carried the body to the car, this time zipped in a big duffel he'd bought at an outlet store nearby. He drove to a lake he'd only heard of. A lake that was said to have no bottom. The girl's body was curiously light, not difficult to deal with at all. Or maybe that was the adrenaline. On the edge of the water, he placed weights he'd also bought on her ankles. He found some round, smooth, heavy stones to put in the pockets of her jacket, where he found five twenties, folded in three. He put them back where he'd found them. Even with the weights, she was light enough for him to swim her body out to the middle of the moonlit lake, then let her sink, which she did quickly, leaving no trace.

When Rigel Voss read about the horse found in Savoy, and how the search was widening, moving out of

Hawley, he knew it was time to return. With any luck, most of the searchers and law enforcement and weird guys with bows and arrows would be gone from the forest. He would execute the rest of his plan, just as he'd dreamed it, every step.

But now here he was, trapped by a thousand-pound moose, hiding in his cellar hole. Just a few miles from the very lake in which he'd sunk Maggie's body.

Jolon's distraction began with a smell. It was a smell that shouldn't have been in the forest in October. A sweet smell, a fragrance. Jolon knew it wasn't coming from the man he'd been tracking. The only smell wafting back to Jolon from the man was Dial soap and sweat. Not even a hint of bug juice. Jolon stopped, sniffed the air. It was lilacs he smelled. As unlikely as that seemed in autumn. He was near an old cellar hole on Hell's Kitchen Road.

Jolon worked in concentric circles around the site. Anyone seeing him from a distance might think he was a bear, crouching on all fours, then standing, snuffing, peering at the trees and sky, then slowly moving his eyes back to the ground.

He'd worked this ground before, and he didn't really anticipate finding anything. But one of Brother Thomas's first lessons was never to expect or anticipate, as if he *was* a bear, without the strange obsession with the future humans have. His second lesson was to keep on where instinct led him. Bear-like again. And instinct led Jolon to search for the source of the flowery smell. He forgot about the man he'd been tracking. Forgot the man might be Reve's Fetch. The smell had enchanted him. A line from a Robert Frost poem came to him then. "The woods are lovely, dark, and deep," he muttered to himself.

The lilac smell persisted. It might be shampoo or perfume, although the searchers were nowhere near him, so there was no woman nearby whose hair could waft that scent on the air. At least no woman alive. People in a forest inevitably made some noise, gave themselves away. Unless they were quiet because they would never make a sound again. Hair could retain scent for much longer than anyone would rationally think, even after death. He remembered the mourning necklace Brother Thomas had worn, made from his dead grandfather's hair. The grandfather who had been a Mohawk tracker. The one who had taught Brother Thomas, telling him the old stories. The snake woman and the creation of the world, the wolf's dance and the moon phases. The animals had come to him, Grandfather Sintum, the foxes lay by him, the birds nested in his hair. Which looked and smelled alive, Jolon remembered, shining black and reeking of wood smoke and bear grease, tied in strong knots on Brother Thomas's neck, long after Sintum was with his ancestors. He hadn't thought of that necklace, or of the stories Brother Thomas told, for a very long time.

Then he stopped still. Slipped thin deerskin gloves on his hands, felt for his knife, reached it out of his pocket. His eye had caught a fleck of dirty white on the ground. Someone else might have taken it for a stone or even a discarded bit of tissue. Jolon knew it was bone. He scraped carefully at the earth, until the domelike shape revealed itself. It was a human skull.

3

I woke from my trance to the sound of my cell ringing. It was Jolon. I didn't push the answer button. I didn't want to talk, I wanted to be there, where he was. Knowing what he knew. I hid the Book away.

I didn't tell anyone where I was going. I didn't want to be stopped or followed. I disappeared and breezed by Falcon Eddy. He turned, put out a hand, but didn't touch me. He shook his big head. "Imagination's working overtime, now," he mumbled. I paused by Nathan's doorway, spied my dad pacing by the window, Nathan with Caleigh, and my mom out on the deck.

I ran to the barn and threw a saddle on Zar. I led him out the far door, out of sight of the house. I'd lost the connection when I closed the Book, didn't know where Jolon's gruesome discovery would take him. But I had a hunch he'd still be at the old tannery cellar hole.

The mist had settled on the hills, and a fine drizzle had started. In spite of it, I'd never gotten to Hell's Kitchen so fast. I remembered the narrow deer trails that I hadn't been on in twenty years. They wound down parallel to Hunt Road, then swerved off toward Hell's Kitchen. I realized that I'd never known the origin of that name. Oh, there were enough Devil's Hopyards and Witch's Hollows in New England that no one batted an eye at evil-sounding names. Nor did I until that day. But when Zar leapt down the last bank onto the road, I thought I saw demon shapes dancing around a fire. Of course they were not demons, and there was no reason I knew of for Zar to pull up and start trembling and snorting.

The figures in the mist probably numbered no more than twenty. But they looked unearthly, surrounded by search-and-rescue vehicles, police cars with lights cutting through the thickening fog—the fire I thought I'd seen. Then I saw the COUNTY CORONER decal on one of the cars and started to shake. There were more shapes in the woods, lurching around what I knew to be the crumbling foundations of the Hallock tannery, which burned in the 1800s and was never rebuilt. Now men and women in red and yellow slickers were climbing over its remains, and down into the cellar hole, where the hides had once been stored.

I rode toward the site, and out of the mist I could see a crouching man look up at me. Jolon.

Then others saw me, called to him, pointed at me. Jolon waved them back, then slid down the bank onto the road. He ran to me, put a hand on Zar's neck, foamed with sweat as it was. "It's all right, Reve," he told me.

I felt dangerous, as if I could do damage. "Whose skull is it?"

"Not your girls'." He shook his head. "I don't know how you knew, but I did find bones, *old* bones, been there decades. Buried in the leaves and clay, inside the cellar hole."

I shuddered. "Were they children? Were there five of them?"

"We don't know how many. But they were children, yes."

"The children that disappeared in 1923."

"Possibly. Probably. But it will be a while before we know for sure. It's like an archaeological dig up there. You don't need to . . ." He saw the expression in my eyes, implacable. "Shit, Reve! They were dismembered. Killed elsewhere, transported and buried piecemeal."

"And Voss?"

Jolon shook his head. "How you know is beyond me, but yes, I *was* following a man in the woods, up to the time I got sidetracked by this."

"It was Rigel Voss."

"He's dead."

"You could have caught him. Again." But I knew he only did what the forest compelled him to. We all did. "The woods are lovely, dark, and deep."

"What?" He looked startled.

"Never mind. What happened to him? The man you were tracking?"

"Well, right now, he's probably still trapped by a moose, not far down the road. I didn't have a tranq gun with me, or I could have brought the moose down. I don't carry a gun of any kind in the woods, but this guy was carrying. He dropped one gun, maybe had another. Figured the best thing to do is what I did, call in for backup as soon as I had signal. Called the station and told them to seal South Road, search for the man, call in Fish and Wildlife to deal with the moose. They'll bring him in. Whoever he is, he isn't invincible. A run-in with a moose will take the stuffing out of just about anyone."

I shivered again, knowing it all. The Book had taken me inside Voss's head, showed me how Maggie had died. A stupid mistake. But it hadn't given me even a glimpse of the girls. If Voss didn't have them, where *were* they?

"Jolon, it *is* Voss. I know he isn't dead. I know he's out there. I *saw* him. In a . . . a kind of vision, or dream. He didn't have the girls then, but . . ." I couldn't speak it. I slipped from the saddle. I leaned against Zar for his animal warmth. I knew that even if the twins were still out here, still alive, Voss was here now, too. "I can't help thinking . . ." I couldn't say it, the word linking my daughters with *these* children, with their horrible fates.

Jolon placed a big hand on my shoulder. "You can't. You shouldn't. It doesn't help anything."

He was right. The bones Jolon found weren't my daughters'. We hadn't found *their* bones. Not yet. I fought the waves of panic.

Around us, the mist was settling to a chill, stinging rain. Jolon dipped his head and his hat brim shed rainbow droplets. "I've got to get back there. We have a lot to do before it gets dark. I'll get a driver for you, and somebody to walk the horse home."

"No. I'll ride. I need to." I swung up into the saddle.

"I'm going to have Bob follow you in the cruiser." He motioned to the uniformed Hawley policeman. "And don't argue!"

I didn't. I had to ride by all the yellow-slickered teams of various kinds, their vehicles. I had to ride by the coroner's van. Another shiver went through me. I looked up the slope to the tannery site, the rocks tumbled on one another like the bones that had been found. The girls' names came back to me, the names my Nan had tolled. Maria Hall. Aggie Green. Liza Sears. Anna Sewall. Lucy Bell.

Two men were lifting a wet black bag out of the hole, their

faces red from exertion and the cold rain. As I rode, the cruiser crawling behind me, I thought those names, and the rhythm of them, matched Zar's hoofbeats no matter which order I thought them in. Lucy Bell, Liza Sears, Aggie Green, Maria Hall. Lucy Bell, Liza Sears . . . over and over, my funeral dirge for them, the other lost children. Not my own. Please God, not my own.

When I returned I found Nathan idly paging through the local paper. There was a photo of the twins above the fold. I winced.

Nathan looked up. "It's about time."

"I went out for a ride."

"Of course. I suppose it didn't occur to you at all that we'd worry? I got a call from Jolon, saying he'd tried your cell, but no go, that he'd closed the forest entrances and wasn't letting anyone use the roads. He wanted us to stay put. I went to tell you, and Falcon Eddy was right outside your door. He didn't see you leave, but when he thought back on it, he said he *felt* you go."

"Then you knew I was fine," I snapped. Sometimes the only way for me to hold it together is to be unreasonable. And I needed to hold myself together then. I felt as if my head would explode with thoughts of those five lost girls.

"But who knew where you were, or what happened after you'd gone? Jolon said that you'd probably head toward the old mill where all the furor is."

"Tannery."

"What?"

"It's an old tannery, not a mill. Where's Caleigh? Where is everybody?"

"Caleigh's with your dad. We didn't think she should know

you'd taken off without saying anything. Your mom's upstairs taking a nap. We didn't wake her. Falcon Eddy went out to search for you."

"Well, now I'm here. I need to go up and change. If that's all right with you."

Nathan flipped a page, not looking at me.

I was chilled to the bone from the wet ride, and wanted a bath, but I just changed into dry clothes and went back down. I wanted to be near Caleigh, who I could now see in the yard behind the house with my dad, playing badminton in the rain. I toweled my damp hair, trying not to think too much. Or at all. Although I did bring *The Hawley Book of the Dead* down with me, sheathed in my Petroglyph bag. I wanted to keep the Book close, in case it would tell me more. I called Caleigh in, and she ran to me, hugged me so hard I gasped.

"Honey, I need you to stay in the house now. Can you do that?"

Her wet face was buried in my sweater, but I heard her say, "I know. A man is coming."

I wasn't really surprised. I kissed the top of her bright head, looked at my dad. I nodded to him. "Maybe. But it'll be okay. They're going to find him before anything else happens."

"Okay. But can Falcon Eddy teach me a new poker game? It's called Horse. Gramps said I had to ask you."

"Sure, honey. But dry off first, okay?" And she trotted off with Eddy and my father in tow.

Nathan was still peevish, still stubbornly using his newspaper as a barricade. I pulled it out of his hands.

"Okay. I was wrong not to tell any of you."

"You were."

"Come have tea with me. At least we don't have Mrs. Pike

glooming at us. That's one good thing about the roads being closed today."

"All right. And you can tell me what happened out there." I knew Nathan's curiosity would eventually overcome his hurt feelings.

I made the Lapsang souchong tea that is perfect for rainy days and for grief. The first sip tasted of earth, and I felt tears spring up behind my eyes. I breathed in the smoky scent to try to stem the rush of emotion. I thought of the bones they were bringing up out of the earth, children's bones. Of how fragile we all are. And my girls. Who knew if their lovely skin still clothed *their* bones? I pushed the tea away.

"They found . . . bones." I struggled to get the word out. I felt Nathan's hand clutch mine. "The bones of the children killed all those years ago."

"The missing children from Hawley Five Corners?"

"Jolon thinks so. It must be them." The names rang through my brain: *Anna Sewall, Liza Sears, Aggie Green.* My body felt charged with grief. Until then I had spoken, moved, eaten what little I had like an automaton. But after those children's bodies were found, the shock that had blanketed me dropped away. The numbness was replaced by grief and fright and anger, and what felt like a skein of fire running through my heart.

"Reve, honey. I know this is hard, but it doesn't really have anything to do with the twins."

At that, I broke completely, absolutely.

"Everybody is telling me that!" It felt like I was retching up knives instead of words. "But what happens to children who disappear, Nathan? What? They die. That's what happens." I leapt from my chair, but then didn't know what to do with my body. My legs jerked under me, as if by their own accord propelled me around the kitchen. I suddenly couldn't believe I'd been functioning as if I was normal. I'd been nurturing the thin trickle of hope that kept me sane. Now the trickle had dried up, all in an hour, since I learned about those children being found. What horrible things had been done to them? And why? I didn't believe in witches or fairies or the protection of the forest. I felt as if I had battery acid for blood, something racing and corrosive driving me. I couldn't be still. I could only rage.

"There must be something more we can *do*. I've been riding and searching and the woods have been scoured and all that we've found are old bones. I don't want Grace and Fai's bones found decades from now!"

"I know, Reve—"

He reached for me, but I batted his arm away. "No, you don't know. You don't know where they are, you don't know how I feel, you don't know anything." My voice was a shriek. Nathan just stared at me.

The door slammed, and Jolon strode into the kitchen, dripping from the mist. He calmly walked to the cabinets, took down three juice glasses. He reached out a flask from his pocket, poured parsimonious shots into two glasses, filled the third to the brim. He took me by the shoulders, sat me down again, though I was resisting all the way.

"You'll drink this. Then you'll maybe pass out and sleep and when you wake you'll have a grip again." He raised the full glass, tilted it toward my lips, but then I took it in both shaking hands and drank. The liquid was heavy and sweet and searing, like nothing I'd ever tasted. I was beyond caring what it was. I drank it like medicine, under Jolon's watchful eye. By the time he poured me another full glass, my hands were not shaking anymore, and the sharp edges of the world had softened and blurred.

4

I awoke to find the darkness closing in. I was in the parlor, the fire crackling. My father with me, the others gone. My mouth felt as if it had been stuffed with sandpaper, and my head ached. "Can I have some water?" My dad startled, then jumped up to pour from a pitcher on the table. "Here, sweetheart." He handed the cold, beaded glass to me, and I pressed it against my sweaty forehead before drinking greedily. "How long was I asleep?"

"Only an hour. It's seven o'clock."

"It feels like midnight. Where's Caleigh?"

"She's playing Monopoly with everyone in the kitchen."

"Jolon?"

"He went back to the tannery. He promised he'd stop in tonight."

I took an inventory of my body and brain, and I felt better. Not a lot, but no longer on the edge of tears or mania. I started toward the kitchen, but stopped when I spied an orange envelope among the mail. I snatched it up. It was addressed to Caleigh, care of me. It had no return address. It was stuffed with something soft and bulky, but it didn't smell of smoke. It smelled of Maggie.

I ripped it open, and her smiley-face cap fell out, the very one she'd been wearing when I last saw her. I brought it to my face, inhaled her scent. Teaberry gum and sandalwood, as if all the years that had passed were a mirage. Then I saw the card tucked into it. A cartoon witch flew across a darkling sky. Inside the message read, "Maybe you can use this for your costume! Happy Halloween, Caleigh. See you soon!"

The Reveal

Joy Tavern—October 31, 2013

1

Halloween dawned hazy, the heat lying over the hill towns like a pall. I woke early, with the birds and the cops out in their cruisers. When I'd shown Jolon the cap, the card, he had ordered a round-the-clock police watch on the house. One black-and-white remained outside the gate; the other parked near the barn.

Officer Bob was on house duty, and saluted me when I disentangled myself from the sleeping Caleigh. I'd tucked her in with me on the couch, and had slept deep, my arms around her.

I stared out at the sky as the coffee brewed, saw the wind pick up as striated clouds rolled over Hawley. Mackerel clouds, we used to call them when I was young, foretelling rain. *The Hawley Book of the Dead* rested on the table, and every once in a while, I flipped it open, but it stayed blank. It would tell me what it would, when it would.

One hundred and twelve hours.

I brooded and watched for the weather to turn from murky to menacing, as the shifting clouds foretold. But then the sky cleared to the rich blue of my laptop screen. Big, lazy, layered clouds continued to roll across the sky. Even in the string of perfect days that autumn, this one stood out. It was as if the best of summer and autumn had merged like waves lapped together. But if the clouds were right, winter would be upon us this night, with little warning. Only someone used to the fickle weather of New England would know those clouds were an omen of great change to come.

I wanted to talk to Nan. I wanted to be the one to tell her of the discovery of the bodies in the forest. If she didn't already know. They were her friends, after all, and it was clear that she still felt their loss deeply. I phoned her, but as usual there was no answer. The hill-town grapevine probably had the jump on me, anyway.

It was a day of waiting. With Rigel Voss possibly still in the forest, I couldn't ride. And I wanted only to be near Caleigh, the one child I had left. I felt brittle, battered, certain the twins were dead, that Rigel Voss had killed them. And now would come for Caleigh. Caleigh, excited for Halloween, innocent of what I felt must have befallen her sisters. She wandered around all day in her wizard robes, and I did my best to keep her busy, happy. The time passed somehow.

Near three o'clock, Jolon came down the drive. I went out to meet him. A strange emotion flickered across his face, although I could see he was trying to suppress it. He looked out past the gate, to the forest beyond. As if he could see something I couldn't.

"What is it?"

"It's only . . . I thought I saw a Harris hawk, just now. They're not native to New England. Thought it might be your Nan's."

I scanned the sky. Saw nothing. "I've been thinking about

her. Those murdered girls were her friends. I want to take Caleigh to Bennington for Halloween."

He nodded. "Safer than her being here. But I thought Nan might have come today."

"She didn't."

"Must have been a redtail I saw, then."

Something jogged my memory. Something I should have thought of days before.

"Jolon." I could hardly keep the excitement from my voice. "When you tracked the girls, the morning after they left, what exactly did you find?"

"Like I told you, I found your tracks and theirs leaving the drive, going down South Road."

"And then what? What happened to the girls' tracks?" Then I remembered I'd nearly ripped his head off when he told me the first time. "Just tell me once more what you saw. Exactly. I promise I won't blow a gasket."

He looked to the sky again, maybe for guidance. "At the edge of the tavern cellar hole, their tracks were . . . just gone. I can't tell you anything more, and I don't know how to explain it."

"There was no sign of them at all, after that?"

"No."

"Have you ever seen anything like that before?"

"No. Sometimes a trail is disturbed. Or a sign is muddled by time or other tracks. But usually I can pick it up again after a bit. Not this time, though. Their tracks were clear as anything, then, well, they were gone."

"You're saying that two girls and two *horses* just vanished, a mile from their home?"

Jolon scuffed a tattered boot in the dirt. "I'm telling you

what the tracks showed, no more, no less. I know it's not what you want to hear."

"How could that be?"

"I know it sounds unlikely." His eyes sought mine. "Reve, I didn't want to tell you, but this . . . this beats me. I honestly don't know what happened. I can't make any sense of it."

But I thought I could.

2

Caleigh grabbed her pumpkin bag for loot and was ready. She skipped to the SUV, bouncing in her excitement, getting so tangled in her wizard robes I had to unwind her twice before she could hoist herself in. Officer Bob followed in the Hawley police cruiser while Falcon Eddy drove us through the beauty of the day, the trees glowing in lemony afternoon light. It was like driving through a medieval church, with arches of maple rather than stone. Golden and airy. I half-expected bells to sound again in those cathedrals of the forest. But the only music was birdsong.

As we passed the first houses in town and the sidewalks began, small witches and action heroes and princesses appeared. A vampire darted out of a green house, cape flaring behind him. All carried bags or pumpkin-shaped buckets for their gleanings, the candy bars and gum and marshmallow ghosts that would be waiting for them at each house. Caleigh whooped, "Let's start here!" I wanted desperately to run to Nan's first. But what if I was wrong? I didn't want to ruin Caleigh's Halloween for a fool's errand. Doubt and hope warred in my brain while we jostled along in a phalanx of Iron Men and mermaids, ladybugs and werewolves. I escorted Caleigh down all the sidewalks in town, with Eddy a few paces behind, looking like he was in costume, too, with his bow, breeks, and quiver. If only I'd been smarter, Caleigh's cool sisters would be slinking beside her, like an honor guard. Not her uncool mother, a guy wielding medieval weaponry, and the police cruiser that crawled along behind us.

Finally we reached Nan's house. The driveway was occupied by the Reverend John Steel's Cadillac, and by a little ghost, a tiger with his tail dragging, a ballerina, and a Shrek. The air was still, charged with the sweet, faintly rotten scent of dying leaves. But even though I felt not the slightest hint of a breeze, the PHINEAS COBB sign creaked on the rusty chain it was suspended from. The curtains of the narrow windows lining the second story were drawn, giving the house an inward look, like it was contemplating something unpleasant.

I struck the brass clapper, and the Reverend Steel answered the door, in shirtsleeves rather than the white suits that seemed like a costume he wore every day, the costume of a southern gentleman. Sweat was trickling down my neck, and I was wearing a tank top. It was hot. I don't know how the kids in furry costumes or big hunks of plastic, or even Caleigh in her wizard robes, could bear it. No wonder the Reverend had shed his jacket.

"Why, Miz Maskelyne!" His "Miz" was drawled, different in inflection than the clipped Yankee word. He looked startled, but I couldn't tell if it was simply his rabbity eyes, or if he was not pleased to see me. "And young Caleigh!"

"Where's Nan? I need to see her," I demanded.

"She's right in the parlor. She'll be glad of some company. I have door duty, and it has been quite hectic. You've come at a rather busy time," he admonished me, as if I had no right to bring Caleigh trick-or-treating to her own great-grandmother's house. But then he seemed to remember his manners. "Do have a treat, both of you," he said, and thrust a wicker basket at us, brimming with Reese's and Almond Joy as well as moon pies and Goo Goo Clusters. "I particularly recommend the Goo Goo Clusters." Caleigh stood on tiptoe to choose a moon pie, then dashed in to see Nan. Falcon Eddy followed her.

I was about to slide by the doorkeeper, too, but something held me back. I realized I'd never seen the Reverend without his jacket before, or in full sunlight. His skin was luminous, like Nan's when she held *The Hawley Book of the Dead*. And on his wrists curled blue tattoos of snakes.

I staggered and he reached out to steady me, but I shrank from his touch. "You! You . . ." I faltered. His smallness, his white skin, the shape of his head—he had seemed creepily familiar to me all the time I'd known him. Now I finally knew why. Those same blue snakes had crawled through my nightmares.

The Reverend was the electrified man I'd seen in the university lab, twenty-four years ago.

I looked into his eyes, and they were as black as the bottom of a deep well.

"Here's Miz Maskelyne, come to visit again!" He pushed me forward into the parlor. Before he turned back to answer the door, I swear he hissed at me.

"What a surprise!" Nan rose and brushed my cheek with her rough hands. She looked the same, her face composed, her braid neat, her red plaid shirt pressed. I couldn't believe that she was living in the same house with such a creature as the Reverend. I scanned the room for Caleigh. She was trying to coax a reluctant goshawk onto her shoulder. Falcon Eddy was nowhere to be seen. Nan must have sent him out to the mews.

"Reve, you look so pale!"

"Nan, you have to tell me the absolute truth. I have to know everything, starting with *him*." I pointed to the door. My hand trembled.

The goshawk fled from Caleigh. The bird landed on Nan's shoulder, its black barred chest ruffled in alarm, its rusty eye indignant. Caleigh shrugged, then busied herself counting and arranging her candy.

"You mean the Reverend?" Nan's eyes had become as searing as the bird's.

Could something so unnatural *be* a man of the cloth? "I saw him," I whispered, although Caleigh would probably hear anyway. "Years ago. At Bay State. In the underground labs. I saw his tattoos. They were doing terrible things to him. Nan, what *is* he?"

The goshawk flapped its wings. I jumped, and Nan shooed the bird off her. It let out a cry like a mad monkey and flew to its perch. "*You* were in the tunnels?" She fell back in her deep chair. Her face was pinched, pale.

"What the hell was going on down there?"

She quivered like one of her hawks readying itself for flight.

"Nan . . . you have to tell me!"

"All *right*!" she exclaimed. "You probably should have known years ago. The Reverend Steel is one of us. And not."

"What do you mean, one of *us*? What does that mean? I know you put some kind of spell on Mom, so *she* wouldn't tell me. Did you disappear the twins, too? I was stupid not to think of it before. Just tell me where they are!"

"I wish I knew." I scanned her old, defeated face. She was telling the truth. "I've done only what was necessary to protect you all."

A sudden horrible idea smote me. "If you know they're dead, you have to tell me!"

She reached for me, a craggy hand open—a plea for absolution, maybe. "I *don't* think they're dead. I think they're with the sidhe."

"Shee? What the hell is a Shee?"

She raised up the hand that had entreated me a moment before. Suddenly imperious, she looked as regal as she did when hunting with her birds.

"Hush. One must be careful when speaking of the sidhe. There were reasons I didn't tell you much, you or my daughters. I suppose I have only myself to blame for your ignorance. I wish I had chosen differently now, but I thought I was acting for the best. To answer your question, the sidhe are the descendants of the Tuatha De Danann. Us, in other words. The Dyers, and others."

"Others? How many *are* there?"

"More than you might think."

A shiver started in my spine. "And you think Grace and Fai are where, exactly?"

"The same place I went, in 1923. And which I returned from. It's not precisely under the ground, or a mirror image of this world, but close enough. I think the twins might be there, with our ancestors."

"This place, it's in the forest?"

"There, but on a different plane. We call it Tir na nÓg."

"The ghosts of our ancestors are there?"

"Not ghosts," Nan said. "They are as real as you or I. Think of it as a kind of heaven. We go there when we die. Like the Rapture for the Christians, our bodies and all. Unless we are taken in, while we're still alive. To protect us."

"Then how will I ever get them back?" I sucked in a sob. In another moment I'd be weeping with frustration.

"Hush, now, girl. Don't let your feelings stop up your ears!" She clutched me by the shoulders. "The story is a long and involved one. I have to figure how to tell it, and you have to figure how to understand. Now listen to me closely. The story does begin, in a way, with the Reverend. He is an immortal, and that fact was . . . discovered. They were performing tests on him in that lab. But he escaped. The Reverend survived the testing, and much worse. I was charged with keeping him safe, after what happened in the tunnels."

All the pieces seemed to fall together, like one of our family jigsaw puzzles. "They were trying to create immortals?"

"Some think they more than tried. But the beginning of this story is long in the past, hundreds of years it was. The Tuatha De Danann had four treasures. The Sword, the Spear, the Cauldron, and the Stone. The Reverend stole them, and they were scattered ever after. He was directed in this theft by a magician named Simon Magus. For their crime, they were made immortal."

My head was spinning. "All right," I said. "Let's rewind. What happened to the treasures?"

"We don't really know."

"Who exactly makes up the *we* you're talking about?"

"The sidhe that are left. They found me, after the incident in Hawley. They taught me what they could. Though the deepest secrets had always been kept by the Dyer women, and those secrets died with my mother. But there's a network, of sorts, of the scattered sidhe. You know some of them."

"Falcon Eddy?" I guessed.

"Yes. And your Wesley."

"Wesley *Knowles*?" She nodded. The 113-year-old caretaker of the Bijoux.

"Las Vegas has been the home of many sidhe families. Because of the stage magic, they can hide in plain sight."

"Families?"

"Yes. Like the Dyers. There are places in which the fabric that separates the worlds is thin. Those are the places we feel most at home. Hawley is only one such place. I'm in contact with many of the families, though I kept most of it from your mother, and all of it from you. So you could live in *this* world well. Better than I could. So you wouldn't be burdened with it all. The Book, the treasures, any of it. I tried to pretend it was all in the past, a set of legends. I can see now I was wrong."

"But these treasures—"

"The treasures themselves carried many protective spells. If anyone attempted to use them for gain, that person would be punished with immortality, and the treasures would be scattered. The Reverend knew all this. Now he suffers. To pay for his sins he must always remain in this world, never move on. Simon Magus, as well. And the treasures? They've never surfaced since the Reverend stole them. All we really know is that they're not together."

"And how do you know that?"

"If they were together, things would be different."

"What does that *mean*?"

"No one knows that either, anymore. But the link between the worlds, the human and the sidhe, is strained now. More fragile, unbalanced."

"But, Nan," Caleigh chimed in. I'd forgotten about Caleigh.

"Everybody wants to be immortal. It's cool." While I hoped she was transfixed by her candy, she'd listened in on everything.

"It's just as well she knows," Nan told me. "I needn't make the same mistake again." She turned to Caleigh, beckoned her. Caleigh came and sprawled on the wide arm of Nan's chair, sucking disgusting blue liquid out of a wax bottle. Nan placed an arm around her. "It is more painful than you can imagine to outlive your friends, your loves. It has gotten the Reverend into more scrapes than you can imagine, child. I've lasted nine decades, and believe me, I'm ready to move on. And don't forget, we know we *do* move on, to another kind of life."

"All right. Let's suppose the twins are in this . . . parallel world. What can I do to bring them back?"

"The danger to them must be gone. Simon Magus and his Fetch must be defeated."

"But how do we do that?"

"Simon's a web weaver. That's how he works his magic. You have to find a way to destroy his web."

"Hey, Mom, you know what?" Caleigh piped up, her face eager, her lips blue from the waxy syrup she'd been sipping. "You know Setekh the Magnificent? He's a web weaver, too."

"What about this Setekh?" Nan's voice was taut with suspicion.

"He's a magician in Las Vegas," Caleigh informed her. "Mom knows him."

Setekh. Before Henry got me the gig writing for him, I'd never had anything to do with him. It was true he made my skin crawl, but how was it possible Setekh the Magnificent could be behind all this?

Nan narrowed her clouded eyes at Caleigh. "Tell us more about this magician, child."

She pulled out her string, shining white in the gloaming. "He gave me this. He taught me to use it."

"Caleigh! You never told me!"

She glared at me. "You never asked."

"I thought you'd gotten it at school. You *know* you're not supposed to take things from strangers!" I was yelling. The idea that my Caleigh had anything to do with the oily magician made me feel sick.

"He wasn't a stranger! He was *nice*!"

Nan whipped the string out of Caleigh's hand, started a pattern, then dropped it like a thread of fire.

"Just as I thought. It's enchanted."

"My string!" Caleigh dove after it.

"Don't touch that!" Nan pulled Caleigh away, threw her toward me. I held her while she cried for her string. Nan reached for her falconer's glove, drew it on, picked up the string. "He can sense us through it, so you mustn't touch it. This Setekh is Simon Magus. The magician commands your Fetch.

"It was Simon Magus who gave the Reverend up to the government. But it's really the Book he wants. He's been searching for it for many years. You see, there's an ancient connection between the Book and the treasures. With the Book, one may summon them. Simon Magus must have discovered years ago that you were the next Keeper. But you escaped his Fetch, without even knowing you did so. He's sent the Fetch again for you now. For you, and the Book."

I thought of all we'd been through. Everything for a lump of paper and disappearing ink. "Why can't I just give it to him? This could all be over."

She shook her head. "No one but a Revelation can command the Book. And the legend is that only a Revelation can use the Book to summon the treasures in times of great trouble. He needs *you*, too."

"So that's what Simon Magus wants? That's why he sent Voss after me? So I would summon the treasures?"

"Yes. Where *is* the Book?"

I shifted Caleigh, lax and weak from crying, to one arm, plunged the other into the Petroglyph bag. "It's here." I lifted it out, warm and fragrant as always.

"You haven't used it!" The panic in Nan's voice shocked me.

"Well . . ."

"Revelation, I *told* you not to. All my own troubles started when I tried to use the Book, without knowing how to. He could sense it, its power, held by hands that couldn't shield it."

I remembered how it had felt each time I used the Book. I remembered how I'd seen a magician in it. Simon Magus, Setekh, whatever he called himself. It was him, I knew it now.

"Nan, I think I *have* been shielding it, even if I didn't know it. Every time I've opened it, I've disappeared. I think the disappearing shields it *and* me. If he knew who I was at Bay State, how did I escape? It must have been because of the disappearing. And he knew about me before I even *found* the Book. He must have known all the years we were in Las Vegas. It's why he was there in the first place. It's why he gave Caleigh the string." My hand stroked Caleigh's hair. Her sobs had subsided to whimpers. "I think the Book itself has been teaching me how to use it. Nan, *I've* seen *him* in it."

"When you've seen him, where is he?"

"In the mountains near Las Vegas. But, Nan, if he knew who

I was all this time, why didn't he try again to send me for the Book, long before this?"

"I suppose he was waiting until you had the most to lose. Don't forget, he's immortal. He has all the time in the world."

"He has all the time in the world . . . but he can't use the Book without me." When Jeremy and I started our act in Las Vegas, the magician Setekh showed up on the Strip around the same time. He'd waited nine years. As Nan said, he could afford to bide his time. Until what? Until I was married, had children. Had everything to lose. Then he killed Jeremy. To create my time of great trouble.

But something else occurred to me. "Why hasn't he gotten it before this? *Way* before?" I thought of all the women in my dreams who had hidden the Book, all the Revelations. Then I had a flash of understanding. "It doesn't do any good to just keep hiding the Book. I need to learn to *use* it. That's the only way to fight him, to keep it from him. That's why he couldn't get it before. All the Revelations in an unbroken chain knew how to use this Book." I held it as close as I held Caleigh. "It's ignorance that we can't afford. He found out everything about us because I didn't know how to keep him from it. That's why he was able to enchant Caleigh with the string."

Caleigh let out a fresh wail. "I want it! I want my string!" She kicked and flailed again at the mention of her string, nearly got away from me.

Nan rose, grabbed her from me like a struggling fish on a line, held her with a strength I couldn't fathom. She took hold of Caleigh's weeping face. "You can't have it, do you hear? It's too dangerous."

Caleigh gulped, then stilled. "Can I still weave patterns?"

Nan looked to me. "Can she use other string?"

"I think so."

"Leave her with me. We have to break the enchantment." Caleigh's head dropped to Nan's shoulder. Her grip loosened, and Nan set her down on the sofa. She'd fallen into a deep sleep.

"She'll be like this until I can disenchant her, now we've taken the string from her. She'll need to stay with me."

"But the Fetch—"

"She'll be safer here. It's really the Book he wants. And you. He wants one of your powers, surely. Simon Magus must have promised it to him in exchange for the Book. That's how he retains his hold over a Fetch."

"Rigel Voss knows I can use it to go to the past. To be with the dead. Maybe he thinks he can make me use the Book, so he can be with his wife again."

"Maybe. But you don't need the Book for that."

"Of course I do!"

Nan shook her head. "Now I need to tell you the last remaining secret. You've always been able to go between the worlds, Book or no. When you disappear, Revelation, you slip between the worlds."

"But I'm really just out of sight. It's like I walk through a curtain, and I'm there, just behind it."

"No. You stay close because we *taught* you to."

I was even more baffled now.

"When you were a child, when you first began disappearing, you didn't come back for hours, sometimes days. And when you did . . . well, you were not yourself. We almost lost you." My mother had said the same thing. "So we had to teach you to stay with us, never to go deep into another world. It's an uncommon sidhe gift, a very powerful one. It might be your ability to travel between worlds that Simon Magus promised to Rigel Voss, years before you had the Book in your possession. In any case, he doesn't want this small fish herself." She placed a hand on Caleigh's flushed forehead. "He would only want her as bait for you."

"All right." I felt hopeless when I said it. I had no idea how I'd be able to leave my Caleigh, walk away. But I didn't know how to break the spell. Nan did. Or said she did.

"I want to know what's happening. Promise me! And don't let the Reverend near her!"

"I can keep the Reverend in check. I've done it for more than twenty years now. The one thing that I'll need from you is a description of the magician's show."

I nodded, then knelt by Caleigh, took her limp body in my arms, buried my face in her damp neck. I felt her breathe shallowly against me, felt her quick pulse. There was a cloying scent around her, like burning sugar. "The enchantment runs deep," Nan said softly. "But I have ways to conquer it. We just need a little time." She stroked my hair, then took me by the shoulders, lifted me up with her strong old hands.

"I'll keep Caleigh safe, I promise you, child. Now you must go." She kissed my cheek with cold lips. "Good luck, Revelation. Although luck is relative. Perhaps I should wish you *on hlone*." I didn't ask what *on hlone* was. I was probably better off not knowing.

The Reverend sat on the front steps, handing out candy. A mummy and a vampire stared at the Goo Goo Clusters in their hands. "Sweet!" said the mummy. "These are heavier than Chunkies."

"Enjoy them, young gentlemen."

"Yeah. We will." And they sped off, never guessing that

they'd taken candy from another kind of monster. I slipped by him, and fled with the pack of kids. The mummy slung his gauze bandages back, and the vampire shoved through a pack of younger children, girls who all seemed to be princesses or ballet dancers. One tripped on a crack in the sidewalk, and I grabbed her before she could fall. She was resplendent in a blue tutu and tiara, and had glitter dusted on her skin. "Are you a ballerina?" I asked.

"No. See the wings?" She pirouetted so I could see the transparent net wings she wore, also glittery. "I'm a fairy." And she marched up to the door to claim her candy from the Reverend.

I felt shaky, bereft of all my girls. I couldn't stop thinking of Caleigh, the enchantment, Simon Magus eavesdropping on our lives for years. He'd even had the audacity to hire me to write a script, disguised as Setekh the Magnificent. But my fury was mixed with a feverish dread. I felt like a mouse with a hawk circling above.

One hundred and twenty-two hours.

This wasn't the kind of magic I was used to. In my world, I was always the one in control of all the magic tricks.

3

Mrs. Pike had brought us bags of Halloween candy, left in bowls on the kitchen table. My mom and I were picking through them for Caleigh's favorites. I knew there would be no trick-or-treaters at Hawley Five Corners. Their parents feared the real ghosts too much.

Jolon, when he arrived, was pale and drawn. Dark stubble shadowed his face.

"Sorry I didn't get here earlier," he said. "It's been a long day. Where's Caleigh?"

"She's at Nan's. We thought it would be safer. Officer Bob stayed to watch the house."

"Good. Though it would have been nice if he'd called the station."

"Can I pour you a drink?" Dad offered.

"Love a beer, but have to get back to file my report. Just stopped to confirm that at least two of the bodies are those of the lost children. Liza Sears and Lucy Bell. But I expect they're all there."

"How was it possible to ID them so quickly?"

"Dental records. Fortunately for us, there was a dentist in Hawley in the twenties, and he kept his records until he died in 1952. His daughter lives in the same house now, and the records have been in boxes in the attic the whole time. It didn't take long to come up with all the kids' records."

Jolon paused, sucked in a breath.

"And we found out that the guy who was staying at Candy Cane Park had a fake ID. His story was a story. He probably was your Fetch, and possibly the guy I was tracking. I was tailing someone in the woods," he told my parents. "I gave it up when a moose got involved. I put a raft of men on him, following the trajectory I thought he'd take from where he was headed, and they came up with squat. So. It's time for *me* to say 'mea culpa,' Reve. At least we can be sure you have twenty-four-hour surveillance now, and the woods are crawling with searchers. We're doing all we can do.

"The one thing that might bollix us up is the weather," Jolon went on. "Supposed to snow tonight. It snows a little, an inch or two, it might help us out, as far as fresh tracks go. Anything more, though—and they're saying it might be half a foot or more—the state will call off the search."

"Why is that?" my father asked.

"We'd need to assess and bring in a team that's been certified in snow and ice search and rescue. Regulations. You'd be surprised how much of a difference even a small amount of snow makes to a search. We can't have volunteers out there getting stuck and needing to be rescued themselves."

I remembered the mackerel clouds of the morning, and nodded. I knew he was doing his best, but it took the heart out of me to think after less than a week the state itself could give up on my girls.

"We'll hope for fair weather, then," my dad said. "Dinner in five. At least have some stew with us, Jolon."

"Got to get back. Those reports, you know."

"Take some away, then. Dad's boeuf bourguignon is badass." As the twins would have said.

Jolon smiled bleakly. "Well. Okay. Eat at my desk."

Dad piled some of the stew, redolent of meat and caramelized onions, into a container. I put it in a shopping bag with a hunk of good bread. Jolon took it from me and, oddly, shook my hand.

"Thanks, Reve." His hand lingered in mine just a heartbeat longer than a friendly handshake called for.

I called Henry, then went out to do night check, accompanied by Falcon Eddy. The temperature had dropped about forty degrees since the afternoon. There was a dampness in the air, and the clouds rolled over the nearly full moon. A few snowflakes drifted down. I could see them falling through the barn light, feel them on my upturned face.

Zar and Miss May were content and sleepy. She was lying on her side in the shavings at his feet. His head drooped over her, his eyes soft and dreamy. He woke with a snort as I opened the stall door to hand in his two flakes of hay. Miss May stretched and groaned, her chocolate sides heaving as she scrambled to her feet and twinkled her short tail at us.

"They seem peaceful, so," Eddy said.

"Sometimes I wish I was one of my animals." I leaned against the stall wall, listened to the horse and goat munch their hay, noses nearly touching. "Eddy? Do you think he knows where they are?" I stroked Zar's coarse mane. "If he did, I think he'd try to take me to them, somehow."

"But, dearie, the horse did take you as far as he could, where our fella Jolon said they disappeared. The tavern cellar hole."

I studied his craggy face. I realized he was right. " 'There are more things in heaven and under earth than are dreamt of in your philosophy.' "

Eddy laughed. "Yeah, as poor bloody Hamlet says."

"You continually surprise me, Eddy."

"Hamlet would have been one of my kinfolk, and yours as well. Tuatha De Danann. Of the Danes."

How did he know Nan had told me? Maybe they communicated with the hawks, like homing pigeons. "Sometime I'd like to know more about the history of the Danann."

"The Tuatha De, as they're more properly called. When we are less fraught, dearie, I'll be happy to tell you. And that time will come, even though it doesn't seem so to you now."

I could hear the wind picking up, roaring through the trees. "We should go back." I turned my collar up, and we plunged out the door into the bracing chill. The few random flakes had multiplied, were falling fast.

I checked my e-mail before bed. What I'd asked Henry to provide was there. A detailed description of Setekh's show. Or Simon Magus, as I was beginning to think of him. Henry had attached photos and video clips of the show, which was called *Web of Darkness*. They made his connection to Caleigh seem scarily real.

Next I took up *The Hawley Book of the Dead*. It was warm from its meadow. The pages wouldn't be blank this time. I was getting to know when the Book had something to tell me.

I made sure I was firmly in the chair in case I was overtaken. When I opened the Book, what I saw first was narrow blue-black writing, which then swirled to a leaden sky blackened by splotches. Dark dots on the horizon shifted closer, until I could see what caused the blackness. Crows. Hundreds of them. Then my vision cleared, and the knowing came.

It was 1862. The height of the Civil War. Just after Antietam, where more than three thousand men and boys had died on the blood-soaked ground. Revelation trudged in the ankle-deep mud, her boots seeping liquid, water mixed with blood. She shivered, tried not to think of it. Hundreds of crows picked at the bodies. She tried to shoo them away, but they just flapped a few feet to another pile of stinking flesh and blood and bone.

It was hot. Maryland in September. She longed for the cool of Hawley Forest. Her skin itched in the wool uniform she'd exchanged for her skirts months before. She'd come south, searching for the Book, and now she'd found it. Her brother Ezra had taken it, tucked in his sack with his Bible, by mistake or design, when he'd run away to join the Union army. She'd found him just before the battle, in a dirty tent in the woods nearby. He was shocked to see her, his dainty sister, in faded Union blue, her face brown from the sun, her hair cut short and uneven with a knife. He'd been loath to give up the Book; he thought it kept him safe, and maybe it had.

"I've killed men to get to that Book, Ez. Don't make me do *you* harm."

He'd handed it over, just as they were called to arms at dawn. She'd fought alongside Ezra; she saw him fall from the bridge over Antietam Creek. Now, the day after the battle, she'd found all the Hawley boys,

> broken, dead, already decomposing in the sun. Her own brother's body bloated with creek water. She sat finally on a rock, her sword by her side. She held the Book close, took in its scent of faraway meadows, and cried until she had no tears left in her. She did not see a man in a tattered shirt creep up behind her, pull his knife, ready himself to plunge it into her back. Suddenly the smell of lilacs swirled heavy around them. It made the man pause to sniff the air, and in that moment Revelation rose and swung her sword. It hit the man's thigh, cut deep. She pulled it away, bloody, then drove it into his chest.

I came up from the vision gasping. Even with a face dirty and swollen with tears and grief and rage, it was plain to see that this Revelation was the woman in the portrait. And the sword was the very sword from the Perpetual Tag Sale. Its jewels had flashed dazzling, even through the muck and blood. I stayed in the present long enough to take in that knowledge, then sank into the Book, into the past again.

> In Hawley, a boy walked down a road. Jordan Sears walked down North Road with a mission. Sent by his father to drive home two cows bought from Martin Klausen. But Jordan, sixteen and willful, wasn't planning on going to Klausen's farm, or on driving cows at all from then on. Or going home, for that matter. He was all aflame with war fever, had made a plan with Luke Miller and Del Hanson to meet on the road and walk to Pittsfield to join the militia. March south to the battlefields with a company of men. Wear the Northern

blue. Carry a rifle on his shoulder. Come back a man himself.

He was walking past the charred remains of Joy Tavern, which had burned the year before. He saw smoke, a big plume of it, rising from the place. It transfixed him. The smoke had a womanly shape, soft in the right places, streaming hair, and white arms beckoning him. He walked toward the smoke woman. He could not help it. Walked straight into those shifting, misty arms. He put his head on her breast and knew no more until he awoke in the same spot.

He rose and splashed his face with water from the stream. He walked to meet Luke and Del, thinking he'd been asleep for an hour or so. But they were not at the crossroads. He walked to Luke's farm. Luke's mother saw him from her window, ran to him, held him to her, asked for news of Luke. Was he on the road home, too?

"But I came to *find* Luke."

She looked at him as if he were addled, placed a hand on his brow. "Honey, Luke's in Virginia, last we heard, near six months ago. Your mama is worried sick. Three years gone and no word! Shame on you, boy!"

"But . . . Luke went without us?" How could Luke get there since they'd made their plan yesterday? How could he himself have slept for three years?

Mrs. Miller gave him another worried glance. "Luke signed up in 1862. Ran away with Del Hanson, and we thought you went with them. The war's over, now. Where have you been?" But he didn't know, couldn't say.

Luke never did come home to Hawley, nor did Del.

Two years later, Jordan married Loreen Wilton. They prospered, but had no children. In 1869, Loreen died after a short illness. In 1871, Jordan married Revelation Dyer, his own cousin and an old maid at thirty-five, although a great beauty still. Revelation was eight years his senior. She kept her own name. It was whispered that she'd fought in the war, dressed as a man. It was also whispered she'd bewitched Jordan. She bore him a child before he died in a sawmill accident, a girl, who bore in due time another girl. That girl's parents died in the Spanish influenza epidemic that carried so many away. Her name was changed to her mother's, to Hannah, when she went to live with her Sears cousins. But she'd been christened Revelation, after her brave grandmother.

Hawley Five Corners—November 1, 2013
The Day of the Dead

1

I awoke late the next morning. I'd slept hard, my cheek resting on the Book. I thought about what I'd seen in it, what the visions could mean. The sword Revelation had wielded, the sword from the Perpetual Tag Sale—it must be the Sword of the four treasures that Nan had spoken of, one of the treasures Simon Magus sought. It surely had come in a time of trouble, one created by the magician spinning his evil web.

The sky was clear, the driveway was plowed. My dad told me of all the changes that had occurred while I slept. "They say we'll either have a nor'easter with lashings of rain, a fierce ice storm, or more snow today. Nathan's gone to town for water and batteries. Jolon said we might be trapped if the storm's as bad as they say."

I hadn't planned on more bad weather. "Dad, do you think you and Mom could go to Nan's, check on Caleigh? Make sure they're okay? Falcon Eddy can stay with me. And bring Nan this." I gave him the envelope with Henry's photos.

"Sure. We can be back before the storm hits."

But they couldn't. It turned out no one could. Not in time.

2

The birds flew all morning and into the afternoon, darkening the sky just as they had in my vision. Crows black as the bottoms of cast-iron pots, looking greasy as if they'd been basted and half-cooked. Their squawks and screeches sounded like children arguing, like old men watching sports on TV, grumbling and murching. I felt the birds, heard them all around the house, like a plague.

Nathan called to tell me he was heading to Northampton, since all the water and batteries in Elmer's had been bought up on Halloween. A brooding restlessness came over me. I was unsettled by the mobs of birds swooping by the windows. Or the coming storm. I wasn't sure which.

I ran down the stairs to the kitchen, opened the refrigerator, the cupboards. I closed them all again, not finding what I sought. Thinking it might be Jolon, I picked up the phone and called him.

The snow had nearly stopped, but at least a foot had been dumped on the forest in the night. Jolon told me the wider search was off, at least for the time being. "I'll still be going out, but the state boys will decide on calling in a snow-certified team. It's drifted too deep in the woods. I'm sorry, but we'll have to wait, for them or for a melt."

"You didn't find anything last night? Any sign of Voss, or . . . anything?"

He puffed out a breath. "No. Nothing."

"I guess that doesn't surprise me." I was desolate, heart heavy with the feeling that I'd never see Grace and Fai again. And I missed Caleigh fiercely.

"Did you see the sky?" he asked.

"The crows, you mean?"

"Crows? I don't know about crows, but you can see the storm coming."

I looked out and saw only trails and clumps of crows, straggling in flight, landing on the barn roof, the fences.

"There's a storm of birds here. Like Hitchcock. Who was that actress? Tippi Hedren? Was she ever in anything else?" My mind ran to non sequiturs. I didn't want to think of what was happening. What *had* happened.

"I'll batten down the hatches here, then come to you. I should be there in an hour or so. The storm's going to be bad, Reve. Bob's still at Nan's, so I can't send him out to you, and even Mrs. Pike's old guys probably aren't out on their Ski-Doos."

"Wait, what? What about Mrs. Pike?"

"Didn't I tell you? She's responsible for the crew of old guys following you around in the woods. She gives the rallying cry. Calls around and tells them where you're riding."

"Mrs. *Pike*?"

"Her husband's the ringleader. Remy Pike."

"*No!*"

"Mrs. Pike's a deep one."

I contemplated this, and looked out again at the storm of crows. It was so much like *The Birds*. "But what about Tippi Hedren?"

"I don't think this will be a night for scary movies. Reality will be scary enough."

I called Nan, for the third time that day. "How's Caleigh?"

"She woke up for a bit, but she still won't eat. Now she's asleep again."

"That's not like her."

"She misses her string, and no other will do. She's still enchanted."

"Did you get the photos?"

"Yes. They're very . . . helpful. I think they'll make all the difference."

"Are Mom and Dad still there?"

"No, they're headed back to you. But it's icing here now."

"I'll call them. Make sure Caleigh . . . just make sure she knows I called."

I tried my dad's cell next, and got a network busy signal. I punched in their landline in Williamstown. My mom answered.

"I'm so glad you made it home!"

"We just got here. The roads are bad. . . . I don't think we can get back to you."

I thought of Route 2, winding and treacherous between Williamstown and Hawley. "No, don't even try. Don't worry, I'll be fine. It hasn't started here yet."

"Is Jolon with you?" Mom asked.

"No, but he's coming. And Falcon Eddy's here, Nathan should be back soon. I'll have plenty of company." I heard the line crackle, cut out, then Mom saying, before their phone went out completely, "Stay safe, Reve. Stay inside."

But of course I couldn't. I had the animals to consider. I pulled on a jacket, slogged through the snow to the barn, arms over my head to fend off crows. They were flying low, cawing so my ears seemed filled with their talk. The air smelled of ozone and sap. I bolted all the barn doors, gave Zar and Miss May their grain, topped up their water, gave them extra buckets. It was early to feed again, but it felt ominous enough that I thought it might be too difficult to get out later. The sky was slatey, the clouds rumpled like tossed bedsheets. The weather forecasters didn't seem to know what the storm would bring—snow, hail, rain—it could be any or all of those, in any combination.

I thought of Grace and Fai—could they still be out in this? One hundred and forty-four hours. Almost a week. Where could they *be*?

The suggestion that they were being hidden by the Tuatha De Danann seemed laughable again. So I did laugh. The sound echoed in the barn, mocking me. There was no one to hear. Eddy was busy with the generator. I could feel the hundred-year storm inside me, no choice but to ride it out. The prickly feeling that someone was watching swept over me. I felt a human presence, almost breathing nearby. I froze.

"Eddy?" I whispered. But my voice was lost in a deafening crack of thunder. I flinched when the scent of lilacs swirled around me. I ran. Overhead, the sky was purple. The crows had fled. The snow had begun again, huge wet flakes big as half-dollars. I ran for the house as marble-sized rounds of ice began pelting me.

I went to the lean-to near the kitchen that housed the

generator. Eddy was bent over it. He'd stripped his shirt off in spite of the cold. He was swearing as well as sweating. He looked up when I shoved the door open.

"Oh. Sorry for the language, dearie. I can't get this thing to turn over."

"Good thing Nathan is bringing batteries for the flashlights, then. And water." No water in the house without power to run the pump, unless Falcon Eddy had some success with the generator. "If he makes it back at all." At least we had enough wood to last through the winter, big storm or no. We'd have heat courtesy of the woodstoves and fireplaces.

"I'll get this going if it kills me." He gave the side of the generator a gentle kick. The reverberation of boot on metal was echoed by another peal of thunder.

"Eddy, you've been out here for a while?"

"Wish I hadn't been. Why?"

"I just thought . . . Never mind. It's starting to snow. And hail. I'll just be in the kitchen, okay?"

"And I suppose I'll be out here."

"I'm making a big pot of beef stew for us all, in case the power goes. We can heat it on the woodstove."

"It wouldn't have Guinness in it, now?"

"It could."

"That's fine!" I could see in his face the boy he'd been.

"I just hope Nathan and Jolon make it."

"If they don't, then more for us."

That was one way of looking at it. I closed the door against the cold, glad at least that I could brighten Eddy up with thoughts of stew.

I started chopping onions and listened for Nathan and the SUV, the whine of Jolon's sled, the thump and roar of the generator starting up. Any sign that soon a door would open and one of the men would rescue me from the fear that tingled up my spine, lodged in my brain like a prehistoric animal. I chopped and braised and poured and stirred, all the time pushing back the panic. I resisted the urge to go for the Book. I didn't need it anymore. I knew, had known since the not-quite-silent barn. No matter what the Book told me, I knew it was Voss, my Fetch, coming for me.

3

The darkness fell early. In spite of the storm, the power still held. Snow fell thick and fast outside the window. I never did hear the whump of the generator, and just before the murky gloaming sank to full blackness outside, Eddy stuck his head in the door.

"Can't get the wretched thing going. It wouldn't hurt to rustle up all the candles and flashlights."

"Already did. What we have is on the kitchen table. But I'm still hoping for Nathan."

He looked out at the purple sky, voiced my fear. "Be a small miracle if Nathan can get up the hill in this. Even with the four-wheel drive. Snow's coming down hard. As much as a foot an hour, now."

"At least Jolon should be here any minute."

"Hope so. Haven't heard a sled, though. Only some big, cracking sounds. Like the trees being yanked up by the roots." He looked worried. I remembered he lived in the desert, wasn't used to this kind of storm. I'd heard the cracking sounds, too, as if cannons were being set off in Hawley Forest.

"This house has stood up to big storms before this. Two hundred years of them. But . . . Eddy?"

He turned back to me.

"You don't think anyone could be out there, do you?"

"In this?"

"When I was out in the barn, I thought maybe someone was there."

"Did you see something?"

I shook my head. "Just had a feeling."

He smiled, patted the quiver full of bristling arrows at his side. "Nothing I can't take care of, dearie. I'll have a look, though, before the storm gets any worse. Just so you won't worry yourself." He grabbed his coat off a hook, shrugged into it, slipped the quiver back into place.

"Back soon."

I hoped he would be.

Caleigh woke with a start. She could feel him in the string she held, the man who was coming for her mother. Not her good white string, blue instead. But she wove the pattern called "The Star" with it. And she saw him clear.

Her Nan was by her. "Is the man there now?"

"He's in the barn."

"All right, love, it's time to begin." Nan took the blue string from Caleigh's fingers, replaced it with her good white string. Caleigh sighed with pleasure to hold her own string again. Her fingers started working it, without her thinking. Her Nan started the same pattern in blue.

In a theater on the Las Vegas Strip, a matinee performance was about to begin. The audience rustled and sighed, flipped through their programs to read about the magic show called *Web of Darkness*.

The stew was bubbling fragrant on the stove. I washed and tore lettuce for a salad. I'd made enough food for three men and one woman with no appetite to live on for days if need be. If any of them made it back. I picked up the phone to call Jolon, but heard only flat silence from the receiver. The landline was out. I unplugged my cell phone from its charger, thinking there would at least be a cell signal. But when the display lit up, there was not even one bar. I walked all over the house, checking for a signal. Nothing in the parlor or on the second floor. I heard the blasts of wind howling round the house. On the third-floor landing, I made out one faint bar, punched Jolon's number, but got only a network busy notice. I tried Nathan's number with the same result.

I was about to head back down when I stopped. I'd set up a reading nook on the landing, an armchair and a lamp under the one round window, now ink blue in the failing light. Caleigh's *At the Back of the North Wind* was sprawled open beneath the chair; a piece of blue string was coiled near it. I picked the string up, tucked it in my pocket.

The landing was usually one of the warmest spots in the house, heat rising as it does. Today it had an icy chill. The door of my office was open a crack, and as I moved toward it, I felt more cold air pouring through the gap. I opened it wider and saw the French doors gaping, the curtains flapping lazily like wet ghosts, saturated with the weight of melted snow and ice. The smell of lilacs was almost overwhelming. I turned on the lights, and they flickered, but that was all. Only the faint light of stormy dusk filled the room.

I ran to the widow's walk, looking for some sign, a reason the doors might be open. They had been locked, and no one had cause to be up on the third floor at all. The darkness was nearly impenetrable. The widow's walk was buried in knee-deep snow, not one indentation to suggest a footstep. But my heart pounded anyway. I looked out over what I could still see of Hawley Five Corners. The pitched silhouette of the church steeple, the gables of the barn. No figures in the fast-falling snow. No Falcon Eddy. The wind seemed to be tearing at the trees, rending them, but the house was strangely still around me. *The woods are lovely, dark, and deep.*

I stepped back to close the storm out, and just then I heard a pop. It was a sound I knew intimately, one that had nothing to do with the storm. The sound I'd heard a hundred times, every time Jeremy and I performed Defying the Bullets, his final trick on this earth. The pop of a gun being fired.

Time seemed to hold me in its rough grip. I tried to hurry, to race down the stairs, leap into my boots, grab a flashlight, but every motion was as slow and ungainly as nightmare flight. The truth was, I didn't really want to know the particulars of that gunshot. I hoped it was my imagination, a cracking tree limb, a branch bowed and snapped by the weight of snow, deceiving me. But the place around my heart that had been hollowed out by the shot that killed Jeremy, that place knew. Even before I got to the barn, snow pelting my face, sinking into the downy stuff up to my thighs. Before I saw the open door, the trail of dark liquid. Before smelling not the iron scent of blood, but the heavy purple one of lilacs, before I saw Eddy's bulk lying in the aisle. I knew I was alone with the man who'd killed Maggie and Jeremy. The man who wanted to kill my daughters.

I fell to my knees, grabbed Eddy's wrist to check for his pulse. Nothing. I remembered something I'd seen on TV, licked my palm and held it to his open lips. No breath cooled it. He would go to Tir na nÓg. If it existed.

Then I saw the yellow square of a Post-it note stuck to his parka. On it was scrawled a smiley face. Below the smiley face were the words *Courtesy of Rigel Voss* in looping copperplate. When I saw that, the fear that had been kicking behind my ribs for hours subsided. A weltering sadness swept over me instead. I'd resisted Falcon Eddy, tried to dislike him. But here he'd given his life to try to protect me. I'd miss him calling me "dearie." I'd miss his big presence in our lives. Another thing for Rigel Voss to answer for.

I sat back on my heels, swept the beam of the flashlight around the barn. No sign of another human presence. I felt alone but for the animals. I heard the swish of Zar's tail, the bump of Miss May scratching her head against the doorjamb, Zar's nervous hooves pacing the stall. I switched on the lights, flooding the barn with a nearly miraculous brightness. I couldn't care less whether I was tipping Voss off to my location. Just knowing he was here for me, finally, filled me with power, and a kind of righteousness. This was my house, my barn, my town, my home. My life. He'd taken enough from me. I was damned if he was going to take more. He'd never have the Book. He'd never have me.

I slid Zar's stall door open, stepped in. Gave him a hug round the solid muscle of his neck, patted Miss May's head. "I'm sorry, kids. There's nothing I can do about Eddy right now. You'll have to be okay. I have to leave you, but I'll be back soon." I kissed Zar's nose, remembering those were the last words Eddy had said to me: "Back soon." I leaned into Zar's neck, smelled his good horse smell. "If I don't come back, someone will find you. They'll be here after the storm. If I don't come back . . ." I kissed him again and looked into his kind eyes. I threw him three more flakes of hay, and left it at that.

I slogged back into the snow, bolted the big slider, trudged back to the house. It was warmer now than when I'd come out. The snow had stopped, and flashes of what looked like lightning lit the sky to the west. For all I knew, Voss had a gun pointed at me, or was lying in wait for me inside the house. But I didn't think so. That wasn't the way it was supposed to play out, and somehow I knew it. It all became clear to me in that moment, what I needed to do to keep myself alive, to end the craziness, to get my daughters safely back.

He hadn't been in the barn. He wasn't in my home. I didn't need the absence of tracks in the snow to tell me. I didn't need the Book. I felt for him with my mind. He wasn't in the Warriner house. That left the church. He would wait until I was beside myself with fear, and then he would come for me. I knew that because I could feel his thoughts now, too. But I kept my own from him as I played the waiting game. Let him think I was terrified.

The lightning flashed again, and rolling thunder followed. I counted. The best I could tell, the lightning strikes were about five miles off. The kitchen lights flickered, went out. I was weary from sporadic, nightmare-laced sleep for days on end. It suddenly seemed like years instead of days since I'd slept soundly.

I needed to stay awake, in control. The barrage of storms, first the heavy snow, now the sudden warming, the lashing rain and lightning, had been blasting Hawley for hours. No phone, lights sporadic, if I was lucky. But I couldn't think of any of it. I had to stay alert for the coming man. It wasn't so bad knowing he would come, and that I'd have to kill him or be killed. But at that moment I hated having to stay awake for it.

I drew all the shades in the house. I scooped coffee, poured water I'd collected in all the vases in the house when it seemed certain the power would go. I heated water on the stove and thanked God for the miracle of propane. I didn't think about anything beyond the steps for making coffee. I went through the motions. I didn't think about Voss. When the coffee was ready, I poured some and took it like medicine, leaning against the counter in the dark. Listening to the storm howl, I felt more alone than ever in my life. I reached for the Book, near me as always. I opened it and fell toward Jeremy.

This time, instead of the Sea Road, I landed on the catwalk of the Bijoux, far above the stage. Jeremy was below me. He didn't wear his mackintosh this time, but the elegant white jacket that meant we were performing the show I liked the least, *Restoration*. Jeremy played the great magician Robert-Houdin, while I was the mystery woman, his muse. The show itself was fine. The only problem with it, from my point of view, was the last illusion, the trick called Without a Net. The illusion that Jeremy thought was my finest, but which terrified me all the same. And here I was again, at the top of the catwalk, without even the harness our prop master Dan used to control my leap, my flight, while I controlled the disappearing and the stunning restoration the show was named for. Not only was I without the harness, when I looked back, I found I was standing on a tiny square of the catwalk that seemed to have disengaged from the rest. A platform hanging in air, with no way down. My heart nearly stopped from fear.

Jeremy waved to me from the stage. "Hello, love."

I was frozen in place on the very edge of that narrow metal grating, unable to move.

"Jeremy," I said through clenched teeth, "where's my harness?" I was afraid even to breathe.

"Oh, that. You don't need that anymore."

"Are you crazy? I'll just go splat on the stage if I jump."

I could see even from that height he'd assumed the look of infinite patience that I'd always found acutely irritating. "Actually, you won't."

"Does this dimension, wherever we are, not have *gravity*?"

He looked around. "Well, we're just in the Bijoux, which I *think* still has gravity. But sweetheart, you're missing the point."

"Look, Rigel Voss is outside, coming to kill me any minute. I have to figure out what to do. And you're not helping!"

"No. I'm only here to make suggestions."

"Well, if this is a suggestion, it stinks!"

"That's my girl, good and stubborn. It's your stubbornness that makes you my bet in any fight. You'll never give up, even when backed into a corner. That's when you're most creative. Now, all you have to do is make the leap."

"And I suppose you'll catch me?"

"No. As ever, you won't need catching. You can do this, my darling."

I looked down. The stage seemed tiny from that height. All reason told me I would die if I jumped.

Jeremy called up to me, "It doesn't take reason, love. It takes faith in yourself."

"I'm a little short on faith right now."

"Then get some help."

"There's no one else here, you idiot!"

"Hmm. I prefer 'wanker.' 'Idiot' is a bit harsh, don't you

think? And it's not exactly true, that no one else is here. I believe in you. And Caleigh does."

"Caleigh's with Nan."

"Well, I know that. But she's with you, too, as I am."

I felt for the string, still in my pocket.

"Just try the first pattern you taught her. What was it?"

I thought about it. "'Witch's Broom.'"

He laughed. "How very fitting."

As I looped the string into "Witch's Broom," the catwalk, the theater, and Jeremy last of all, faded and softened like wax melting. I heard him call to me once more, "Hold fast, my good witch, and believe."

Then I saw Caleigh, with Nan beside her. Hail pelted the roof of Nan's house, drowning out the speech between them. Caleigh's hair was damp with sweat. I could feel her heart hammering with my own, echoing the thrum of thunder. Her eyes opened, and I knew she felt all the tendrils working out from her to me. I felt them, too.

Nan placed Caleigh's own white string in her fingers, the string Simon Magus had given her. I gasped. But then Nan said a word, and Caleigh sat up, looped the string around her fingers. She wasn't afraid. She would get it right this time, so everyone could go home. Nan held sharp sewing shears, waiting. They were all old and simple patterns, tried and true. "Lightning." "The Sword." "The Star." "Sunrise." And finally, "The Twins." Then she began one that I knew was called "The Web of Darkness."

4

After the string eased from my hands, I made a mental inventory. I went to the closet where I'd last seen the sword, hoping Mrs. Pike hadn't moved it. I scrabbled around in the dark of the closet, and my fingers touched the intricate scabbard, tucked behind the scrim of jackets and coats. When I slid the sword out, its jewels gleaming, it seemed right in my hand, balanced and lighter than it appeared. The blade shone bright even in the dimness of the hall.

I remembered the vision of my great-great-grandmother with the sword on the battlefield of Antietam. Lightning flashed again, closer this time. I knew I should get to the church before the storm worsened. But I felt the pull of the Book once more, knew it was part of the magic I was crafting. I ran to it, and its soft leather felt hot in my hands. I opened to the first page. In purpling ink, words I hadn't seen before appeared: "This is the Book of Revelations. Use it for Hurts and Triumphs, for Healing and to make Death come." I flipped gently through the pages. All were now filled again with writing. Many hands had written in the Book. Early pages were written in a script I didn't recognize. Further in I saw the Five Corners place names I knew of old—Joy Tavern, Camp Rock, Hell's Kitchen Road. The stories were interspersed with quotes from the book of Revelation. I got to later pages, thick with writing I knew. My breath caught in my throat. My Nan's writing. Describing the disappearances, first of her friends, then of the town itself.

I thought of them, Nan, my ancestor of the portrait, all the Revelations. I willed them to help me. I turned to a random page, a random sentence. It felt like a prayer. It felt right. My eyes fell upon this: "And he had in his right hand seven stars: and out of his mouth went a sharp two-edged sword." I would take the sword to the church. What would happen then, I had no idea. I only knew Rigel Voss was waiting for me there. I took up the sword and the crushing weariness left me. I felt the generations behind me, with me. I tucked the Book in my jacket pocket, and went out into the snow.

5

If the devil had made his way to the church, he might have melted a path to it. Rigel Voss had not, but I could see a faint indentation in the snow, the violet shadow of a trail that meant someone had traveled there. I slogged in the snow, up to my waist, using the sword as a walking stick. The wind had risen to a howling screech. Branches rent from trees flew by me. Lightning cracked and split a tree just at the top of the drive. The storm was everywhere. Icy rain pelted my skin. But I took my bearings, headed for the church. The sword propped me up. It felt light; it was no burden. I had my hand on its hilt as I struggled through the snow and ice. I knew I could still escape, leap onto Zar's back and have him trot me out of there, striding chest-deep to the village where I would be safe. But then this cat-and-mouse game Rigel Voss was playing, had been playing for months, would continue. I knew he would not be caught. Simon Magus would keep him hidden. If Voss saw me leave, he might let me, then disappear as he had every other time, only to surface again. We'd never be free of him. I knew it was foolish, knew it might mean my own death, but I had to face him. I wanted to. It must end here. I was ready.

The lock of the big white doors had not been touched, but I saw that the hummocky valley in the snow led to the side door. It was standing open, its padlock nowhere to be seen. The snow had drifted into the foyer, into the aisle between the pews, like a bride's train. The smell of lilacs warned me again. I pulled the sword from its sheath and held it before me. It was bright and thin and looked as if it could slice a man to the bone. I gripped the hilt softly, as if my hand was made for it, rather than the sword itself fashioned for human hands. A light seemed to emanate from it. The church had never been wired for electricity. I switched on the flashlight in my other hand. I stepped inside slowly, pivoted until I had a view of every corner of the square, plain nave.

Then I saw him. The black shadow of a man. It looked as if he might be praying, he sat so silently, so still, head bowed. I shone the flashlight full on him, and he turned. He seemed so normal, neither a devil nor fiend. Just a man with a quiet face, thinning hair. He looked younger than the man I'd seen in the visions. He looked innocent.

He shielded his eyes, said, "Revelation. There you are."

In Las Vegas, on the Strip, in his theater, Simon Magus climbed up his silks. The houselights dimmed. The show was about to begin. He'd weave his web of darkness.

Voss said my name as if he knew me. And he did, I realized. More intimately than some of my friends. He'd studied me, followed my every move.

I dropped the flashlight. It clattered on the wooden floor,

spilling light. I reached to grip the sword hilt with both hands, my heart pounding. I stepped quickly and silently into the darkness at the front of the church. After all the years scrambling around in dusky theaters, my eyes adjusted swiftly; I could see well in the near-dark. Voss turned to the right, the left, looking, searching. He ran to where I'd stood. He was rattled, and hadn't expected to be. I performed my one turn, my perfect visible vanish. I held the sword close so that it would be encompassed in the vanish as well.

"God damn it, where are you?" He scrabbled for his own flashlight, then spun its beam. I thought how ludicrous this all was, and couldn't stifle the laugh that rose in my throat. He ran toward the sound. I'd forgotten that I could still be heard, my voice penetrating that shimmery between-worlds place. I stepped aside, feeling the displacement of air as he passed. He slammed into the rail behind the pews, spun again, seeking.

"I'll find you. You know I will. I always do."

The heavy velvet curtain parted. The audience gasped. The magician, elegant in his swallow-tailed tuxedo, hung suspended from two long silken ropes, high above them. Then, from utter stillness, he swung and twirled, spun the ropes, spun them and wove them, arcing his body through the air. Plunging, swooping, he began weaving a miraculous, intricate dark blue web.

Voss ran again, again I stepped aside, felt his bulk rush past my body. I risked speech. "Where are my girls?"

And suddenly I knew for sure that he had less knowledge of them than I had. I felt his frustration, not only with me, but with Grace and Fai as well, for eluding him. I knew the answer didn't lie with him. He pulled out a gun then, shot toward where I'd stood only seconds before. Low, so he might shatter a kneecap, wouldn't kill me. He still needed me. But he was shooting blind. I stepped behind him, slid the point of the blade to the base of his skull.

"I want you to drop the gun." I felt the shock run through him. He hadn't thought that I could best him, even for a moment. I pushed the point of the blade in, just a little. In the shadows, I couldn't tell whether I drew blood, but I think I did. Something clattered to the floor. His gun. "I don't have them. I don't even know where they are."

"That's better." I eased up on the sword. "But you killed Maggie. And Jeremy. I want you to tell me why."

"I never meant to kill the girl. Her death was . . . a mistake."

Hatred coursed through my blood. It felt too huge for me to contain it all. I could have killed him then, but I needed to hear the truth. He told it.

"I lost everything because of your disappearing act. And when I found out about the research they were doing, I knew you must have been in on it, some way. How you did it—that's all I started out wanting to know. I wanted my life back. You ruined my life!"

"That wasn't Maggie's fault, or Jeremy's."

"I had to find you. I had to *know*. If I could explain it, I could make it right. Make you show them, my boss, my wife. So they'd know that it was real. That I wasn't crazy. But I didn't find you. After that girl died, my best chance, I knew it was too late. And then, when my wife died too . . . I found out about the experiments, how it's possible to go between the worlds. How to be with the dead again."

I'd just been with my own dead husband, and all Voss wanted

was to be able to do the same. Talk to his Alice, be with her again. The irony made me laugh.

"Shut up! It's not funny! You *know*. It all had to do with you. Why would you be there, otherwise, in the tunnels? You and the guy in the electric chair. *He* could go between the worlds, talk to the dead. I knew you could, too. So I had to find you. I need to *know*!"

"What about Simon Magus?"

"Who?" He didn't react when I said the name. I realized he didn't know who had enchanted him.

"Never mind. Go on."

"No one would ever believe I hadn't meant to kill the girl. You'd already made me a murderer. I had nothing to lose. When I finally found you, I waited months, figuring, getting to know your routines, the theater. Everything. You had no idea."

I shuddered. That he'd breathed the same air we did. "You made me kill my own husband."

He spat the words out. "You as good as killed my wife, my child. You *made* me kill your friend, your husband. We're just the same. We're both killers. I just want what's mine by right. I need to be with her again!"

Voss dropped and whirled so fast I didn't anticipate it. He grabbed my waist and used his body weight to pull me down. The sword fell, must have hit him on its way to the ground. He roared as blood spurted from his leg. Startled, I must have reappeared. He took hold of my wrists, gripped them with one hand. I could smell his sweat, mixed with lilacs and his blood now, like molten metal. "Tell me!" he roared in my face. I willed myself to disappear again. He reached for my throat, but his hand hit my chin and I bit at the fleshy palm beneath his little finger.

"Shit!" He let go of me, and I scrambled away, rolled under

a pew. I could see the glint of the gun just inches from me. He saw it, too, and lurched toward it. The blood was pumping from his leg. I saw it spread, wet and dark, on his pants. Jeremy had bled to death. It had taken only moments after the bullet severed the artery in his neck. I'd tried in vain to stanch the awful spurting while his eyes went dark.

I knew what I had to do, but it took every ounce of courage I possessed not to let the dread I felt paralyze me. I reappeared, rolled out from under the pew, and bolted for the door. Voss had whipped off his belt, was tying it around the bleeding leg. He looked up, saw me, dropped the tourniquet, and ran for me. I didn't dare vanish. I had to keep him running. I ran out the church doors blindly, floundered into the drifts. I heard his breathing, harried as if he were the hunted one. I could feel him behind me, his rushing presence. He was a big man, with more blood in him than Jeremy. How long would it take?

I ran toward the house, brightly lit again, the power on for the moment. I feinted and zigzagged, to tire him, to make the blood flow faster. I didn't dare look back. I had to keep him moving. I rushed through the back door, tried to slam it in his face, but he caught it. Our fingers touched; his were cold as fish in a stream. I ran through the parlor, hurling vases and lamps behind me, tossing small tables in his path. He was so near. I knew he could catch me at any moment. I could almost feel his breath as it battled in his lungs.

At the third-floor landing, he snarled my name, lunged for me. I felt his hand brush my shoulder. In another stride I was in my office, through the still-open doors. I turned at the railing of the widow's walk to see him rushing toward me, all the color drained from his face. I climbed onto the railing, looked out for one split second at the houses, the barn, the church steeple. Our tracks in the snow. The ground, so far below me. I didn't know if I could do it, after all. Sweat broke out on my forehead in spite of the cold. The icy rain pelted my face again, and I could hear the faint booming of the church bell.

And then I leapt. Made the leap of faith.

Simon Magus had done this countless times. He'd never wavered. But this night, in his fifth pass through the growing web, he reached for silk, found only air. He slipped, slid, grasped at the web to regain his balance. The audience groaned. There was no net.

Simon Magus was slipping through the web of his own making. He clawed at the ropes, but couldn't gain a purchase. He heard the cries of women, then a voice said, "I'll cut the string now, Caleigh. Don't be afraid." He reached once more, into thin air. Then he fell. Before he hit the stage floor, he heard the voice again, using his own magic word against him. *"I-undias!"*

Voss's hand gripped my ankle, but still I soared. I felt weightless and powerful, as if the wind held me, kept me from harm. I soared over Hawley, saw it all laid out before me. I saw the first Revelation in this New World, this New England, her long hair trailing behind her, her eyes blazing, holding a sword up. My sword. The blue snakes on her wrists writhed like living things. I saw Hawley as it was, like the mural on our dining room wall, all the old houses and barns resurrected, lights burning in the windows. I saw Grace and Fai on their horses, Queen Anne's lace in their hair, riding through Hitchcock Meadow. I flew between the worlds.

*

I landed softly in a swell of snow. Only a few flakes drifted down. The clouds parted, and the full moon cast her lemony glow on Hawley Five Corners, on dying Rigel Voss. His hand flapped, reaching for me. He gripped my arm, and I knew everything. Even without the Book, I knew it all.

In the days after Maggie's death, Rigel Voss tried to be normal, tried to make sure Alice wouldn't suspect anything. But he was distracted, couldn't sleep, and when he did, he had dreams that shook him to the core. He would wake drenched in sweat, panting. Once he woke up yelling, he didn't know what. Alice smoothed his hair, wiped the sweat from him with a cool washcloth. She didn't ask, but he could tell by her silence that she knew something was horribly wrong.

He still dressed in his suits and went to "work." He would drive to another town, sit in a library, and scan the local newspapers for mention of his terrible deed, then find a dark bar where he could drink the afternoon away. For the first time in his life, he couldn't make a plan, had no idea what to do, except try to protect Alice from the truth while he waited for the torrent of discovery and punishment to break over him. It didn't matter that he'd never meant to kill the girl. He played the scene over and over in his head, how it would be when Alice found out her husband was going to prison and she'd have their child alone. But it didn't happen that way. She never did find out what he'd done, yet the reality was worse than anything Rigel Voss could have imagined.

Five days after he'd killed Maggie Hamilton and dumped her body, he returned home to find his old friends Rivera and Lindley sitting in an unmarked car outside his house. His heart started racing, like a marathon was pounding through his chest.

Alice was on the screened porch, as usual. She waved to him as he pulled up. He thought of driving around back, ignoring the agents, but they saw him and stepped out of their car. He had no choice but to park behind them, greet them.

"Rigel, good to see ya." Rivera didn't take off his sunglasses. Neither did Lindley. Voss didn't like not being able to see their eyes.

"Looks like you got a pretty good gig." Lindley patted him on the lapel. "Still wearing the nice suits. What, you get consulting to Monsanto, GE? I hear the pay's kickin'."

Voss forced a pale smile to creep over his face.

"Yeah, it's a shame we didn't come here to shoot the breeze. I could go for a cold one." Rivera was a bullish man, ugly and smart, smarter than Lindley, who'd gone to Princeton but was languid as melting butter. Voss wondered if Rivera had been promoted, if he had Voss's old office now. It was the last thing that mattered, though. Rivera wasn't here for congratulations.

"We hate to trouble you and the missus." He nodded toward Alice, who had opened the screen door, taken a few steps out toward them, now stood at the top of the stone steps. "It's about that college kid. Maggie Hamilton. She's gone and disappeared. Have to ask you a few questions. Hunter wants to know can you come to Springfield."

It was bad. Worse than he thought. They wanted him to come in. He turned toward Alice. He could see her fingers plucking at the ribbons of her dress, knotting and unknotting them. A pink cotton maternity dress, the white ribbons at the collar fluttering in the breeze where she'd loosened them. He said, "Let me tell my wife." The words were thick in his throat.

He slogged up the steps, knew their eyes were following

him. When he got to her, he saw her face was white, the freckles like dark constellations. "Honey, I have to go back to work. Only for a little while."

"Rigel, you were just *at* work." She nodded toward Rivera and Lindley. "They've been sitting out there for the last two hours. Didn't they know where you were? I brought them Cokes, asked them to come in, but they wouldn't. Just said they'd wait for you in the car. What's going on?"

He was hot all over. He scraped the sweaty hair from his forehead. "It's . . . nothing. Glitch in a surveillance. They need me back there. Please, Alice, just go in the house. I'll be back soon."

She folded her arms, scrunched them over her breasts. "Not till you tell me what's really going on." She narrowed her eyes at him, and it was like she read his mind. She could do that, he knew. He just wished she wouldn't do it now. "You didn't go to work, did you? That's why they came here. You weren't at Bay State, or at the field office. You haven't been going, have you?"

He couldn't look at her. He looked at the flat blue slice of river.

"Shit, *shit*. How are we going to live, Rigel? This baby could come any day. What about the insurance, tell me that? Do we still even have health insurance?"

He didn't know what to say. This was only the beginning, and he wished she wasn't so upset now, because it was only going to get worse. He reached out to her, to comfort her, but she spun away, tripped, and she started falling. He saw the surprise on her face. He leapt to catch her, but his foot caught the iron railing and he fell hard on the stones. By the time he got to his feet, he saw Rivera and Lindley running, and Alice's body still tumbling, her head lolling and hitting each stone, her hair dark and wet with blood.

He never was questioned about Maggie. That day and the days until the funeral were a blur to him. He remembered Rivera bringing him coffee at the hospital, which he drank because it was there in his hand. He remembered a doctor with a pale meaty face explaining that they'd tried to save the baby. He remembered falling into their bed that night, waking in his bloody clothes. Although he didn't remember cradling Alice's shattered head to him, that's what he must have done. Her sister, Emily, came out for the funeral, with their mother. He didn't remember where they stayed, or what they said. He remembered the graveyard, and someone pressing a clod of dirt into his hand, hearing the thump as it dropped on the coffin.

He remembered most clearly the day after the funeral, when he packed a bag, unplugged every appliance, got in his car and drove. His first stop was a house just off the common in Amherst. It was a grand house, Victorian, not as old as some but you could tell it was owned by someone wealthy. He went up the walk, didn't bother to knock, just opened the door and stepped into the sunny foyer, stopped and reached for his Glock. He listened until he heard the buzz of a coffee grinder. He followed it, found his way into the kitchen, where a black-haired man in a blue bathrobe was standing at the sink. Voss stepped lightly up to him, stuck the gun in his back, whipped his hand over the man's mouth. The coffee cup clattered, but the man didn't make a sound. Didn't even struggle. Maybe he'd been expecting something like this, someday.

"Okay, Professor," Voss said into his ear. "You're not going to try to get away. You're going to walk with me to your study, turn around, and lock the door." The man did as he was told. As soon as he'd thrown the bolt, Voss let him go. "Sit down," he told the man, who sat in an expensive leather armchair. Voss kept the gun to his head. "All you need to do is tell me all about the experiments, everything you know. I won't hurt you. I'll go away and you'll never hear from me again. Unless you tell anyone I was here. Or you tell me lies. Do you understand?"

The professor did understand. He told Rigel Voss everything. The scientists had a big government grant to study this man, to test whether he truly had the power to communicate with the dead, to bridge the gap between the worlds of the living and the dead. He told the scientists amazing things, things he could know only by this ability. It was uncanny, what he had told about their dead mothers, uncles, brothers, wives. He told them he could go there, to where the dead were. When they'd hooked him up to an EKG, the results were really quite remarkable. Unfortunately, just a few days since, the man had escaped. Nowhere now to be found. Poof. Abracadabra.

Were there photographs of this man? Any way to trace him? Unfortunately not. They never knew his real name, it turned out. And curiously, all the photos they had taken of him had vanished.

No, he had no knowledge of any red-haired girl. A girl *had* been seen in the tunnels, as Voss himself knew. But no one at the university knew who she was. She might have been involved in the escape. Another thing the man had told them, under duress, was that there were more beings like him. That was really all he could tell Voss. But for Voss it was more than enough. It gave him something to hope for, even beyond avenging his wife.

The professor accompanied him to the door, as if they were old friends. He shook his hand and wished Rigel Voss good luck in his endeavors. Then he'd said a word in parting that Rigel Voss didn't understand and never could remember.

From that day, he called himself by many names. Only once again by the name of a star, when he had the opportunity to kill off his old self, to be resurrected as anybody and nobody. But the day after Alice's funeral was the day Rigel Voss truly disappeared, began his quest to find the red-haired girl, who must either know how to speak to the dead, or knew the man who could. Rigel Voss had never seen the man's face. But he had seen the red-haired girl. He would find her. He would find out how to do it, how to go to his own dead, to his Alice. He would hold her again, tell her he loved her beyond everything. He would keep her from all harm, in between the worlds, where they might be together, forever.

6

I knew he'd never get up again. Blood bubbled between his speaking lips. I bent to hear the words. "How," he whispered. "Just tell me . . . *how.*" Rigel Voss was insane, he was obsessed. And now I knew beyond a doubt that he was enchanted. Who knew where the insanity stopped and the enchantment began? It had brought him to his death, and he still couldn't let go. But I knew that kind of crazy. I thought of his wife, his Alice, falling. I thought how he had loved her.

I leaned in, whispered back. "I'm sorry." His eyes dulled. Snow melted on his cheeks and forehead, on the dark stain of blood that ran from thigh to ankle.

I was going to tell him I didn't know how it was that I could walk between the worlds, how I could visit with my dead again. Then I realized I *did* know.

I told dying Rigel Voss, my compatriot in grief, "It's magic."

7

I knelt by the dead man in the bloodied snow. I didn't feel the cold anymore. The Book was still in my pocket. I opened it, felt myself falling from the wintry landscape of Hawley Five Corners, through time or space to land on the Sea Road, among the yellow blooms of gorse. This time I ran to the end of the path, to the seawall, threw myself into Jeremy's arms, pressed into his mackintoshed shoulder.

"If I had died, if he had killed me, would I be here with you now forever?"

He took my face in his hands, gazed at me, his eyes the color of sea. "It couldn't have happened that way. We wouldn't have let it. You have things to do in your world, Reve. And we both know it isn't my world anymore. So now, you have to let me go." He pulled me close then, hummed in my ear, a song we both knew. David Bowie's "Golden Years." The band had played it at our wedding. We swayed together, our bodies melded. We danced on Kilcoole Beach, danced one last time, while Jeremy sang the familiar words to me, until the sun dropped below the Irish Sea.

In the last of the light, when I felt Jeremy slipping from me, the beach dissolving around us, I grabbed his hands, held them as tightly as I could. I felt the golden band of his wedding ring, wrapped my fingers around its substance, felt his flesh turn to air, cold air. I opened my eyes to the falling snow of Hawley. I was back. Rigel Voss lay near me. I thought of all he had gone through to assuage his longing for Alice, his dead wife. In my palm lay Jeremy's wedding ring, that circle of gold we had buried with him. It felt different, changed. The outside of the band was no longer smooth. I turned and went to the house, to the light.

When I examined the ring, I found our initials, and the date of our wedding, which we'd had engraved inside the band. There was an inscription now on the outer side of the ring as well, words I knew would be Jeremy's last gift to me: HEARTS HOLD MAGIC.

He was right. The magic I would always remember, when all was said and done, was the magic of our hearts beating together. Dark, and deep.

Then the next line of the elusive Robert Frost poem reminded me: *but I have promises to keep.*

I dragged the cold, stiffening body of Rigel Voss to the barn. When I finally dropped him near Falcon Eddy, I looked for signs that one was good, the other evil, but I found none. I grabbed a tarp and spread it over their bodies. I went to the church, found the sword. It glistened with Rigel Voss's blood. I brought it to the house. Cleaned the blade, and sheathed it. I had a hunch where it belonged. I went up to the third floor, to my office. To the portrait of my ancestor, the Revelation I now knew had fought in the Civil War. I looked for the thin crack in the wall below the portrait, slid the sheathed sword in. The wall absorbed blade, scabbard, and hilt, then closed as if the breach had never been. I knew it would be there for me if ever I had need of it again.

8

Bits of ash float onto surfaces, like snow that will never melt. I'd gone to Caleigh's room in the night, found the old school notebook she'd written her visions in, then to the twins' rooms for their phones. I inscribed all our experiences onto the thick pages of *The Hawley Book of the Dead,* as Nan had done after the deaths she'd caused decades ago. Then I deleted the texts, burned Caleigh's notebook. There will be only this record in the Book, for the next Keeper, the next Revelation.

Hawley Five Corners—November 2, 2013

When I wake, I am cold. Colder than I've ever been. Frozen inside. I don't want to move, just let my aching head stay welded to the floor, looking at the snowy field of burned pages. The white expanse of ash covering the rug by the hearth, my jean-clad legs. I think it's the ash-snow that makes me cold, and for a moment I wonder how it has fallen in the house. I think how strange a house it is. A house and town of wonders and spirits, not exactly evil, not exactly good. I hear the furnace kick in, and even though I feel the blast of heat from the floor register near me, I'm still freezing. I can see the sun shine, weak but with promise for the coming day, when the morning mist lifts.

I sit up, finally, pull a shawl from a chair and arrange it around my shoulders. My knees pop as I rise stiffly and survey the wreckage from my battle with Voss. Chairs are knocked over, candle wax drips from tables, glass shards are strewn over the floor.

I have no idea what to do, but only wander across the room, stare out the window, down the drive. I can see no tracks in the fresh dusting of snow that must have fallen after I'd killed Voss.

I step outside, and more cold finds me, but not the relentless cold of November. It's as if the turn toward spring has begun, rather than the trudge toward the winter solstice. Warm currents of air puff at me. From where? I hear the whine of a chain saw in the distance. Then I hear my cell phone chime out the tone that tells me I have messages. I run to find it.

There are two messages. The first is from Nan. It is brief, but it makes my knees weak with relief, makes me smile: "Caleigh is herself again. The web is broken."

The second message is from Henry. "You're not going to believe this, Reve, but Setekh fell out of his web tonight. They say he was struggling in the ropes, then it looked like the ropes broke, and he fell. The whole audience saw him hit the floor. But then something really strange happened. Every single person who saw it says his body kind of . . . disintegrated. Into motes of dust, that flew away. And now he's gone. None of his personal effects are at the theater, his house is empty. Like he never existed. Some trick, huh? It's causing a sensation. Wish I represented that guy! But nobody can find him. Anyway, call me."

I stand and stare down the drive, still expecting, not hoping, certain some shift has occurred. Either the night-cracking thunder, or Caleigh and Nan cutting Simon Magus's web, must have cracked something else. The wall between worlds.

Two riders come through the mist, knee-deep in it, so I can't see their horses' legs. But they are not ghost horses. I can see their breath, hear muffled hoofbeats. One black horse, one gray. On their backs are Grace and Fai, turning to each other, laughing.

I run. The shawl falls from my shoulders, plumes into air. I run into the mist, and my own feet disappear. I am up to my waist in mist and snow when I stumble into Brio, bounce off his chest, reel between him and Rikka. I grab at Fai's boot and Grace's knee. The horses, startled, pull away and I fall to the ground.

"Mom!"

"What are you doing?"

They both dismount in a flash, and Rikka and Brio tear to the paddock for a reunion with Zar over the fence. I look up at my daughters' alarmed faces, and thank God they are the same, the same round cheeks and freckles, their wild red hair shining, not tangled with leaves and burrs, clean and bright as new copper. I clasp their ankles, booted and chap covered. I breathe in their good, horsey smell and weep.

Then a hand is on my shoulder and through my tears I see Fai's still-tanned face, looking concerned.

"Mom? Is something wrong? Is Caleigh okay?"

They help me to my feet, and I grasp twinned hands and arms, touch cheeks, soft hair, then hold them as tightly as I can and sob into their necks. My girls, returned to me. They just stare at my hugging, patting, crying self.

Grace says, "What is *up* with you?"

My throat is so full I can't get one word out, but I let them go, the better to gaze at them.

Fai scans the yard, the barn, the rime of snow clinging to everything. "Where did this snow come from? The trails were fine. No trees down, no snow, no ice. Until we got in the gate. Did you all have some freaky storm or something?"

How can I explain enchantment, theirs or mine? How can I explain the storm, or their weeklong hiatus with their ancestors, which they clearly don't remember? Or the search for them that had lasted one hundred and sixty-one hours?

But Grace doesn't wait for my answer. "Hey, I'm really hungry," she tells us. "Let's go untack. I feel like I haven't eaten in *days.*"

"Umm, I'll take care of the horses." I can't explain the deaths, not yet. Poor Falcon Eddy, whom they never knew. And Rigel Voss, whom for years no one knew. "Go in and get a snack." Then I remember I have to account for Caleigh's absence. "Oh, and your sister's fine. She's at Nan's."

"Aren't you going to yell at us for riding when you told us not to?" Grace taunts me.

I should, but I feel my love for them pumping through my veins. "No. I'm not."

They don't argue. I watch them walk to the house together, their arms around each other, laughing and teasing. I hate to let them out of my sight. But there will be time for telling it all later, and time for just contemplating my girls, full of life and vigor.

I start toward the barn, to the tasks I must still perform. I startle at a resounding crack behind me. Branches fall away, and Jolon steps out of them, drops his chain saw, and runs to me through the wet snow and mist. He grabs me up in a fierce embrace. "You're all right, you're okay!" He is shaking with cold or relief, I don't know which. His hands grip me as if he'll never let me go. He looks haunted, sleepless, an extreme version of himself.

I realize in all the furor of the night I'd felt a heavy ache, and that was the way I missed him. "Where were you? Why didn't you come last night? I thought . . ." I can't go on. My throat is filled with sudden tears again, for everything we'd gone through.

"There's a forest of trees down from here to Hunt Road. I had to chainsaw my way in. It took me all night, with the ice and snow. But I saw the tracks of two horses by the gate . . . the twins?"

I nod. I can't speak about the twins. Not yet. "Thank God," Jolon whispers into my hair, his sweat and cut-pine scent clean on the air. "All I could think, the whole night long, was if I lost you, you'd never know. You'd never know how I thought of you. For years I tried, but I never forgot you. It may be too soon to tell you this. Or you may never want to hear it." He looks in my eyes then, asking. I open my lips to speak, but I can't.

He is tender, his bruised, scratched hands move softly on my shoulders, my face. "Ah, Reve, I have to tell it." And he whispers his secret, that is no secret to me: "I've never loved anyone but you."

I remember the last lines of the poem that has been circling in my head.

The woods are lovely, dark, and deep,
But I have promises to keep,
And miles to go before I sleep,
And miles to go before I sleep.

I take Jolon's hand, close my eyes. I feel his arms encircle me. I breathe in his warmth, his good woodsy smell, feel how real and solid he is.

I don't know what the future might hold. We may indeed have promises to keep, and miles to go before we sleep. But at this moment, we have all the time in the world.

ACKNOWLEDGMENTS

No book is written in isolation. Thanks are due to many who have helped me, who have accompanied me for hours or days or years on the road to *Hawley*.

Thanks first and foremost to Aimee Swift, co-founder of the Valley4Writers and my most constant companion on the write road: the best friend, critical reader, and writing buddy a person could hope for. May your books be as well loved and well tended as *Hawley* was by you.

To Kate Miciak, my brilliant editor, who has the truest feel for the shape of a story, and incredible patience to cultivate it. Also many thanks to Libby McGuire, Jennifer Hershey, Kim Hovey, Maggie Oberrender, Jennifer Garza, Julia Maguire, Marietta Anastassatos, Vincent La Scala, and Kathleen Lynch.

To my amazing agent, Alexandra Machinist, who pulled this book out of the slush pile and got it where it is today—in the hands of readers. You are a true superhero. And at Janklow & Nesbit, to Stephanie Koven and Michael Steger.

To my UK editor, Selina Walker, and her wonderful team at Cornerstone, especially Glenn O'Neill.

To Rick Reiken, from whom I learned that it is possible to make a living as a writer.

To the Splinter Group: Janice Sorenson, Dori Ostermiller, Michael Hoberman, and David Lovelace, who welcomed me into their homes and writing lives.

To the other co-founders of the Valley4Writers: Stephanie Greene and Elizabeth Macalester. Scribblitas rule!

Thanks to Carol Cassella and the many members of the Seattle7Writers, for inspiration and coolness. Hope we can bring your spirit to the East Coast.

To Save Your Life Writers: Karen Amerman, Carleen Fischer Hoffman, Eva Kealey, Donna Liese, Missy Haddad, and Susan Staples.

To Joy Harjo, for early encouragement, and grace. To Maribeth Fischer, for the Seaglass conference. To Carolyn Parkhurst, for being the first to tell me I could sell this book. To Jacquelyn Mitchard, for lucky #119 earrings.

Thanks to the people of the western Mass hill towns, especially to Jay McMahon, for the history of magic and the Hawley Forest. And to Jim Martin, Cummington police chief (retired), for search and rescue information.

At the Odyssey Bookshop, thanks to everyone who has worked with me, past and present: for your patience, and your insights into the book world I wouldn't have found elsewise, particularly Joan Grenier, owner of the Odyssey, and Emily Crowe, manager extraordinaire.

I am very grateful to friends who helped me along the way: to Carlotta Hoffman, for her spectacular visual sensibility, and to Leon Caragulian, for helping me negotiate weird Las Vegas. To Tracey Eller, for great photographs. To Nancy Grossman, for keeping my chi moving. To Diane Vincent, Elisabeth Brook, Anne Chamberlain, Jeanne Russo, Peter Vanamee, and Toni Lake, for friendship, cabins, stalls, and suppers.

Many thanks to my mother, Jennie Karpinski, for always having my back. Also to my aunts, Yvonne Szarlan and Stephanie Kuc, for love and cakes.

And finally, to my husband, George E. Browne III: thank you for feeding mutts, cooking dinners, and most of all for your belief in me. You're last on this list, but first in my heart.

ABOUT THE AUTHOR

CHRYSLER SZARLAN lives in western Massachusetts with her family, works part-time as a bookseller at the Odyssey Bookshop, and rides her horse in the Hawley Forest whenever possible. An alumna of Marlboro College, she jogged racehorses and worked as a magician's assistant before graduating from law school, after which she worked as a managing attorney with Connecticut Legal Rights project. She is deep into her next novel of the Revelation Quartet.

www.chryslerszarlan.com

ALSO AVAILABLE IN ARROW

The Last Grave

Debbie Viguié

'Fans *of Buffy* and *Charmed* will love it ... I enjoyed it immensely.'
Independent on Sunday

Police Detective Samantha Ryan is doing whatever she can to forget her terrible childhood in a dark and evil coven.

But escaping who you are isn't easy.

She is called in on a bizarre and horrific murder case, one that is steeped in the occult, and Samantha is soon led deep into a powerful coven. As she works to uncover the connection with the murder, an earthquake rocks the Bay Area.

That's when Samantha has a premonition: Something is coming. Something evil.

'One of the most beautifully written and scariest books I've ever read' – Nancy Holder, author of *Buffy the Vampire Slayer*

'Dark, bloody, emotional and scary, and so darn well-written that it's almost impossible to put it down ... this novel is an insanely good read.' – *USA Today*

AVAILABLE IN ARROW

The Magicians

Lev Grossman

Quentin Coldwater's life is changed forever by an apparently chance encounter: when he turns up for his entrance interview to Princeton he finds his interviewer dead – but a strange envelope bearing Quentin's name leads him down a very different path to any he'd ever imagined.

The envelope, and the mysterious manuscript it contains, leads to a secret world of obsession and privilege, a world of freedom and power and, for a while, it's a world that seems to answer all Quentin's desires. But the idyll cannot last – and when it's finally shattered, Quentin is drawn into something darker and far more dangerous than anything he could ever have expected...

'A gripping fantasy thriller that will please all the older Harry Potter fans out there'
Yours magazine

'This is a sophisticated, subtle novel that is also magical fun. I can't imagine any lover of well-written classic fantasy ... who won't adore it'
The Times